3

THE
VERSIPELLIS
MYSTERIES

THE SHADOW OF DEATH

RHEN GARLAND

Published in Great Britain 2021
by Amethyst and Greenstone

Copyright © 2021 by Rhen Garland
Illustrations by Adam Garland
The Coventry Carol. Trad

ISBN 978-1-8384604-4-0 (Paperback)
ISBN 978-1-8384604-5-7 (eBook)

First Published 2021

DRAMATIS PERSONAE

Elliott Caine/Versipellis	Private Enquiry Agent
Giselle Du'Lac/Angellis	Private Enquiry Agent
Abernathy Thorne/Shadavarian	Private Enquiry Agent
Aquilleia Aquileisi Thorne	A Psychic
Veronique	Thorne's Labrador
Reverend Newton Popplewell	The Vicar
Araby Burgoyne	The Survivor
Merric Burgoyne	The Earl of Cove
Cornelius Burgoyne	The Great-Uncle
Amicarella Burgoyne	The Great-Aunt
Sybilla De Banzie	Amicarella's Step-Grandaughter
Marcus De Banzie	Her Husband
Melisandre Salazar	A Guest
Nanny Wyck	The Nanny
Dr Tenniel Mayberry	The Doctor
Luci Lutyens	A Rakish Young Man
Sebastian Lees	Araby's Old Friend
Theodora Lees	His Wife
Leander Lees	Their Son
Davaadalai	The Butler
Chymeris	Versipellis' Sister
Phoenixus	Versipellis' Brother

PRONUNCIATION GUIDE

Versipellis — Ver-si-**pell**-is
Shadavarian — Shad-a-**vair**-ian
Angellis — On-gel-is
Aquilleia — A-kwee-**lay**-ah
Xenocyon — Zee-noh-**sigh**-on
Abditivus — Ab-**dity**-vus
Chymeris — Ky-**meh**-ris
Phoenixus — Fee-**nick**-sus

Astraea — Ast-**ray**-a
Filicidae — Fill-**ee**-sea-day
Aranea — A-**ray**-knee
Asteraceae — Aster-**ray**-sea-eye
Pythiacace — Pie-thea-**catch**-ay

Cove Castle Floorplan

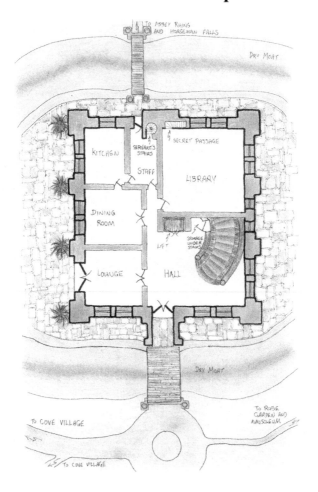

The Isle of Cove
February
Midnight
1825

The dark winter waves swelled and crashed along the bleak coastline as the full moon peered through racing storm clouds and cast its shifting light upon a small, windswept island.

Resting just off the southern coast of Westrenshire, the tiny, wooded island sat at the end of a narrow causeway, accessible only at low tide, that led from the mainland village of Penwithiel, to the island's tiny harbour village of Cove.

Down in the harbour, under the cover of protean clouds and dappled moonlight, a small group of men bearing swords were silently disembarking from one of the fishing boats. The leader of the group nodded his thanks to the young fisherman who had used his father's boat to smuggle them into the village earlier that day. The young fisherman, who was barely thirteen, nodded back and watched as the armed men left the jetty and followed the narrow, winding lane that led away from the harbour and up the hill beyond.

The group made their way along the lane and came to a halt at one of the small cottages that lay on the outer edge of the village. Their leader walked silently up the tidy, well-kept path and tapped lightly on the front door with a gauntlet clad fist. After a few brief minutes, the door opened and they were joined by a quiet, unarmed young man dressed in black; a young man with hazel eyes. He nodded silently at the men, closed the door behind him, and joined them as they continued along the lane to the top of the hill.

They arrived at a point where the path diverged; one path leading right, towards Cove Castle, and the other heading left, towards the cliffs and the island's only waterfall: the Horseman Falls.

Taking the left-hand path, the men finally arrived at an ornately carved door, seemingly set into the side of the hill itself; a door that would lead them to the heart of an evil that had tormented the islanders and their children for many years.

The leader paused at the doorway and gestured, the young man with hazel eyes moved to the front and knocked a strangely rhythmic tattoo on the solid barrier. Moments later, the door slowly swung open.

The red-robed figure on the other side of the threshold looked at the hard faces of the gathered men and swallowed hard. "They are all here. I have done as you instructed, I have betrayed my brethren…" He looked at the quiet young man, an expression of fear on his face. "But have I done enough to be forgiven?"

The young man nodded. "Yes, you have done enough. Now go, and never return to this place."

The doorkeeper nodded jerkily and hitching up his robes, ran past the quiet man, and down the path that led to the village as the troop of men silently entered the torchlit passage and made their way to a chamber, hidden deep within the hill, that was their final destination.

As they descended, the distant sound of chanting became apparent. The young man caught the eye of the leader of the mercenaries he had hired and made a gesture. The leader nodded, and tapping two of his men on the shoulders, pointed at the doorway. The armed men settled against the wall and stood guard as the others continued down the torchlit passageway towards the distant voices.

The Temple of the Inner Sanctum

The black-robed figure slowly lifted the bejewelled and wickedly sharp knife from its velvet bed; light from the flickering braziers placed around the opulent chamber caught the gleaming edge of the blade as the figure turned their burning gaze upon the grey-clad acolyte kneeling before them, and in a rich, strangely gravelly voice, intoned, "Who entreats entry into the sacred upper echelons of this most devout order of the Priory of Cove?"

The acolyte pushed back their heavy cowl, revealing a tumbling mass of dark hair surrounding a proud, cruel face. The young woman raised her voice for the words she had spent many months practising. "I, Josephina of the House of Burgoyne, do entreat entry into this most sacred order."

The dark figure leant forward; their eyes fixed on the young woman's face. "And by what vow do you entreat entry from your Master?"

The young woman smirked, the ugliness of the expression at odds with her fey beauty. "By the vow of blood, and by the offering of a sacrament, do I entreat entry from my Master."

The Master smiled back. "And do you swear fealty to this order, to keep its secrets, and those of our Brothers and Sisters?"

The acolyte smiled. "I do!" She held out her open hand.

As the glinting blade paused over the centre of her palm the figure spoke again. "And do you wholeheartedly promise to imbibe to excess, to feast to excess, to fornicate to excess, and to bring rich offerings to our altars?"

Josephina nodded proudly. "I do!"

The blade was placed against her palm, and slowly drawn

to her index finger. As her blood welled up and dripped onto the floor, the black-robed figure enveloped her bloody hand in his. "Then, my daughter, we bid you welcome. Welcome to the Temple of the Inner Sanctum!"

Cheers rose from the massed brethren lining the smooth walls of the huge cave that was home to the debauched Priory of Cove. Men and women clad in robes of white, grey, and red roared their approval as the Master removed the acolyte's grey apparel and dropped it to the floor, revealing a sheer white cotton gown beneath. He removed a deep red robe from the altar and draped it around her shoulders.

The Master raised his voice. "Let it be known that Josephina is now and forever a Sister of the Holy Inner Sanctum; the highest of the high within the Priory of Cove." He ran a burning eye over his rapt congregation. "Let it also be known that Sister Josephina will replace the blasphemer Jerome as my right hand!"

Josephina turned proudly to face the thirty men and women whose cheering echoed around the massive, ornately decorated chamber as each man and woman drank a toast from their full goblets of deep-red wine. Judging by their bleary eyes and slurred words, these were not their first draughts of the evening.

Josephina snapped her fingers at a white-robed acolyte kneeling next to the altar. "Fetch the offering!"

As the acolyte stumbled out of the room in their haste to perform her bidding, their cowl fell away, exposing the face of a young girl; her light blue eyes and pale face framed by a mane of silky, white blonde hair that spread across her shoulders as she flew to one of the side chambers to retrieve the gift Sister Josephina had brought as sacrifice.

Josephina turned back to the Master with a look of exultation. "If it would please the Inner Sanctum, I have brought a suitable offering for the altar."

The white-robed female returned to the hall, carrying a terrified young child in her arms. The little boy's wide-eyed stare took in the proud young woman and the huge black-robed figure next to her; as the Master approached with a searingly unpleasant smile, the little boy began to cry.

A murmur rustled among the spectators, and several stepped forward, ugly gleams in their eyes; the Master took the child and laid him on the ornate stone altar as the young acolyte carefully placed a silver salver covered in bay leaves by the child's feet.

"No!"

Josephina and the Master spun round as one of the red-garbed monks pushed back his dark-red cowl to reveal a face very similar to Josephina's. He held out his hand to the Master. "No! Father, you swore after what happened last time: no more children!"

The black-robed figure glared at the younger man. "How dare you, you impudent brat! I banished you from this order for your insubordination, and you defy me again to enter this hallowed space. How dare you raise your hand to me! I spared your life the first time your impudence raised its head, Jerome, and only then because you were my son — but no more! From this day on, you are no son of mine! Guards, remove this blasphemer!"

As two grey-robed men grasped his arms, the red-robed monk shouted, "This has gone beyond what this place was supposed to be, Father! This was to be as the Hellfire Club: nothing more than drinks, frolics, and play! What you have done here is sacrilegious to the very nature of this club!" He turned to the proud young woman beside the Master. "Josephina, how could you?"

The Master laughed. "Did you really believe that I would be prepared to stop at just one child? After the wealth of ages of our family's true nature had been revealed to me? We are the rulers here, Joseph…not the cattle who serve us! That child was only the most recent of our offerings…and he will not be the last! Take him!"

As the guards dragged the still-shouting man out, Josephina turned to the Master and held out the jewelled blade he had just used on her. "Father?"

The Master smiled and stroked the side of her face, the similarities in their features all the more apparent in their identical expressions of expectant, exultant cruelty. "No, my daughter…this is your offering, and your gift to possess."

As the white-robed acolyte tied the crying child to the altar, another of the red-robed monks stepped forward. "Brother Jerome is right! Thomas…my lord, you cannot do this!"

The Master snapped his fingers at another grey-robed follower. "Prove your fealty and destroy this usurper!"

The young man, swaddled in his too-large robes, stared at the Master and shook his head. The Master's eyes opened wide, the whites gleaming in the flickering orange glow from the braziers. He crooked his finger at the fearful young man and crooned, "You dare refuse a direct order from me? Come here, Brother Phillipe…come to your Master…"

As the terrified young man again shook his head, shouting came from the long corridor that led to the doorway: from the direction in which the protesting Jerome had been dragged.

The Master's head snapped round as the sounds became clearer: shouting, mingled with the sound of sword play. Gritting his teeth, he turned back to his daughter and gestured at the bound child on the altar. "There is still time for you to prove your allegiance, my daughter! Kill the child!"

Josephina nodded; a rictus grin that was a travesty of a smile disfigured her face as she rushed to the altar. Standing beside the feebly moving little boy, she took a handful of bay leaves from the salver and threw them onto the burning brazier; then, gripping the dagger with both hands, she began the ritual. "I, Josephina, child of the House of Burgoyne, and Sister of the Inner Sanctum of the Priory of Cove, make this sacrifice of flesh, blood, and fear—"

As she raised the dagger above her head to strike, Jerome suddenly appeared in the doorway. Running across the cavernous room, he wrenched the blade from her grasp, and threw it onto the altar. As Josephina screamed in anger, he dragged her towards the far wall.

Several bloodstained men bearing swords ran into the room, and paused to take in the sight of thirty unarmed, drink-sodden men and women cowering against the walls. The armed men faced the brethren, all except one man who stood by the door, a heavy sack on the ground next to him.

The young man with hazel eyes slowly made his way through the crowd until he stood before the black-robed lunatic whose followers called him Master.

The Master turned his burning eyes on the troop of armed men and bellowed, "Infidels! Blasphemers and usurpers hear me — I shall have vengeance upon you all!" His fiery gaze rested upon all in the room; but when it came at last to the hazel eyed man before him, he paused for several moments before bursting into incredulous laughter. "Popplewell? Well, I'll be damned if it isn't my good and true friend the Reverend Popplewell! Have you finally decided to join us and throw away your foolish desires for love and harmonious dwelling, old friend?"

The Master grinned as he drew himself up to his full height, head and shoulders above the silent man before him. "And how is your delightful wife? Oh, of course, how could I forget? She's roasting in hell because she stole her own life... such a shame about your faith condemning her, old friend. And your son only just buried — well, what little they could find after we of the Inner Sanctum had finished with him!" He roared with laughter as several of the younger acolytes stared at him in horrified revulsion.

Josephina echoed her father's laughter, then turned her burning dark eyes on the vicar and sneeringly sang, "Lully, lullay, thou little tiny child, bye bye, lully, lullay. Lully lullay, thou little tiny child, bye bye, lully, lullay." Her eyes flashed. "A song for dead children in your sacred book, Reverend!" She screamed with laughter as she twisted against her brother's tight grip. Jerome's face was deathly pale as his eyes flickered from his father, to his sister, before resting on the gentle face of the quiet man.

Newton Popplewell, the Burgoyne family vicar, turned his steady hazel gaze from the sadists before him and walked to the altar. He looked at the terrified child with kind eyes and gently patted the boy's bound hands, then paused as he noticed the discarded blade. He leant down to the little boy's ear. "Close your eyes, my child."

As he stepped back, the vicar reached up and removed the neatly wound white cravat from his throat. He kissed it and placed it on the altar before turning back to the Master, a faint smile on his lips. "Thomas Burgoyne, Earl of Cove...you shall not take another child as you took mine." And with a sharp lunge, the young man plunged the bejewelled dagger straight into the Master's heart.

Josephina's laughter ceased, and there was a sudden dead silence before her screams began. She writhed against the grip of her brother, who gazed in stupefied shock as their father, Thomas Burgoyne, Master of the Priory of Cove, gaped at the knife in his chest. His black eyes burned as he looked into the intent, hazel eyes of his killer, then he dropped like a felled tree.

As the vicar untied the mute child, a man appeared in the passageway, desperately pushing his way through the fighters; he stopped next to the altar and Popplewell handed the child to him. "Look after your boy, Samson; he will take some time to heal." The man clutched the child to his chest, and nodded. "Yes, Reverend…and thank you, sir."

The vicar shook his head. "Go to your wife, my friend; return your child to the safety of his home."

As the relieved man left with his son, Popplewell turned his attention to the rest of the Monks of Cove, who stood flinching from the swords of the armed men before them. "Now, apart from Thomas Burgoyne, who else was a part of the Inner Sanctum? Come along now, gentlemen…ladies, don't be shy — we know for a fact that none of you are!"

Jerome shook his head, a stunned expression still on his face as he held his sobbing sister. "I was unaware of the existence of an Inner Sanctum until the…events of last month were made known to me. Reverend, I am so very sorry."

Popplewell nodded to him. "And I believe you, Jerome; however, the murder of my child was not the first carried out by this diabolical coterie…several children have gone missing from Cove, Penwithiel, and further afield over this last year. Your father was the instigator of the heinous crimes committed here, and he did not act alone. I know this, I also know that I am willing to be…merciful to those who admit their crimes and tell us where they hid the bodies, so that we may give those innocents a Christian burial. So, members of the Priory of Cove, tell me: there were four members of the Inner Sanctum present on the night my son was murdered, one was the Master; who are the other three? And where are the bodies of the children you murdered?"

There was silence.

Popplewell raised his voice. "Remove your cowls, and let us see who inhabits this place of death."

No one moved. Popplewell looked at Fellwell, who raised his sword.

9

The cave was suddenly filled with the sound of rustling, as several hoods were lowered, and one in particular caught his eye. The white-robed blonde stared silently at the floor as Popplewell stood in front of her. "Well, well, Nanette, and you not yet sixteen. Whatever will your parents say?"

The young girl turned her tear-streaked face to glare at him, her blue eyes blazing with hatred. Then she tossed her head and stared at the floor.

As Popplewell scanned the room, one of the red-robed men sneered, "You have no power here, Popplewell. You're a vicar, not an avenging angel, and Brother Grimstone will enjoy teaching you that in due course!"

Popplewell moved to stand before the arrogant man. "And is Brother Grimstone here?"

The sneering man cast a supercilious glance around the room. "No," he muttered.

Popplewell nodded. "I'm not surprised." He called over his shoulder to the leader of the mercenaries he had hired. "Fellwell?"

"Yes, sir?"

"What did you do with Grimstone?"

Fellwell paused. "Grimstone?"

"Yes, Grimstone."

Fellwell shrugged. "I couldn't say, sir, but Feldspar might know. Feldspar!"

The man lounging by the doorway with his sack looked up from cleaning his nails with the tip of his dagger. "Sir!"

"Do we have Grimstone, Feldspar?"

Feldspar paused. "I don't rightly know, sir. Shall I check?"

Fellwell nodded. "Please do."

Feldspar saluted. "Yes, sir!" He tucked his dagger back into his belt, lifted the heavy sack and emptied its contents across the floor. Several of the robed men and women cried out, and not a few were violently sick as the severed heads of their more bloodthirsty friends bounced free from their material confines and rolled across the floor, leaving bloodied, gory streaks on the rough stone.

"Do any of these belong to the man you're looking for, sir?" asked Feldspar.

Popplewell nudged the head nearest to him with his foot, and the unmistakable features of Sir Grimstone Covey stared blindly back at him through glazed eyes. He nodded at Fellwell. "This is he." He turned back to the red-robed man, who stared at him in horror. "I am very much in the way of being an avenging angel, Markham. Yes, I know who you are, and I also know that you were present on the night my son was murdered."

Fellwell dragged the complaining man to the altar. Popplewell cast his gaze over the silent room as he walked towards Jerome and Josephina. "There was at least one more whose identity I know, and one who is unknown to me; speak now, or suffer the consequences."

Josephina spat at him in rage. "Rot in hell with your wife and brat, you bastard!"

Popplewell stood before the struggling woman. "And here is the third of the Inner Sanctum; take her with Markham."

As Fellwell took her by the arm Jerome stared at the vicar. His face turned grey as he realised the implication of Popplewell's words. "What are you going to do with my sister?"

Fellwell pushed Josephina against the altar, next to Markham. He stepped back and nodded at another of his men, who silently raised his crossbow and fired. The bolt left the machine with an oily twang, followed almost instantly by a meaty thud as it hit the sneering Markham in the heart. The deathly silence erupted into screams from the monks as another member of the Inner Sanctum died before them.

Popplewell looked at Jerome. "You were there when we

discovered my son's body; you saw what had been done to him. He was five years old, Jerome. You were there when I had to tell my wife her only child had been murdered; you were there when we discovered her body at the foot of Horseman Falls. You tell me, Jerome: what do you think I should do with your sister?"

Jerome stared at him in horrified silence before turning, almost against his will, to look at his sister. "Are you truly saying that — that Josephina was...oh my God!" He fell back against the wall and raised his eyes to Popplewell's. "But she only entered the Inner Sanctum tonight — I don't understand!"

Popplewell looked at the young man with gentle eyes and patted his shoulder. "Your sister has been a dedicated follower of your father's perversions for quite some time, Jerome. I'm truly sorry to be the bearer of such news." He turned back to the tear-streaked, yet still proud and arrogant woman before him. "I will say it again: there is one more of the Inner Sanctum whose identity is unknown, speak now and mercy will be shown...but if you hold your tongue, you will suffer, Josephina!"

The dark-haired woman laughed at him, hysteria evident in her high-pitched, screaming laughter. She ignored the corpse at her feet and propped herself against the altar as she spat her contemptuous response. "You presume to threaten me? You fool, you ridiculous preaching fool, with your words of love and brotherhood! We have brotherhood here, bathed in blood, and fear, and power! You and your pathetic wife and brat...what did you have that we couldn't take from you whenever we wished? Answer me that!"

She continued to laugh as Popplewell bent towards her. But when he whispered in her ear, her laughter stopped dead and her face froze. She shook her head, her dark eyes wide and tinged with fear. "You cannot do that; it is impossible!"

Popplewell studied her. "Is it, now? With all your self-proclaimed power, can you not do it? It is a simple thing, an easy thing…for those of us who have the ability." He raised his hand to Fellwell, who nodded and gave the order for his men to remove the monks from the cavern. As the terrified hedonists were marched from the room, Popplewell looked at Fellwell. "Now that they have seen what can and will happen if they do not speak, see if any of them are willing to divulge the whereabouts of their previous victims." Popplewell paused, his hazel eyes thoughtful. "Feel free to use any and all methods you feel suitable under the circumstances to…extract that information."

Several of the monks cried out in both fear and protest as they were dragged from the chamber. A slight smile crossed Fellwell's face; he and the reverend had talked about what would be acceptable…and what would not, but none of the monks had been privy to that little conversation; it would be enjoyable watching them squirm. His smile widened. "It will be my pleasure, Reverend."

Popplewell nodded. "I will join you shortly."

Fellwell turned and left the chamber, slamming the iron-bound outer door shut behind him as he left the three people in the opulent, treasure strewn room to stare at each other in silence.

Jerome took in a shuddering breath. "I will ask you again, Popplewell: what are you going to do with my sister?"

Popplewell smiled faintly. Moving away from the altar, he removed his coat, threw it across what had been the Master's throne, and began to roll up his sleeves. "Don't worry, Jerome, I will not kill her; she will be punished in a rather different manner than eternal damnation in hell. I will make her an unwilling ally in my fight against the evil nature that festers deep in the heart of your family!"

13

Josephina stared at him in silence, an expression of genuine fear on her tear-streaked face.

Taking a deep breath, Popplewell turned back to the altar, and the silent scions of the House of Burgoyne.

He raised an eyebrow. "Shall we begin?"

○

London
An Evening in September
1900

Piotr Rose tipped a shilling to the young girl who had reunited him with his topper and coat before turning towards the door of his club and the chill autumn air of the bustling street beyond. He paused on the threshold and inhaled — the scent of burning coal was a favourite of his; it was the smell of movement and industry.

His son Simeon joined him, hastily wrapping his scarf around his throat. "I'm sorry, Father, Mr Reynolds was rather insistent about knowing the rates for purchases made before the close of business today."

Piotr settled his hat on his head and screwed his monocle in with a little more force than was necessary. "I trust you weren't too generous with your figures?"

Simeon laughed as the two men walked back to the main road to hail a hansom cab, weaving between the assorted pedestrians, vendors, and bawling paperboys whose collective clamour, odour, and constant movement embodied Piotr's ideal of the true essence of a city. "Not at all — I remembered his attempt to buy the goldsmiths we were in talks with, and without a word to us!" Simeon shook his head at the memory. "I gave him the full price. He tried to barter, but I insisted. Carat for carat, he is unknowingly willing to pay us five percent over the usual…but only for blue and yellow diamonds of greater than two carats per stone."

Piotr nodded thoughtfully as he dodged a wily young street urchin who had spotted them from the other side of the street, and had fixed his bright eye upon the elderly man's fob watch. Piotr slapped the boy's groping, inexpert hand away and tossed a penny to him. "Practice, young man! Everything works better with practice. Better luck next time."

As they continued down the street, Piotr checked the time on the ornate little watch that had caught the urchin's eye. They had left their club at the usual time and would be home before eight o'clock; his daughter, her husband, and their young son would be joining them for dinner that evening, and both he and Simeon were under strict orders from his wife not to be late. He tucked the watch back in its pocket and turned his attention to the business at hand. "How many carats in total?"

Simeon paused as they fought their way through a jostling crowd outside a theatre. "He wants a minimum of four hundred carats in blue and one hundred carats in yellow."

Piotr's monocle popped out of his eye. "What on earth does he want that many diamonds for? A tiara?"

His son shrugged. "In truth, Father, I don't care. He can glue them to his mistress and present her to the Prince of Wales as a birthday gift if he wishes, so long as he informs His Royal Highness that the gems came from the Rose Diamond Company!"

Piotr chuckled. "As you say, my boy, as you say!"

Both men laughed as they stepped into the main thoroughfare, and made their way towards the rank of waiting hansom cabs.

They were halfway across the wide, busy road when a

covered carriage, seemingly without a cabby at the helm, suddenly appeared at the end of the street, scattering pedestrians as its four black horses thundered directly towards the two men.

As the warning shouts grew louder, Piotr and Simeon turned, but the carriage was upon them. Screams erupted from the horrified witnesses as both men were struck by the careering carriage. Their bodies were thrown through the air like rag dolls before landing with sickening thuds by the kerb.

As people gathered around them, Simeon painfully turned his head to look at Piotr, whose sightless eyes gazed past his son's face. "Father…"

Several hundred yards down the road the carriage slowed, and made its way down several side streets until it came to a halt at Euston train station. As the sweating horses steamed in the chill September air, the traces that led from their bridles into the curtained cab slackened, as the person within dropped the reins they had threaded through the carriage wall to give sufficient privacy to carry out their murderous work.

After a pause, the rear door opened and the figure responsible for the outrage stepped down from the cab. Without a backward glance, they made their way towards the waiting train that would take them home.

PART
I

The elderly man sat in his study in a state of shocked silence, a full glass of sherry untouched on the desk before him. After what he and his old friend Cornelius had discovered earlier that evening, he was amazed neither of them had died from sheer horror!

Cornelius had shakily agreed to retire to his rooms under the orders of his family's very protective butler, Davaadalai, who had furnished him with a sizeable supper tray consisting of curried mutton with rice, a large bottle of whisky, a chilled soda syphon, and strict instructions to the rest of the servants not to disturb him for the rest of the evening.

The three men had agreed to keep the discovery secret from the rest of the family, including the master of the house. But such a thing could not be kept secret for long. As soon as Cornelius' sister Amicarella found out, most of the village of Cove and the mainland settlement of Penwithiel would know!

However, his friend Cornelius had agreed to his suggestion of outside assistance, so long as it was as discreet as possible...at least, until such time as discretion could go to the devil!

So, there he sat at his writing desk, staring at the inoffensive sheet of vellum beside his sherry glass. How on earth could he put into words the hideous truth of what they had discovered that evening? He paused before lifting his pen. Tapping it on the side of the inkwell, he tried to control the faint tremor in his hand that threatened to spatter the dark-blue ink across the blank sheet. It had been so very long; were they even at the same address?

Finally, he began.

My dear Versipellis.

I am aware that it has been many, many years since we last met, but I have great need of your services.

You will hopefully remember me and my history, so I shall not go into details of our shared past; but in the event of you needing a little reminder, and the possibility of this letter being read by unwanted eyes, allow me to explain my predicament, in the hope that you will recall my old name.

I am now very nearly in my sixtieth year of life in this most beautiful part of the earth. I still live on the Isle of Cove, having followed my dear father into the Church, in the service of the Burgoyne family... I trust that will be enough to ensure that you remember me and are willing to renew our very old friendship.

Perhaps, instead of informing you of the terrible events of the past hour, I should instead start fifteen years ago, with the beginning of this most ungodly tale, which I hope your presence will bring to a swift and appropriate conclusion.

The Isle of Cove has seen its share of tragedy, as you will recall if you remember my family's sad history, but I digress.

Fifteen years ago, several of the island's children fell victim to evil...perhaps a strong word, Versipellis, but evil is the only word I can use to describe the horrors that befell this place. In little over one week, seven children fell victim to a murderer whose identity was never discovered, a murderer who seemed intent to glory in the most hideous of abuses.

The murderer appeared to take their cue from the obscene acts committed here seventy-five years ago by the Monks of the Inner Sanctum of the Priory of Cove, a group of men and women who likened themselves to the Hellfire Club of old, but whose minor indiscretions were supplanted by the evil will of the Master, Lord Thomas Burgoyne, who for his egregious sins was killed in 1825.

Fifteen years ago, the nightmare only ended when the great-niece of my friend Cornelius Burgoyne, dear Araby, was attacked in her own bed...her screams brought the family butler to her aid and I am thankful to say that she survived her injuries – but her attacker escaped.

Out of fear for our children's lives, every single child who remained alive on the island was sent to family and friends on the mainland for their safety, all the parents agreeing that the children would only return fifteen years after that last attack in Cove Castle.

Well, my friend, those fifteen years have passed, and this advancing Yule is the date for our children's return. Sadly, of the eight children sent away, only three have survived, and they are no longer children; at least one is now married with a child of their own. But they will all return to the island, and young Araby shall return to the Burgoyne family home for the first time since she was found, desperately injured, in her room.

But why am I disturbing you now, after so very many years of silence?

This evening, my old friend Cornelius and I made a

discovery…a discovery of such hideous import that the only person I could think of who could possibly help us was you. You see, Versipellis, on the night young Araby was attacked in her room, the same night that the murders on the island stopped, her fifteen-year-old brother, Master Alistair Burgoyne, went missing…

As the elderly man continued his missive, a sudden thought came to him. Of course, Versipellis' contact Lord Lapotaire was a member of his own club in London. He would send the letter to him via the Mercury Club.

The Mercury Club was somewhat lesser-known than the more popular and fashionable clubs in London, but rather more dangerous. The members of this particular club were not your average hedonistic wastrels, not at all; its clientele consisted of politicians, adventurers, artists, authors, and scientists of both sexes. It was considered quite shocking by some…but not by all.

He looked at the hastily written letter; reading it through, he scrawled his signature at the bottom and blotted it carefully, before tucking it into an envelope on which he wrote the name 'Versipellis'. Then he took another piece of paper and wrote a covering letter to Lord Lapotaire, requesting the conveyance of the enclosed letter into the hands of the man they both knew as Versipellis.

He tucked the second missive into an envelope, addressed and blotted it, and rang the little bell on the desk. After a few moments, the door opened and the Burgoyne family butler, Davaadalai, entered the room. Well over six feet tall, with dark, straight hair that fell in a thick plait to his waist, his impassive face wore its usual expression of calm patience. He bowed to the elderly man, and lifted one jet-black eyebrow.

The elderly scribe smiled with relief. As he was about to seal the letter to Versipellis, he had a sudden thought; he opened one of the desk drawers, and rummaged. Finding what he sought, he paused to study the sepia photograph; two young people stared back at him from the stiff card. Turning it over, he wrote their names and the date the image had been captured on the back before tucking the photograph into the envelope addressed to Versipellis and sealing it. Placing the letter inside the envelope addressed to Lapotaire, he sealed the second envelope, and turned to the waiting butler. "Davaadalai, will you please see that this letter is taken to the village for posting; it needs to be with the postmaster before the next collection."

Davaadalai bowed smartly and took the package, his dark eyes flashing; he was well aware of the import of the awful discovery earlier that evening. "I shall see to it personally, Reverend Popplewell."

○

The Mercury Club
London
15th December

The terribly upright and rather stiff young man, clad in the exclusive and equally stiff plum serge uniform of a Mercury Club attendant, moved silently through the Club's plush, leather-scented library. He entered the adjoining reading room, materialised silently at the elbow of Lord Lapotaire, and gave the sort of polite, deferential cough one would wish were the only type of throat clearance one would ever hear, but that was so often instead a thunderous phlegmatic emission that left one wondering if one's neighbour might expire from the worst possible form of plague.

Lapotaire looked up from his newspaper and his reclining position in the comfortable armchair, and raised a weary eyebrow at the young messenger. Since the birth of their twins, he and his wife Bunny had not enjoyed much sleep; in fact, the Mercury Club was the only place where both could hope to get any kind of rest. His dear wife was currently in the bowels of the building, being pummelled by one of the many exceptional and violently professional masseuses in the Turkish Bath.

The young man bowed and held out a silver salver on which lay a sealed packet. "A letter for you, sir." Another idiosyncrasy of the Mercury Club was that within her hallowed walls, no one was allowed to use their titles.

Lapotaire sat up with a groan, took the proffered envelope, and the young man disappeared as silently as he had arrived. Lapotaire opened the thick packet, removed a second, sealed envelope, and retrieved the single page of writing addressed to him.

Sipping his cocktail, he ran an eye across the beginnings of the letter; a request for assistance from the Reverend Newton Popplewell of Cove Rectory, Cove Village, The Isle of Cove, Westrenshire. Lapotaire rolled his eyes; how on earth had a provincial vicar managed to find the contact details of a government minister?

He reread the sender's address with a faint smile; the people of the aforementioned settlement had obviously been unhindered by imagination when it came to naming their little part of the Empire!

As he began to read the note, his dark eyebrows slowly lowered over his nose. Short to the point of brusqueness, it contained a polite but brisk demand that he not open the other letter, but that he must instead forward the sealed envelope post-haste to the mutual friend they knew as 'Versipellis', whilst offering absolutely no information about what lay within, other than it was 'imperative that the letter be forwarded immediately, as the information therein is a matter of life and death, and Versipellis' agreement to investigate must be settled before Yule,' which was a little matter of six days hence.

Lapotaire rubbed his eyes and swore under his breath. He remembered all too clearly what had occurred the last time he had acted as Elliott's messenger boy: the hideous murders aboard the paddle steamer in New Zealand; the panic as the machine of government began to understand what Versipellis had discovered about Lady Carlton-Cayce; and the flurry of damage control in both hemispheres as the establishment fought to contain the knowledge that one of its paramount beauties, the serial wife of several of the richest businessmen in Britain and Europe, was actually a man.

Lapotaire shook his head. Thank God they had managed to keep that little snippet secret...the Americans would have been laughing about it in their scandal rags for months!

He narrowed his eyes. The fact that said person had disappeared before they could be arrested, and that most of their wealth had disappeared with them, still rankled...even though, as it turned out, they hadn't been the murderer.

Lapotaire glared at his nearly empty glass. He was sure that Elliott and Thorne had been a party to the disappearance of Lady Leonora Carlton-Cayce, as the gentleman had been known, but there was no evidence to prove it. Lady Carlton-Cayce's most recent paramour, Sir Wesley Eade, was dead, the other guests weren't talking, and most of the paperwork that could prove her male identity had apparently been blown over the side of the paddle steamer during the escape of the actual killer.

Lapotaire shook his head. It had been a complete and utter mess, but the British Establishment had survived for many years and dealt with greater scandals, worse infamy, and rather more questionable bedfellows and habits than most people were actually aware of.

He dropped the letter on his lap and tapped his index fingers together. After the debacle Elliott and his associates had created in the southern hemisphere, Lapotaire had been forced to spend what should have been his honeymoon in his Whitehall office, dealing with the painful aftermath of what had become known as 'the New Zealand issue'. He was actually rather amazed that he and Bunny had managed to find both the time and the privacy to create the twins at all!

As he mulled over this obvious sore point, a sudden thought came to Lapotaire's mind, slowly followed by a fiendish grin as he recalled the events of a few short weeks ago, when he and his wife had been invited to the nuptials of one Abernathy S. Thorne of London, England, and one Madame Aquilleia Aquileisi of Cividale Del Friuli, Italy. He nearly laughed out loud at the symmetry of the events — Elliott and Thorne owed him this much!

Thorne had mentioned at the wedding that he and Aquilleia were planning a winter honeymoon across Europe, visiting her family in Italy before travelling to Egypt and one of the most prestigious and ornate hotels in the civilised world: the Eridanus Eau De Nile, situated on a small island three hundred and fifty miles up the Nile.

Lapotaire smiled. Well, now...if, as the Reverend Popplewell insisted, the events detailed in the sealed letter were for Versipellis' eyes only, and unsuitable for the attention of one of the Government's youngest ministers, then he was duty-bound to pass the information to his dear friend, in the hope of their immediate travel to the descriptively named home of the resolute reverend, and the solving of whatever was of too great an import to share with him. Such a terrible shame that it would interfere with Thorne's honeymoon plans. He sniggered, ignoring the chorus of harrumphs and the outbreak of emphatic newspaper rustling that erupted from the men and women sitting around him in the club's reading room.

Lapotaire crumpled the letter into his lap, picked up his glass, and tossed back the last of his cocktail. He tugged at the bell pull just behind him, and a few seconds later the young man who had delivered the offending letter reappeared and bowed. "Yes, sir?"

Lapotaire heaved a happy sigh. "Mr Perch, I need this letter to be taken to an address that is held in the private guest section of the club books. The gentleman's name is Mr Elliott Caine. When you have seen to that, I would like another Martinez, with a touch more gin, if you please."

"Yes, sir."

As the young man accepted the packet and began to turn away, Lapotaire raised his hand, and the young man turned back to face him.

Lapotaire smiled as he settled back in his armchair. "As soon as you possibly can, please."

"Of course, sir, right away."

The messenger walked back to his desk. Pressing a button in the side of the exquisitely carved piece of furniture, he blew down a speaking tube that led directly to the bar, opened the large black-bound ledger that nearly covered the desk, flipped to the private guest section at the back, and copied out one of the addresses within.

A boy not much older than twelve appeared, clad in a similar plum-coloured uniform. "Yes, Mr Perch?"

The club rule of not using titles or forms of address that would elevate an earl above a baron had also been applied below stairs. It had caused some minor issues at first. Several of the servants who had come to work at the club had previously been employed by fine houses and finer families, and were deeply aware of their own standing. As such, they were rather unhappy to find that they would lose that elevation if they chose to accept the generous employment terms offered…it had caused a thinning in the applications which had rather pleased the club management.

The older man handed the packet, the slip of paper, and several coins to the boy. "Take this letter to this address as quickly as possible please, Mr Frank."

The boy bobbed his head. "Yes, Mr Perch."

As the boy shot through the front door, a sharp whistle came from the speaking tube as the bartender responded. Mr Perch gave the drink order, which arrived a few minutes later.

Mr Perch walked back into the library, where Lapotaire was still ensconced in his comfortable chair. His mouth was slightly open and his eyes closed as he serenaded his still-harrumphing fellow-members with several choruses of falsetto snoring, interspersed with occasional bass ululations.

Mr Perch placed the Martinez on the table next to the sleeping man and walked back to his desk with a smile.

A Private Residence
London
15th December

Chymeris looked at the grandfather clock in her plush apartments and frowned, she consulted her marcasite wristwatch with irritation. He was late, again! She ground her teeth as she waited for Trevenniss to bring the carriage to the front. Would she always have to suffer fools?

Pressing her full lips together she stalked to the nearest window, twitching one of the heavy brocade curtains back to glare at the street below. She took a calming breath as she gazed down at the scene before her. London was approaching the cocktail hour in style: couples wandered arm in arm down the bustling street; a flower girl on the corner bawled her wares and their prices; a newspaper lad jockeyed with her for position, screaming out salacious titbits about the latest outrageous murder of a young girl whose mutilated corpse had been discovered not so far from that very street.

Chymeris smiled at the paperboy's language; his joyful use of grisly terms for the young woman's death, employed to encourage buyers, delighted her. She laughed at one particular term, spoken in terms of great enjoyment. That particular corpse wasn't even one of hers, but she could appreciate passion and enjoyment in one's hobbies!

She gazed at the scene and took another deep breath. She so loved the city; fame or anonymity was yours for the asking…as long as you had the wealth, charm, and beauty to take it. Chymeris understood better than most how money, a charming manner, and a pretty face could make most people ignore the more socially unacceptable aspects of one's personality.

She smoothed the front of her black velvet evening gown, a light smirk on her newly acquired face. This one had belonged to a young, but not entirely inexperienced street walker Trevenniss had brought her just a few nights earlier. The young girl had been quite lovely; long blonde hair, wide, almond-shaped blue eyes, and a rather pleasant voice. To be more precise, she *had* been lovely when she arrived; shortly after she had been shown into Chymeris' private rooms, her rapidly cooling corpse had been removed by Trevenniss and disposed of in several locations along the Thames. If only the young paperboy below knew!

She smiled again. The only one who knew just what she

was capable of was trapped inside her mind — but not for very much longer!

She moved to the malachite table in the centre of her sitting room. On it rested one item: a simple wooden jewellery box. She opened the lid, and the Lark and the Spur winked at her from their cushioned velvet bed, the purple diamonds glowing in the flickering gaslight.

Her smile broadened; soon…soon, one of her brothers would be trapped within one of the stones. Perhaps she would use the second stone on her other brother — and then at last she would have what she had wanted for so long!

Her smile twisted then another expression suddenly rippled across her face. Seemingly against her will, her dainty left hand rose and the sharp, manicured nails ripped down her left cheek, leaving deep, bloody gashes in the peachy skin. She gasped in pain and turned to face the mirror that covered the wall opposite her. Deep brown eyes that were not hers gazed out of the murdered girl's face as her brother Phoenixus, utter hatred glowing in his eyes, laughed defiantly inside her head.

Her breath hissed between her teeth; he had never managed to take control of her in that way before. If he could find the strength to fight her after so many years, perhaps her plans should wait until he had been permanently dealt with.

A deferential knock sounded at her door. Her head snapped round and she clapped her hand to her face. "Enter!"

The door swung open and Trevenniss entered, his benign face blank in the manner of a good servant. His voice was as colourless as his appearance, but his eyes were lustful as he looked at his mistress. "Your carriage is ready, my queen."

Chymeris ran her hand across her wounded cheek, the bloody marks disappearing rapidly under her touch. "I've changed my mind. We shall not go to the theatre this evening. It's time I dealt with at least one of my brothers, and sooner rather than later. We will pack and leave for Horseman Falls tonight." She smirked, an unpleasant light in her newly acquired blue eyes. "How nice to finally return home...I wonder if my old student is still there!"

Trevenniss bowed his head as she swished past him into her private chamber. As he turned to follow her; the door slammed in his face.

○

The Road to Penwithiel
Friday the 21st of December

Araby Burgoyne scowled at the open bonnet of the profusely gaseous and collapsed automobile. The dratted machine had decided that country roads were simply too hilly to be borne by its creaky springs, and had deliberately chosen to expire exactly between settlements in order to make it harder for them to reach their longed-for destination. She sighed: never trust a friend who swears their miracle of modern science will get you to Timbuctoo and back again in safety.

Araby straightened up and kicked the nearest tyre in a none too ladylike display of irritation. They were still miles away from the tiny harbour village of Penwithiel and the causeway that would carry them back to the Isle of Cove, and then home...home to Cove Castle, after so many years away.

As she stood, lost in thought, sharp tapping on the motor's window caught her attention. Araby sighed and opened the door. "Yes, Nanny?"

A very elderly lady, bundled in multiple layers of rugs, furs, and scarves, peered at her young charge and lowered the walking cane she had used to tap on the window. "Are we nearly there, my dear?"

Araby shook her head. "Not yet, Nanny."

The lady turned her head slightly. "I'm sorry, my dear, what did you say?"

Araby leant into the car and bawled. "NOT YET NANNY...THERE'S SOMETHING WRONG WITH THE MOTORCAR!"

Nanny tittered. "There's no need to shout, dear child, I'm not deaf!"

The young man standing quietly on the other side of the automobile gave a snort of laughter which faded rapidly at Araby's pointed glare. She raised an arched black eyebrow at him. "Don't just stand there, Perry, do something!"

The young man fiddled with his cufflinks petulantly before reaching into his breast pocket and removing his cigarette case. "Like what?"

Araby faced the young man angrily; it had been one of his gambling friends who had procured them the ropey vehicle they were currently trapped with. But as she opened her mouth to put the young man firmly in his place, she heard a distant sound behind her. That sounded like another automobile!

She ripped off her hat and flung it into the car, almost hitting Nanny as she slammed the door shut. Then she pointed furiously at the passenger seat until Perry got the idea, thrust the cigarette case back into his pocket, and climbed back in to continue his sulk.

Araby pulled her threadbare serge coat closer, perched against the driver's door, and assumed her most tragic expression, her thick, scandalously short hair fluffing around her head like a dark halo as the approaching car swept into view. She ran a swift eye over the vehicle and realised that, whatever its current cargo, it was quite large enough for the three of them and all their meagre belongings to fit in a corner of one of the rear seats. An immaculately dressed, well-muffled chauffeur sat rigidly to attention in the front, while the passengers, however many there were, were hidden inside the pram-like cover that protected them from the freezing December weather.

Araby allowed herself a rueful smile; she didn't have to try too hard to manifest a tragic expression, since she was cold, damp, tired, and hungry...and they were still miles away from where they needed to be!

Her heart leapt as the vehicle began to slow down. The chauffeur looked at her over his bottle-end glasses, his bright green eyes at odds with his dusty, dark-blond hair. He cleared his throat. "Are you requiring assistance, miss?"

Araby smiled in relief. "Oh, yes! Yes, I am...that is, we are; there are three of us. Is that acceptable — I mean, is there enough room?"

The chauffeur nodded. "That should be fine, miss. We can take you on to the next village, if you like?"

Araby smiled gratefully. "Oh, thank you so much!" She opened the door. "These kind people have offered to take us to the next village, Nanny. I should be able to find a mechanic who can deal with this blasted machine there."

Nanny leant out of the vehicle and gave Araby a sharp tap on the hand with her cane. "No coarse language! Whatever would the family think if they heard such profanity?"

Araby rolled her eyes as she helped her elderly chaperone out of the car. As she guided her towards the other motor, she gestured at Perry and mouthed "Get the things". Perry scowled, but at another sharp glare from Araby he snapped his mouth shut, hurried back to the still-steaming wreck, and collected the few items of luggage they had brought for Christmas, carrying them to the rear of the other motorcar.

As Araby and Nanny approached the passenger side of the car, the chauffeur climbed out of the motor and raised a warning hand. "Not in the front, if you don't mind, miss: my passenger wouldn't like it!"

Araby looked at the passenger seat and heard a faint whine as a black Labrador, looking much the worse for wear, sat up. Sorrowful brown eyes met Araby's as with a reproachful look at the uniformed man, the dog sank slowly back out of view.

The chauffeur doffed his cap, took Nanny's arm, and guided her to the rear door. He tapped deferentially at the rear window and turned to Araby. "What's your name, miss?"

She blinked. "Burgoyne — Miss Araby Burgoyne. This is Nanny — I mean Miss Wyke, my chaperone, and this is Mr Perry Challick."

The chauffeur looked at her sharply. "Burgoyne, eh? In that case, miss, perhaps we can take you a little bit further than the next village." He swiftly opened the door. "Ladies and gentleman — Miss Araby Burgoyne, Miss Wyke, and Mr Challick!"

He gently deposited Nanny in the nearest seat, then stepped out of the way and gestured for Araby and Perry to climb in. As he turned to close the door, he winked at a smartly dressed, dark-haired woman sitting opposite the other two inhabitants of the vehicle; she smiled at him in response as he closed the door. Moving quickly, he deposited their scant luggage in the boot, next to some rather swish leather-bound steamer trunks. Climbing back into his seat, he gave the poorly Labrador a gentle head scratch before taking off the brake and continuing down the long road to their destination.

Inside the car, polite social interaction was taking place. Araby, not a foolish young woman by any stretch of the imagination, had taken in the contents of the car as the chauffeur opened the door, ready to flee or use her hatpin accordingly. Luckily however, the inmates of the vehicle seemed, on the surface at least, to be rather safe-looking travel companions. The smartly dressed dark-haired woman, who had remarkable violet eyes, looked far too elegant to be a maid, so Araby judged her to be more a companion than a servant. Opposite her sat a man and a woman, they too were quite striking: the woman a vibrant redhead with sparkling blue eyes and a charming smile, the man of medium height, with short dark hair, and clean-shaven.

Though seated, the man still bore a walking cane with an unusual handle, that of a snake eating its own tail. He was a stranger, yet at the same time strangely familiar. Araby frowned; she felt she should know him, but she was quite sure she didn't.

She smiled uncertainly and ploughed on. "Good evening, and thank you so very much for your assistance; we might still have been there tomorrow if you hadn't arrived!"

The elegant redhead smiled at her. "Not at all: you must have been freezing! Miss Wyke, please do wrap this rug around your knees; that should help a little with the cold."

Nanny flapped an ineffectual hand. "Oh no, please don't go to any trouble on my account!"

The lady shook her head. "Please, Miss Wyke, I insist."

Araby took the warm rug with a word of thanks and tucked it around the feebly protesting lady's legs. As she accepted a blanket for her own legs and settled back in her seat, she addressed the redhead with a bright smile. "As your chauffeur said, I am Miss Araby Burgoyne, returning home for Christmas with Miss Wyke and Mr Challick. Might I enquire as to your names?"

The dark man smiled faintly, his canines flashing in the thin, watery light that penetrated the curtains. "Do you not recognise me, Araby?"

She looked at him sharply as he gestured towards the woman sitting next to him. "Allow me to introduce my wife,

Giselle. This lady is our friend, Aquilleia Thorne, and as for the chauffeur — don't let him fool you, that is our dear friend Aquilleia's husband, Abernathy, who enjoys amateur dramatics and all that terrifying pastime entails! The rather unwell Labrador next to him is Veronique. As to my name, all will be revealed at Cove Castle."

Araby stared at him. "You — you are going to the island?"

His smile widened. "Of course we are." He looked at the driver's seat, and raised an immaculate eyebrow. "Or we would be if a certain person would put their foot down with a little more pressure!"

Thorne raised his voice over the thrumming of the engine. "I heard that, old friend!" He grumbled quietly but pressed his foot somewhat harder on the pedal. Beside him, Veronique whined and threw him another reproachful look as she leant back in her seat, her silky black ears flapping in the breeze.

As the motor car sped through the watery winter sunlight, Araby sat back and smoothed the warm rug over her knees. She wasn't quite sure what was going on, but the vehicle was heading in the right direction. She frowned; how could strangers be heading to her old home? Home...she paused at the thought of that word and what it entailed: the long narrow causeway to the island that could only be used at low tide, the incredible views of the English Riviera from the top of the cliffs, and the little beach where she and her friends had spent so many innocent summers. Her face twisted. Innocent until that summer, fifteen years ago...

As the car rocked gently on the road, Araby pulled herself away from the thoughts that began to seethe in her mind; yes, there were elements of her past she would have to face at Cove Castle...but not yet.

Penwithiel Harbour

As the motorcar pulled smoothly to a halt, Araby woke with a start and caught the dark young man's eye. She blushed and gently nudged Nanny's knee. "Nanny, Nanny… we're here."

The elderly lady looked up blearily and pouted. "Oh, are we? And I was having such a lovely dream…" She paused and seemed to remember where she was, she looked at Giselle and gave a surprisingly girlish giggle. "I do beg your pardon, I'm sure!" She looked around in a bemused manner. "Already on the island? Fancy!"

Araby shared a brief, understanding look with Giselle and shook her head. "No, Nanny, we've just arrived at Penwithiel. Do you remember Penwithiel? That's where the causeway is that leads to the island."

Nanny frowned. "Oh, yes…yes, of course." She turned back to Giselle and her husband. "I do beg your pardon — so rude of me to sleep."

The young man smiled and shook his head. "Not at all, Miss Wyke, travelling can be very tiring."

The chauffeur opened the door and assisted his wife, then turned to Araby, who smiled and accepted the offered hand.

As she stepped onto the narrow, cobbled road, Araby took in the view. From what she could see, Penwithiel hadn't changed much at all. Though one long, sinuous cobbled road was the sum total of the village's spread, Penwithiel was quite sizeable for a village, consisting of a church, a public house, a school, a post office, a police house, a village hall, and several low fishermen's cottages. These were all built of the same local stone and covered in a brilliant white limewash that blinded the unwary eye with flashes of the reflected sunlight that cut through the scudding clouds, pushed by the same winds that tossed the sea into foam-topped waves beyond the harbour.

A wealth of memories spun into Araby's mind: picnics on Rosebay Head overlooking the sea, games of tennis and croquet on the lawn, and the dances at the village hall. She had been too young to dance, but she remembered sitting by the table, watching her brother and his friends.

Araby blinked rapidly in the stiff breeze and turned back to the motor as the dark man alighted and held out a hand to his wife. As she stepped out of the motorcar, a sudden gust of wind caught her ornate veiled hat and nearly carried it down the street.

Her husband guided her to the relative safety of a doorway as Perry climbed out of the car and stared at the pub and the church, his thoughts very much like Araby's; they had returned to a place at once familiar and strange. It had been many years since they had walked on these worn cobbles; Araby had been twelve and he barely eight when they and the others had been sent to the mainland for their safety.

Araby jumped at a sudden shout behind her. Turning, she saw the chauffeur, or rather Abernathy Thorne, approaching a short figure she definitely recognised. The two men engaged in a brief discussion that involved Thorne turning back and gesturing not just to his friends, but also Araby, Nanny, and Perry, and which ended with a firm handshake and a sum of money changing hands.

Thorne made his way back to the little group. "Apparently we have missed the low tide, so we won't be able to drive to the island, but I have managed to hire us a boat." He gestured towards the elderly man. "This gentleman has agreed to take us to the island — but it seems we are not the only guests expected on the isle!"

Araby hurried to the redhead's side. "Oh, please let us pay for our journey to the island!"

The young woman's husband smiled at her and shook his head. "We won't hear of it, Araby. Perhaps we should make our way on board."

He gently took his wife's arm, escorted her to the boat and assisted her aboard. Then he stood on the well-scrubbed deck of the vessel and waved at Thorne, who glared before stomping back to the motorcar. He slammed the door with rather more vigour than was necessary, handed the grumpy Labrador's leash to his smiling wife, and began to struggle with the contents of the boot.

Araby dug her elbow into Perry's ribs and gestured at the motorcar. Perry heaved a sigh, tucked his cigarette case back into his pocket, and made his way over to offer assistance. Thorne accepted with a magnanimous smile only slightly touched with relief as the two men dragged the contents of the boot to the waiting fishing-boat where they were helped by Mossy's young grandson.

Araby guided Nanny aboard the old vessel and settled her in one of the bench seats before turning to look at the couple who had kindly provided them with transport. She bit her fingernail: there was something about him, but she couldn't put her finger on it.

The subject of her appraisal had paused to talk with the captain; five foot nothing, built like a tree trunk and pushing eighty from the other side, Mossy Stumps had been born and raised in Penwithiel and was proud of the fact that he had never left: "Everythin' 'ee need is right here. If 'ee don't think so, then go an' find out what it's like out there where no one knows 'ee, cares about 'ee, or worse, sees 'ee as easy pickins!" This was his response to any of the young ones who complained about the lack of dances, theatres, and other forms of civilised entertainment in the little village.

As Araby looked on, Mossy smiled at the ravishing redhead and touched his forelock before turning his attention to her husband. A strange expression crossed his face as the younger man talked with him, their voices too low for Araby to hear, before Mossy gave a huge guffaw of laughter, clapped the other man on his back and bellowed, "Welcome back, young sir! I very near din't recognise 'ee! And married now, too!"

The dark-haired man smiled and shook the proffered paw. "It's wonderful to be back, Mossy. I trust your lovely wife Maybell is well?"

Mossy grinned, the various gaps in his smile adding to the overall effect of 'hardy seaman'. "She yem, sir. Still goin' is old Maybell!"

Araby sat next to Nanny in one of the little seats bolted to the side of the small boat, stared hard at the young couple, and chewed her fingernail. Nanny lightly slapped at her hand, Araby caught her chaperone's judging eye and guiltily placed her hand back in her lap. She knew she had sensed something familiar about the young man when they met, but she still couldn't place him. And Mossy had recognised him — indeed, treated him like an old acquaintance!

Mossy addressed them. "Now, we'm can't go just yet. There's a few others we'm needing to collect, they should be comin' soon..."

A tiny motorcar appeared at the top of the hill and made its way rapidly down the main street before pulling to a halt next to the village hall. A smartly dressed young man climbed out of the driver's seat and tore off his goggles. He stared out across the harbour, a genuine smile on his face as he took in the view.

Araby's breath caught in her throat; she knew that face! It had been so very long, but she still recognised him. She stood up and without thinking waved at the new arrival. "Sebastian! Sebastian Lees — over here!"

Nanny tugged at her sleeve, and hissed under her breath, "Araby! Ladies do not behave in such a way!"

Araby ignored her and turned back to the handsome young man. He flung up a hand in greeting, then ducked around the motor and opened the rear passenger door. A very elegant, dark haired young woman in a deep-red travel dress got out and smiled at the man. They both turned back to the motorcar as a little boy of not much more than six exploded out of the vehicle and ran to the water's edge, speedily followed by a nanny and a smartly dressed maid clutching a carpet bag. Araby's heart, which had leapt into her throat on seeing Sebastian for the first time in nearly fifteen years, plummeted into her boots as the young family approached the boat with their servants and luggage.

The young man assisted the lady in red and the little boy aboard, then turned to the others with a charming smile. "Good morning, ladies and gentlemen. Araby!" His smile deepened. "My dear Araby, it's marvellous to see you again after so long. Please allow me to introduce my wife Theodora, and our son, Leander. Theodora, this is my very old friend Araby Burgoyne, and these are Nanny Wyke and Perry Challick. Gosh, Perry, it's been a while!"

As Perry pumped the proffered hand, the young woman smiled politely at Araby and Nanny, who had already started to coo over the little boy. In a pleasant voice touched with coolness, she murmured, "I am very pleased to meet you; Sebastian has told me so much about his life on the island."

Araby plastered a polite smile on her face and shook the fingertips of the offered hand. Nanny smiled vaguely and began a conversation with the Lees family nanny.

Mossy checked a battered piece of paper. "One more for the journey." He looked over at the pub, and a sad expression appeared on his face. "An' I think I'm knowin' where that one may be! If you'll 'scuse me…"

He disembarked from the little vessel and stomped towards the pub. As he approached the front door, it was flung open and he was joined on the doorstep by a tall, dark young man who appeared with alacrity, as though propelled at great speed from within the dim little building.

Dressed — festooned was perhaps a better word — in a collection of richly coloured brocade and velvet, clutching a hardback book in one hand and an open bottle of red wine in the other, the young man turned and addressed the slowly closing door in a voice as rich and sumptuous as the clothes he wore. "And let that be a lesson to you!"

He swung round, nearly collided with the captain, and took a step back. "Ah, Mossy. Might I endeavour to inveigle my way aboard your most salubrious vessel?"

Mossy regarded him with an amused but slightly pained expression. "I can't rightly say, Mr Lutyens…but I can take 'ee back to the island if tha'll do?"

The dark young man gave a bark of laughter and clapped the short man on one broad shoulder. "Indeed it will, Mossy. Absolutely capital of you!"

He wandered down to the boat, taking the occasional swig from the wine bottle. Nanny squeaked something under her breath as he trotted down the gangplank and beamed at them. "Ladies and gentlemen, let us hope Mossy gets us all to the island in one piece, shall we?"

He grinned as his gaze drifted across their faces, pausing on Giselle and her amused husband, skimming across Aquilleia, Thorne, and a curious Veronique, before alighting on Nanny, Perry, and Araby. He shook his head as though trying to clear his vision and his expression became incredulous. "Araby? Good God, Araby!"

Araby smiled tentatively, aware of the shocked grumbling coming from Nanny. "Hello, Lucius. It's been a long time."

Lucius Lutyens smiled at her, this time with genuine happiness. He caught her hand and gently pressed a kiss against her thumb. "You always called me Luci, remember?"

She smiled. "I remember, Luci. How have you been? Do you remember Nanny and Perry Challick...and Sebastian? Of course, you won't know his...wife and son, Theodora and Leander."

A slightly distant light appeared in Luci's eyes. "Oh, yes, of course. How could I possibly forget Miss Wyke and young Perry?" He smiled at them, then his gaze settled on Sebastian and the smile faded. "Dear Sebastian, we meet again. What a pleasure it must be for you!"

His smile returned but didn't quite reach his eyes. He nodded to them before choosing a seat as far removed as possible from his fellow-travellers. He took another swig of wine, opened his book, and proceeded to become engrossed in the marvellous tale within.

Araby flicked a quick glance at Sebastian, who was standing next to his seated family. He caught Araby's eye and gave her a troubled smile before turning his attention back to his wife and child.

Thorne leant in to Aquilleia and murmured, "Well, that was awkward!"

Giselle caught her husband's eye and raised an immaculate auburn arch. It promised to be an interesting weekend!

The Isle of Cove
The Jetty

Cornelius Burgoyne stared at his pocket watch and grimaced. As he tucked the watch back into his waistcoat pocket and smoothed his bristling walrus moustache, a sharp voice rose next to him. "Do stop fussing, Cornelius! We knew they would arrive too late to use the causeway; at least Mossy will get them here in time for dinner."

Cornelius bent a pained gaze on his sister. Amicarella Burgoyne, known to her nearest and dearest as Ami, sat in her mechanised bath chair, awaiting the return of the island's surviving children with interest and hope. Five years younger than her brother, her mind was as sharp as it had been when she and her brother had married into the family more than forty years earlier.

Several years after her marriage to Edward Burgoyne, Ami had fallen ill with Heine-Medin disease and had been confined to her bed. The paralysis had destroyed her marriage to Edward, who had drunk himself to death in the company of his mistress several years later, but instead of languishing in ill-health and widowhood, Ami had thrown herself into living in a way that had taken various friends, but not the family who knew her, by surprise.

The sharpness of Ami's mind had clashed with the weakness of her legs, and her nephew Merric, the Earl of Cove, at that time only twenty, had witnessed his beloved aunt's unhappiness and so had thrown himself into his studies to try and help her. Even if Ami could no longer walk unaided, the mechanised bath-chair Merric had created for her, as well as the lifting platforms in the castle, ensured that she could keep up as well physically as she could mentally.

Ami cast an exasperated and lively eye over her brother. He could be a worrier at the best of times, but something was different today. Yes, she knew it was time for the island's children to return, though in spite of their efforts far fewer had returned than they had hoped, but there was more to his expression than simple concern. It was almost as though he were afraid of something, and he wouldn't share it with her!

She pursed her lips thoughtfully. Well, she knew her brother better than he knew himself. He might not tell her now, but he would most certainly tell her later...if he knew what was good for him!

She paused at the thrumming sound travelling over the water, and poked her brother in the ribs with a ring-bedecked finger. "That sounds like Mossy's boat now."

They were joined on the end of the jetty by another man who had made his way down the lane from the rectory. Tottering but still upright, Reverend Popplewell dropped the small carpet bag he was carrying to the ground and pressed a gentlemanly kiss on Ami's hand. He nodded at Cornelius and gestured at the scudding clouds in the bright-blue sky. "Cornelius. A lovely day for the return of our past, wouldn't you say?"

His friend flashed a quick look at his sister before nodding uncertainly. "As you say, Popplewell, a lovely day. Oh, by the way, your suite has been readied for your stay."

Popplewell nodded and gestured to the carpet bag at his feet. "Thank you, Cornelius. I have packed for the next few days. I thought I would travel up to the castle with you...and with the children."

Ami, who had caught the look as well as the glance the men shared, cast a gimlet-eyed glare at them. So, it was something they were both aware of, and both were keeping it from her. She pressed her lips together. This would require special attention; she didn't know what they were up to, but she would find out…she always found out!

The reverend smiled at her. "And how are your other guests settling in?"

Ami settled back in her cushioned chair as she watched Mossy's boat appear from the other side of the cliffs. "As well as can be expected, I believe." She paused, turned a slightly mischievous smile on Popplewell, and added brightly, "Do you know that my dear step-granddaughter Sybilla is one of the most celebrated mediums in London? Of course you do — but has Cornelius told you that she and her lovely husband Marcus have offered to hold a séance for us this evening, and their marvellous friend Melisandre has offered to assist? Isn't that thrilling?"

Popplewell caught Cornelius's embarrassed glance, blinked rapidly and turned his gaze to the approaching boat. "Yes…thrilling!" he echoed faintly.

As the laden vessel pottered towards the jetty, Ami paused in her enjoyment of Popplewell's religious squeamishness and turned to look towards the village, her lively blue eyes scanning the butter-yellow stone buildings that wove their way through the neatly tended gardens and bare trees. Her gaze wandered up the sun-dappled lane that headed towards the bluff, and beyond, to Cove Castle herself.

Built of the same yellow stone as the pretty village nestling at her feet, Cove Castle was a thirteen-storey castle fortress, not counting her extensive cellars, complete with three-foot-thick walls, arrow slits, and narrow spiral stair-cases that sprouted like mushrooms from every conceivable surface. Tight, tapestry-lined corridors wound their way around the many rooms and seemed to head nowhere in particular, while tiny hidden courtyards, romantic balconies, and massive fireplaces grew in abundance. She was beautiful in summer, with her rose gardens, rhododendron walk, and the glowing sunshine streaming in through the myriad stained glass windows, and she was sumptuous in the dead of winter, with her sheepskin rugs, roaring fireplaces, and tapestries. However, in spite of the cosy fires in nearly every room and the bright sunshine beating in through every window, she was also absolutely freezing!

Designed and built by the same ancestor who had been given the island by Henry VIII, this generous gift had occurred at the same time as the dissolution of the monasteries that had led to the destruction of Cove Abbey, whose desolate but picturesque ruins lay to the south-west of the house, and whose wrecked walls, windows, and relics had been salvaged to build and grace the new master's home.

Up at the castle, in a room that, in spite of the bright sunlight, was also lit with the golden glow of gaslight, a naked woman stood at one of the thickly draped windows and gazed out to the village and the distant jetty below.

She paused, a thoughtful expression on her face as she lifted her jade cigarette holder to her red lips and inhaled. Carefully placing the holder on an ashtray sitting on the small table under the window, she gathered her peignoir from the back of the well-upholstered velvet armchair, wrapped the thin Chinese silk tightly about her slender figure, lifted the holder and tapped the ash from her cigarette. She twitched back one of the creamy lace window panels, brought the holder back to her lips, and resumed her silent watch.

In the comfort of her luxurious suite of rooms, Sybilla De Banzie, niece to Ami and Cornelius, and Acclaimed Medium to the Finest Families in London and Europe (or so it claimed on her calling cards), gazed with calm calculation at the small clot of people huddled on the distant jetty, her light grey eyes also taking in the slowly approaching boat.

Tall and slim, in her early thirties, with a wealth of dark

hair piled atop her elegant head, a vivid streak of silver hair at her brow caught the bright winter light streaming through the window and glittered, the silvery strands mimicking the light in her almost colourless eyes. She knew how to use her unusual appearance to great benefit in her art, and her very healthy bank account was a testament to just how good she was in her chosen profession.

She turned at a slight noise behind her and smiled as her husband Marcus pressed a kiss on her neck. He wrapped his arms around her as the boat moored and the slightly unsteady passengers gathered at the gangplank.

A similar age to his wife, as fair as she was dark, and with brilliant blue eyes, Marcus De Banzie had been honourably discharged from the Grenadier Guards with several campaign medals to his credit, and several creditors clamouring for payments owed in relation to his superb collection of outfits, motor cars, and accommodations suitable for an elegant man about town and his equally fabulous wife. It wasn't that they couldn't afford to pay: far from it, they simply adhered to their motto, which they had lived by for several years: why pay, even if you had the funds to do so?

Their parties were renowned among the younger residents of the more stylish parts of the capital. The occasional cost of propping up the De Banzies' lifestyle was unimportant to those acquaintances more than happy to support them in return for the superior fun their spectacular company provided.

However, even their closest acquaintances were slowly becoming aware of previously hidden concerns. Whispers of the more socially unacceptable side of their lifestyle were becoming louder; peculiar goings-on, disappearances, strange late-night wanderings, and the entertaining but highly questionable characters who were part of their inner circle. These whispers now followed them even into salubrious clubs and wealthy households, but Sybilla's psychic abilities far outweighed any alleged nefariousness...for now!

They were more careful these days; indeed, they had to be, for there were certain entertainments they both enjoyed that they could never, would never, give up!

Marcus pressed another kiss on his wife's neck, and tightened his arms around her as they watched the disembarking passengers. "What do you think, my love? Will one of them have the answer?"

Sybilla smiled, the curve of her lips sharpened by an unpleasant light in her ash-coloured eyes. "I believe so, my darling. Either one of them, or someone else in the family. By the time we've finished with whoever has the information we seek, they will be desperate to speak!"

They both laughed as she let the lace curtain fall, and turned to kiss her husband.

○

The Boat Arrives

With the smoothness of many years' practice battling the elements, Mossy pulled the craft alongside the battered, barnacle-clad jetty that served the village of Cove. As his grandson leapt from the boat onto the rickety wooden structure, Mossy grinned and doffed his cap to Ami, Cornelius, and Popplewell. "'Ow you be doin' ma'am, sir, Vicar?" He turned back to the bay they had just entered and waved an expressive hand. "She'm do be lookin' lovely today. And none too choppy neither, even if them aboard do say otherwise!" He threw a thick coil of rope to his grandson, who tied the boat up and hopped back on board to help the slightly green passengers disembark.

Araby helped Nanny ashore, then immediately flung

herself at her great-uncle Cornelius. "Gruncle! Oh, it's been so long — too long!"

Cornelius looked rather embarrassed, as he always did at her nickname for him, but privately he had always been rather touched by the sentiment behind it. A gentle smile appeared as he awkwardly patted the slim arms wrapped around his neck. As she pulled away from him with a watery smile, he gently stroked the side of her face. "My dear child, welcome home."

As Araby turned to greet her great-aunt, the other returnees disembarked. Sebastian and his family stood to one side as Lucius, making every attempt not to look at the young man, gave Cornelius and Popplewell a nod, greeted a smiling Ami with a cheerful kiss on her cheek, and headed towards one of the tidy little cottages that lined the natural harbour.

One guest alighted without any sign of queasiness, and assisted their equally capable companion to a more stable setting before approaching Cornelius. Elliott's calm dark-brown eyes met Cornelius' questioning, watery blue gaze as the two men stared at each other. At an almost imperceptible nod from Elliott, Cornelius moved towards him, and spoke. "My God, I can't believe it! We had hoped you would return, but..."

He turned to look at his niece, who was giving Ami a tearful hug. "Araby, my dear, look who has come home to us...your dear brother, Alistair!"

Araby spun round, almost dropping Ami, and stared at the dark young man who had assisted her and her travel companions. As her wide brown eyes took in his gentle smile and outstretched hand, she collapsed in a dead faint at her great-aunt's feet.

Nanny tutted and nudged her with one tiny foot. "Oh Araby, really! A lady at least tries to aim for someone who will catch her!" She tittered as a rather embarrassed Perry held her arm and alternated between looking at her and Araby, who was draped perilously close to the water's edge.

Help arrived in the form of both Sebastian and Lucius, who, on hearing the commotion, had turned in time to witness Araby slump to the floor. Luci and Sebastian almost clashed heads in their attempt to be the first to Araby's side. As they each clasped an arm and began to prise her off the cold wooden boards, Araby began to come to. Luci and Sebastian glared at each other before assisting her to the end of the jetty, where a weathered bench took in the changing seasons year in, year out.

As they settled her, Sebastian's wife Theodora approached, rummaging in her bag. She sat next to Araby and waved a vial of smelling salts under her pale nose. A sudden fit of coughing racked Araby's slender frame. As she sat up and pushed the vial away, she caught Theodora's eye and smiled weakly. "Thank you...Mrs Lees. And you too, gentlemen, please do forgive me..." Her voice trailed off as Elliott walked over and knelt beside her, smiling.

Araby shook her head as she reached out a trembling hand to touch his face. "Alistair, how...I don't understand."

He caught her hand and kissed it. "All will be revealed tonight, my dearest sister. There is so much to talk about, so much time we have lost, and there is new family for you to get to know."

Cornelius nodded. "Yes! Yes, of course. Oh! Pardon me, Ami!" His ears turned pink with embarrassment as he nearly fell over his sister in her bath chair.

She prodded him sharply in the ribs. "You should know by now that if I am not ahead of you, I am never more than one step behind you, Cornelius! Now, Alistair, come here and let me have a look at you..."

Elliott smiled and swung his cane with a flourish as he

was subjected to Ami's gimlet-eyed scrutiny. After several minutes had passed, she nodded. "You look very well, young man, but don't ever run away like that again! You scared us into fits!"

Elliott laughed as he kissed her proffered cheek. "I promise, Aunt Ami. May I introduce my wife, Giselle?"

Cornelius, now recovered from his near-collision, swept over to the smiling redhead and bent his moustache over her hand. "Charming, charming."

He waved a hand towards his sister and Popplewell. "Allow me to introduce my sister, Amicarella Burgoyne. Alistair, you of course will remember our dearest friend and familial confessor, Reverend Popplewell?"

Elliott nodded as he extended his hand to the elderly vicar with a smile. "How could I possibly forget you, Reverend? You are indeed one of the family's oldest friends."

Popplewell shook the proffered hand with a strange smile. "I hoped you would not have forgotten me, young man. It is wonderful to see you again, and to meet your lovely wife." Giselle smiled as the elderly gentleman bent over her hand in turn.

Ami studied the ravishing redhead before she spoke. "Has anyone told you, my dear, that you bear a striking similarity to the renowned contralto, Giselle Du'Lac? And you share her name, too…quite a coincidence."

Giselle smiled, ignoring the look that passed between her husband and Thorne. "They have, yes…though sadly I don't possess her talent for singing." She looked at the others. "There is indeed much to talk about, but may I suggest that we retire to the castle and refresh ourselves first? I wouldn't presume to speak for anyone else, but I am rather chilly!"

The others murmured agreement; various formal introductions were swiftly dealt with, and the correct amount of conversation was concluded with extreme speed in the rapidly cooling afternoon air. Cornelius turned and waved at a large open carriage waiting near the bench; two young men immediately climbed down and set about loading passengers and luggage. Ami waved cheerfully as she made her way up the lane in her mechanised bath chair, and the others waited patiently to set out on the short but cold journey through the village and up the hill to Cove Castle.

As the small procession departed the village, Lucius stood in silence by the abandoned bench before making his way back to his tiny cottage. As he entered the trim stone building, the ornate purple door closed behind him with somewhat more force than was strictly necessary.

As the slam echoed across the little bay, a curtain twitched in the bedroom of the house next door. The person within sat back in their armchair and continued their vigil.

○

Cove Castle
The Dining Room

Mabe Burnthouse, the Burgoyne family cook for more than forty years, glared at the impassive mountain that was Davaadalai, propped her large red hands on her substantial hips, and snapped, "I don't care! You know it's my kitchen, and I says' we don't eat no curry three days in a row! Mr Burgoyne might like it, but he's not the one who has to suffer the aftermath like Mrs Burgoyne, now, is he? He can have the bisque, the fish, the venison, and the pudding that Mrs Burgoyne requested and like it, and that's my final word on the matter!" She stalked out of the dining room, her bristling, aproned form moving surprisingly quickly as she stomped back into the kitchen and closed the door firmly behind her.

Davaadalai continued checking the settings on the

immaculate dining table with a faint smile. It was the same every time Mr Burgoyne requested a curried dish for dinner; his sister allowed it for two days in a row — no more, no less — then issued a request for a simple menu. The cook always supported Mrs Burgoyne, and he always supported Mr Burgoyne. This tourney had originated many years earlier, and remained a game that all continued to enjoy.

His dark, almond shaped eyes scanned the heavily furnished room from the forest-green velvet curtains to the massive Gothic-arch fireplace, decorated with evergreen boughs from the gardens, and back to the Elizabethan dark-oak dining table that could seat twenty, and that was currently set for seventeen. He tweaked one of the name cards that sat on a spotless china plate, then wiped a non-existent smudge from the gold-edged dish before smoothing the puckered green cloth that dressed the table and best showed the ornate display of gold, white, and red chrysan-themums gracing the centre of the table.

He checked the place settings; husbands and wives were placed the correct amount of space apart, the current master of the house, Lord Merric Burgoyne, Earl of Cove, sat at the head of the table, and the future master of the house would be seated in his correct place as the highest ranked male guest. That had required moving Mr Burgoyne from his usual place to the position of second male guest of honour, just to the left of the hostess. Lord Burgoyne had been rather embarrassed at the idea of moving his aunt and uncle, but both Cornelius and Ami had insisted that the proprieties be observed. It had been more difficult to place the other guests, as there were rather more men than women. The seating arrangements for the next few days would also require some degree of artistic licence, as Mrs Burgoyne had insisted that young Leander Lees dine with the adults on Christmas Eve and

Christmas Day, instead of in his parents' suite with his nanny.

Davaadalai exhaled. Luckily, apart from the master of the house, none of the guests were titled, which meant there ought not to be any issues over placement at table. He closed his eyes and rubbed the bridge of his aquiline nose, remembering the one occasion at the beginning of his tenure as butler at Cove when he had accidentally placed a baron above a viscount. The only person who had noticed was the viscount — the baron had been too drunk to care — but the viscount had been rather strident about the social faux pas. Davaadalai sighed; that had been the most uncomfortable occasion in his career as a butler. Not his life, but definitely his career!

He tore his near-black gaze away from the past and back to the matter at hand. Yes, all was quite suitable, the gleaming china place settings were immaculate and just the right distance from the glasses, cutlery, cruets and the neighbouring diner. The crystal was polished to eye-watering brightness, and the steady sunlight coming through the huge south-facing windows set the sparkling glass and polished silverware to brilliance, throwing vibrant rainbow hues against the yellow stone walls. Davaadalai removed a small ruler from his inner pocket and remeasured the space between an empty tureen and a full cruet. A satisfied smile appeared on his usually expressionless face: perfect!

He left the dining room and entered the great hall. Walking past the thirty-foot-tall Christmas tree that had taken both footmen and several maids several hours to haul in and decorate, Davaadalai paused by one of the towering windows overlooking the castle entrance. He smoothed his thick black pigtail as he waited for the arrival of Cornelius and the last of their guests.

He heard Mrs Burgoyne before he saw her. The mechanised bath chair that her nephew had built for her spat out bullet-like sounds as she appeared, barrelling up the lane followed by a trail of black smoke, and piloted the noisy vehicle onto the drawbridge spanning the twenty-foot-deep dry moat which guarded the castle.

Davaadalai opened the front door and bowed from the neck as she approached. "Mrs Burgoyne."

Ami, having had time on her return journey to think about various things involving Cornelius and Popplewell, looked up at him through narrowed eyes. Davaadalai was notoriously devoted to her brother, but she knew full well that subterfuge was not something Davaadalai would play along with...unless it was at her brother's behest. She pursed her lips, deciding that bluntness would be best. "Davaadalai, do you know what my brother and the reverend are up to?"

Davaadalai cultivated his smoothest butler face and gazed at a point somewhere above Ami's left earlobe. "I couldn't say, madam. I trust the arrangements for the guests are to your satisfaction?"

Ami settled back into her cushions and sniffed. "The rooms are of course perfect, thank you, Davaadalai." She paused, a pained expression on her face. "I trust the menu this evening will not contain...curry?"

Davaadalai's lips twitched. "No indeed, madam, Mrs Burnthouse has taken your instructions to heart and created a menu that does not contain curry."

Ami smiled and patted her stomach. "That is a relief...my digestive system will thank her later!"

The full carriage swayed up the hill and came to a halt just in front of the drawbridge. Davaadalai turned and clapped sharply. Three maids and two footmen appeared, seemingly out of nowhere, and began to organise the guests, all of whom would be staying at the castle for the holidays.

Before the murders fifteen years earlier, Sebastian had

lived with his parents in the village. Both had passed on in the intervening years, and though he had inherited his family home, it had been agreed that he, his wife and son, and young Perry, whose parents had also passed shortly after he had been sent to the mainland, should stay at Cove Castle for Yule, Christmas, and New Year before heading to their homes on the island.

Perry climbed out of the carriage and stared at the massive building in silence before turning and assisting Nanny out of the vehicle. The elderly lady gazed at the castle in a somewhat happier silence than Perry, sighing contentedly as one of the maids guided her through the front door and explained that she world escort her to her suite of rooms. The maid took the elderly lady not up the stairs, but towards a nook in the far wall; she carefully settled Nanny into a small, well-cushioned chair, blew down the tasselled communication tube, waited for the answering whistle, and intoned, "First floor". As the floor beneath them jolted and began to rise, the maid just managed to keep a straight face as Nanny forgot her previous objections to coarse language and turned the air a becoming shade of periwinkle as they made their juddering ascent.

On the upward journey, the maid explained how to use the mechanism, and that the moving floor had been built over several years by Lord Burgoyne, to better enable his aunt to move easily between the ground floor and the upper reaches of the castle. The topmost level, some thirteen floors above, held the family chapel, with its walled roof garden and fernery. This floor had previously been impossible for Ami to access due to the substantial number of steps between the ground floor and the roof.

Nanny, with an embarrassed titter about her unladylike remarks, explained to the smiling young maid that the mechanism had already been in the castle when she had lived there, but she had never used it.

As Nanny, the maid, and the platform disappeared through the ceiling, Araby climbed down from the carriage and, like Perry, stared at the place that had been her home for the first twelve years of her life: a place she hadn't seen for fifteen long years. A huge wave of emotion hit her as she walked across the drawbridge towards the huge front door that stood open, waiting for her. She reached out hesitantly, as though afraid it might disappear; as she touched the ornately carved dark oak, she whispered softly, "I'm back — I'm home!"

"Araby!"

She turned and was engulfed by a strong pair of arms encased in rough cotton covered with a strange concoction that smelt of engine grease and tea leaves. She recognised the strange miasma immediately. "Uncle Merric!"

Merric Burgoyne, brother of Araby's mother Sabine, and as the eldest male in the family, heir to the Burgoyne family estate and title, smiled with genuine happiness as he held Araby at arm's length and gazed at her. A slight frown creased his gentle face as he took in the hollows in her cheeks and the shadows beneath her jaw. "You need to eat more, my dear...whatever would your mother say if she knew you were neglecting your health?" He patted her hand and tucked it under his arm as he walked her into the hall. "Never mind, you are home, and most welcome you are too. I'm sure Mrs Burnthouse will attempt to force-feed you your own weight in seed cake!"

Araby gave a watery laugh as she blotted at her eyes with her free hand. "Mrs Burnthouse? She's still here?"

Merric smiled. "Of course! She's as much part of the family as any of us, and she remembered that seed cake was your favourite, so there will be plenty of it this holiday!" He looked at her questioningly, a searching light in his soft blue eyes. "And how long will you be with us, my dear?"

A thousand thoughts ricocheted around Araby's mind, but one stopped before her mind's eye and stayed there. She looked shyly at her uncle. "I think — that is, I do believe, that I have come home for good."

Merric kissed her hand. "I am very glad! Come, we have put you in the Blue Suite on the third floor. Sybilla and her husband Marcus are in the Pink Suite next to you, and Sybilla's friend Melisandre…" He paused. His next words were uttered in a different tone that made Araby take note, even though he sounded nonchalant. "Do you remember Melisandre Salazar? She used to visit with Sybilla when they were at boarding school." He frowned slightly as Araby shook her head. "Well, it's understandable if you don't; she was a little older than you, and spent most of her time with Sybilla and Alistair. She seemed to be at a loose end this Christmas…she has no family, and Sybilla suggested — well, you know Sybilla! Anyway, Melisandre is in the Green Suite on the same floor as you." Araby blinked as her uncle's stream of consciousness continued into the grand hall and then as they went upstairs.

Elliott entered the great hall and looked at the massive stone staircase. Ami looked up at him. "How does it feel to be home after all these years, young man?"

He smiled. "As strange as it must feel for you, Aunt Ami."

Ami smiled back and caught the butler's eye. "Davaadalai, will you please escort Master Alistair and his lovely wife to their suite?"

The butler gave a sweeping bow and indicated the stairs, where Merric and Araby were just disappearing from view.

As Elliott and Giselle began their ascent, Merric and his niece turned down one of the many narrow and heavily furnished corridors that issued from the central staircase, making their way towards an ornate spiral staircase at the far end. Araby smiled as she took in the familiar stained-glass windows and tapestries. She turned to her uncle. "So, Sybilla and Marcus have already arrived?"

Merric nodded, and a slightly cynical look appeared on his usually good-natured face as they climbed the wrought-iron treads. "You know what Sybilla and Marcus are like; if bed and board is offered at another's expense, we will never be rid of them!"

Araby shot her uncle a teasing look. "This Melisandre of whom you speak: you say she spent some holidays here, but I don't remember her at all. Who is she?"

Merric paused, and to Araby's astonishment, a faint redness appeared around his neck and crept up to his cheeks. He coughed and ran a finger around the inside of his necker-chief. "Melisandre is one of Sybilla's dearest and oldest friends, or so I am gushingly told by both Sybilla and Marcus. The last time she visited was many years ago — it must have been fourteen or fifteen years ago. She seems to have fallen on rather hard times lately, so she assists Sybilla with her seances. Sybilla insists that she's a highly gifted young woman whose psychic abilities are even better than hers." Merric waggled his eyebrows conspiratorially, "But just between us, I have long been of the opinion that Sybilla's gifts are more dedicated to the taking of payments than her questionable abilities as a medium!"

Araby smiled and gently slapped her uncle's arm. "Don't be a cat, Uncle!" She scrutinised him closely. For as long as she had known him, her uncle had been obsessed with machinery and had categorically refused to observe the social niceties necessary to wooing and winning a bride, but the flush that had crept up his neck suggested that finally, in his fortieth year, he just might succumb!

Araby hid a smile and allowed herself to be escorted to

her rooms. The Blue Suite was a pretty, light, feminine apartment with views to the north and the mainland. It was also far removed from the little suite of rooms that had been hers all those years ago. Araby blinked and tried to force her mind away from the hideous memories that rose inside her, threatening to flood her...

Merric felt her fingers tighten their grip on his arm. He took in the sudden pallor of her cheeks and guided her to the chaise at the end of her bed before hurriedly tugging at the bell pull. As he waited, he cursed himself for mentioning the last time Melisandre had visited the castle: that very same holiday, fifteen years ago...

A sharp knock made him jump. "Enter!"

A smart young footman appeared and bowed from the neck. "Yes, Lord Burgoyne?"

"Brandy, please, Ellis — immediately!"

"Yes, sir."

The footman left the room. As soon as the door closed, his calm disappeared and he sprinted to a cupboard. Removing a key from a heavy chain on his belt, he unlocked the door and entered. A few moments later, he reappeared with a tray containing a decanter, two glasses, and a plate of biscuits.

Locking the door behind him, he moved with practised speed to the Blue Suite and knocked on the door. Merric flung it open and stood back as the footman placed the tray on the dressing table, bowed and left.

Merric poured a generous measure of brandy into a glass, looked at his niece and doubled it. He poured a second glass for himself and sat down, watching her as she gulped down the brandy. He took the glass from her trembling hands and held out the plate of biscuits. "Eat these, Araby, it will help." He shook his head; it was wonderful to finally have her home where she belonged, but the damage that had been done to her fifteen years ago might never be mended.

Araby bit into a buttery biscuit. It was one of Mrs Burnt-house's best oatmeal and raisin creations, soft and chewy, but it tasted like ashes in her mouth. She raised her eyes to her uncle, who was looking at her in concern, and attempted a smile that didn't fool him at all. "I'm all right, Uncle, it's just — memories of that night…" Her voice trailed off as the sounds and smells came back to her.

Tears leaked from Araby's closed eyes as Merric knelt by the chaise and gently held her hand. "You're back home with us, Araby. We will protect you, child, always."

○

Elliott and Giselle's Suite
6:15pm

Elliott stood by the full-length mirror in their room and studied his reflection, smoothing his dark-red cravat and brushing a non-existent speck of lint from his lapel.

Giselle smiled at his expression as she jammed yet another handful of pins into her mass of red hair; having not yet replaced her maid, Lilith, dealing with her almost sentient tresses was something of a challenge!

As they finished their preparations for dinner, a soft tapping came at their bedroom door. Giselle looked up from where she had been fighting her hair by the dressing table and shared a sharp look with her husband as he made his way to the door and called out. "Yes? Who is it?"

An elderly voice responded. "It is I, Reverend Popplewell… We didn't have the chance to introduce ourselves properly or speak at the jetty…"

Elliott hurriedly opened the door, then looked at the

elderly vicar with a gentle smile. "It has been an age...Mellior."

Popplewell smiled. "Indeed it has...Versipellis. May I come in?"

The young man stood back with a smile. "Of course."

As the elderly man walked into the room, Elliott checked the hallway beyond. The thickly carpeted corridor was utterly silent; not even a murmur from behind the other rooms could be heard as he pushed the door shut, locked it, and turned back to the man standing in the middle of the large, lavishly appointed room. He clasped Popplewell's hand. "My dear old friend, it has been far too long! How have you been?"

Popplewell gripped the younger man's shoulder tightly. "As well as can be expected, my friend." He turned to the redhead still seated by the dressing table and smiled. "Lapotaire had informed me that you would be accompanied by your wife, but I had no idea that the lady in question was Angellis. My dear friends, you finally found each other...I am so very happy for you both."

Elliott smiled. "Then perhaps the social niceties should be observed. We know each other from our lives in Astraea; however, we need to be aware of our identities here. Therefore, my darling wife, may I present Reverend Newton Popplewell, whom we know as Mellior. My friend, may I present my extraordinary wife, Angellis, whose name in this realm is usually Giselle Du'Lac, though for the time being she is to be known as Giselle Burgoyne. I think it best we continue the ruse in public at least, so you may continue to call me Alistair. In this realm, though, the name I have used for many years now is Elliott Caine."

Popplewell nodded, an amused expression on his lined face. "I must admit that sometimes I do lose track of our multitudinous names and titles."

He turned back to Giselle and bowed over her hand; Giselle smiled. "Dear Mellior, it is lovely to see you again. Would you like to sit down?"

As Popplewell settled himself into one of the overstuffed but very comfortable armchairs, another knock sounded at the door. Elliott again called out, "Who is it?"

Thorne's voice responded. "It is us."

Elliott grinned, ran a hand over his hair, and opened the door with a flourish. Waving them in, he turned back to Popplewell. "Of course you must remember Shadavarian, though here his name is Abernathy Thorne, his wife Aquilleia, and their very spoilt Labrador, who is known here as Veronique, but whom we also know as Xenocyon."

Popplewell stood up again and smiled as Thorne bounced across the room, rapidly followed by an excited black Labrador.

Thorne gripped the proffered hand. "Mellior! It's wonderful to see you again, even in such strange circumstances." A soft violet light appeared in his eyes. "You remember my wife, Aquilleia?"

Popplewell turned with a smile of genuine delight and pressed a light kiss on her slender hand. "How could I not remember Aquilleia," He smiled at her gently, blinking through suddenly teary eyes. "I spent many years working with your remarkable mother, my dear...of course I remember you."

There was a slight pause as he pressed a handkerchief to his eyes, sat back in his armchair, and collected himself. Veronique sat down in front of him and gently prodded at his hand with her damp nose until he stroked her ears.

Alistair turned to Thorne and Aquilleia and waved his hand towards a settee. "Let us discuss why we are here, shall we?"

As the others headed towards the seating area,

Veronique, assuming the invitation included her, promptly launched herself at the plushly upholstered and well-sprung velvet settee. As she made contact, the springs rebelled violently and flung the startled Labrador several feet into the air, depositing her without a remaining shred of dignity in a tangled heap of legs next to a laughing Popplewell.

As Thorne and Aquilleia, caught between laughter and genuine concern, fussed over her, the embarrassed Labrador picked herself up off the floor, shook herself thoroughly and slunk to the far corner of the room, where she turned her back on the others with a dismissive sniff, curled up with her nose by her tail, and closed her eyes.

As the others settled themselves on the now vacant settee, Elliott had a sudden thought and rang the bell by the side of the bed. After a few minutes, the young footman who had been called by Merric arrived at the door. Ellis had been newly assigned to the first, second, and third floor suites, and was determined to be seen as well-suited to his new and more powerful role within the castle. The young man smoothed his waistcoat and his hair and quickly checked his breath with his hand before straightening up and knocking smartly.

The door was opened almost immediately by the man Ellis knew to be Alistair Burgoyne. He nodded formally, and intoned, "You rang, sir?"

The man nodded. "Yes, ah, Ellis, isn't it? Yes, we would like a bottle of champagne and glasses for five, please."

"Of course, sir." Turning to leave, he spotted the canine sulk going on next to the bed and hid a smile. As the door closed behind him, he again made his way to the little cupboard. Entering the tiny room, he closed the door behind him, blew down the connecting tube that led to the kitchen and waited.

After a few seconds there was a responding blast and a tinny voice at the other end responded. "Ready."

Ellis recounted the order down the tube. After a few minutes, a strange sound began to echo below: a low rumble like distant thunder, accompanied by an occasional high-pitched squeak, as the dumb waiter approached from the kitchen below.

Ellis opened the hatch and glared at the slow-moving platform. An idea popped into his quick mind; perhaps he should suggest to the butler that the cables needed a spot of oiling. Surely the butler would take it as the mark of a young servant working hard to prove his worth. Ellis swelled slightly. Then again, would the butler see it as a novice footman insulting the butler who should have oiled the cables in the first place? Ellis deflated at the thought of incurring the wrath of Davaadalai as the loaded platform appeared before him, bearing a silver tray with not one but two bottles of champagne, glasses, and a plate of toasted almonds.

Moving swiftly, Ellis checked the contents before an idea came to him. With a smile he placed a small plate next to the almonds, and opening a large jar in the cupboard on his left, he removed several dog biscuits and arranged them on the plate. Balancing the tray on his hip, he again knocked at the door. Elliott moved to one side as the young footman carefully set out the drinks tray, nodded and left the room.

Elliott turned to the others. "I know it's only forty minutes to the cocktail hour in the lounge, but I thought that as we are re-establishing old friendships, a glass or two might go down well." There was immediate agreement; he opened one of the bottles and poured a full coupe for each person.

As Elliott took care of the drinks, Thorne saw the plate of biscuits and placed them on the table next to the settee with

64

a smile. Veronique, whose eyes had snapped open at the knock on the door, realised there was a plate of something edible beside Thorne, stretched in her best nonchalant fashion, inflicted her most derisive sniff upon the vengeful settee, and sat next to Thorne expectantly.

Elliott raised his coupe with a smile. "To old friends."

The others raised their glasses. "To old friends."

There was a companionable silence, broken only by the crunching of a marginally placated Labrador enjoying her treats as they sipped their drinks, before Elliott took his seat next to Giselle and looked at Popplewell over the gold-edged rim of his glass.

"So...Popplewell, we are here. Before we descend the stairs and begin our surreptitious investigations, talk to us. Your letter spoke of a terrible discovery; please continue where your missive finished. What did you and Cornelius discover that was so very terrible that you need our help to discover the truth? And, why exactly have you insisted on my pretending to be Alistair?"

Giselle looked at the elderly Other. "But first, shouldn't Cornelius be here, as you say it concerns him and his family?"

Popplewell shook his head. "Cornelius and I discussed this before I sent the letter, and we both agreed that in order for him to continue unchanged in his demeanour with the family and servants, plausible deniability was best. You are to investigate, and keep him in the dark as much as anyone else in the family, until the time comes for the truth to be revealed."

He paused. "I did mention in my letter that the butler, Davaadalai, is part of our little...troupe, didn't I?"

Elliott nodded. "Yes, you did; can he be trusted to keep a secret?"

Popplewell nodded enthusiastically. "Oh indeed, he is

absolutely devoted to Cornelius." He paused. "Rather unusually so, to be honest; the butler is usually attached to the master of the house, but Merric is so...relaxed is probably the best word to use about his position within the family. He is utterly content to allow Cornelius and Ami to deal with the day-to-day running of the estate, because it gives him greater freedom to create his machines."

Elliott sipped his champagne and nodded at Thorne, who passed another biscuit to the now-placated Labrador, surreptitiously removed a notebook and several pencils from his breast pocket, and began to take notes.

Elliott leant forward and looked at Popplewell. "Very well, please begin."

Popplewell took a gulp of his wine and looked at the others. "In my letter I spoke of the killings here fifteen years ago; unspeakable evil was committed here of a type I thought had been long forgotten! That I hoped had been forgotten..." His voice trailed off, he took a deep breath and continued. "Seven children — seven — were murdered in various despicable ways here on the island. The eighth and last victim thankfully survived an attack in her own room, here in the castle—"

Aquilleia raised her voice. "Araby Burgoyne?"

Popplewell nodded. "Yes." His face grew pale, "I was in the house with Cornelius and Ami when it happened. My God, Versipellis...I can still hear her screams in my nightmares!" He cleared his throat before continuing. "We ran to her room..." He paused, "Ami followed us; she was in her bath chair, and had to use the moving platform." He took a gulp of his drink. "Araby was huddled on the floor next to her bed, absolutely covered in blood! The skin across her back and arms had been ripped...torn by something hideously sharp. We realised her injuries were severe — so severe that Cornelius and Davaadalai carried her to the village, in order to get to the mainland and seek help, while Merric and I woke the rest of the staff and began to search the house."

Thorne looked at him; the elderly man appeared greatly upset. "What is it that you are pained to tell us?"

Popplewell grimaced. "As she was being carried from the castle, Araby managed to inform Cornelius that as she was being attacked, she had smelt bay leaves."

Alistair nodded. "Go on."

Popplewell took a deep breath. "During the search, we realised that her brother was not in his bedroom. We thought it strange that he had not come to her aid; how he could not have heard her screams was beyond me, as they were enough to wake the dead! We searched the house and grounds but found no sign of the assailant, and equally, no sign of her brother — he was nowhere to be found! But we did find a note on his dressing table. In it, he stated that he found the life planned for him dull, that he had no desire to be the second male in a house that would never be his home, and that he had decided to leave the island and live a life of his own somewhere else. Several items of clothing and a carpet bag were missing from his bedroom, but that was not the worst of it!"

Giselle sat forward; her coupe almost empty. "Please, continue!"

Popplewell sat back, a miserable expression on his face. "That letter, believed to be written by Araby's brother, carried the scent of his cologne...Bay Rum!"

There was a silence before Elliott spoke. "So, you believed the scent on the paper suggested he was responsible for the attack on his sister, and by implication, the murders committed on the island?"

Popplewell nodded, he looked ill. "Yes, God help us, until our appalling discovery a few days ago!"

There was a sudden crunch as Thorne gave Veronique

another biscuit. He looked up. "Sorry!" He sat back and continued with his notes, a faint pink tinge about his ears.

Popplewell continued as Elliott refilled Giselle and Aquilleia's coupes. "Cornelius is a great collector of fine wines; he has a suite of rooms in one of the sub levels of the castle which homes his extensive wine cellar…there are certainly enough rooms to choose from down there: the castle is a rabbit warren! Anyway, in the process of searching out more room to extend his cellars, he came across a corridor that even I didn't know existed. On that corridor was a locked room which bore, in its centre, the entry hatch to an oubliette."

Aquilleia frowned slightly, and Thorne caught her look. "A type of dungeon built into the floor, usually quite deep… the only way in or out is through the hatch in its ceiling."

Aquilleia grimaced as Popplewell continued, now looking nauseous. "We entered the room. You will of course know what I mean when I say that evil has a scent; well, this room stank of it! The room itself was empty, apart from the hatch in its centre…" Popplewell paused and swallowed. "The oubliette contained a broken wooden chair, and seated on the chair was a corpse. The air in that room was dry, so the corpse had mummified. My friends, that corpse was the mortal remains of young Alistair Burgoyne!"

There was silence as the reverend sat back in his chair, pressing his handkerchief to his mouth. Elliott refilled his glass before leaving his chair and standing by the window. "That still doesn't explain why you suggested that I pretend to be…"

Popplewell patted his lips with his handkerchief. "I — that is, Cornelius and I — thought that if one of the people staying here were the guilty party, then seeing you, and hearing you claim to be Alistair…well, it might shock them into a confession."

Giselle took a sip from her coupe and looked at Popplewell over the rim of her glass, one auburn eyebrow arched. "It could also lead to them trying to kill my husband, in the belief that they are finishing what they started fifteen years ago!"

Elliott shared a look with Thorne, who nodded. "From the remains, could you estimate how long had he been there?"

Popplewell took a deep gulp of his champagne. "The carpet bag of clothes from his room was in the oubliette with him...he must have been thrown into the dungeon the same night he went missing."

"Could he have taken his own life?"

Popplewell shook his head. "The door to the outer room was locked from the outside, and we found no key amongst the items on his body."

Aquilleia looked sick. "So, he was thrown into the oubliette and left to die? That would have taken days!"

Popplewell sat forward. "No: we discovered that he had suffered a massive blow to the head. It was horribly obvious to us that he would have died within hours of being thrown into the dungeon."

Thorne nodded as he nibbled an almond. "That's a little less unpleasant, but not by much!"

Popplewell nodded. "It meant our suspicions about Alistair were unfounded. He was not the murderer, but another victim of the same killer."

Elliott nodded as he returned to his seat. As he settled into the settee, he looked at Popplewell. "What did you do with his remains?"

"We didn't want anyone else to know of our discovery...if we had removed him to a room in the castle, he would have been found and the whole island would have known about it in less than a day! So, we left him exactly as we found him."

He looked at Elliott. "I have to admit to feeling unhappy about the lack of proper respect shown to the dead, my friend. It felt so very wrong to leave him in that place, and it still does: a child, on his own...in the dark."

Giselle sat forward and gently touched his hand. "But you do understand why, don't you? If the person who killed him still has the keys to the oubliette, it could be a way of discovering the killer." She looked at Elliott. "And if they do check to see if Alistair is still there, it might keep you safe from harm." She took another sip from her coupe. "It feels very strange to refer to a corpse and one's husband by the same name, especially when one's husband is pretending to be said victim!"

Elliott raised his glass to her. Popplewell nodded unhappily and took another sip of his drink as Thorne spoke. "What can you tell us of the other victims — you say they were all children?"

Popplewell nodded sadly. "Yes, all between the ages of six and fifteen. Alistair was the eldest, and young Timothy Lutyens the youngest."

Giselle tapped her fingernail against her lip. "Lutyens... any relation of the velvet-and-wine-appreciating Lucius?"

Popplewell nodded as Thorne continued with his rapid note-taking. "Yes, Lucius is Timothy's elder brother. Poor Lucius never really came to terms with his brother's death; it left him...damaged is the best word, I think. That was when he took to drink, and the society of some rather questionable company on the mainland."

Aquilleia looked up from playing with Veronique's ears. "How old was he when his brother died?"

Popplewell thought quietly for a few moments. "He was a little older than Alistair, I think...maybe eighteen or nineteen. He left the island shortly afterwards and didn't return for several years..." He looked at Elliott his face grave. "Ami was informed by some friends in London that he had fallen into the company of some disreputable and genuinely unpleasant people there, and she asked me, as a friend, to find him and bring him home. So, Cornelius, Davaadalai, and I headed to the den of iniquity we call our capital to rescue both Lucius and his soul before it was too late."

Thorne looked up from his notes. "And did you succeed?"

Popplewell looked unsure. "I truly don't know. I believe we managed to reach him before he did anything that could truly have corrupted him… But what he saw, what he experienced in that place, with those people and at that young age, I cannot say!"

Giselle nodded. "But you don't believe he had anything to do with the murders on the island?"

Popplewell shook his head forcefully as he shifted in his seat. "Absolutely not! Lucius became a drunkard due to his brother's death. If he had been responsible for those murders, he would not be punishing himself with his dependence on alcohol." Popplewell closed his eyes. "The harm done to his brother was not caused by someone who would punish themselves for their actions, but rather by someone who would exult in what they had done!" He finished his drink in one gulp and stared into the distance. "He discovered his brother's body…"

There was silence as the guests realised the horrors the louche young man had suffered.

Thorne raised his eyes from the notebook. "Why did Ami ask you to rescue Lucius — why not his parents?"

Popplewell shook his head. "Both his parents had died two years before, leaving Lucius to raise his brother. Timothy was four years old at the time of their deaths, and Lucius just sixteen, but he managed remarkably well as a provider for his brother, until the boy's death two years later. The police officers from the mainland believed him to be guilty — chafing at being trapped in the position of parent to his much younger brother — but those of us who knew Lucius were able to allay their suspicions. He adored his brother."

As he fell silent, an incredibly loud metallic crashing shook the very floors and walls of the room. Veronique leapt to her feet from her prone position by the now empty biscuit plate and let loose a volley of barks, her hackles bristling as Thorne hurriedly comforted her.

As the cacophony faded, Elliott looked at Popplewell with a raised eyebrow.

The elderly man smiled. "It's quite all right; it's the dinner gong, another of Merric's inventions. It's loud enough for him to hear down in his workrooms. The first gong is the warning that it is five minutes to cocktail hour, then there is a second gong to remind people that the cocktail hour is underway, and then there is the main dinner gong. Perhaps we could continue our discussion after dinner, or even tomorrow?"

Elliott offered his arm to Giselle and addressed Popplewell. "That sounds a very sensible idea, my friend. Well, ladies and gentlemen, shall we?"

Thorne finished scribbling in his notebook before standing up and looking at the still-grumbling Labrador. "I need to get Veronique settled before coming down; I'll be with you shortly."

Aquilleia smiled as she took Thorne's arm. "*We* will see to Veronique…" She turned to face the others. "We will meet you in the lounge."

Five people and one very vocal dog left the room and separated; one pair and a Labrador made their way to a suite on the same floor, where Veronique knew her bed, toys, and treats were waiting, while the other group of three headed down to the lounge for that most excellent and civilised time of day; the cocktail hour.

○

Sebastian and Theodora's Suite
6:55pm

Sebastian offered his arm to his wife. As she linked elbows with her husband, she addressed their nanny. "Harriet, please see to it that Leander is in bed no later than half past the hour."

The nanny bobbed gently. "Yes, ma'am."

Sebastian led his wife from the room. As he was about to close the door behind them, Theodora called out to their son. "No night-time wanderings, Leander! I doubt very much that the Burgoyne family would approve!"

The faint response from the other side of the door seemed to be in the affirmative; she nodded firmly. "Correct answer. We will see you in the morning; good night, Leander."

As they walked towards the stairs, a dark shape watched in silence from the shadows at the far end of the corridor, their mind fixed on the thought of a child once again being within their reach.

○

The Lounge
7:00pm

Marcus waved the cocktail shaker and with a flourish, poured the strangely coloured concoction into two ice-filled glasses. He presented one glass to his spectacularly gowned wife, who accepted the offering with a private smile, and gave the other to Ami, who was in the midst of a spirited and somewhat condemnatory statement about the dyspepsia-inducing qualities of curried mutton. She paused mid-rant to stare at the brilliant blue drink, then looked at her step-granddaughter and the smiling man. "What on earth is this?"

Marcus smiled charmingly. "Oh, a little of this, a little of that...and a touch of something new we discovered during our little jaunt to Curacao."

Ami looked at the glass with trepidation. "You know I don't drink, my dears..."

Sybilla placed her hand on Ami's arm and cast a quick glance at her husband. "It's quite all right, Ami...it tastes something like orange cordial!"

Ami smiled. "Oh, well...orange cordial never did anyone any harm."

As she raised the glass to her lips Davaadalai appeared at her side, bearing a silver salver on which was a small glass of milk. "Your usual pre-dinner aperitif, madam."

There was only the faintest emphasis on the word "usual", but it still garnered a sharp glare from Sybilla, which Davaadalai blithely ignored. In his position as butler, he knew that a servant had to be utterly respectful at all times, to all guests, and all family members...however, in the case of Sybilla and Marcus, this rule had been relaxed on the private orders of both Merric and Cornelius, after an incident a few years earlier involving a Ming vase from Ami's suite which had somehow found its way into Sybilla's steamer trunk. The incident had been brushed over for Ami's sake, but the rest of the family and the faithful servants remembered! They had found the best approach to Sybilla and her husband's increasingly desperate attempts to be the centre of attention was to treat them with an air of polite dismissal that killed most of their endeavours within the family circle stone dead.

However, what they got up to beyond the castle walls was anyone's guess!

Ami looked somewhat relieved; placing the blue drink on the salver and picking up the inoffensive glass of milk, she saw the look that Sybilla and Marcus shared, and felt suddenly defensive as she snapped, "Doctor's orders."

As Davaadalai bowed and walked away, Ami cast her eyes around the room for a topic, any topic, on which she could discourse with her step-granddaughter. Her gaze flickered across the ribbon-festooned Christmas tree beside the roaring fireplace without actually seeing it, taking in the evergreen boughs, Christmas cards, and lit candles that covered the mantle. She did love Sybilla, but sometimes it was like talking to a portrait: a very lovely, but still, cold, and rather distant portrait. The child was more like a shop dummy than a human; perfectly arranged in her exquisite gowns, with immaculately coiffed hair, and lovely pieces of jewellery...

Ami paused as she looked a touch more closely at the diamond necklace around Sybilla's white throat. Strange; she could have sworn...she shook her head. No, that was silly! There were of course only a certain number of the best kind of settings for truly perfect gems. The necklace simply looked very similar to one belonging to an old friend of hers in London, which had gone missing some months earlier. That was it; that must be it.

She looked at Sybilla and against her will, her mind turned to some of the more lurid gossip she had heard about the couple's conduct in London. Some unpleasant things had occurred, and some nice people had lost expensive jewellery...among other things.

A sudden noise, brash and jarring, filled the room, making Ami jump and spill her milk. She turned to glare at Davaadalai, who had sounded the gong; why on earth was she so jumpy? She shook her head firmly. It was merely gossip: horrid, spiteful, squalid gossip meant to damage a wonderful, beautiful young woman and her equally handsome and charming husband!

Having made up her mind, Ami turned back to Sybilla and asked her about her gown. A spark of life appeared in the cool grey eyes as the young woman began to talk animatedly about the various expensive items she had purchased recently from the House of Worth.

Ami, not really one for silk knickers, silk camisoles, nor indeed silk stockings, listened politely, her eyes glazing over at the vocal waterfall that poured forth from Sybilla about undergarments, gowns, and the matching accoutrements that the finest gentlewomen in the city must have in their possession.

Cornelius, standing next to Merric, nudged his nephew with his whisky glass and nodded at the two women. "Look at that expression on Ami's face…she looks more glazed than the plates! What on earth d'you think Sybilla's going on about?"

Merric took a sip of his drink. "Knickers."

As Cornelius choked on his pre-dinner whisky, Merric grinned and clapped him firmly on his back; his uncle had owed him that cough for years!

Cornelius regained his breath and twinkled at his nephew with a twitching moustache and a raised eyebrow. "Knickers?"

Merric's grin widened as he nodded. "I overheard Ami asking about Sybilla's gown. I believe Sybilla decided to start at the bottom…literally, and work her way up and out!"

Cornelius frowned as he watched the two women. "Why on earth would she do that? Your aunt absolutely loathes anything to do with buying clothes."

Merric shrugged. "Possibly trying to find something

Sybilla will talk about, and the only thing that Sybilla will talk about is…?"

They answered the question together. "Sybilla!"

Cornelius looked at his nephew with a pained expression. "I happen to know that she has asked Ami for a greater allowance. Apparently two thousand a year is not enough!"

Merric took a gulp of his drink with a frown. "Well, she certainly showed her true colours with that little demand."

Cornelius nodded. "The colours in question being the brass of her neck and the gold of her dreams! Grotesque creature!"

They both glared at the offending woman and sipped their drinks. Cornelius regarded Merric as he lifted his drink to his lips, and a thought came to him; as his nephew was in a sharing mood, he might as well ask the question! He hid a smile. "So, whose knickers were you thinking about?"

He watched with pride and enjoyment as his nephew's drink suddenly reappeared in a fine spray that narrowly missed the tall, and impossibly glossy aspidistra that hid them from most of the room. Merric shot his uncle a look as he mopped himself with his handkerchief and checked the aspidistra for damage.

Cornelius chuckled, the twinkle in his blue eyes more obvious as he turned to look at the young woman sitting next to Araby, and who he well knew was responsible for his nephew's change in demeanour. Slender, with a wealth of honey-blonde hair pinned atop her elegant head, Melisandre Salazar had arrived at Cove Castle only the day before with Sybilla and Marcus, and luckily, was nothing like either of her friends.

When they had arrived, Melisandre had been left utterly embarrassed when she realised that Sybilla hadn't bothered to ask if she could bring a guest. Fortunately, the castle was more than big enough to fit in an extra person, and any irritation was lost as soon as Ami remembered that Melisandre had visited the island several times many years before.

Merric had walked in late in his usual outfit, one a loco-motive engineer might dismiss as unkempt, taken one look at Melisandre, flushed from ankle to hairline, and bolted back to his room. He had then kept them waiting while he dragged a hot flannel across those parts of him that were visible, and covered the rest with a cobbled-together evening dress that hadn't been out of mothballs for over a decade.

Both Ami and Cornelius were surprised and concerned in equal measure; Merric had never expressed any interest in the opposite sex, and they had believed that the title would die out with their nephew, as with the disappearance of Alis-tair there were no other male Burgoynes left, but the appear-ance of Melisandre had changed that situation. She was as taken with him as he with her; but there was at least one person who was not as happy with the burgeoning relation-ship as the others.

○

Sybilla and Marcus' Suite
The Night Before

There was a delicate crash as the exquisite glass bottle of hideously expensive perfume shattered against the far wall.

Marcus rolled his eyes and held up his hands in a placa-tory gesture. "Darling, my darling...it will be all right."

Sybilla turned to face her husband; fuming rage had turned her usual cold mask into an ugly, blotchy mess. She took a deep breath and screamed, "It was your idea — your idea — to bring that insipid idiot here, and now look! After all our plans! My uncle was to die unwed, without issue, and leave the land and castle to me and Araby! Now, thanks to that mewling little bitch, he might be married by next year!"

She flung another perfume bottle at the wall. Marcus approached her carefully; if she continued like this, she would soon start in on his cologne collection, and that would never do.

He gently placed his hands against the side of her face and crooned softly. "Calm down, calm down…"

He sat her down on the edge of the bed and stroked her hair as she wiped the tears from her eyes. Sybilla looked at her husband and bit her lip. "We need that treasure, Marcus! We need to find what is hidden!"

He tightened his arms around her. "I know, my darling, and we shall have it. When have we ever let a little thing like living relatives get in the way of the things we need, hmm?"

Sybilla smiled at him as he kissed her forehead. "You say the most marvellous things, my love. We made our plans, but this does alter things. Tell me, how can we deal with this threat?"

Marcus smiled faintly. "I've had one or two ideas about Araby, and a few interesting thoughts about Melisandre and Merric have emerged over the last few hours. Would you like to hear them?"

Sybilla laughed as she settled into her husband's arms to listen to his intriguing plans of murder.

The Lounge
7:15pm

Sybilla shared a knowing smile with her husband as she sipped her second cocktail of the evening. Yes, the possible complications caused by Melisandre and Merric were an irritation to their plans, but they could still be dealt with. Accidents could always be relied upon to happen, especially if they were planned thoroughly in advance!

There was a cough from the door, and as some of the guests turned, Davaadalai made an announcement. "Mr and Mrs Alistair Burgoyne, and Reverend Popplewell."

The bright tinkle of social chatter paused as everyone in the room stared at the arrivals: some in curiosity, others in mild disapproval, and some in shock.

Although Elliott had been introduced as Alistair to some of the family at the jetty, not everyone in the household had been made aware of apparent return of the missing scion...until now.

In the silence that followed, Sybilla's glass slid from her nerveless fingers and smashed on the parquet floor. The others in the room turned their attention from the newly announced couple to Sybilla as she gazed in utter horror at her cousin, her mouth opening and closing as though about to speak. Her slack-jawed husband also stared in disbelief at the silent couple in the doorway, his attention so fixed on them that he did not see his wife's eyes roll back in her skull, and so failed to catch her as she dropped in a dead faint on top of her shattered glass.

○

The Great Hall
7:30pm

Cornelius stood by the open front door and frowned at the panting young footman running back up the hill from the village. As the young man approached, he barked, "Well?"

Ellis paused to get his breath. "Sir, Dr Mayberry said to

tell you that he's on his way now, sir, and he'll be here as soon as possible.

Cornelius nodded. "Good lad. Get yourself to Mrs Burnt-house and tell her I said for you to have a stiff whisky."

"Yes sir, thank you, sir!"

As the footman made his way to the kitchen, Cornelius glared at Merric, who was sitting half-hidden in the window seat by the door. "What on earth was the silly woman thinking? Dropping like a sack of potatoes onto broken glass — I ask you!"

Merric shrugged uncomfortably as he shifted in his seat, unpleasant memories of the last twenty minutes playing through his head: the deeply unpleasant crunching sound as Sybilla's slim form had crumpled to the floor and landed on the shattered remains of her cocktail glass, followed by Marcus' shocked swearing; then the change in his voice from irritation to fear as blood had begun to seep from under the unconscious woman and pool around her still form. The sudden sense of panic in the room had been swiftly dealt with by Davaadalai, who had immediately sent Ellis down to the village to fetch Dr Mayberry, as Marcus had carried the unconscious Sybilla to the suite they shared.

Elliott, still in his guise as Alistair, and Giselle had accompanied a shocked Ami and Melisandre up to the suite as a deathly pale Araby stood in silence by the stairs. On realising the seriousness of Sybilla's accident, Araby had immediately attempted to escort Nanny back to her room, whereupon she had been told in no uncertain terms by the elderly lady that regardless of the evening's events, she was still very much ready for her dinner, and would be staying where she was.

As an irritated Nanny returned to the lounge to await the dinner gong, Araby paused at the foot of the staircase and shared a look with Sebastian. He smiled at her; as a frequent visitor to the castle many years earlier, he could well remember just how forceful Nanny could be about mealtimes!

Theodora caught their shared look. Her dark eyes flashed, then she turned without a word and walked upstairs.

Sebastian turned as she left him, and looking back at Araby, he paused before bowing slightly and following his wife. Araby stared after him in silence.

A few moments later, Thorne and Aquilleia appeared at the top of the stairs and descended to the great hall. Thorne looked at Araby with one eyebrow raised. "It's very quiet… has someone said something naughty?"

Araby's eye twitched and she shook her head. "No… Sybilla dropped her glass and fell upon it, and there was blood…blood everywhere!"

A large tear trickled down her pale cheek. Aquilleia exchanged glances with her husband, then gently took Araby's arm and led her back into the lounge. "Is a doctor coming?"

Araby nodded. "Yes, Dr Mayberry…he lives in the village, he's been with the family for years."

Aquilleia nudged her husband in the ribs, and looked towards the little bar. Thorne nodded and made his way past the two maids who, under the watchful eye of Davaadalai, were clearing the bloody mess that was the obvious aftermath of the Sybilla-versus-cocktail-glass debacle.

Thorne arrived at the bar and eyed the contents: well stocked, with champagne, spirits, and a decent-sized ice cupboard; he noted the ornate silver ice pick, grimaced, and instead turned his attention to the open bottle of champagne.

"Allow me, sir." Davaadalai materialised by his side and began to set out glasses. "Champagne for three, sir?"

Thorne nodded. "Yes, thank you, Davaadalai. I understand there has been a slight disagreement between Mrs De Banzie and a glass?"

The butler paused as he opened a new bottle. "Yes, sir. The lady appeared taken aback at my announcement of Mr Alistair and his wife; she dropped her glass, then fainted upon the shards. She has been taken to her room, and the doctor sent for."

Thorne frowned as the butler finished pouring the welcome libations. "You say she appeared taken aback?"

The butler nodded. "Yes sir." He paused before leaning his not-inconsiderable height into Thorne's ear. "I would go so far as to say that the lady looked as though she had seen a ghost! Your drinks, sir."

Davaadalai pushed the tray forward, bowed and returned to the maids, who had now finished their unenviable cleaning task and were more than ready to return to the kitchens and enjoy the strong cup of tea and plate of biscuits that Mrs Burnthouse would insist on pressing upon them.

Davaadalai checked the damage to the exquisite Persian rug; with a slight frown, he pulled one of the immense potted plants a little further forward, then bowed to Thorne and shooed the maids from the room. Thorne collected two full glasses and made his way back to his wife and Araby, who had seated themselves as far as possible from the area of Sybilla's accident.

As he placed the champagne on a little table, he caught his wife's eye and nodded imperceptibly towards Araby; Aquilleia raised her eyebrows and shook her head. As Thorne returned to collect his glass and the champagne bucket, Aquilleia placed her hand on Araby's. "Would you rather go to your room for a rest? It must have been a terrible shock for you."

There was a faint titter behind them. They all turned to look at Nanny, who was sitting behind one of the many aspidistras that conspired to turn the large room into a veritable jungle.

Nanny tutted at them as she wagged a condescending and wrinkly finger. "It would be churlish in the extreme to avoid an organised dinner party purely because someone could not manage their emotions." She sat back and shook her head sadly. "I fear Sybilla simply doesn't have what is required in her chosen path…she is far too headstrong; she really should be more gracious and willing to please, which is the right and proper behaviour for a woman of her advancing age. And she really does drink far too much — that is quite telling in a woman's character!"

Aquilleia's mouth dropped open and she closed it with a snap. She glanced at Araby, who sat in embarrassed silence, ignoring Nanny and staring at her untouched glass of champagne.

Thorne suppressed a grin as his wife raised her full glass with a faint smile and drained it. Turning her violet eyes to her amused husband, Aquilleia crooned, "A little more champagne for me please, darling."

Ignoring the tutting from Nanny, she faced Araby with a look of concern. "I'm sure your family would understand, Araby…especially considering what happened to you here."

The sudden darting look from Araby was a little too wild-eyed for Aquilleia's liking, and she suddenly wondered what Popplewell had not told them about the attack on the young woman so many years before.

The younger woman took a deep breath. "They told you about — about what happened to me?"

Aquilleia and Thorne shared a glance; thinking rapidly, Thorne decided the best way forward was a convincing lie. He shrugged in a relaxed manner as he settled back in his armchair, and smiled gently as he sipped his drink. "Please don't misunderstand us, Araby; your brother chose a most inopportune time to leave the island, and it was thought appropriate that he be filled in on what had occurred since he left. As his friends, we were privy to those discussions, nothing more. I trust that helps?"

Araby nodded silently, and as she lifted her gaze from her glass of champagne, Aquilleia was relieved to note that the whites of her eyes were no longer as wide and glassy as they had been.

Araby took a deep breath. "Truth be told, I…I can't actually remember that much of the night when Alistair disappeared. It was Christmas Eve, I remember looking for him, and then I went to my room, and — someone was there. They attacked me, then Gruncle — I mean great-uncle Cornelius — and Davaadalai came and saved me." Her face paled. "I can't remember the attack, just a scent…it was familiar…" She took a gulp of her drink, and blinked hard.

Aquilleia gently patted her hand. "If you ever want to talk about it, we're here, Araby, as are Alistair and Giselle."

Araby blinked rapidly. "Thank you. I think…I think I shall take your advice and go to my room for a rest. I don't really feel…" She looked at Aquilleia, "I feel awful for asking, but would you please tell Uncle Merric?"

The three of them ignored the harrumphing from behind the aspidistra as Nanny let her disapproval be known. Thorne stood up as Araby began to rise from her seat. "Of course we will let your uncle know that you have retired for the evening. Come, we shall find him, and see to it now."

As the three of them left Nanny to her displeasure behind the aspidistra and made their way back to the great hall, they met both Elliott and Marcus walking down the sweeping staircase. Thorne looked at Elliott, then addressed Marcus. "I say, old chap, we've just heard; how is she?"

Marcus smiled charmingly, his strong white teeth glinting in the flickering gaslight. "Much better than we had feared… her arm landed upon the glass first, hence the amount of blood. At Sybilla's insistence, her maid Eliza has cleaned and bandaged the wound and dressed Sybilla in another gown, so hopefully both dinner and our little séance can proceed as arranged!"

Aquilleia stared at him, her violet eyes flashing. "You mean continue with the evening? Is Sybilla truly well enough?"

Marcus held up his hand; his well-practised smile now looked slightly forced. "I assure you; this is entirely Sybilla's choice! She is determined to carry on and enjoy the evening we have planned; a superb meal, followed by a séance, then revisiting happy memories with her much-loved cousin Alistair and his lovely wife Giselle."

Elliott smiled lazily and endeavoured to ignore the not particularly well-hidden eye-roll that Thorne directed at the back of Marcus's head. "As you say, Marcus, if Sybilla believes herself to be well enough, who are we to deny her the evening."

Thorne raised an eyebrow. "Then you had better speak with the Earl of Cove; he has sent for the doctor, and the gentleman is already on his way."

Marcus frowned. "He shouldn't have done that. I shall speak with him immediately; please excuse me."

Thorne stepped back to allow Marcus to pass. "Of course."

As the irritated-looking man walked briskly towards the lounge, Thorne caught Elliott's eye and glanced at Araby. Elliott nodded imperceptibly and leant against the bannister. "Well, it would appear that dinner is going ahead after all." He turned to the young woman with a gentle smile. "It will return some of the time we lost all those years ago, Araby; I am greatly looking forward to being reacquainted with my dear sister."

Araby looked at him in silence, a strange expression on her mobile young face. As she opened her mouth to speak,

Nanny arrived behind them and prodded Araby's leg with her stout walking cane. "Araby, I insist that you stay for the dinner; it is the height of poor manners to walk away from an arranged soiree just because you feel unwell! What on earth would your dear parents say about your lack of thought for the arrangements of others?"

She suddenly noticed the others present and her usual titter made itself known. "Oh, do forgive me, I didn't see you there. Araby, please assist me back into the lounge; I believe it is nearly time for the gong!"

She held out her arm peremptorily to Araby, who paused before silently taking it and escorting her back into the lounge. As the two women walked away, Elliott, Thorne, and Aquilleia could hear the elderly lady continue her haranguing long after they had passed into the lounge and settled beyond the aspidistras.

Elliott, Thorne, and Aquilleia shared a look as they were joined at the foot of the stairs by Giselle, who had finally managed to make her escape from Sybilla's suite.

She stopped next to Elliott who smiled at her. "I trust all is well with the injured party upstairs?"

Giselle shook her head, then paused as Marcus suddenly reappeared and went upstairs, Giselle's eyes followed him until he disappeared, then she turned back to the others. "I don't think Sybilla is in any fit state to be dining, conducting a séance, or doing anything that requires more than absolute rest! It is my honest opinion that she should be taken to a hospital immediately."

Elliott frowned. "So, her injuries are not superficial?"

Giselle shook her head. "One or two are relatively minor, but she has a deep cut to her wrist that is the absolute opposite: it took us quite a while to stop the bleeding. Another of the shards cut through her gown and into her thigh…" She looked around hurriedly before continuing in a low voice.

"But those injuries are not all I saw…as we were waiting for her maid to arrive, Melisandre and I assisted Sybilla in undressing…I saw other, older marks on her wrists, further up her forearms, and on her torso."

Elliott stroked his chin. "Scars, or bruises?"

"Both." She frowned. "But there are some, on her torso and legs in particular, that form a sort of pattern upon her skin: winding vines and leaves…I can't explain them."

Her husband's expression was grim. "Almost as though they had been deliberately carved into her skin?"

Giselle nodded slowly. "Yes…yes, I think so."

Elliott took a deep breath and exchanged glances with Thorne. "This case is more unpleasant that I thought. We need to ask certain questions, and I think there is only one person from whom we shall get an honest answer. Where is Popplewell?"

Aquilleia shook her head. "We don't know…we haven't seen him since we left your suite to see to Veronique."

Elliott opened his mouth to speak, then paused as Davaadalai appeared next to him.

The butler cleared his throat deferentially. "Reverend Popplewell was somewhat shaken by the events in the lounge, sir, and retired to his rooms for a rest…he is quite an elderly gentleman, but he assured the master that he would return downstairs at the third gong."

Elliott nodded. "And when will that be, Davaadalai?"

The butler consulted his silver fob watch. "In just over ten minutes, sir. If you will excuse me, I must see to the arrangements."

As the butler headed for the kitchen, Thorne turned and offered his arm to his wife, who took it with a smile, then turned to Elliott and Giselle. "Ten minutes gives us just enough time to pour a glass or four of champagne." The four of them smiled as they made their way to the bar.

As they entered the room, the ornate wrought-iron bell by the front door rang. Davaadalai stopped mid-stride on his journey to the kitchen, and made his way back to the front door.

As he pulled the heavy door open, a strong gust of chill wind accompanied and speeded the entry of the two people on the doorstep. The first in was Luci Lutyens, who looked both utterly fabulous and utterly freezing in his spectacular but thin emerald-green velvet smoking jacket; he paused just inside the door, smiling lazily at the butler as he straightened his garish purple and gold cravat. Before he could say a word, however, he was pitched into the hall by the equally freezing, but far more warmly dressed gentleman behind him; Dr Tenniel Mayberry.

Tall and massively broad, with a sizeable corporation, and a vibrant red beard and mutton-chops so luxuriously thick that they could have been utilised as a scarf, and frequently were in severe weather, the doctor stood on the threshold and glared at the foppish Luci with an expression of good-natured irritation. Davaadalai hurriedly closed the door, shutting out the freezing wind that threatened to undo the hard work of the many blazing fireplaces.

Luci waved a genial hand and looked at the butler brightly. "Drinks?"

Davaadalai's mouth twitched; he inclined his head. "In the lounge, sir."

Luci clapped the tall manservant on the shoulder. "Marvellous!" He trotted away as Davaadalai turned back to the second guest on the threshold.

Dropping his battered Gladstone bag with a rattling thud on the tiled floor, the doctor removed his equally battle-scarred hat and overcoat, revealing a mustard and salmon tweed suit that even Thorne might blench at. He handed his overgarments to the impassive butler and in a booming voice touched with a soft Scotch burr he barked, "Patient, where?"

Davaadalai draped the doctor's hat and coat over his left arm, bowed, and led the doctor upstairs.

○

The Lounge
7:56pm

Elliott raised his eyes from his contemplation of the flickering gaslight on his wife's glorious red hair as a booming laugh echoed from the great hall and Cornelius, Ami, and the owner of the laugh, Dr Mayberry, entered the room. The doctor was smiling. "Well, my friend, if you insist, I would of course be honoured to stay. Will it be another of Mrs Burnthouse's marvellous curries?"

Ami raised her eyebrows at his smile, her expression both arch and pained. "No, it will not!"

As Ami leant back in her bath chair, she saw Elliott, and turned to look back at Mayberry. "Of course, I'm sure you will remember each other. Dr Mayberry, may I present our dear great-nephew Alistair...long lost, but now happily returned to us. Alistair, you must remember Dr Tenniel Mayberry..."

Alistair stood up and held out his hand. Dr Mayberry paused, looking at Alistair with a questioning expression, before grasping the offered hand. Alistair spoke first. "How could I possibly forget the man who fought so valiantly to save my mother's life? It is a great honour to be reunited with you, Dr Mayberry. May I present my wife Giselle, and our friends Mr Abernathy Thorne, and his wife Aquilleia?"

A slight moistness appeared in the doctor's brown eyes at Elliott's words; he blinked rapidly, and his voice, usually a bellow that would chase off a stampeding elephant, was suddenly quiet as he gruffed over the firm handshake, "My dear boy, welcome home." He took Giselle's slender hand in his massive paw and pressed a gentle kiss to the air just above her thumb. "A pleasure, Madam, an absolute pleasure."

He harrumphed slightly as he did the same to Aquilleia's hand, and gave Thorne's hand a firm shake. Thorne winced as he smiled through clenched teeth; damn, that was a powerful grip!

As Thorne tried to shake sensation back into his crushed hand, Cornelius addressed the butler, who was standing by the little bar. "Champagne, please, Davaadalai. Oh, and Merric thinks it might be best to push dinner back by say, fifteen minutes, to allow Sybilla time to organise herself before she comes down. So, dinner for a quarter past the hour, if you please."

Davaadalai bowed, his face inscrutable as he opened another bottle of champagne and poured two coupes. He presented them to Cornelius and Dr Mayberry, left the room, and made his way to the kitchen.

As he entered the well-lit, manically busy room, Mrs Burnthouse turned from her omniscient position by the range and glared at him. "Go on, what now?"

Davaadalai growled something unspeakable under his breath. One of the maids paused in the middle of spooning soup into a tureen, and gawped at him before hurriedly turning back to her work.

He gritted his teeth and spat. "That bloody Sybilla…"

Mrs Burnthouse nodded as she settled herself into her chair. "I heard she chucked herself onto some glass at the sight of young Mr Alistair…she always was a dramatic tart!"

Without turning, she addressed one of the footmen, who was making some highly offensive hand gestures to Ellis.

"And you can stop those shenanigans too, Poulson. You're not far enough up the ladder to get away with it, my lad!"

The young man paled and immediately devoted himself to polishing the silver; Ellis, seated next to the terrified young man, also got back to his work.

She glared at the butler. "You'd better not be coming into my kitchen to tell me that my dinner's off because that silly tart's done herself a mischief!"

Davaadalai shook his head as he poured himself a sherry and knocked it back in one go. He waved the glass at the cook, who paused before nodding. He poured an equally large measure and placed it on the small table next to her chair. "No, it's only pushed back until quarter past. Will that cause any issue with the dishes?"

The cook paused in reaching for her drink, an irritated expression on her red face. She sat back in her seat and folded her arms across her substantial bosom, then shook her head. "Shouldn't; the soup's done—" She addressed the young maid who was still spooning soup into the tureen. "You'd best stop ladling, Jeanie — pop it all back in the pan 'til I give you the nod!" She turned back to Davaadalai. "The fish and the salads are cold, the venison will have to rest anyway, and the vegetables can be kept warm...No, it should all be fine — but only for fifteen minutes, mind, and no more. I won't allow overcooked vegetables to be sent out of my kitchen because of that silly cow!"

Davaadalai nodded as he eased himself into his well-stuffed chair opposite the irritated cook. These two particular armchairs had been a gift from Cornelius and Ami when they had married into the family, and were for the sole use of the butler and cook — woe betide any other servant who dared to place their person there.

The tired and now very crabby butler took a deep breath as he gazed into the open door of the range, watching the dancing flames for a few seconds before heaving his long body from the chair with a sigh.

The cook watched him as he walked towards Ellis and Poulson. Taking various item of polished silver from the pile the younger man had already worked his way though, he caught the cook's eye. "I forgot to mention ...Doctor Mayberry will also be staying for dinner."

As the cook rolled her eyes, grabbed her glass, and took a healthy gulp of sherry, Davaadalai turned to the other footman. "Ellis, with me."

Ellis leapt to his feet and followed the butler to the dining room, where the two men had less than fifteen minutes to reorganise the table to accommodate an extra setting. Moving swiftly, they set about changing the various place settings, moving the towering bowls of fruit, multiple cruets, and the fiddly display of chrysanthemums at the centre of the table, which had been an utter nightmare to order and that had begun shedding petals a full three days earlier than expected; all had to be rearranged to enable the placement at table of the unexpected guest.

○

The Lounge
8:14pm

As the final measurement between a cruet set and the newly placed setting for Dr Mayberry was checked and found to be acceptable by the still-irritated butler, Ellis shot back to the kitchen to assist with the serving of the meal.

Davaadalai stretched his neck, smoothed the front of his waistcoat, and walked back into the hall. Standing by the gong, he glared down his aquiline nose at his silver fob watch, counting down the seconds before he hefted the ornate wood and leather beater and struck the innocent and inoffensive gong with extreme force. He gritted his teeth as the unmelodious crashing sound echoed through the castle.

Placing the beater back on its plinth, he walked towards the lounge. He should have known that Sybilla would find a way to make the weekend all about her. Even if her fainting fit had been an accident, it had been a very well-timed accident indeed. Pushing the evening meal back fifteen minutes, and making him reassign the seating to make room for Dr Mayberry — all because of that selfish bloody woman!

With a disdainful sniff he walked to the lounge door, bowed low and announced, "Dinner is served."

As he awaited the arrival of the guests, a faint sound came from the stairs behind him. Turning, his eyes narrowed at the approach of the aforementioned Sybilla, draped limply on her dashing and concerned husband's arm, as they made their way very slowly down the stairs.

There was a high-pitched whirring sound followed by a dull clunk from the niche at the far end of the hall as the moving platform arrived and Ami disembarked. She hurriedly wheeled herself off the moving platform and applied a burst of speed to her motorised bath chair to reach Sybilla's side, where she immediately began to fuss over her. Davaadalai, meanwhile, stood in stony silence as the De Banzies made their grand entrance into the lounge.

Luci, propped by the bar with a full coupe in one hand and a nearly full bottle of champagne in the other, turned at the sudden change in atmosphere. He took in the vision that was Sybilla, and snorted with laughter as he raised his glass in her direction.

Now clad in a hideous but painfully expensive confection of purple-black silk that fitted tightly from throat to narrow waist, and which fell in swagged profusion from her bustle into a puddle of material that swept the floor behind her like a bridal train, Sybilla smiled weakly as she and Marcus became the centre of attention for the others in the lounge.

Davaadalai, standing by the door, dispassionately considered the overall effect of Sybilla's outfit. Her light eyes and naturally pale skin looked almost bleached against the couture gown's raven-feather tones, and with her mass of thick, dark hair coiled and secured with amethyst and jet pins, she resembled nothing more or less than a human-sized bruise!

Davaadalai's lips twitched at this thought as Melisandre entered the room and immediately stole the attention from Sybilla, throwing her friend's pale and tragic look into the shadows with her stunning teal velvet gown and glowing, honey-blonde beauty. As she entered and was warmly welcomed by many of the guests, her eyes turned from each friendly face until they rested on Merric, whose tentative, welcoming smile widened as he approached her.

Popplewell quietly made his appearance and bowed to Ami. She smiled at him, and nodded to Cornelius as she began to hand out the paper slips that identified which lady each gentleman would escort into dinner.

Davaadalai, standing rigidly by the lounge door, permitted himself a smile. Several of the placements had afforded much amusement to both himself and Mrs Burnt-house. His enjoyment increased dramatically at the sudden, unguarded expression that appeared on the face of the charming Marcus as he realised that neither the beautiful Melisandre nor the regal Theodora were to be his lady for the evening. The look of horror that appeared on the smart Grenadier's face as he realised he would be escorting a coquettish, and tittering Nanny into the dining room was something the butler would cherish forever.

○

The Dining Room
8:20pm

Once the gentlemen had escorted their ladies to their seats and taken their places at table, the dinner began. A fine fish bisque that Mrs Burnthouse had been fighting for several hours made its presence felt with its warming orange creaminess. A light lemon sorbet followed, to refresh the palate before the next course. A selection of cold meats, fish, and salads was brought to the table, its swift arrival keeping conversation to a minimum as the guests enjoyed the second stage of what was to be an eight-course meal.

After the entremets had been cleared and replaced by another sorbet, this time a delightfully pink raspberry ice, the chatter became slightly louder as the guests relaxed into the meal and enjoyed the wine and champagne that flowed with every course.

As the sorbet bowls were removed and most of the servants left the room, Merric stood up, tapping a spoon lightly on his glass. As the conversation around the table died down and all turned to face him, he turned pink under their scrutiny. "Ladies and gentlemen, family and dear friends, we are finally reunited for the first time in many years. A great crime was committed here on the Isle of Cove against all our families — by whom, we may never know — but now it is time for us to return to our families, to start afresh, with no thought of past evils."

As he spoke, Elliott, Giselle, Thorne, and Aquilleia sat back in their seats and casually watched the others. Ami was silent as she watched her nephew, her thin, ring clad fingers pressed together on her lap. Cornelius and Popplewell kept their attention on their glasses and looked faintly sheepish, while Dr Mayberry looked pugnacious — although that might have been his reaction to the singular lack of curry on the evening's menu. Luci was unusually quiet, his dark eyes sunken as he listened to Merric and gazed at the bowl of chrysanthemums without seeing it; Sybilla looked pale, tragic, and bored — very, very bored — while Marcus looked politely interested as he stroked his wife's bandaged wrist. Melisandre's expression was rapt as she watched and listened attentively, much to the silent irritation of her friend, Sybilla.

Sebastian sat in a state of silent questioning, his eyes flickering from Merric to Araby, and back to his wife, while Theodora sat in passive silence, her dark eyes giving away none of her knowledge of her husband's uncertainties. Araby, however, was not quite so prudent, she sat openly staring at Sebastian until Nanny prodded her foot under the table with her ever-present walking stick. Perry noticed Araby's wince and the glare she directed at the elderly lady as he gripped his glass, trying desperately not to quaff the entire coupe before Merric had finished speaking.

Last but not least of those in the room, the butler Davaadalai stood by the door, almost on guard, as he too cast his dark eyes around the room, studying each guest and family member in turn. He caught Elliott's eye and bowed his head slightly; being a party to Cornelius and Popplewell's scheme, he knew the young man was not who he claimed to be. He had been present when they had discovered the contents of the oubliette, and was an avowed ally to the cause that Elliott and the others had been charged to investigate — the discovery of the person, alive or dead, who had brutally murdered the island's children and abandoned young Alistair Burgoyne to die alone in the dark. Davaadalai knew that was the only way to free the family and the islanders from the terrible shadow of death and grief that had hung over them for so very long.

As the guests dealt with their own thoughts, some only vaguely aware of Merric's words, the Earl of Cove turned to Elliott and Araby, who sat opposite each other. Elliott's dark eyes were untroubled as he listened to Merric, while Araby's face was touched with two spots of high colour on her cheeks after Nanny's violent prod had summoned her back from her daydreams.

Merric raised his coupe high. "My dear nephew, Alistair, and my dear niece, Araby, on behalf of the Burgoyne family, after so very many long years, I bid you both welcome home."

As the other guests round the table raised their glasses in a toast, Sybilla and Marcus shared a long look. Failing singularly to raise their glasses, they sipped their champagne. Merric turned and raised his hand to Davaadalai, who nodded, crossed the room, and knocked once on the door to the kitchen, which was immediately opened as several servants entered carrying various dishes, sauces, and on a massive platter, the main course: roast haunch of venison with game chips and cress.

As the dish was carried across the room and placed on a separate table, the servants again departed, leaving only the butler and the footmen behind to serve the guests.

Merric stood by the table, gripped the fiendishly sharp bone-handled carving knife in his left hand and the equally ferocious looking fork in his right, and began to slice the perfectly roasted meat off the bone, placing it on a platter nearly as large as the plate bearing the haunch. He took his place back at the dining table as the meal was served by Davaadalai and the two young footmen.

The sound of chatter and clattering cutlery grew as the meal continued, and glasses were frequently refreshed. As the two footmen left the room, Davaadalai stood with his back to the door and watched the meal in silence. The courses were exceptional as ever; Mrs Burnthouse had once again worked her magic. The butler hid a smile as Cornelius and Dr Mayberry tucked into the game chips with evident enjoyment — and not a pinch of curry powder in sight!

As the butler continued his unblinking supervision, recharging glasses and monitoring when to call in the next course, Elliott, Giselle, Thorne, and Aquilleia applied themselves to the game in hand, and began their careful, seemingly innocent questioning of the guests around the table.

Aquilleia turned to look at Ami. "Mrs Burgoyne, I believe your family is one of the oldest in England, dating back even beyond the Doomsday Book; there must be quite a family history, but we have never been able to get Alistair to talk about it. Your name is ancient, but the title was bestowed by Henry VIII, I understand?"

Ami shrugged. "The family has most certainly existed in various guises for many, many years. We learned how to survive the vices that could ruin us, and took the various attempts to destroy the family, from within and without, in our stride." She sat back in her seat. "You must understand, my dear, that survival is the most important thing for the family name. Any family name is far more important than the title attached to it. A name can convey loyalty, honour, and strength…or it can convey terror, fear, and darkness. A title is much like the plumage of a peacock — beautiful, flamboyant, and graceful — but if you take away the plumage, what do you have? Nothing but a plucked chicken. An unmarred family name can survive for many generations without a title, if it is strong enough."

Cornelius coughed and turned a pained eye on Elliott, then glared at his sister, who caught the look and smiled brightly before addressing Elliott with a twinkle. "Never mind, my dear; one day all of this will be yours — as long as the death duties don't take it first!"

Merric laughed as he sipped his drink. "I don't intend to shuffle off this mortal coil any time soon, Aunt Ami!"

Ami shrugged. "Well, my dear, you aren't getting any younger, and as yet you have no issue — so who will inherit, if not Alistair?"

Merric flushed, took a large gulp of his drink, and steadfastly refused to look at Melisandre, whose face had also become rather pink.

Aquilleia noticed and smiled. She turned to Cornelius. "There is something else I don't quite understand, Mr Burgoyne."

Cornelius smiled. "Call me Cornelius, please, my dear. What don't you understand?"

She looked at him, then glanced back at Merric. "I cannot quite understand why you are not the Earl of Cove — you are the eldest male Burgoyne, after all..."

Cornelius sat back in his seat. "Ah, yes, there is a little tale to be told about that; I am not related to the Burgoyne family, I merely married into it, as did my sister Ami. My dear wife Raine, rest her soul, was sister to Merric's mother Drucilla. Merric is the twin brother of Araby's mother, Sabine, and as such the eldest Burgoyne male by bloodline; therefore, *he* is the Earl of Cove."

Thorne took a sip from his coupe. "Then you took the family name, sir. May I ask why? It is rather unusual."

Ami smiled at her brother. "Because it has always been an expectation of the Burgoyne family that any male marrying in will take the family name to enable its smooth continuation; again, we return to the name being the most important thing to the Burgoyne family." She sighed as she took a sip of her champagne. "Our father was deeply unhappy when he realised that we were both marrying into this house, as it meant the end of our family name. Luckily for us, however, our father-in-law, Jerome, was quite happy for us to unofficially keep our family name." She paused, reflecting. "He was nowhere near as strict as I believe his father, Thomas Burgoyne, was."

At least two people paused in their conversation to remember their own personal experience of the hideous old Master of Cove: one with hatred and condemnation, the other in remembered enjoyment...

In the sudden silence that descended, Cornelius patted his lips with his napkin and racked his brains for some way to lighten the dark tone the conversation had taken. He turned to Dr Mayberry with a slightly desperate expression. "Have you seen the new traction engine that Cove Farm purchased last month, Mayberry? Rather a marvellous piece of machinery..."

Ami took another sip of her champagne as she watched her brother struggle to change the conversation. She placed her coupe back on the table, waved her hand at Sybilla, and spoke over her brother's harrumphs. "I'm sure most of you are aware that my dear step-granddaughter Sybilla is one of the pre-eminent psychics in London..." Sybilla glanced down at the table in a fine display of insincere modesty. "I am very pleased to inform you all that she has agreed to undertake a séance for us this evening. Isn't that marvellous?"

Several guests made noises of intrigue, at least two showed deep displeasure, and another two were amused. Aquilleia showed great restraint in her reaction, coming as she did from a place of hidden knowledge; Luci, however, laughed out loud. Ami gave him a sharp look which he acknowledged with a winsomely guilty expression and a wave of his perilously full coupe, which didn't go down well with either Ami or the outraged De Banzies.

Of the two who were not appreciative, Popplewell's reaction was purely down to his faith, as was that of the other disapproving guest. Theodora's facial expression was one of deep offence; she looked askance at her husband on the other side of the table, but Sebastian failed to notice due to his conversation with Araby. Theodora bit her lip and stared across the table, silently willing her husband to look at her, but Sebastian continued to focus on his old friend.

His wife sat back in her seat; as the remains of the venison were removed and the palate-cleansing rum punch arrived, she silently planned her next move.

○

The Séance
10:30pm

As the final course was cleared, the gentlemen escorted their ladies from the dining room to the library, where the séance was due to take place.

Theodora, escorted by Popplewell, saw her opportunity; she gently disentangled her arm from the elderly man's light clasp, approached Merric, and curtsied smartly. "My lord, I am sorry if I offend you, but I have no desire to be present at such an entertainment. If you will please excuse me, I must attend to my son."

Merric blinked, and stuttered. "Of course, Mrs Lees...absolutely."

As he bowed, she curtsied again, before turning to look directly at her husband, who was escorting Araby. She deliberately caught his eye before turning her cool appraisal to the young woman on his arm. She looked Araby up and down before returning her gaze to her husband, who flushed angrily as she swept past them and made her way upstairs.

Giselle and Aquilleia exchanged glances before Aquilleia winked at her friend, then turned a concerned countenance to Marcus, who was standing by the door. "Will one fewer in the party cause Sybilla and her guides any issue?"

Marcus shook his head with a smile as Melisandre joined them. "Not at all, Sybilla will not be touched by anything the mundane world could possibly threaten her with. Shall we go in?"

As he extended his arm to Melisandre, Merric suddenly appeared by her side. "Yes, shall we?"

Melisandre turned her bright-blue eyes to Merric and curtsied with a smile as she took his arm. A little knot of warmth grew in the happy lord's stomach as he escorted her past an obviously irritated Marcus and into the library.

According to Sybilla's demands, which had been somewhat mitigated by Ami before Cornelius translated them into a polite request for his nephew, Merric had instructed Davaadalai to set a round table large enough to seat all his guests in the centre of the massive, book-lined room.

As the guests milled around, searching for their named places, Davaadalai waited by the door. At a nod from Marcus, Ami looked at Cornelius, who managed to catch Merric's eye; he smiled encouragingly at his nephew, who stared at him with a nonplussed expression before understanding finally dawned. He raised his hand to Davaadalai, who drew the servants out of the room before pulling the heavy oaken door shut. The echoing thud of the door silencing everyone with its note of finality.

Luci turned from his cavalier slouch at the small bar set up between Cornelius' collections of Dickens and Punch, which had taken him less than a minute to find, and smiled brightly. "Drinkies?"

Marcus flashed him a dark look from his place at the far end of the room, well away from the door that led back into the hall. "No, Mr Lutyens, not at this time. For the safety of all, I must ask you not to take any glassware to the table."

Luci looked at him silently, an unreadable expression on his usually mobile face. With a shrug he turned back to the bar, refilled his coupe with the excellent champagne on offer and knocked the glass back in one. Ignoring Marcus's glare and Ami's sharply raised eyebrow, he set the coupe on the bar and took his place at the table. He turned to Elliott. "You remember me, Alistair; I never was one to accept advice. however bossily it was issued."

He cast an insolent glance at Marcus and waved his hand. "As you were, old man."

Marcus gritted his teeth, then turned to Sybilla, who was gently sinking into the large chair at the top of the table. "My dear, are you ready?"

Sybilla closed her eyes and took a deep breath. She held it for what seemed an abnormally long time before slowly nodding. "I am ready…"

Marcus turned down the gaslights and approached his wife. Lighting the solitary candle in the centre of the table, he turned to look each guest in the face, as he dramatically proclaimed, "Will you all please be seated and take the hand of the person next to you. Under no circumstances are you to let go until you are told that it is safe to do so."

As he sat next to the silent Sybilla, those who were still standing took their seats. Dr Mayberry looked rather bullish, but caught Ami's gimlet eye and sat down without a word.

They clasped hands with only a modicum of embarrassment, and after a suitable pause, Sybilla began. "I call upon my guide, he who protects and leads what passes through the veil, to stand by my side. Come to me, my friend, and assist us here in this, the longest night of the year. Can you hear me?" Her voice softened to a whisper. "Can you hear me?"

A sudden loud knocking echoed around the large room, making all at the table jump…except Sybilla and Marcus.

Sybilla smiled, her pale eyes still closed. "My guide, we

contact you in the time of both the dark moon and the longest night…both times unite in helping us heal an ancient loss. Many years ago, an evil was committed here…can you guide us? Can you guide us to one who can help us discover the truth?"

The candle flame bobbed suddenly, ruffled by a soft breeze that seemingly came from nowhere. As the light flickered, a faint sound came to the ears of the people around the table…the sound of a child's laughter.

Sybilla shook her head, her eyes slightly unfocused. "There are children…so many children…" Her eyes widened as the child's voice became a keening cry. "And they are angry!"

A faint gasp came from Elliott's left. He darted a glance in the direction it came from, but the lowered gaslights made it impossible for him to see who had been taken aback.

Sybilla closed her eyes and began to hum, swaying gently from side to side. To her left, Marcus turned his gaze from the lone candle and frowned at his wife as her breathing became laboured and a faint mist began to form around her…

In the dim light, Sybilla opened her unfocused eyes and slowly turned to Elliott; she tilted her head to one side as though listening to voices only she could hear, smiled faintly, and nodded. "You are known to others…*the* Others. Many guises…and many lives." Elliott and Thorne shared a dark look across the table.

Sybilla continued, her voice almost sing-song in its intonation. "There is one…someone you are concerned for…" She shook her head slightly then tilted it, as though to hear better. "A brother in arms — oh, how he suffers!" She shuddered and her eyes widened as she looked at Alistair. Her soft voice suddenly became thick and guttural. "He must burn… burn to be free — burn!"

She began to slump in her seat. Against his own advice, her husband dropped his neighbour's hand, moved to his wife's side and supported her. Melisandre shook herself free of her neighbours' hands, left the table, and turned the gaslights up, then poured a glass of brandy and handed it to Marcus, who gently pressed the glass to his wife's lips. She took a sip and coughed, then sat up and pushed the rest of the glass away with a grimace. "What — what came through? Oh, I feel so sick!"

Ami patted her hand. "There, there, my dear. I don't think it was your usual guide. Someone much stronger, judging by your words — and, if you'll pardon my bluntness, the smell!"

Dr Mayberry looked at them. "I recognised that smell: sulphur, or as the laymen might know it, brimstone!"

Elliott, Thorne, Giselle, and Aquilleia looked at each other silently as the people around the table rather self-consciously released each other's hands, and not a few gazed longingly at the small bar. Luci took in their expressions with a barely hidden smirk before he stood up and with considerable enjoyment, announced baldly.

"I don't know about you, my friends, but after that lovely lot of twaddle, I could do with a drink…a large one!"

As he walked to the bar, Marcus glared at him from his position beside the whimpering Sybilla. "How dare you, you…Philistine!"

Luci poured himself a large refill from the champagne bottle, threw himself into a comfortable chair and hooked his leg over one of the arms before turning a rather malicious grin on the outraged husband. He took a sip from his glass and wagged his finger. "Now, now…careful, Marcus: you never know what might be revealed in the heat of an argument."

The angry man opened and closed his mouth like a landed fish, his handsome face an ugly shade of puce as

Sybilla, realising the situation was no longer under their control, made a sudden, magnificent recovery. She hurriedly sat up and placed a calming hand over his. When she spoke, her voice was soft and trembling. "Darling, please will you escort me to our rooms? I feel a trifle unwell."

Marcus's head snapped round to look at her, and the veins in his neck bulged as he stared at his wife. He took a deep breath, then escorted Sybilla silently from the room.

Luci polished his thumbnail on his velvet jacket. "Spectacular performance!"

Ami glared at him. "Luci! Must you?"

He laughed. "Yes, darling Ami, I must, as well you know!" His dark eyes flashed. "I don't take kindly to the murder of children being used for entertainment." He took in the sudden upset on her face and smiled gently. "Ami, dear Sybilla and her marvellous husband are simply too much for a simple country boy to take seriously! They are both so very, very…well, 'city' is probably the best term; probably because it is far more polite than some of the others that leap unerringly to mind!"

Ami's eyebrows snapped down. "Lucius Aloysius Lutyens, that is enough!"

He raised his glass to her with a polite smile. "Ahh, the full address! The fun must come to an end, then: as you wish."

As the guests refilled their glasses and light social chatter began, no one witnessed the door to the large armoire in the corner of the room slowly close, as the person within tucked themselves away until all had left and they could return to their quarters.

○

Sybilla and Marcus's Suite.
11:45pm

Sybilla sat on the edge of the bed and watched with a concerned expression as Marcus stalked to the bell pull and tugged it hard. A few minutes later Ellis knocked on the door. As the door was flung open, the young footman took in the dark-red face and bulging veins in the neck of the seething man before him and silently took the barked order for champagne.

Ellis returned to the cupboard and set about the order; carrying a tray loaded with champagne, coupes, and almonds, he headed back to the suite, where he was swiftly admitted by a still puce Marcus. Ellis dealt with the cork, poured the drinks, and left the room as quickly as possible, bowing smartly as he left. From the bell to delivery, less than five minutes had passed. Ellis was pleased — it beat Davaadalai's record by a country mile!

Marcus closed the door with rather more force than necessary and turned to his wife, jaw clenched. "Well, that was an interesting evening. That bloody parvenu, Luci — what I would love to do to that grubby little dandiprat!"

Sybilla stroked his face gently. "Patience, my darling. You know he isn't on our list…" She thought for a moment. "But if you need a plaything, we could alter our plan slightly. We could kill Melisandre — and if we plan thoroughly, we just might send Luci to the gallows for her murder!"

She raised her delicately arched eyebrows at her husband. "I know you've had your eye on Melisandre for quite some time; that's why you kept inviting her for dinner and week-ends at our home. Don't be shy, my darling; I knew it wasn't charity towards a friend who had fallen on hard times, even if that's what people thought!" She smiled. "Now, if we plan carefully, in one evening we could enjoy our entertainment with Melisandre, place evidence there to implicate Luci, and then kill Merric, making it appear that he took his own life over his love's brutal murder. Two birds with one stone!" She paused, and tapping her finger against her lips, looked at her husband. "But we would have to find somewhere suitable first: quiet, and out of the way. What do you say, my love?"

Marcus looked at his wife in silence, then placed his hands on her silk-clad neck and pressed a soft kiss to her forehead. "You truly are spectacular, my darling! That sounds like a perfect evening." He looked with concern at his wife's pale face. "We've had no time to speak privately after what happened in the library. Sybilla, are you all right?"

Sybilla looked at him silently before moving to sit at the dressing table, where she began to remove the jewelled pins from her hair. "It was the shock of seeing…" She paused; her pale face uncertain. "You know as well as I do, Marcus, that my cousin Alistair could not possibly be sitting downstairs."

Marcus sat on the edge of the bed and kicked off his shoes. "I can't explain it, my love. He is the very image of Alistair, but as you say, we know it can't be him…" He shook his head. "Something is afoot; someone else has a game in play, and we must keep our eyes open. We can't lose the prize now!"

Sybilla settled in her chair and smiled at her husband. "We know we can't rest on our laurels, as the sanctimonious reverend would say; we cannot rest until we have found it! Now, the map!"

Marcus walked to the wardrobe and pulling their trunk down from the top, placed it carefully on the bed. He opened it, rummaged through, and removed a small leather tube.

Heading back to the dressing table, he carefully unrolled the tube and placed various pots and jars at the corners to secure it. He looked at his wife. "I think it would be best if I did the first reconnoiter alone, my darling. After what happened earlier, it is more sensible for you to rest."

Sybilla smiled. She stood and glided towards her husband. She stroked his face with a smile, then wrapped a slender arm around his neck and nibbled his ear. "I have lost more blood than that in our more…playful moments, darling!" She sat back, thinking. "But I take your point. It has been quite a tiring, stressful evening, and I do need my rest — especially if we are to deal with this talented usurper, whoever he is."

She looked at Marcus with an arch expression. "You go alone tonight, darling, and see what you can find." She smiled. "And while you are out there, see if you can find somewhere suitably private for an evening with Melisandre!"

She tilted her head to one side and lightly stroked one pointed nail along his jaw. "But now, tell me, my love, was the séance a good enough performance for our dear family? Do you think our target understood?"

Marcus stood up, took both coupes from the tray, and placed one before her. "It was absolute perfection, my darling. You were marvellous this evening, and I sincerely believe our mark understood quite clearly what was meant about the children. I was watching, and I saw their reaction…" He gave her an appreciative look. "That piece about the "brother in arms who must burn to be free" was quite spectacular; who was it for?"

Sybilla frowned as she took a sip from her coupe and perused the map on the dressing table. "I didn't say anything about a brother in arms, my darling. Whatever are you talking about?"

Marcus stared at her as she continued to study the map.

A soft, deferential knock sounded at the door. Marcus was about to call out when Sybilla shook her head and mouthed "Eliza". He walked to the door and admitted his wife's maid, who was clad in a long dark cloak that covered her from the floor to her neck. As she entered the room, she removed the cloak to reveal a shockingly masculine outfit comprising of a tight black shirt, fitted black trousers, and black ballet slippers. She smiled at her master and mistress. "I did well, yes?"

Sybilla poured more champagne into her coupe and handed it to the young woman.

"You did marvellously, Eliza...that little touch of the child's laughter was spectacular; your talents as a ventriloquist make you an invaluable addition to our little circle."

Marcus ran his finger across the young woman's jawline as she smiled at them both. "In more ways than one!"

○

The Kitchens
1:20am

Mrs Burnthouse and Davaadalai sat by the well-scrubbed table with full snifters of port and raised their glasses in a tired toast. An evening well done, even if Sybilla had very nearly ruined it!

The cook finished her drink and washed her glass. Placing it on the draining board, she nodded at the butler. "Goodnight; see you in..." She checked the clock on the wall. "Three and a half hours!"

Davaadalai groaned, downed his port and rinsed his glass.

They lit their oil lamps, left the kitchens, and sought their rooms; Davaadalai's was in the first-floor servants' quarters and Mrs Burnthouse's on the second floor.

Davaadalai climbed the spiral staircase in a state of extreme tiredness. He entered his room, closed the door, and for the first time since he had moved to Cove Castle, locked the door behind him.

Heading towards her room, Mrs Burnthouse paused as a strange sound came to her ears, almost like the rustling of bats or the skittering of spiders. She turned up the gas lamp on the wall before looking down the corridor; there was nothing behind her, and nothing but the closed doors of the maids' rooms on either side of her. She listened intently and realised that the sound came from directly above her...

She swung her oil lamp into the air and stared at the ceiling that stretched along the dark corridor before disappearing round the corner to where her rooms were situated. She could see nothing, but she could swear she had heard something...

With a pugnacious set to her jaw, the cook turned down the gas lamp, set her shoulders, and stomped down the dim passageway to her rooms. She flung the door open, glared into the small sitting room beyond, slammed the door shut, and locked it.

Several minutes passed in silence. Then, as the little clock on the far wall struck half past the hour, the door on the corridor which led to the guest chambers slowly opened and a small figure appeared. Looking furtively up and down the silent passage, Eliza silently closed the door before making her way down the long, dark hallway, back into the servants' quarters.

As she headed to her room, Eliza heard a sudden sound ahead of her and pressed herself against one of the closed doorways. She held her breath as someone appeared at the top end of the corridor. Tall and obviously male, the figure walked past without seeing her and continued down the servants' staircase.

Eliza turned to see which room they had been visiting. The corridor turned a corner and ended with two doors: that of the room given to Rose Marshall, the Lees family's maid, and the entrance to the small suite belonging to Mrs Burnthouse.

Eliza's face split in an unpleasant grin. A gentleman caller, either for a young slapper or an old baggage! If that spicy bit of information didn't get her a few extra bob, she'd be surprised!

The young maid continued to her room, happy thoughts of extra money adding to the events of the past few hours flying around her head. Being the plaything of a wealthy couple had its disadvantages, but certain society doors had a little more give if you were introduced as a companion rather than a maid, and Sybilla and Marcus had offered her the promotion that very night. They were tiring of the beautiful but pure Melisandre, whose naivety had so intrigued them at first; they had come to the conclusion that corrupting a virgin in order to bring her into their rather exclusive fold required a great deal of time, effort, and planning they simply didn't have the patience for. And besides, why should they bother? When they had a willing playmate prepared to encourage and support them, and who was quite capable of enjoying the same strange pleasures as they?

Eliza smiled, looking at the simple but expensive gold bracelet on her wrist. There were of course the obvious gifts from Marcus and Sybilla — money, clothes, and some nice little pieces of jewellery as recompense for certain liberties they enjoyed — but as Sybilla's paid companion she would earn a far better wage, don better clothes, wear the jewellery she had been given, and finally, which to the young but not inexperienced Eliza was far more important, Sybilla and Marcus had promised that she would have a maid of her own.

Eliza's smile widened. Today had been her last day as a servant. Tomorrow she would be introduced at table as

Sybilla's companion, and the rest of her life would be far more enjoyable. She entered her bedroom, closed the door, and locked it behind her.

In the dark hallway, one of the many doors closed slowly as the person within pondered the unreliability of modern domestic staff.

○

The Sub-Levels
Saturday Morning
2:30am

Cove Castle had been built in the days when 'trust no one' had been the standard by which you lived your life — and hopefully survived! Therefore, the massive building had been designed, planned, and built with that in mind. Several different architectus had been employed, all of whom had met their end shortly after making interesting suggestions and alterations to the previous plans of the castle. Their deaths were against the wishes of the family monk, who had pleaded in vain for the lives of various workers who had been executed to prevent knowledge of the myriad hidden passages from falling into the wrong hands. Not just those hidden passages, but also the catacombs and dank dungeons built within the castle walls, across the estate and into the sprawling ruins of Cove Abbey and the smugglers caves below...

Deep in the bowels of these sub-levels, below the cellars where Cornelius kept his best wines and the basements where Merric built and tinkered with his machines, a lone figure bearing a lantern was approaching a room they had hoped never to enter again.

An eldritch creak sounded from protesting metal as the

figure passed through the elderly door that led from one of the many secret passages into the catacombs, which spread like an ant's nest within the foundations of the castle keep.

As they stepped around a corner, a faint prickling crept up the back of their neck. Swinging round with a gasp, they waved the lantern above their head. The heavy black robe swirled as they turned, but they could see nothing in the thick darkness. Swallowing hard, they turned back to their chosen path. It had to be done, so it was best to get it over with quickly.

After several minutes of walking, they came at last to a locked, iron-clad door, stained with dark-orange rust which had wept from the iron studs and streaked down the damp oak like bloody tears. Their heart seemed to beat in their throat as they remembered the last time they had stood before that door.

Removing a key from one of their pockets, they unlocked the door and slowly pushed the heavy oak slab open. The room beyond was pitch black, but as they entered, the lantern clenched in their left hand introduced soft light to the small, cell-like room beyond. While the outside of the door had been damp, the room beyond was dry and musty. It was also empty, save for a heavy metal grate in the middle of the floor which guarded the entrance to one of the family's oldest, most unpleasant, and best-forgotten historical possessions: the oubliette.

Pausing on the threshold, the figure gritted their teeth and entered the room. They approached the rusty metal grid, carefully leaned over, and gazed into the dungeon below. Caught in the glow of the lantern was a single piece of furniture, an ornate but broken wooden chair, and seated upon it, the mummified, still-recognisable corpse of young Alistair Burgoyne. His sightless, sunken eyes stared blankly up at the entry to the oubliette, his thick hair was ruffled around a dark mass of dried blood on his temple.

The figure above recoiled from the desiccated corpse, their breath stuttering in their throat as they ran back to the open doorway. With clumsy fingers they relocked the door before stumbling away, the candle guttering as the lantern jerked in their shaking hand.

As they fled the dingy catacombs, a dim figure behind them watched as they ran into a passageway leading to the house and gardens. The waiting figure struck a match and relit their candle stub; they turned to stare at the barred door before approaching the enclosed room and removing two metal pins from their pocket.

After a few moments the door swung open and the figure silently entered. Several minutes passed before they reappeared, wearing a thoughtful expression. Their suspicions were correct: the man upstairs could not possibly be Alistair Burgoyne! Marcus turned with a satisfied smile and followed the fleeing figure along the passageway.

The distant figure flung open a wooden door and ran into the dark garden, where they paused in the clearing beyond the door and gulped the cold morning air, their heart hammering in their chest.

As they paused to catch their breath, Marcus stepped out behind them and pushed the door closed, the thud echoing in the foggy rose garden. The figure jumped, and spun round to stare at him.

Marcus smiled again, his white teeth flashing in the light from his candle. "Well, fancy meeting you here! Let's cut to the chase, hmm? Based on what we have just witnessed in the dungeon, we both know that the man who calls himself Alistair Burgoyne, isn't!" He rubbed his chin with a rueful expression. "We were aware of your many and varied abilities. You certainly showed an innate skill on your little jaunts to our home — we spent some wonderful weekends there, didn't we? But I digress." He shot the silent figure a smile. "While we knew Alistair had been killed — we discovered his body in that particular little suite of rooms some years ago, we never realised that he was one of your victims! You've done very well to commit murder and never be suspected — well, not yet, at any rate! In light of certain pertinent information that we need, it's time our friendship...changed slightly. Bearing in mind certain photographs taken for our mutual delectation, I daresay you and I can come to an arrangement!"

The robed figure blinked rapidly, then raised their eyebrows. "Saw what in the dungeon? I don't know what..."

Their voice trailed off as Marcus looked at them in silence.

The figure swallowed. "Are you trying to blackmail me? Is that what you want, money?"

Marcus laughed. "Oh, there's no need for me to blackmail you; not when I already am!"

The figure looked uncertain. "What?"

Marcus's smile widened unpleasantly. "We knew of your previous crimes; they became known to us a short while after you did what you did." He laughed. "Why do you think we invited you into our little circle? We knew just what you were capable of." He paused thoughtfully before continuing. "Well, we thought we did. Concerning this particular little murder, to be honest, we weren't sure if you were the guilty party." His smile became even more unpleasant. "It appears we lost that little bet! We knew of — most of your peccadilloes and proclivities all those years ago, and at the time, we pondered several options. Informing the police would have ensured justice for your victims, but who are we to judge someone by their amusements? we came to the conclusion that a willing helper in our little activities would be rather pleasant. Then we also realised that we rather like money, and blackmail is quite simple. Money is lovely, especially when it belongs to someone else, and one can profit from someone else's hard work — or in your case, inheritance… we are aware that you have given us nearly all of it, and have very little of real worth left; therefore, in the light of that pertinent piece of information and our shared mutual interests, we are prepared to make you a deal."

A desperate expression crossed the face before him. "Go on."

Marcus nodded encouragingly. "We are looking for a room hidden somewhere within the building, or possibly between the castle and the ruins of the abbey. Either a single large room, or several smaller rooms, but very well hidden and accessed solely from a secret passage. we want you to help us find it."

The figure blinked. "Why?"

Gritting his perfect teeth, Marcus kept a grip on his manners. "That is our business, not yours…but I assure you it would be worth your while. we have no desire to inform anyone of your highly questionable actions on this night or any other night, including what you must have done to hide a certain item in a certain locked room below us. We rather enjoy our little business arrangement, and it would be a terrible shame for all of us if it were to end! Think about where such a room or rooms could be, and I will talk with you again after lunch. I bid you a good evening — or rather, good morning!"

Marcus walked away briskly. As he headed for the path leading back to the castle, his mark watched him go; their fearful expression slowly replaced by one of contempt. They were joined by two other figures: one a slight shape robed in grey, who stood behind them and gazed at the floor in worshipful servitude, the other a huge, silent figure who wore no robe and towered over the other two; their leathery hide untroubled by the freezing fog.

The first figure folded their arms under their thick black robes and looked at their associates with an amused expression. "It appears that our blackmailer has finally decided to reveal himself. I should have known it would be him; it appears that we have to deal with yet another little problem!" They nodded thoughtfully. "As for the photographs, I know of only three that show my presence, and I made damn sure the camera couldn't focus on me by moving." The figure turned to their larger confederate with a smile. "One of the many things you taught me, Filicidae: never allow them to keep your likeness."

The black-robed figure gestured towards the grey-robed figure behind them. "Back to the business in hand. I think our faithful acolyte would have a bit of difficulty dealing with that one, since he is rather large; would you like to see to him?" They raised their lantern and looked up at the towering figure. "Best if it were done sooner rather than later; then you can change before we return to the castle." They smiled up at the hideous creature. "I think it best that the people in the castle only see your human side...until the time comes to finally unveil you!"

The massive figure next to them laughed, the guttural, wet sound grating upon the ear. Then they pushed through the dank, foggy foliage of the garden, and followed the distant figure back towards the castle.

Moving with a speed belying their size, the dark shape shifted to the left of the path as Marcus paused, pulled a pipe out of his pocket, and proceeded to light and smoke it. The coiling wisps of smoke merged with the rising fog to create an ocean of white visible even in the dark moon as the tendrils wrapped around the distant figure. As Marcus stood in silent enjoyment of his pipe and the prospect of even more money to finance his and Sybilla's lifestyle, the watcher in the woods slinked deeper into the shadow of the dark leaves around them.

The creature paused, then began to advance on the unsuspecting man, the chill dampness of the fog clinging to their leathery hide and thick fur as they made their way through the overgrown rhododendron walk.

Marcus took a deep pull on his pipe and smiled. A serendipitous encounter; if anyone knew where the hidden room was, it would be—

A sharp snap echoed like a gunshot from the thick rhododendron hedge to his left. Turning sharply, he peered into the shadows, but could see nothing. He turned towards the castle; it was still some way to the drawbridge and the front door. He looked towards where the noise had come from and sighed. If they wanted to dissuade him from his very generous offer, he would have no alternative but to dissuade them first. And if they refused to assist him, he would have to choose between telling the authorities what he had witnessed — after all, it was his civic duty — or perhaps a few hours' discussion in his well-equipped London cellar might help them change their mind!

He smiled, and tapping the pipe against the sole of his shoe, he tucked it back inside his breast pocket. When his hand returned to his side it was grasping a truly vicious-looking blade. Over a foot long and curved, with an ornately carved ivory handle, the kukri had been a gift from Sybilla for their first anniversary, and had been used by them both over the years in their private play, and their private hunting.

Marcus weighed the knife in his hand. A smile came to his lips as he thought of the last time he and Sybilla had used the blade, just a few days earlier in London. A new friend from the streets had spent an interesting evening at their

Mayfair house before leaving via the sewers and making their way out into the Thames.

Marcus's smile broadened. So many waifs and strays in the big city. That particular playmate had been washed up on the riverbank next to several other body parts that, oddly enough, had nothing whatsoever to do with him and Sybilla — well, not that time! Dismembering a corpse took time and effort which they had both agreed could be far better spent on disposing of said corpse in one lump and returning home to an entertaining evening with one's spouse, and a glass or two of freshly fortified wine…

Marcus heard a faint snuffling in the shadows behind him, somewhat closer than before. He gripped the blade, straightened up and smiled languidly into the shadows. "Is that you? I only want your help to find the room. Now, if you try and go against my suggestion, I'm afraid I shall have to cut you out of our nice little arrangement and either inform the authorities about your many mistakes all those years ago," — his face hardened — "or organise an evening you will not live to see the end of! Do you understand me?"

The shadows moved slightly in the mild breeze that swept up from the harbour below and made the fog swirl towards him. Marcus retched — what in God's name was that foul stench?

A raw, gurgling sound came from the distant shadows. Marcus froze as a huge figure moved away from the dark trees and stepped onto the path. "Afraid…yes, it is you who is afraid — I can smell your fear!"

Marcus gaped at the approaching figure which, with a sudden snarl, began to run. Using one arm as a prop, it moved towards him with frightening speed.

Still gripping the blade, Marcus turned and ran towards the lights of the castle. The hideous sound that he now knew to be the creature's laughter echoed in his ears as he made for the sanctuary of the distant building.

The dark pathways glowed in the swirling fog as the terrified man approached the drawbridge — but there, on the bridge, was the black-robed figure who had so obviously refused his demands. As he attempted to push past, the figure pushed back their cowl and pointed a pistol at him. With a snarl, Marcus ran back across the bridge and towards the narrow path that led down the hill to the village.

As he took that path, another figure garbed in grey robes appeared and also threatened him with a pistol. Marcus turned again, and ran into the thick shadows on the far side of the garden...

Whimpering in terror, and his heart pounding in his throat, he ran through the dark garden. Veering off the path, he pushed his way through damp vegetation, hacking at the thick branches with his blade in a desperate attempt to escape.

Casting a look over his shoulder, he saw the hideous shape gaining on him, and screamed. He ran so fast he thought his heart would burst as he shot out of the dark foliage and into the open...

As the dark shape of the following creature disappeared above him, Marcus's despairing screams faded as he fell three hundred feet from the cliff to the crashing sea below.

○

Aquilleia and Thorne's Suite
3:15am

In the dim light afforded by the dying embers of the banked fire, Aquilleia's eyes sprang open. Her violet irises swirled with silver light as she sat up in the large bed she shared with her husband and turned towards the door. Across the room, Veronique also sat up, and looked at her mistress with a questioning whine.

Aquilleia's eyes flickered as she reached out with her mind and realised that one of their number was no longer to be found — neither in the castle, nor on the island.

She carefully climbed out of bed, taking care not to wake Thorne. He snored faintly, turned over, and continued to sleep as she walked past the dying fire, knelt by Veronique's bed, and comforted the worried dog, gently stroking the silky ears as she whispered her thoughts to the concerned Labrador. In the stillness of the dim room, Aquilleia tried to remember what she had felt and seen: bone-numbing fear, heart-pounding terror, a sense of sudden freedom, the roaring sound of water, then darkness. This was followed by an image of waves, and a brief flash of a rather shabby bathing machine.

Having perused the images in her mind's eye, Aquilleia studied her sleeping husband and decided that what she had witnessed could wait until morning. She opened one of their trunks and removed a handful of biscuits for Veronique.

Before she returned to her husband's side, she struck a match and looked at the clock on the mantle: 03:17. She blew out the flickering light and returned to the warmth of the well-blanketed bed. As she settled back down, Aquilleia wondered whether or not Marcus De Banzie had actually been murdered — and if so, by whom, and why?

○

Sybilla and Marcus' Suite
4:00am

Sybilla woke with a sudden gasp. The soft gaslight she had left on for her husband's return lit the room as she turned to look at the clock. Four in the morning: he should have returned by now!

Throwing back the covers, she hurriedly pulled on her peignoir. In spite of the fire Marcus had banked up before leaving for his reconnoiter of the castle's hidden chambers, the room had become quite cold in the intervening hours…

Sybilla seized the poker, prodded the dull embers, and threw a large log on the grate. She checked her pristine fingernails for damage as the fire caught with a sharp cracking sound, and the room slowly began to warm.

She walked to the window and tweaked back one of the thick curtains, but she could see nothing in the dark, foggy grounds. With a sigh, she let the curtain fall, poured herself a glass of brandy and returned to bed. Pulling her thin peignoir about her, Sybilla plumped up the pillows and settled to await Marcus's return.

○

Yule Morning
The Dining Room
8:00am

Dr Mayberry wandered over to the breakfast table and helped himself to a huge portion of kedgeree. He paused to judge one or two of the other dishes on offer, and added a poached egg, two sausages, and a substantial portion of devilled kidneys to his already heaped plate. As he made his way back to the table, Veronique peeped out from under Thorne's chair and whined softly. Mayberry's plate jumped, and deposited one perfectly cooked pork sausage directly in front of the Labrador's twitching nose.

Continuing to his seat, he shared a smile with Thorne, who finished his bacon and eggs and headed back to the buffet to peruse his second round: several thick slices of toast, a helping of butter that could have comfortably covered the dining table, and enough strawberry jam to drown a badger.

Veronique pricked up her ears and watched as he returned to the table. A single rasher of crispy bacon soon joined the pork sausage in her belly.

As Thorne sat down beside his wife and devoted himself to his breakfast, Elliott and Giselle entered the room. They greeted everyone cheerfully before considering the victuals on offer. As they settled themselves at table with several small but well-loaded plates, Ellis entered and refreshed the tea and coffee pots.

As Elliott and Giselle ate their breakfast beside Thorne and Aquilleia, the four of them shared a glance. Once Aquilleia had explained her vision that morning, they had realised that informing the family that she was a psychic who had had a vision about Marcus dying might not be the best way of breaking the news. Having considered several possible options, they had decided on a roundabout course of action. They needed to find out whether there was a bathing machine on the island without raising any suspicions, and after some thought, they had determined the best person to ask.

Cornelius entered the room, waved a vague good morning to the room in general, and applied himself to a thorough study of the breakfast table before loading one plate with a healthy serving of pheasant hash, and another with several rounds of buttered toast. Thorne coughed, rather relieved that the company were completely unaware just how big a lie he was about to tell.

He dabbed at his lips with his napkin. "I say, Cornelius, I'm rather fond of the occasional winter dip — excellent for the circulation, don't you know? Where on the island is best for a good swim? And is there somewhere I could possibly change? You know, like a bathing machine?"

Cornelius sat at the table and nodded as Ellis poured him a cup of tea. He took a massive bite of his buttered toast and pondered Thorne with a slightly pained expression as he chewed. Swimming, in this weather? Well, it took all sorts, he supposed!

He nodded thoughtfully as he sipped his tea. "Yes, there is a bathing machine, but it's a little out of the way, not down the usual path to the village. If you take the path to Horseman Falls and follow it all the way down, it ends at Horseshoe Bay. There's a battered old hut there." He took another bite of his toast. "It *was* a bathing machine many years ago but the wheels rusted, so now it's just a hut." He smiled, old memories of past trips to the bay returning. "Horseshoe is a lovely bay for swimming. Sheltered, but the rip tides that form further out can be deadly. Don't swim out too far past the point!"

Thorne nodded his thanks, exchanged a glance with Elliott, and returned to his breakfast as Merric and Ami entered the room. The Earl of Cove met Melisandre's eyes with a gentle smile before turning to his uncle. "Blessed Yule, Uncle. Is everything arranged?"

Cornelius nodded happily. "A blessed Yule to you too, Merric, and you, Ami. Yes, indeed: Davaadalai has set up the targets, and he and Mrs Burnthouse have organised luncheon to be served outside a little before one. That gives us plenty of time to finish breakfast and gather on the lawn." He glanced down the table at the doctor, who on the appearance of Merric and Ami had risen from his breakfast and greeted them both before sitting back down and becoming engrossed in his kedgeree. Cornelius waited until Ami had settled into her usual place at the far end of the table before waggling his eyebrows at his nephew. Merric leaned down to his uncle. "I thought it would be a sensible idea to include Mayberry in our little weekend," murmured Cornelius. "With all that happened last night, it might be an idea if he stays on for a little while — just to make sure all is well, you know?"

Merric nodded. "As you say, Uncle."

Thorne allowed himself a slightly nonplussed expression as he swallowed a mouthful of toast. "Forgive me, Cornelius, but, what exactly did you mean when you said that the butler had set up the targets?"

Merric smiled as he poured his aunt a cup of tea, and replied for his uncle. "The Burgoyne Yule morning shoot; it's been a fixture of our calendar for — gosh, absolute years... since well before my time, certainly." He frowned slightly. "I'm surprised Alistair hasn't told you about our Yuletide extravaganza. It was a great favourite of his...many years ago."

Elliott smiled, his long canines flashing in the watery light that poured in through the massive windows. "I wanted the family festivities to be a surprise."

Giselle smiled as she caught Elliott's eye. "My dear, you know how I *love* surprises!" She turned to Cornelius. "Has it been a part of the family's Christmas for so very long?"

Cornelius blinked, knowing that the conversation had very nearly derailed the entire purpose of the presence of the man claiming to be Alistair. He took a deep gulp of his tea, settled back in his seat, placed his fork on his plate of pheasant hash, and patted at his lips with his napkin. "Oh my, yes! It was a fixture before Raine and I were married, back in '52. I believe it was first started by my father-in-law, Jerome, sometime after the unpleasantness back in '25."

Thorne hid a smile as he sat back in his seat. "Unpleasantness?"

Cornelius, who had just savoured a forkful of his pheasant hash, coughed and took a hasty sip of his tea. "Ahh, well, yes...that! Um." He flicked a glance at his sister. If he could tell he was waffling, so could Ami!

Merric put his cup down. "Our family has an interesting, and somewhat bloody past, Mr Thorne, as indeed do most landed families...well, as do rather a lot of families in general, but an aristocratic family can be made or broken by things the average family would never have to deal with. Choosing the correct side in a war and placating the new inhabitant of the throne if we chose unwisely is an art form, and as such part and parcel of enabling both the family and the family estates to survive. Warfare, treason, good marriages, bad marriages, good servants, bad servants, death duties, debts, dry rot and rising damp — these are just a small part of what most of the upper classes have to deal with."

A faint smile appeared on his face as he took a sip of tea. "Our family decided that those minor inconveniences were far too trivial for the Burgoyne name, and so added a propensity for hedonism, sadism, and child murder to the already full list of commitments! It all came to an end in 1825, when the then Earl of Cove — Thomas Burgoyne, my great-grandfather — decided that the hedonistic group he had set up to emulate the grand debauchery of the Hellfire Club no longer suited his more...sophisticated palate. Instead, he created a secret society within that club consisting of three or four men and women, one of whom was his seventeen-year-old daughter Josephina: my great-aunt." He nodded at Thorne's raised eyebrow. "Oh yes, apparently she was an enthusiastic follower of her father's peculiarities! This Inner Sanctum the Priory of Cove decided that child sacrifice was the ultimate sin, so they kidnapped and murdered twelve children from various villages on the mainland. Their depravity culminated in the murder of a child from the village of Cove...the boy's mother took her own life, leaving her grief-stricken husband alone."

Cornelius shook his head. "Poor Popplewell!"

Melisandre looked at him curiously. "Popplewell?"

Ami, who had been quite subdued, spoke. "Popplewell's father was the vicar here in Cove when Thomas committed his evil acts against the innocent. Popplewell's half-brother was the last child murdered by the Inner Sanctum; his father's first wife killed herself shortly after the child's body was found." Ami took a sip of her tea. "Thomas Burgoyne decided to open up the Inner Sanctum to the wider members of the Priory and found no shortage of followers willing to join him in his more extreme practices...so Popplewell's father led a revolt against the Earl of Cove and his followers. If he had not have stood up to them, they would have killed every child for miles. Thomas Burgoyne was killed in front of his daughter Josephina and his son, Jerome. It was known that Jerome had nothing to do with the abuses his father and sister perpetuated against the people of Cove. After the death of his father, he took the title, and refused to punish Popplewell's father for his actions. He was a far better man than his father ever was! I married Jerome's son, Edward, and Cornelius married his daughter Raine."

Aquilleia raised her voice. "And what of Josephina? What happened to her?"

Ami shot a look at her brother. "We...well, she vanished shortly after the death of her father. We are not sure what happened…" She paused. "Legend has it that the Nightwitch took her."

In the silence that descended upon the table, Giselle looked at the gathered faces. "The Nightwitch?"

Cornelius nodded, looked rather uncomfortable. "An ancient family legend, my dear. It was believed that many, many years ago the Burgoynes were cursed, and that when a member of the family does something truly terrible, she — that is to say, the Nightwitch — she comes for them, and takes them!"

Giselle looked at the silent Ami. "Takes them where?"

The elderly woman's response was terse. "The only place that would accept them: hell!"

She stared into her now-cold cup of tea. Thorne's ears pricked up. He exchanged glances with his wife as Ami continued.

"The reverend was…changed, understandably so after the deaths of his son and wife. Some ten years after their deaths, he left the island for a living somewhere in the north of England, where he married again. We heard from him sporadically. He and his wife were expecting a child, and then we received the worst possible news: she had died bearing their son. He returned to us, but left his child with family on the mainland; he visited them quite often. Then, it must have been thirty or more years ago, he went to visit them and never returned. He passed in his sleep, and his son came to Cove to carry on his father's work, just as his father, grandfather, great-grandfather and so on had done before him."

She smiled as she finished her tea. "The Popplewells have been the custodians of the Burgoyne family's souls for the last eight hundred years, and long may that particular tradition continue."

Giselle raised an eyebrow. "Eight hundred years?"

Ami shrugged as she spread honey on her slice of toast. "Both families have been going for quite some time!"

The peaceful atmosphere was suddenly shattered by a loud, metallic boom. Giselle blinked, and her teacup rattled as she nearly dropped it back into its saucer. "Oh…!"

Cornelius smiled. "It's quite all right, my dear. It's the Calling Gong, similar to the dinner gong, but, ahh, not quite! It's another of Merric's little creations: it means that we have ten minutes to retire to our rooms and prepare before heading out for the shoot."

Giselle laughed, her white teeth gleaming in the sunlight. "But I've never fired a gun in my life!" She ignored Elliott's raised eyebrow; both she and her husband were quite aware that she could hold her own exceedingly well when it came to firearms.

Ami smiled. "Oh no, my dear…not guns — far too loud and noisy! Archery — you know, bows and arrows? It's fun!" Ami's eyes suddenly widened and she turned to her brother. "Oh, Cornelius, I nearly forgot. After everything that happened yesterday, dear Sybilla has one of her heads again. She said she would rest this morning, then meet us at the glade for luncheon at twelve."

Several people exchanged glances as she delivered this piece of news. Elliott, Giselle, Thorne, and Aquilleia did so covertly before returning to their breakfasts. Cornelius and Merric also shared a dark look, though for somewhat different reasons. As they turned away from each other, Cornelius grumbled under his breath, "Now, why am I not surprised!"

Ami was slightly hard of hearing, though not nearly as deaf as Nanny, and was more than capable of hearing a slight to her darling step-granddaughter even if hissed from more than twenty feet away. She shot him a look, pushed away her half-eaten slice of toast, and left the room.

At the dining room door, she was halted by the appearance of Davaadalai, who, having struck the calling gong, was now the bearer of some rather unwelcome news for Cornelius. He handed the older man a piece of paper before turning to the table and judging which localised whirlwind had made the biggest mess; his bet was on a mixture of Cornelius and Dr Mayberry.

Cornelius read the note with an incredulous expression. He turned to his faithful retainer. "Good God, man! Snow? We haven't had snow in these parts for, well, nearly fifteen years!"

Davaadalai inclined his head. "Nevertheless, sir, it has been confirmed by several of the fishermen at Cove that a snowstorm will be with us before the end of the afternoon."

He took a deep breath; he already knew the answer to the next question. "Do you wish to cancel the Yule shoot, sir?"

In response, Cornelius' voice was loud and rather tragic — an exact mirror, in fact, of the truly appalling red and green ascot that currently sat in a fashionably puffy manner around Thorne's neck, and that resembled nothing less than the aftermath of a disaster in a newt colony. "Cancel? Never! The Yule shoot has been a Burgoyne family tradition for many, many years. A little snow will not stop us!"

He addressed the others with a slightly forced smile. "So, friends, family, and honoured guests, in spite of the approaching weather, I suggest we wrap up in our warmest winter fashions and convene by the front door in ten minutes to begin the day's festivities."

There was excitement in the air as everyone stood up and began their ascent — in some cases, rather a long journey — to their rooms, to prepare for the forthcoming and somewhat chilly adventures.

Ami shared a look with Merric before making her way past her irritated brother towards the lifting apparatus at the back of the hall. She wheeled herself into the small platform and blew down the connecting tube. "First floor, please."

There was a sudden jolt as the rising platform began its creaky journey. Once it settled at the first floor, Ami opened the little gate and wheeled herself towards the next lifting platform at the far end of the corridor.

As she passed the suite Sybilla shared with Marcus, the door opened and Sybilla looked out, a hopeful expression on her face. As she saw her step-grandmother, it was replaced by a look of worry.

Ami paused, taken by the young woman's expression. It was quite unusual for Sybilla to show emotion. She said it was to prevent frown lines; but it also prevented lines that showed you had laughed or cared.

Ami held out her hand. "My dear child, you look quite unwell! Last evening's events have obviously taken a terrible toll on you...I shall call Dr Mayberry."

Sybilla shook her head vehemently. "No! I mean, no, thank you." Sybilla paused. "I didn't ask earlier, but...have you seen Marcus this morning?"

Ami stared at her step-granddaughter. "No, my dear, I haven't. Why?"

Sybilla swallowed, and when she spoke her voice was a whisper. "He...he couldn't sleep, so he went for a walk. It was quite early, not even light, and he hasn't come back."

Ami patted the slim white hand that clutched her arm. "There, there, my dear, I'm sure all is well...he probably went for a swim, or down into the village for a walk. He will return shortly, desperate for a good breakfast. And speaking of food, you need food to calm your nerves and help you overcome that migraine. I'll tell Davaadalai to bring you a tray, and I shall also tell the others to keep an eye open for your lovely husband. Don't worry, my dear Sybilla, you just need to rest."

With a gentle smile, Ami continued on to her suite of rooms, leaving Sybilla staring after her. As Sybilla slowly closed the door, one of the doors opposite her suite also closed, and the person within smiled.

○

The Drawbridge
10:35am

As Cornelius led the gathered guests and family from the front door to the glade that was the starting point for the shoot, he permitted himself a proud smile. In spite of the threatening weather, this weekend was actually progressing in a very enjoyable fashion. It was rather nice to have the children back on the island. He paused, and closed his eyes; a sudden thought blowing his previous good mood away like the storm they had been threatened with — he had almost forgotten what he, Popplewell, and Davaadalai had discovered in the dungeons; how could he have forgotten?

In the distance, a heavily laden table overseen by a fussing Davaadalai beckoned. Cornelius frowned: people were already there. How strange — he couldn't recall inviting anyone else. As they got closer, he recognised the figures: Luci and the Pepperbelles. That was all he needed!

Luci was already on his second coupe of champagne when Cornelius and the others arrived. He greeted them with a smile worthy of a host and gestured expansively towards the groaning table. "Superb spread, my dear Cornelius! Ami, my darling, thank you so much for the invitation. I ran into some old friends and thought they might like to meet up with the old gang, as it were. Araby, Alistair, Perry, Sebastian — I'm sure you remember the Pepperbelles, Felix and Fern?"

Araby's jaw clenched as she looked at the brother and sister who had been the cause of some of the more unpleasant memories of her early years at Cove Castle.

Tall and bony, with thin blond hair, pointed features, and judgemental eyes that gave one the sensation of being glared at by a malnourished and ill-mannered ferret, Felix Pepperbelle was the island's querulous, aspiring firebrand. Fully equipped with delusions of both artistic and political adequacy, he was a dedicated and vocal proponent of anything that would not only upset the applecart, but fling it, along with its contents and driver, into the very river of history and replace it with his shining vision of the future... which revolved around his hitherto-unrecognised artistic genius and unsurpassed political intellect.

He was clad in an uninspiring but expensive set of khaki-coloured tweeds that he had purchased from Savile Row and roughened on a cheese grater to make them appear well worn. His ever-present flat cap was perched at what he believed to be a jaunty angle. He ran his thumbs along the edge of his pockets as though they were braces, and bestowed on the assembled group a smile that sat oddly on his pursed and disapproving face. "Morning, morning...and how is everyone on this bright and hopeful day?"

Cornelius gave what could only be described as a lacklustre response as he cast his eyes back to the castle. What was keeping Merric? Dealing with this sort of thing was something the reluctant lord was simply going to have to get used to...and he could damn well start with the odious Felix and his execrable sister, Fern!

The aforementioned Fern, the elder sibling by a few minutes, while not nearly as tall as her brother, was equally as bony. Her oxblood day outfit, though expensive, was quite badly fitted, designed as it was for a woman several inches taller and with rather more curves than sharp edges. Her

135

over-jacket bunched in unbecoming folds around her armpits, and her bustle appeared to be on a par with the backs of her knees, lending her quite possibly the most peculiar shape ever inflicted on the female form. With her scrawny neck protruding above her ill-fitted jacket, her bulbous eyes that glared myopically at the guests, her total lack of chin, and her bustle scraping along the floor behind her, she gave the appearance of a goose preparing for war. Her brother's most devoted supporter, and his equal in pettishness, Fern also lacked social ability, decency, tolerance or politeness — and the less said about her table manners, the better!

Cornelius gritted his teeth and glared at Luci, who took a sip from his glass and smiled back in his easy, charming manner. He knew full well the depth of the reciprocated feelings between the Pepperbelles and Cornelius. His smile deepened; this should be an interesting morning!

Cornelius scowled. Hopefully they would be gone before the snow began; he had no desire to offer those two pontificating wretches a room for the night!

As he opened his mouth to speak, the nasal whine that passed for Fern Pepperbelle's voice suddenly broke the silence as she guffawed loudly, her large teeth giving the visual effect of a braying donkey. "Alistair? Luci, I actually thought you said Alistair! Good joke there!"

Cornelius glared at her. "And why would you think it funny, Miss Pepperbelle?"

She looked at him incredulously. "Oh, I say — after what he did? And then lacking the courage to admit it and running off like that…I always knew he was a bad lot, a murderous, capitalist—"

She almost doubled over as her brother elbowed her in the ribs with extreme force. He smiled in a distinctly obsequious manner at Cornelius. "What my sister was going to say was that we haven't seen Alistair for many years—"

"Then your wait is over!" Cornelius, his face almost purple with rage, pointed a trembling finger at Elliott. "This is Alistair Burgoyne. And in answer to your sister's revolting display of ill-bred, ill-mannered malice, there was never any proof that Alistair attacked or murdered anyone! In fact, there is rather more evidence to the contrary!" He stared down the now slack-jawed siblings before him. "I have had enough of both you and your sister, Felix. Neither of you will ever be welcomed here again, nor will either of you receive any form of hospitality from this family while I live! Begone, you greedy, sanctimonious, grasping wretches! Begone, or I shall practise my archery skills on you!"

Felix gaped at Cornelius and turned to look imploringly at Luci, who instead raised his glass with an expression of extreme enjoyment. "Well, Felix, Fern…it would appear that we have just seen hoist and petard made manifest! It has been long in coming, but it was a beautiful thing to witness! Do not wait upon the order of your passing, my dear Pepperbelles; the path to the village lies before you!"

As the two shaken siblings began their cold journey back to the cottage they shared, Cornelius turned to Luci. His face was still purple but his voice was quiet. "I wish you to leave as well, Luci. I am angry at your thoughtlessness, and I have no desire to damage our friendship. Please go."

The louche young man looked at Cornelius in silence, then nodded, finished his drink, bowed to Ami, and walked towards the same village path the Pepperbelles had taken.

Ami looked at Cornelius with a concerned expression. "Cornelius…"

He held up his hand. "No! Lucius needs to learn that we are not here for his amusement. However much he has suffered, that does not excuse his behaviour in bringing the insufferable Pepperbelles here today."

Davaadalai approached and coughed. Cornelius turned. "What?" he barked.

Davaadalai smoothly extended the drinks tray, on which were several rummer glasses full of mulled wine. "Your Yule archery drink, sir."

Cornelius blinked. "Oh, thank you. Yes…now, back to the shoot."

Merric suddenly appeared on the path from the castle, looking a little flushed. He stopped at Cornelius's side. "I'm sorry I'm late; I was a little sidetracked!"

Ami gave him a faint smile. "By one of your machines, I suppose. You've just missed the removal of the Pepperbelles from our shooting party." She threw a look at her brother. "And the casting out of Luci!"

Cornelius set his jaw. "He needs to learn." He caught his sister's eye and tugged at his tweed jacket. "Now don't start, Ami. I know Luci has always been one of your favourites." He glanced at Theodora who, at the first raised voice, had taken Leander to the edge of the clearing. "However, he can be a little…" Cornelius paused as he tried to think of a word to describe Luci's behaviour that would be suitable in polite company.

As he floundered, Sebastian leant down to Araby and murmured, "Thoughtless is the best word I can think of!"

As Araby smiled up at him, Ami turned cold eyes on the young man. "That will do, Mr Lees!"

Sebastian straightened up. "I beg your pardon, Mrs Burgoyne. Please excuse me." He walked over to his wife and child on the edge of the clearing.

Davaadalai handed a small velvet bag to Merric, who took the bag, shook the contents, and smiled at Elliott. "Like old times; draw for your position."

Elliott dipped his hand into the bag and withdrew a slip of paper, on which was written the number 6. He returned the smile and approached the table. Alongside the food and drink was a map of the castle, gardens, and grounds, encompassed by a circle and split into twelve sections like the face of a clock. Elliott looked at the section numbered 6; immediately south of the castle, it covered a large section of the more unkempt grounds.

As Merric completed the draw, his uncle raised his voice. "I forgot to say, Merric, Popplewell asked to be released from the shoot...he needed to return to the rectory for something...don't know what. But he promised to be back in time for the Yule luncheon."

As Merric looked at his uncle and frowned, Giselle approached, looked at him with a raised eyebrow and showed him her number: 2. Merric blinked and shook his head with a slightly forced smile. "Part of the game is not to let anyone else know your number."

She nodded thoughtfully. "So, I go to my section...what happens next?"

"You have to find the target; they are always hidden. You fire an arrow — only one — and you must try to aim for a gold. Then, and only then, you travel to the other segments in turn, working clockwise, find the target, and try to achieve gold there. The person with the most golds wins."

Giselle smiled. "But how can you tell who has won the most?"

Merric gestured towards a separate table covered with full quivers, against which were propped many short bows. "The bows are numbered and have a coloured strip of ribbon attached. You take the bow that matches your number, and the arrows whose fletching match the ribbon..."

Cornelius drained his Yule cup, set the glass on the table and waved his hands for attention. "Ladies and gentlemen, you are now each in possession of your starting section, your bow, and a quiver of arrows. Remember, there are twelve targets and only twelve arrows, so you must make your shots count! It is now…" he consulted his fob watch, "nearly eleven o'clock. We will reconvene here no later than half past twelve to check together for the winning arrows. Then, depending on the weather, we will either take luncheon here, or move our Yule repast to the dining room."

He smiled at the gathered throng, the argument over the Pepperbelles' ill-breeding and the ensuing dispute over Luci a distant memory as he oversaw one of his favourite yearly events. "Ladies and gentlemen, the very best of luck to you all!"

○

The Path to Horseshoe Bay
10:50am

Elliott paused at a sudden sound from the narrow path behind him. As he gripped his bow and turned, he was suddenly joined in a loud and friendly manner by a very happy Veronique, who was followed at speed by Thorne and Aquilleia. He nodded at his friends as he stroked the Labrador's ears.

"Have you seen Giselle?"

A faint but clear expletive came from within a particularly thick hedge of rhododendrons as Giselle fought her way through. Trust her luck to land her with the one segment on the archery clock with no through route to where her husband and friends would be waiting!

As she finally managed to push herself through the thick vegetation and appeared on the other side, flushed and somewhat rumpled, she raised an admonitory finger. "Not a word!" She removed the worst of the leaves and groaned as she struggled to control what had been a neatly pinned Gibson Girl bun before it had finally given up the unequal struggle against the thrashing foliage. She desperately pushed the escaping pins back into her hair. "I really need a maid!"

Aquilleia smiled and helped her friend repair the worst of the damage while Elliott, Thorne, and Veronique looked on. Then the party began the journey to their destination: Horseshoe Bay.

This began on a clear path, which after several yards led them into an overgrown clearing dominated by the remnants of Cove Abbey. Not much of the ancient ruins remained: a low length of wall suggesting the refectory's foundations, a narrow, partially collapsed tower that could once have held a flight of stairs, and the remains of the nave, all overgrown with thickly twining brambles. The chill winter sunlight touched the stonework with a soft light diffused by the faint mist hovering in the still air. Elliott studied the dark clouds gathering in the distance; the air wouldn't be still for very much longer!

They walked past the ruins, following the well-trodden path that wove its way through the overgrown meadow which was all that was left of the abbey gardens, before cutting through a thick hedge. From this point, the path was narrow but well-tended — to begin with! After some few hundred feet the path narrowed again, and a thick hedge of untrimmed rhododendrons filled what appeared to be the only route through.

Thorne advanced to push past the greenery, and Aquilleia touched his arm. "Be careful!"

He smiled at her. "Always, my love."

He disappeared through the hedge, whereupon the others heard a sudden and strangulated swearing. Elliott was approaching the bank of plants when Thorne reappeared, looking somewhat pale. He looked at the others as he caught his breath. "As my dear wife said earlier, be careful; it gets a touch narrow from here on in!"

The others pushed through carefully behind him and found themselves on an exposed bluff that commanded stunning views of the English Channel and the Westrenshire coastline, including the small village of Penwithiel — and the exposed causeway that led there.

Giselle raised an eyebrow as she looked over the cliff's edge only a few feet away. "How high up are we, do you think?"

"Well above what I feel comfortable with, I can assure you!" Thorne replied. "The path down to the bay continues to our left, and I suggest we follow it. Personally, I would feel much happier somewhat closer to sea level!"

They made their way down the path, which clung to the side of the cliff and wound its way along part of the island's rocky coastline, then paused as the path seemed to disappear under a waterfall.

Elliott nodded. "The Horseman falls. Well, we are in the right place...but I can't see a way to get past the water."

It was Veronique who discovered the route, her keen nose sniffing out the very narrow and overgrown path that continued behind the falls. Once past that obstacle, the path dropped rapidly, leading from a rocky landscape into gorse, before suddenly opening up into a surprisingly beautiful, perfectly formed bay. The small beach was golden sand, the water beyond a deep and sparkling blue, in spite of the dark clouds threatening the western edge of the horizon.

Elliott turned to the others. "Well, to paraphrase…I see no bathing machine."

Thorne looked at Aquilleia, who nodded. He knelt beside the fidgeting black Labrador. "Veronique, we need you to find someone; his name was Marcus, and we think he is here. My friend, I ask you to seek."

Veronique shook herself, then lowered her head and sniffed the sand. She turned, spied a rocky outcrop a few dozen feet away, and began to run towards it, her quivering black nose pressed to the ground before her as she headed unerringly for the far side of the beach.

As the party followed Veronique over the rocks, they spotted what they had been searching for: a rather dilapidated bathing machine. On the beach before it lay the mortal remains of Marcus De Banzie.

Aquilleia sighed. "Sometimes I wish I wasn't always right about these things."

Thorne gently squeezed her hand as they made their way across the rocky foreshore to the little hut. Situated on an area of soft golden sand directly below one of the bay's many cliffs, the hut was in desperate need of repair. The wheels had rusted to the point where no amount of oil would ever enable them to work properly again, and what had been rather splendid pink and green painted stripes were bleached by years of exposure into grubby yellow lines.

Marcus's body lay in front of the hut, between the machine and the sea. The first thing they noticed, aside from Marcus being dead, was that he was not wearing evening dress, but what Thorne's practised eye identified as an expensive tweed ensemble in a rather becoming shade of midnight blue that would render the wearer almost invisible at night. As they began their search, Thorne made a note of the tailor's label; a suit of that shade would be a very handy addition to his wardrobe!

Elliott looked at Thorne. "What do you think?"

Thorne carefully turned the corpse over and studied the back of the well-fitted suit: he could see no blood, and aside from some slight bruising to the face, no obvious wounds.

He placed Marcus back in the position in which they had found him and pushed down on his chest. Water trickled from the corner of Marcus's mouth and ran down his cheek.

Thorne sat back on his heels as Giselle and Aquilleia entered the bathing hut to search inside. "There are bruises on his face, but no obvious signs of injury that could be considered a cause of death...no stab wounds, bullet holes, or signs of strangulation. His clothes are still sodden, and there appears to be water in his lungs, so Aquilleia's vision appears to have been quite correct: death by drowning."

He carefully opened the jacket; the leather and steel sheath buckled against Marcus's side was empty. Thorne pointed at it. "This looks as if it should contain a very large knife...judging by the shape of the sheath, I would say possibly a kukri." He examined the area around the body. "It isn't here...I wonder if he dropped it as he was running, or perhaps lost it in the sea?" He looked up at the cliff, then faced the sea. "It could be up there, or out there...I'll take Veronique for a wander later and see what we can find."

Elliott nodded. He crouched next to the corpse and pointed at the face of the dead man. "What do you make of his expression?"

Thorne frowned. He had been trying not to look at Marcus' face; death treats people differently. He knew that in their line of work most of the dead people they dealt with would have met their makers in a less natural way than the average person, but the rictus of horror on Marcus' face was unnerving. His strong white teeth were fully exposed and his cheek muscles stretched up to his opaque blue eyes, which were wide open, staring blindly out of his grey face. Thorne carefully closed the open eyes and looked at Elliott as he sat back on his heels. "Fear?"

Elliott nodded. "That's my thought. If he had been running, as Aquilleia saw in her vision, something must have been chasing him. Something that caused him to feel absolute terror. Something that wasn't afraid of a strong, capable military man, armed with a kukri."

○

The Garden
10:50am

As the family and guests made their way to their assigned starting sectors for the shoot, one person had already begun their plans for the removal of one or two people who, though entertaining, had sadly come to the end of their usefulness. One murder down, several more to go!

Making their way through the woods, they headed for their destination; not their given sector on the archery clock, but an ancient storage building on the far side of the rose garden.

Covered with the unkempt remains of several rambling roses that had been left to their own devices and achieved dominion over the unprotesting shed, the small building was almost invisible from the path that passed within a few feet of its ramshackle door. Years of damp coastal weather had left the wooden slab warped and twisted on its hinges, leaving a gap just wide enough for an adult to enter.

Squeezing through the narrow opening, they entered the dingy space beyond. Moving carefully through the junk-filled room, they made for a dark, dank corner that contained an ancient, mouldy archery boss, several tired old bows, and a long box lying on its side. Opening the box, they looked at the contents in silence before removing four arrows fletched with white turkey feathers, tucking them inside their quiver alongside the arrows allotted with their bow; the longer arrows covering the new additions in the leather envelope.

Replacing the lid of the box, they left the building and hurried back to their sector to search for their target.

Passing a thick stand of trees, they arrived at the edge of their area and began the laborious task of searching for the target. After several minutes' fruitless rummaging they finally spotted it, bolted to a high branch on a winter-bare elm. Drawing one of the twelve arrows they had been given, they drew back on the bow, and sighting down the shaft, loosed the arrow, which hit the centre of the target with a satisfying thunk.

Nodding sharply, they turned from the boss and continued through the trees until they reached the edge of the dry moat that encircled the castle. They surveyed the open area carefully, but apart from the rising, chill breeze whispering in the trees, they could hear no other sound; even the birds had ceased singing.

They walked briskly around the building until a particular window came into view. Removing a turkey-fletched arrow from the quiver, they aimed at the edge of the window and loosed it. The arrowhead made a sharp retort as it hit the stone ledge and spun away. The figure noted where the arrow had landed before turning their attention back to the window. After a few minutes, a figure appeared from behind the gauzy curtains, and looked at the figure below with some surprise. "Oh, it's you. What on earth are you doing down there?"

The figure did not speak, but swiftly pulled an old arrow from their quiver, drew back and released in one smooth movement. A sharp cry rang out, followed by a distant thud, as Sybilla fell backwards onto her bedroom floor, the white-fletched arrow embedded in her heart.

Horseshoe Bay
11:10 am

Aquilleia gasped, her eyes widening at the image that appeared in her mind. A window, a white arrow, a billowing cloud of peach-coloured light…then nothing. She grasped at Giselle's arm as she sank onto one of the benches in the hut, her voice a whisper as she told her friend the vision that had suddenly arrived.

As Elliott and Thorne continued their examination of the corpse of Marcus De Banzie, Giselle appeared at the door to the bathing hut, an expression of concern on her face. "Thorne, Aquilleia needs you!"

Thorne sprang up and hurried inside the dilapidated wooden shed followed by Veronique. Aquilleia turned on the bench as her husband entered the tiny space, her face deathly pale, her eyes swirling with silver light.

She took a deep breath. "There has been another death."

The Mausoleum
11:10 am

Merric jumped at a sudden sound in the bushes behind him. He held his breath, listening as his heart pounded in his chest. Several minutes passed in silence before he took a deep breath and returned to his task: quickly removing a large sackcloth bundle from its hiding place by the mausoleum door, and taking one of the many pathways from the castle grounds to the village. As he walked down the bare path, he realised that this bundle was much heavier than the many previous sacks he had carried…but needs must and all that — and now, more than ever!

He walked in silence; the narrow path lit by the watery silver sunlight of the December morning. Shafts of dappled light passed through the leafless trees and caught the small pockets of mist in the fallow fields around him as he approached the stile that served as access to the only official road on the island. The imaginatively titled Cove Lane led from the causeway in Penwithiel through the village and up to the castle; but for those who knew of it, the narrow foot-path was by far the quicker route to the castle. The lane was only ever used for large deliveries and vehicular approaches.

Reaching the stile, Merric shouldered the bundle and clambered over. The heavy sack became an unwieldy obstacle as he wobbled precariously on the rickety wooden steps. He steadied himself, climbed down the other side, and continued his journey onto Cove Lane. Pausing just before he reached the Reverend Popplewell's house on his right, he stooped below the thick laurel hedge and hurriedly made his way past as he followed the lane down to the harbour.

As he passed the twin rows of cottages where Luci lived on one side of the lane, and the Pepperbelles on the other, he spotted Mossy's boat in the harbour and picked up his speed, scuttling towards the little vessel that bobbed at its mooring on the jetty.

As he reached the boat, Mossy appeared from inside the wheelhouse. Merric handed the large bundle to him with a relieved smile. "Usual rates, Mossy, and let me know when the, ah, response needs collecting! If you'll excuse me, I have to get back…Yule shoot, and all that."

The elderly man grinned back, his pink gums glistening as he dumped the heavy sack in one of the bench lockers on deck, pulled out a sackcloth bag of his own, and set about his large lunch.

Merric walked back down the narrow lane towards the path. As he passed Luci's cottage, he shook his head. Presuming to invite the Pepperbelles to the Yule shoot was, perhaps, a rag too far. He only hoped that his uncle would forgive their old friend; they had been through far too much together to allow the likes of Felix and Fern Pepperbelle to come between them!

As he walked back towards the path, lost in thought, a sudden noise came from his right. The footman, Ellis, appeared, climbing carefully over the same stile he himself had used only a few minutes before. Merric blinked; had the footman seen him? Without a second thought he flung himself over the nearest hedge, landing with a damp-sounding squelch in Reverend Popplewell's well-tended vegetable garden.

Using his elbows, he wiggled towards the hedge and peeked through the evergreen leaves. Ellis stood in the middle of the lane and carefully smoothed his uniform, brushing away one or two minuscule specks of lint before making his way down the little lane to the village.

As he passed the reverend's cottage the footman spotted Mossy in the distance, veered from his route, and headed for the jetty.

Merric held his breath as Ellis approached the elderly man, who waved a brown bottle and a pewter cup at the young servant. As the two men sat on the edge of the jetty, their attention focused on the contents of the bottle, Merric pushed his way back through the hedge, brushed himself down, and groaned at an unpleasant stain on his cricket jumper that was beginning to reveal its smell.

With a grimace he climbed over the stile, various thoughts leapfrogging each other in his mind as he began the walk back up. His mind focused on one thought in particular: Melisandre. Merric took a deep breath and patted the contents of his pocket; the small satin-covered box and its sparkling contents had been an opportune find amongst the many other glittering items he had discovered in the lower vaults of the castle.

He glanced at his pocket watch — good grief! It was now far too late for him to take part in the shoot; he had barely enough time to return to the castle and change before seeing Melisandre.

As Merric increased his speed, rather a silly smile appeared on his face. There was something very important that he needed to ask the beautiful young woman who commanded his thoughts — right after he had returned to his room and changed!

As the young lord made his way back to the castle, various hopeful scenarios running through his mind, down in the village, Popplewell had paused in his daily perambulation around his little garden, taken a sip of his tea, and pondered the strange spectacle of the Earl of Cove vaulting over his hedge and into his well-manured potato patch.

○

The Luncheon
11:36am

Cornelius stalked into the foggy clearing with a grim expression. Three golds, two reds, three blues, and the rest of his arrows missing in action. Blast!

Davaadalai saw his expression, guessed the reason, and poured a large glass of whisky, which he handed to the irate man in silence.

Cornelius nodded his thanks at the butler, accepting the drink with a grunt as he peered up at the sky. "What do you think? Should we risk it, or remove to the dining room?"

Davaadalai bowed from the neck. "I took the liberty of sending a footman to place a telephone call to Mr Stumps on the mainland, sir. Luckily, the gentleman in question was still in the village, having just made a delivery of fish. Ellis was able to confirm the weather reports with Mr Stumps, sir, and on the basis of the information received, I regret to inform you that removing the luncheon to the dining room is the only possible option, Mr Stumps is certain that a severe weather front is approaching." Davaadalai coughed. "I am informed, sir, that Mr Stumps's knee is very bad today."

Cornelius rolled a pained look skywards before giving the butler an aggrieved nod. Mossy's knee was the barometer by which all local weather was judged; if Mossy's knee told him bad weather was approaching, then bad weather was approaching!

He sighed and took a final gulp of his drink. As he handed the glass to the butler, Merric and Melisandre appeared; her face was faintly pink, matched by the flush on Merric's neck as the Earl of Cove smiled in a slightly confused manner and blurted, "We're engaged!"

The butler managed to catch the dropped glass as Cornelius stood stock still for a moment, then caught his nephew's hand in an enthusiastic clasp. He bellowed his congratulations, his disappointment at the foreshortened outdoor festivities forgotten, as Ami, Sebastian, Theodora, and Leander arrived.

Ami beamed and turned to Davaadalai. "The Yule archery shoot luncheon must become a celebration of the engagement! Davaadalai, will you ask Mrs Burnthouse to see about a suitable cake, please?"

The butler bowed as several footmen appeared and began carrying the tables, food, and drinks back inside.

Ami turned to Merric with a smile. "Sybilla's head should be quite settled by now, and hopefully Marcus has returned from his walk. Oh, she will be so very happy for you both! I will go and tell her immediately!"

Merric's face set slightly as his aunt bustled off in her bath chair, leaving the rest of them to make their way back to the castle.

Cornelius turned to Davaadalai. "We must recall the rest of our guests, Davaadalai. I have no idea where most of them are, but please see to it that they are informed of the change in plan and the imminent threat of inclement weather."

The butler bowed. "Of course, Mr Burgoyne." He marshalled his footmen as Cornelius followed Ami, Merric, Melisandre, and the Lees family back into the castle.

Standing just outside the drawbridge, Ellis awaited the return of the bows and quivers, his carefully cultivated 'resting servant' face politely blank as family and guests relinquished their weapons into his custody. Once the last of that particular inventory of bows were handed in and everyone had entered the castle, he rubbed his eyes. Perhaps the several drams of whisky he'd had with old Mossy had been an error in judgement; he was now rather tired, slightly queasy, and not a little hungry. He was also not looking forward to what was planned for the rest of his day: several hours spent walking the grounds, retrieving arrows from the targets, the gardens, and possibly from the properties of several irate locals! He knew just how bad Cornelius was at losing rather than loosing his arrows — the last few Yule shoots had led to them purchasing enough spare shafts to threaten a second Agincourt! With a sigh, he waved a hand at the young under-footman loitering with intent in the alert, invisible manner of a well-trained servant.

As they collected the bows and quivers, Ellis paused. "Master Alistair and his friends aren't back yet. When they do return, just put their bows in the under-stairs cupboard; we can put them away later. Come along — those gathering clouds look unpleasant and we've got plenty of work yet to do."

The two footmen walked through the rapidly chilling gardens to the ramshackle storage shed, where they shoved the unprotesting equipment into several of the large boxes in the damp-smelling room.

Picking up a much larger quiver, Ellis turned to the younger man and handed it to him, along with a pencil, a piece of paper with numbered and coloured drawings of the arrows' fletching on one side, and a diagram of the archery clock on the other.

He grinned. "This is your lucky day, Smithers. Now, this side shows the arrow colours and styles, and this side shows the grounds with the section numbers and targets. You're looking for twelve of each type of fletching...don't forget to right down which, if any, were found in the targets, and which colour they were in. And be advised, the last time Mr Burgoyne shot an arrow, it was at this year's Midsummer Fete and the bloody thing ended up all the way down the hill in the reverend's garden...the good vicar was not very impressed! Apparently, it nearly decapitated his prize sunflower!"

Smithers rolled his eyes as he took the quiver, but made sure Ellis didn't see; he knew his place. "Yes, Mr Ellis."

Ellis smiled. Mr Ellis...he liked the sound of that! "Right, off you go then. Remember, bring it all back here and put it all away in the correct quivers. Got it?"

Smithers nodded. "Yes, sir."

"Good." Ellis looked at the clouds scudding across the wintry sky. "Mossy reckons on bad weather for the next few days...if it gets bad before you've finished collecting the arrows, come back in, and you can continue after the worse of the weather has passed. No use panicking over stuff that won't be used for another six months!" He clapped the young man on the back and headed into the castle. Entering the great hall, he tugged his jacket straight on his way back to the kitchen.

As he entered the bustling room and drank in the incredible smells coming from the range, there was a shrill whistle from the connector tube in the corner. Hurrying to the apparatus, he checked the piece of paper gummed to the wall behind it and noted the suite number and the guest. The lovely Sybilla — wonderful! He lifted the tube and in his best butler's voice intoned, "Yusss?"

There was a pause, then the sound of sobbing from the other end of the line as Ami clutched the connector tube and wept. "Oh, send someone — send someone, please! She's dead...she's dead!"

The Bathing Machine

PART
II

The Lounge
12:10pm

In the face of the dimming winter light and the approaching storm, the gas lamps in both the lounge and dining room had been lit. Their warming light made the burnished brass fittings gleam, and touched the smiling faces of the guests and family with a golden glow as they drank a toast to the happy couple, unaware of the tragedy unfolding above.

Polite chatter, laughter, and the popping of champagne corks echoed through the room as people sidled between the rampant aspidistras and settled themselves into the armchairs and sofas to await the buffet gong. Merric and his fiancée Melisandre chatted with Sebastian and the aloof Theodora; Nanny cooed over young Leander, who seemed rather more interested in his tin soldiers and the battle campaign he was waging across one of the fine Persian rugs; Araby sat next to Nanny and tried not to stare at Sebastian, but instead attempted to carry on a conversation with the newly arrived Reverend Popplewell about missionary work in the Ganga Basin; Perry did his best to blend in with the scenery immediately next to the bar; while Cornelius and Dr Mayberry were involved in a quiet and decidedly murky conversation about the most scandalous and salacious murders of the last few years.

As they chattered and sipped their drinks, Ellis appeared in the doorway, his face deathly pale as his eyes searched the room for Davaadalai.

In the immediate aftermath of the call from Sybilla's suite, he had raced up the servants' stairs, followed by two of the maids and the slower-moving Mrs Burnthouse.

As he approached the suite, he saw that the door had been left open; as Ami had entered in her bath chair, she had been unable to close the door behind her. As the footman entered the suite, he shivered. The room was freezing cold; one of the large windows was wide open, allowing the snow-scented air to chill the room and its inhabitants to the core.

As Ellis entered the freezing room, he saw Ami's bath chair, overturned beside the connecting tube by the bed. Bending down to right it, he saw Ami sitting on the floor at the end of the bed, cradling her step-granddaughter's body. Sybilla's eyes were open, her mass of dark hair floating around her pale, still face like a cloud. The untied peach peignoir exposing her bare breast and the wooden shaft of the white fletched arrow embedded in her heart.

Ellis knelt next to Ami. "Mrs Burgoyne? Oh my God... Mrs Burgoyne..." But Ami was oblivious to Ellis's words as she held her step-granddaughter's body and wept.

Running feet sounded in the corridor outside and Eliza, Sybilla's maid, ran into the room and stopped at the sight before her. Her mouth moved convulsively, then she fell to her knees and began to scream.

Faced with a murdered woman, a weeping aristocrat, and a screaming servant, the youngest of the two maids immediately had a fit of hysterics. Mrs Burnthouse stepped forward and slapped both shrieking maids hard across the face. As the younger maid stared at her and Eliza burst into gulping sobs, the housekeeper turned to the third maid, who looked calmly back at the cook. She remembered being slapped by Mrs Burnthouse many years ago. It had made enough of an impression for her never to show any form of hysteria — at least, not within Cook's immediate vicinity.

Mrs Burnthouse nodded at her. "Mary, escort Lily and Eliza back to the kitchen. A cup of tea and a large brandy each should set them right, and that goes for you as well! Stay with them. Now go!"

As the maids left the room, Mrs Burnthouse turned to Ellis. "I'll stay here with Mrs Burgoyne; you go and tell Davaadalai, so he can tell the others." She glanced at Ami and gestured the footman to the door. As they moved out of Ami's hearing, the housekeeper shook her head and sighed. "He'll just love this! The silly tart always did want to make sure everyone's eye was on her. Well, she got what she wanted, but not in the way she would have liked!" She glared after the three young maids. "We're thirty feet up here; I doubt they heard that silly girl screaming down in the main quarters. Go and tell Davaadalai before those girls blurt it out, and hurry up about it."

She made her way back to where Ami sat and dragged the chair from the dressing table next to the elderly woman. Carefully arranging her large form on the seat, she sat next to the weeping woman as Ellis hurried down the stairs.

Standing by the door to the lounge, he cast his eye around the brightly lit room and spotted Davaadalai standing by the connecting door. Ellis sighed with relief and made his way through to the butler's side.

Cornelius paused in his discourse with Mayberry about the possible motives behind the notorious Jack the Ripper case, and took a sip from his coupe. As he settled back in his chair, he spotted Ellis sweating by the door. He sat up slightly, and watched the footman cross the room to

Davaadalai. Such obviously emotional behaviour was unusual in a good servant. The young man leaned towards the butler and whispered something that left the usually imperturbable Davaadalai looking as close to shocked as Cornelius had ever seen him. The butler's eyebrows met over his aquiline nose and his large black eyes widened as he stood motionless, almost statue-like. Then he blinked and gestured the young footman back to the kitchen. Ellis obeyed, only too happy to leave the bright room and return to the kitchens for a cup of tea and a very large brandy.

Davaadalai took a deep breath and approached Merric; bending, he informed the seated man of the discovery upstairs. The happy smile on his master's face slid away as he listened, and a sudden silence descended as the assembled guests heard the butler's quiet words.

Melisandre looked at Merric with a horrified expression. As she gathered her skirts and began to rise, Merric shook his head. "I don't want you to witness this, Melisandre. Please stay with Araby; I shall return."

She sank back into her chair as the family and Dr Mayberry made their way to the first floor, leaving Melisandre, Araby, the Lees family, and the oblivious Nanny as the room's sole occupiers.

The silent group made their way upstairs. They paused as the bell at the front door rang. Davaadalai swerved from his route and opened the front door to admit Elliott, Giselle, Thorne, Aquilleia, and Veronique.

Elliott saw their faces; clearly, they no longer needed to try and find a way to inform the gathered family that Aquilleia had seen the death of Sybilla in a vision — but broaching the news of Marcus' death might be interesting!

Merric looked at him from the top of the stairs. "I think you should be with us, Alistair."

In the lounge, all was quiet. Theodora smoothed her son's

silky hair, then cast a glance at the silent Araby, who caught the look and rose from her seat. A determined expression appeared on her pale face, and she addressed Melisandre. "Let's not speak of what might have happened upstairs — at least, not until we know more. Let's take the air on the terrace."

Melisandre accepted Araby's offered arm, her expression one of deep worry as Araby escorted her to the terrace just beyond the lounge door. Nanny, dozing peacefully in her chair, snored faintly as the door to the terrace clicked shut behind them.

Theodora looked coolly at her husband as their son continued his game of soldiers, blissfully unaware of the situation seething around him. She placed her cup of tea on the little table next to her chair. "Were your…friend's family always this unusual?"

Sebastian heard the slight pause before her use of the word 'friend'. He dragged a hand through his Macassar-laced blond hair and scowled. "You cannot judge Araby solely by her family, Theodora. She *is* my friend, and that will not change! As to her family — well, whose family is perfect?"

His wife smiled faintly; her almond-shaped eyes dark. She understood the bonds of true friendship, but though she had many female friends, she had never formed such a friendship with a member of the opposite sex. To her mind, to do so would be almost akin to adultery.

She contemplated her husband, wondering what it would take for him to realise that continuing his friendship with a young, unmarried woman of notorious family was both socially and morally questionable. Such foolishness, thoughtlessness, and sheer naivety could well result in a negative impact on her — and more importantly, on their son.

Theodora found herself pondering what kind of man she had married. Perhaps her father had been correct in his instruction to treat marriage as a business. Indeed, that had originally been her plan, but on meeting Sebastian, she had instead chosen to marry for love. Well, it had been love on her side, at least. Being brutally honest with herself, she had to wonder if it had been perhaps, not love of *her*, but love of her father's many successful businesses on the part of Sebastian….

She paused, thinking on her family's recent tragedy. The deaths of her father and brother in a London carriage accident several months earlier had rendered her mother stricken to her bed by grief, and the shock had led to her sudden death a few days later. In that most horrifying and bewildering of times, Sebastian had proven himself a worthy addition to the family, working almost beyond endurance to continue her father's business concerns in the capital. Perhaps she should give him the benefit of the doubt, until such times as he proved himself…one way or another.

She tilted her head to one side and studied her husband's countenance. "True, husband, but for one family to be connected with so many deaths, across so very many years, is at best questionable, wouldn't you say?"

Sebastian stared at her, and Nanny's snores became louder as the silence between husband and wife grew.

○

Sybilla's Suite
12:20pm

Cornelius looked down at Dr Mayberry with raised eyebrows. "Is there anything you can do?"

The doctor gave him an incredulous look as he covered Sybilla's body with a blanket. "She has an arrow embedded in her chest, Cornelius — it is my humble professional opinion that she'll nae survive! Good God, man, she was dead before she hit the floor." He stood up with a groan as his knees complained, and looked at the covered corpse with a thoughtful eye. "Damn good shot, though, whoever it was... the shaft went straight through her heart — impressive!"

Elliott spoke from the door. "And in your professional opinion, doctor, was she shot from within the room...or without?"

Dr Mayberry looked from the corpse to the window and frowned. He looked at Elliott, then nodded slowly. "Hmmm...yes, I'd say she was shot from outside. Look."

He knelt back down and whisked back the blanket in a businesslike fashion, ignoring Cornelius's flinch as his niece's naked body was again exposed to their scrutiny. Sybilla lay on the wooden floor, her thin silk peignoir a peach-coloured halo about her still form. The slender arm thrown across her chest almost touching the white-fletched arrow that stood several inches proud of her left breast. A small quantity of blood had puddled around the base of the shaft, its shiny, congealed surface a dark-red mirror.

"As you can see, the blood has dried, so it has been a few hours since she was killed. The amount of blood is minimal and in one neat little spot. That implies that she was thrown to the floor, where she landed on her back and she did not move again after she fell, suggesting that death was instantaneous." The doctor carefully turned her onto her side. "The arrow has entered her heart, but it has not passed all the way through her torso. In my professional opinion, she has been dead since...I'd say late morning. Before twelve o'clock certainly, and she was indeed shot from outside. If she had been shot from within this room, the arrow would have passed through her body and be embedded in the wall, rather than her heart." He gently placed Sybilla back into her original position and stood.

Elliott looked at Cornelius. "Wouldn't the draw of the bow have something to do with the distance the arrow could penetrate?"

Cornelius stared at him blankly, then attempted to gather his wits about him. The sight of Sybilla's corpse had thrown his mind back to the footman's shocking announcement in the lounge and the horrifying scene that had met them as they entered the freezing suite on the first floor.

Dr Mayberry had been the third to enter the room, behind Merric and Cornelius; he had pushed past the two shocked men, hurried across the room, and knelt next to Ami and Sybilla. He caught the eye of the housekeeper, who nodded at him, heaved her form out of the spindly little chair, and left the room for the sanctuary of her kitchen and a large port.

Mayberry glanced at Sybilla, his jaundiced doctor's eye immediately seeing that he could do nothing to help her, and turned to the weeping Ami. Touching her face, he had swiftly realised she was shivering and dangerously cold; gently disentangling her from Sybilla, he lifted the weeping woman and placed her back into her bath chair.

Merric had stared in dumbfounded silence at the body of his second cousin, then he had recalled Mrs Burnthouse from the hallway and issued instructions that the ladies of the house of Burgoyne were to come to Ami's room to support her in her hour of loss; under no circumstance were they to leave her alone. Mrs Burnthouse had nodded, and gone to inform Araby and Melisandre of their instructions. While Giselle and Aquilleia had assisted the doctor in escorting the weeping Ami to her suite, Merric had fetched Mayberry's medical bag, then returned to his aunt's room, where Mayberry had administered a sedative.

Cornelius brought his mind back to the present, and nodded

unhappily as he answered Elliott's question. "The draw of the bow would be a factor, but the bows are not very powerful compared to some. The draw weight is twenty pounds for the ladies, and forty pounds for the men." He paused; his left eye twitching before he suddenly barked. "I don't understand why Marcus isn't here. He should be here, dammit!"

Elliott shared a look with Thorne as he approached the corpse. There would be time enough to announce that little item of news later; in the meantime, it would be interesting to see what they could find out before the matter of Marcus came to light. "As you say, he should be here," he murmured. He looked at the naked figure, his eyes lingering on the white-fletched arrow; "Thorne, what are the chances of fingerprints?"

Thorne snorted. "Doubtful: we were all wearing gloves, and I don't recognise that particular colour of fletching from the quivers that were handed out."

Elliott turned to Cornelius. "Do you recognise the fletching?

Cornelius looked even more uncomfortable. "It looks like one of our older arrows...we keep several dozen spares in the old games shed, along with the rest of the archery equipment."

Elliott nodded. "How many people know of the extra equipment, and the whereabouts of the games shed?"

Cornelius's voice was quiet. "The family, friends, most of the village, anyone who has stayed here..."

Thorne looked at Elliott. "So we can narrow it down to, what, thirty to fifty people maximum? Joy!"

Mayberry's tufted red eyebrows bristled. "You can moderate that insulting tone, young man! This is a house of death, not a place for cheap insults and laughter!"

Thorne looked at the doctor silently, his green eyes calm.

Elliott held up his hand. "Dr Mayberry, what do you make of the marks on her body?"

The doctor pulled his irritated glare away from Thorne, and back to the body; he sighed and knelt back down. "These wounds on her wrist and her thigh were the result of landing on the broken wine glass. These others, well, I recognise what they are…but I'm not sure in this particular context, shall we say? They are certainly…"

Elliott looked at him. "Deliberate?"

The doctor nodded slowly. "Aye, deliberate is the word. But they're nae tattoos; I'd say they look more like scars." He frowned, "But they've nae healed clean: they're raised…"

He paused, then threw back his head and bawled, "Popplewell!"

His voice boomed out of the open door and down the empty corridor to where Popplewell was sitting in a little chair on the landing, lost in his thoughts.

Upon hearing the doctor's call, he sighed, rubbed his eyes, and slowly eased himself from the comfort of his chair. A few moments passed before the reverend appeared at the door to Sybilla's suite. He looked down at the doctor with a raised eyebrow. "You screamed?"

The doctor paused at this unexpected appearance of humour, then pointed at the markings. "You're a well-travelled man, Popplewell; what do you make of these markings?"

The elderly vicar got down on his knees alongside the corpse, removed his spectacles from his breast pocket and squinted at the trailing marks that began just above both of Sybilla's wrists and continued up her arms and across her shoulders, wrapping around her waist and between her breasts before making their way down both her slender legs. The scars were a delicate shade of purple that stood proud of her deathly pale skin, the design that of a trailing vine with tendrils, leaves, and flowers.

Popplewell removed his glasses and sat back on his heels with a sigh, then looked at Mayberry. "Much the same as you, I believe, Mayberry. You've seen similar, of course?"

The doctor nodded. "Aye, out in Africa…Abyssinia, to be exact. Quite common amongst several of the tribes, made by rubbing ash into cuts in the skin, although, their designs are rather more…abstract." He coughed as he twitched the silk robe aside to uncover a further design. "This, however, is not something I have ever seen before — and certainly not something I ever thought to see on a white woman!"

Thorne, who had been lounging in one of the plush armchairs, listening and making unobtrusive notes, looked at the doctor. "May I see?"

The doctor shot to his feet and turned to Cornelius. "My dear Cornelius, I must object!" he bellowed. "As a doctor, my presence and that of the good reverend here are beyond reproach, and…Alistair is here in his capacity as family, but this gentleman is superfluous to the requirements of this investigation. I object to a man who is neither doctor nor priest examining a deceased woman's intimate parts!"

Elliott smiled at the doctor's slight pause before the use of his assumed name, his canines flashing. "It's quite all right, doctor. My friend and I have spent quite a few years in the study of investigations and detection; that is how I have become successful in the years of my absence. We are known to the authorities, and should you require their approval, I shall be honoured to issue you with the details of our contact in the government. Please let me assure you, Dr Mayberry, that Thorne and I have an extensive background both in the unusual, and in the solving of criminal cases."

Thorne smiled at the perturbed doctor as he moved next to him, set his monocle in place and peered intently at the markings on Sybilla's arms and torso, and at the design that had so offended Dr Mayberry: a simple open flower just below Sybilla's pubic bone. After a few moments' thought he nodded, turned back to Elliott, and declared with absolute conviction, "Hanabira."

Elliott leant forward, cast a swift look at the design, and nodded at Thorne. "I concur."

He turned to Mayberry and Popplewell. "That's why the design didn't seem quite right, gentlemen. It isn't African; it's Japanese, but created in a very similar fashion. Small cuts are made in the skin and a substance — usually ash, as you say, doctor — is rubbed into the wound, creating a raised design caused by deliberate scarring of the tissue."

Cornelius ran his hands across the back of the chair he was using to hold himself upright. He turned his pale face to the doctor. "Mayberry, would you please cover her?"

As Mayberry complied with his friend's request, Cornelius turned to Thorne. "I will not ask how you know such things, but what on earth is that...that *thing* doing on my grand-niece?"

Mayberry took a deep breath. "Perhaps that is a question best put to her husband, as Sybilla cannot tell us. It's certainly something a husband would be aware of. Do we have any idea where Marcus is?"

Cornelius dragged a hand through his hair. "The servants have searched the castle and he isn't here; short of searching the gardens, and the village...he seems to have vanished off the face of the earth!"

A voice came from the doorway. "Have you not told them?"

They turned as Giselle and Aquilleia entered the room. Aquilleia's face was deathly pale as she sat carefully on the edge of the bed.

Cornelius looked at her. "Told us? Told us what, my dear?"

Elliott glanced at Thorne. "I'm afraid Marcus won't be able to answer any of your questions, Cornelius. I'm sorry to inform you that when we visited Horseshoe Bay, we discovered the body of Marcus De Banzie by the bathing machine."

There was complete silence, followed by several strangled epithets from Cornelius and Mayberry as Elliott detailed their discovery on the beach.

Cornelius blinked rapidly. "Good God!" He paused for a moment before turning to Elliott. "Is it possible…could Marcus have killed Sybilla and then taken his own life?"

Elliott shook his head in response. "The evidence suggests that Marcus died several hours before Sybilla; it would have been quite impossible for him to have killed his wife."

Aquilleia turned her violet eyes to her husband. "There is something else; something here, in this room…information about someone we know."

Thorne stood up from his crouch next to Sybilla and gestured about the room. "Can you narrow the field down, my love?"

Aquilleia closed her eyes and fell silent. Mayberry stared at her, then shot a hard glare at Elliott before turning back to Cornelius. "I canna believe you're playing a part—"

Thorne gave Mayberry an equally hard look as Aquilleia began to hum under her breath. After several minutes had passed, she opened her eyes and pointed to the wardrobe. "Not within, but above."

Elliott approached the imposing piece of furniture, pausing at the dressing table to appropriate the chair. He turned back to Aquilleia. "Not within, but above, yes?"

At her nod he stood on the chair; even with the added height he could barely see over the top of the door. He turned back to Thorne. "Would you mind, old man?"

Thorne looked at his wife with a wry smile. "Would I mind, he asks." He kissed his wife's hand, climbed onto the chair and looked down at the top of the wardrobe. "What would we like to see first? The small trunk or the leather tube?"

Elliott rolled his eyes at Giselle. "Just bring them both down."

Thorne handed the two items down to Elliott, who placed them on the bed. He cast a quick glance at the corpse still in the middle of the floor and turned to Cornelius and Mayberry. "Before we begin our investigations, perhaps we should move Sybilla's remains somewhere more…agreeable? And it might be an idea to marshal some servants to fetch Marcus from his rather damp resting place."

Mayberry turned to Cornelius, who was now sitting on the chair he had appropriated, looking quite sick. Mayberry took in his pallor and harrumphed, then addressed Elliott. "I think it would be best if Cornelius came with me. Davaadalai can organise the collection of Mr De Banzie's body, and provide a suitable temporary resting place for him and his wife." He turned back to his friend. "Cornelius?"

Cornelius looked up at Mayberry. "I shall wait until I have seen the contents of the case, Mayberry, and then I shall come with you."

He took a deep breath and sat back, his eyes on Elliott, who nodded and turned his attention to the small wooden trunk. As he carefully undid the leather straps and opened the lid, Popplewell made a hissing sound between his teeth, and turned away. Elliott, Giselle, Thorne, Aquilleia, Mayberry, and a horrified Cornelius stared at the ugly array of knives, blood-letters, and other equally sadistic-looking surgical implements lying within the bespoke trunk.

Elliott looked at Thorne in silence and held up a speculum oculi. Thorne winced as he turned back to the contents of the case and picked up a small black-bound book. Flicking it open, his eyes widened at the contents; he snapped the book shut with a curse which made Elliott look at him sharply. Thorne handed him the book and turned back to Aquilleia as his friend looked through the pages with a nauseous expression. It was a book of carefully posed photographs featuring Sybilla, Marcus, and the many victims of their sadistic habits. As he was about to close the book he paused and stared at one of the photographs, a look of incredulity on his face. He turned to Thorne. "Look at this!"

Thorne shook his head. "I've seen enough. We had to see such things in the case at Marmis Hall...I don't think I would—"

Elliott thrust the photograph under Thorne's nose. "That is exactly why I am asking you to look at it! Who do you see?"

Against his will, Thorne looked at the photograph. The image showed six people. Sybilla and her husband Marcus were standing either side of someone for whom death would have come as a blessed relief, and there was a very blurred outline of someone who had moved when they should have been still, but the other two people were clearly visible. Thorne's eyes grew wide as he took in the image. He turned to Elliott, a look of disbelief on his mobile face. "Oh, my Gods!"

The three other men in the room each reacted differently. Popplewell refused to look, instead staring at the far wall, his jaw clenched; Mayberry glanced briefly at the photograph, his doctor's eye telling him all he needed to know about just how evil Sybilla and Marcus had been.

Cornelius pulled himself out of his chair and forced himself to look at the image. The ruin his niece and her husband had created out of what had once been a human being sickened him to his core. He forced his attention to the other people in the photograph; the blurred outline could have been anyone of either sex, but the other two were a rather fussy-looking middle-aged man and a not unattractive woman in her early thirties. He frowned and pointed at the man who stood to Sybilla's right. "Isn't that the society nerve chap — the one who was killed trying to murder Lady Bunny Ellerbeck?"

Elliott nodded slowly, a faint green light flashing in his eyes. "Dr Weatherly Draycott was an adept in the art of sadism." He looked at Thorne. "And the other?"

Thorne shook his head in disbelief as he gazed at the image. "I can't believe it; that's—"

Elliott nodded. "Chymeris, in her guise as Sophie Havercroft!"

Mayberry looked at them from under massive eyebrows. "You know of these people?"

Elliott nodded. "In our work as investigators, yes. We cornered Draycott during his final killing spree at Marmis Hall."

Cornelius's face turned a sickly shade of green. He pointed at the book. "I will speak with Merric about this, but here and now I want you all to swear to me that you will keep this book, the contents of that case, and the information contained within a secret from Ami. If she ever discovered the truth about Sybilla it would kill her."

Popplewell turned from his silent study of the far wall. "I agree. If Ami ever found out; it would utterly destroy her."

Elliott looked at him. "There is a small issue, Cornelius. Ami discovered the body and Sybilla was unclothed: the markings would have been visible to her. I am not sure how we can hide that."

Aquilleia spoke, her voice quiet. "Ami's mind was blinded by the discovery of her step-granddaughter's body…she does not remember the marks, only her sorrow."

At Aquilleia's words Mayberry's face turned a rather concerning shade of purple; he looked as if he were about to explode.

Cornelius spoke again. "Swear to me: not a word to Ami."

Elliott, Giselle, Thorne, and Aquilleia nodded. "Agreed."

Mayberry nodded reluctantly, his face still a dangerous hue. "Aye, very well." He paused. "And if we are talking about keeping secrets…" He turned to Elliott and held out his hand. "Dr Tenniel Mayberry at your service, young man." He glared at him over his gold-rimmed glasses. "I don't think we've been formally introduced — because I know for damn sure Alistair would never have turned to detection as a line of work. The boy was sickened by the sight of blood…it was how I knew he wasn't responsible for the murders fifteen years ago! So, who are you, and what the hell is going on here? Where is the real Alistair, and what have you done with him?"

Elliott smiled. "First things first, doctor." He turned back to Thorne. "What about the contents of the tube?"

Thorne took a deep breath and unrolled the length of leather. As it opened, he relaxed. Having seen the contents of the case and the black book, he had been concerned about the tube, but it unrolled to reveal a rather scrappy-looking map showing what appeared to be part of Cove Castle.

Giselle peered at the markings on the leather and pointed to a scrawled word on the upper edge. "Does that say 'treasure'?"

A voice came from the doorway. "May I see that?"

They jumped as Merric wandered over to them, skirting Sybilla's covered body. He grimaced as he saw the map. "Oh dear, were they after that? Most unfortunate!"

He made his way back towards the door, leaving the others staring after him. Thorne flicked a waspish glance at Elliott and called after the Earl, "What is unfortunate?"

Merric paused at the door, and looked back with a slightly apologetic expression. "There has long been a belief that buried somewhere within the family estate lies the wealth of the Burgoynes…and not a little of the fortune the original inhabitants of this island had gouged for themselves." He saw Thorne's raised eyebrows and continued. "The monks of Cove were eradicated by the first Lord Burgoyne on the orders of King Henry VIII during the dissolution of the monasteries, but before their demise they had been diligent in their work. As monks, they had what was referred to as the 'right of shipwreck', namely the right to help themselves to goods from any vessel dashed upon the shore. But the monks of Cove Abbey went one step further and actually lured ships to their doom. They were wreckers who dispatched ships for over three hundred years before their final ruin at the hand of the king's man: our ancestor."

Elliott looked at Merric. "Again, Merric, why did you use the term unfortunate?"

Merric paused, and a slightly shamefaced expression appeared on his good-natured face. He darted a glance at Cornelius as he spoke. "A few years ago, I needed more space for my workrooms, so unknown to anyone in the family, I began to knock down one or two of the lower-level walls…" He sat in one of the armchairs and tugged at his bright-yellow cravat. "While knocking down an old cupboard, I discovered the back of it was an artfully concealed door with a tunnel behind, leading to a room." He glanced at Cornelius again. "It was quite a large room, circular and cave-like, with what appeared to be a — well, an altar, in its centre. There were several rooms leading off this main room, one of which was full of what could only be described as…treasure."

Cornelius looked at his nephew, incredulity on his face. "A room with an altar? You mean to tell us that you found the

Inner Sanctum of the Priory of Cove *and* the Burgoyne family treasure, and you didn't think to mention it?"

Merric looked at his uncle with an apologetic expression.

"I'm sorry, Uncle, I should have told you at the time, but, well, other things happened, and at the time I just didn't think it was important. I covered the door and pretended that what lay behind it didn't exist…until a few months ago when we needed money to deal with the leaking chapel roof." He looked at his uncle with a faintly pugnacious set to his jaw. "So, I had a word with Mossy, and he agreed to take several items to Benchester for me…he has a friend in the auction house there. The items were sold and the proceeds, minus the percentage for the auction house and a small fee for Mossy, were delivered to me a few days later."

Elliott studied him. "Merric, what happened that was more important than this discovery?"

Merric glared at him. "It was fifteen years ago, Alistair. Can you remember anything of great and terrifying importance that happened here fifteen years ago?"

Elliott looked at the angry nobleman, his faint smile somewhat more pronounced. "Why do you ask me that, Merric?"

Merric glared at him. "Why do you think?" He took a step forward. "I don't know who you are, but I do know who you aren't — and you are not my cousin Alistair, so who are you?"

A loud harrumph came from Mayberry. He glared at Elliott, who cast a questioning look at Cornelius.

Cornelius stared at the tufted rug beneath his feet for some time before he raised his eyes to his nephew. "In honesty, Merric, I cannot complain about you hiding things; you are not the only member of this family to keep secrets. I don't know how to say this gently Merric, so I shall simply say it. A few weeks ago, Popplewell, Davaadalai and I found the body of young Alistair hidden in an oubliette on one of the sub-levels; in a moment of madness, we decided to keep our discovery quiet. Popplewell has friends who were in a position to investigate our discovery and hopefully uncover the identity of Alistair's killer — for mistake me not, he had been murdered, and his body abandoned in the dark."

Merric and Mayberry stared in stunned silence as Cornelius continued.

"This gentleman came here in the guise of Alistair in order to shock Alistair's killer, our belief being that this was one of the large group of family and friends who were here fifteen years ago, and that Alistair's murder was directly related to the appalling deaths on the island at that time. Alistair was not the killer, as we had feared — may God forgive us — but he was possibly one of the last victims of that evil monster!" He looked at them. "And now someone has been terrified into action!"

Cornelius heaved a sigh. "I would like to formally introduce you to Mr Elliott Caine, his wife, Giselle Du'Lac, his friend, Mr Abernathy Thorne, and his wife, Madame Aquilleia. They have the backing of Lord Lapotaire of the Government, and that should be good enough for you both!"

Merric and the doctor were silent, then Merric held out his hand. "Mr Caine."

Elliott smiled and shook the offered hand. "My lord. We must send a message to our contacts in London to inform them of recent events here. Afterwards, we shall assist you in the removal of Marcus and Sybilla, and find young Master Alistair a more suitable final resting place."

Cornelius cleared his throat. "There is one of those — what's the blasted thing called? A telephone — at the Post Office in the village; they also have a telegraph machine."

"That should make our job easier, and far quicker, thank

you," Elliott replied. "We shall return shortly; please do not move the bodies until then."

As Merric went in search of Davaadalai, Popplewell slowly made his way back to the small suite of rooms at his disposal and sat in his chair with a heavy heart, his mind whirling between the recent and distant past. Meanwhile, in the room Sybilla had shared with her husband, Doctor Mayberry sat with Cornelius and the two men stared at the covered body, contemplating the frightening speed with which the recent, disquieting events had occurred.

○

The Post Office
1:20pm

Elliott, Giselle, Thorne, and Aquilleia collected Veronique from her patient vigil at the head of the stairs, wrapped themselves in their warmest winter coats, and set off for the village, to relay the day's disturbing events to Lapotaire. As they walked down the snow-dusted footpath, Elliott shook his head. "Lapotaire is not going to be very happy!"

Lapotaire's response to the news of the deaths, rendered somewhat tinny by the recently installed telephone line, was exactly as Elliott had surmised, merely somewhat louder. "Good God, man! You appear at a tiny island in the middle of nowhere and suddenly there's a corpse — or three! I can't believe this! No, I take that back. I can believe it, and I do believe it — why on earth should I be at all surprised? You—"

Elliott held the receiver further away from his ear and grimaced at Thorne, who grinned at him from the other side of the glass privacy panel. Turning, Thorne smiled winsomely at the postmaster's wife, who was diligently wiping the immaculate counter next to the booth. She caught his smile, bobbed hurriedly, and turned her attention to the spotless glass panels of the telephone booth. Elliott and Thorne watched keenly as she finished cleaning the impossibly tidy area around him and went about her business, showing absolutely no sign of eavesdropping whatsoever: the sign of a master at work.

Elliott became aware that the cursing at the other end of the line had become a somewhat glacial silence. He hurriedly pressed the infernal instrument to his still-warm ear and lowered his voice to a whisper that the postmistress, hopefully, couldn't hear. "Now, Lapotaire, remember your blood pressure..." He caught Thorne's eye and sighed theatrically as he rubbed the bridge of his nose. "I doubt very much that your health concerns are entirely our fault, Vyvian! You have been the guiding light not just for us, but also for the seven other agents you have at your disposal within the Espion Court, for quite some time now..."

Thorne snorted as Aquilleia waved at them from outside, pointed at Veronique, then at herself, and finally at the pathway that wrapped around the little harbour. Thorne watched with a gentle expression as the two most important beings in his life began their perambulation around the harbour.

He turned back to Elliott as Giselle looked up from her perusal of various items of boxed chocolate that the post office sold under their second guise of dealers in general stores. She cast a swift glance at her husband before bestowing a bright smile on the postmistress. "May I please have a box of the violet and rose creams?"

As the postmistress saw to her request, Giselle raised an eyebrow at her husband and made a hurrying gesture. Elliott nodded as the disappointed postmistress rang up Giselle's purchase, her till being too far from the booth to overhear anything of interest...which was just how Giselle and the others wanted it.

He turned his attention back to the outraged voice on the other end of the line. "Now, Lapotaire, we just need some information..."

○

The Oubliette
4:00pm

Less than four hours had passed since the discovery of the murders, and they had been spent in unpleasant industry. The remains of Sybilla and Marcus had been removed to a suitable place of rest, where they had been joined after a time by the remains of Alistair Burgoyne.

There had been a small issue with the removal of the boy's body from the oubliette; there were no steps into the tiny dungeon and no means of easy retrieval, until Giselle and Aquilleia had an idea to keep Merric, Cornelius, and Mayberry busy in the dark corridor outside the room by throwing a mild fit of the vapours. As the ladies entertained themselves, Elliott watched in silence as Thorne walked around the room, then turned to nod at his old friend. Elliott slowly lowered the lantern as Thorne's Otherness woke beneath his skin, his green eyes filling with lavender light as he backed into the darkest part of the room, disappearing into the shadowy recess in the far wall...before suddenly reappearing in the shadows of the oubliette below.

Throwing the carpet bag up to Elliott, he carefully wrapped the mummified corpse in a length of cloth and pressed himself back into the shadows of the oubliette, before reappearing in the shadows next to Elliott, bearing the mortal remains of Alistair Burgoyne, as Merric and

Mayberry arrived at the door. The doctor glared at them both in querulous silence before turning his professional eye to the body Thorne carefully placed on the floor by the hatchway.

The doctor gazed at the mummified remains of the boy he had helped into the world; the deep gash over Alistair's temple the most obvious injury on the desiccated remains. Mayberry's voice was husky as he spoke. "Aye, the wound to his head is severe. Between that and the amount of blood he lost," — he gestured at the dark stains on the boy's night-gown and the dried marks on the floor of the oubliette below — "he would have died maybe two or three hours after the first blow. I believe — I hope — he was unconscious when he died."

He stood up and wiped his eyes, then turned to Cornelius, an expression of extreme anger on his face. "I knew it wasn't him! He couldn't stand the sight of blood! But we still thought it was him, we didn't even try to search, and all these years the poor wee one's been trapped down here in the dark..."

Mayberry's eyes again filled with tears, and this time he didn't try to hide them. He glared at Elliott as they coursed down his cheeks. "Caine, you had better find this murderer before I do, for I tell you now that if I get my hands on them, I will kill them!"

He turned and left the room as Davaadalai and Ellis, under the direction of Merric and Cornelius, arrived to remove the oddly weightless remains to the cold storage room off the kitchen, while Elliott, Giselle, Thorne, Aquilleia, and Veronique made their way to Popplewell's rooms for a long-overdue discussion.

Popplewell's Suite.
4:20pm

In the small private suite that the Burgoyne family had assigned for his personal use, Popplewell sat in silent thought, the events of the last few hours mingling with memories of things that had happened many years ago. One in particular stood out: his memory of the destruction of Cove Abbey, and the creation of the castle.

The ruined remnants of Cove Abbey sat almost central to a massive clearing some few hundred feet west of the castle, the destroyed walls of the refectory, kitchens, and cloisters the only remains of what had been one of the Catholic Church's jewels in its English crown — shortly before a Burgoyne ancestor had given his backing to King Henry VIII and received the island and the estate as a reward. Upon viewing his new domain, it dawned on that particular Burgoyne that he had been very well paid indeed for his service.

Shortly after his arrival, the order had been given for the dissolution of the Catholic Church in England. Being the kind of man who would willing shy away from using his own income if he could legitimately use someone else's instead, Lord Burgoyne had swept an appraising eye over the abbey and realised that he no longer had to bring building supplies to his new estate when he could simply use the building supplies on hand to build a castle.

The order was given to clear the abbey. The abbot had begged for his monks to be spared — indeed, the Burgoyne family monk had begged his master to allow them to flee across the Channel to France — but the king's man was firm. Even though he had been raised in the faith, he knew it was more than his life was worth to disobey an instruction from the king. An order from the highest authority in the land could not be countermanded, and so the monks had been taken from the abbey and thrown, one by one, from the top of Horseman Falls into the crashing sea below.

As the abbot witnessed the last of his monks murdered before him, he turned to Lord Burgoyne and his men and wept as he passed a judgement upon the Burgoyne family: a curse that would follow their heirs until the day the final Burgoyne family member breathed their last. As the men approached him, the abbot cut his hand on a sliver of glass he had hidden in his sleeve and struck Lord Burgoyne in the face, smearing his blood upon the young man as he proclaimed his curse. As Burgoyne's men ran to his aid, the abbot backed away from the lord, never breaking eye contact until he fell from the cliff.

In the immediate aftermath of the dissolution, the abbey had been stripped of her treasures. Stained glass windows, icons, triptychs, and carved pews had been taken for the Burgoyne family's private chapel, and an intricate wooden staircase that had led to the abbot's private rooms provided the link between the third and fourth floors in Cove Castle.

In the careful demolishing of the abbey, they found a series of hidden passages and chambers that linked the abbey with the beach a few hundred feet below. In these passages and rooms, Lord Burgoyne had made a discovery of such monumental import he had suddenly realised that although he was the king's man, there were some things the king didn't need to know about.

The monks of Cove had been keen adherents of the right of shipwreck, but the sheer amount of treasure Lord Burgoyne had discovered in the hidden vaults below the Abbey far outweighed the possibility of its presence being the legitimate spoils of the right of shipwreck, and far more likely the results of the thought 'there is a ship…wreck it'.

Gold, silver, precious gems, jewellery, barrels of brandy, and more were amongst the treasures taken from vessels lured onto the rocks by the monks of Cove.

As the treasure was removed to his new home, Lord Burgoyne's mind lingered on his new-found and very great wealth; if he had listened to the abbot's words prior to his death, he would have known that his actions were following the very path of the curse the abbot had cast. He began to see shadows, he felt threatened by his own men, who had been loyal to his family for longer than he had lived, he also began to suspect his loyal wife of adultery, but his overwhelming fear was that someone planned to take his treasure and inform the king of his treachery…and that would never do.

Cove Castle was in the early stages of construction; the foundations were laid with several levels of cellars built, but his desire to keep his treasure rooms hidden was paramount in his mind. In the guise of talking to the unsuspecting man who had designed the foundation of the castle, Lord Burgoyne took him for a walk to the abbey ruins…a walk from which the man failed to return.

To the eternal horror of the Burgoyne family monk, Lord Burgoyne worked his way through several other architectus; using them to design new rooms, hidden passages, and secret doors before dispensing with their services via the long walk to the ruins, and the equally long drop from Horseman Falls.

His cruelty had been slow to appear…but on the night the castle was finally finished, his madness took full control. His wife and children had arrived that same night from their lodgings in Penwithiel and he had taken great enjoyment in showing them the thirteen floors of the castle keep. He repeatedly scanned his wife's face for proof of her perfidy and cast dark looks at his faithful retainer, Bardier, who had been given the task of protecting her and their children while the castle was being built.

As they descended into the cellars, Lord Burgoyne struck. Drawing his sword, he brought the hilt down on the back of Bardier's head with a sickening crunch, and grasped his screaming wife by her wrist. Their three youngest children had clung to their mother in terror, while the eldest, a boy of eight, had fled up the stairs.

Lord Burgoyne dragged his wife down several corridors to a small room he had carefully prepared for just this purpose. He threw her and his three children into the narrow little cell, then uncovered a pile of stone and lime mortar and began to brick them in.

As his wife screamed and wept, clutching at her children, the eldest child had reappeared with the Burgoyne family monk. A look of utter horror twisted the monk's face as he watched the lord to whom he had sworn an oath of fealty attempt the murder of his own wife and children. He struck at the madman, landing a powerful blow on the side of his skull which rendered him unconscious, then pulled the stones away to release the lord's wife and children from their half-finished tomb.

As the monk guided them upstairs, he paused beside Bardier; the injured man was unconscious, but alive. The monk slung the wounded man onto his shoulder and continued to the main part of the house. Fortunately, in his desire to murder his children, his wife, and the man he believed she was having an affair with, Lord Burgoyne had ordered that the house be empty of servants until the following day, which gave the monk enough time to do what had to be done.

Carefully placing the injured Bardier on one of the many empty beds in the castle, the monk gave the silent young woman several words of advice, her tears dried as she realised the evil nature of the man she had married. She wiped her face and tended to her children and Bardier, as the monk returned to the crypt and studied the face of the still-breathing Lord of Burgoyne.

As the young man slowly opened his eyes and looked into the face of the person who had foiled his dastardly plans, the monk, a quiet, unassuming man by the name of Mellior, began to roll up his sleeves…

Popplewell woke suddenly, his heart pounding as his mind returned to the present. He poured himself a glass of water and sat back with a sigh. So much suffering, caused by the family and to the family ––and so much of it at his hands.

As he sat in thought, a light knock sounded at his door. He took a deep breath. "Who is it?"

"It's Elliott. Giselle, Thorne, and Aquilleia are with me… may we come in?"

Popplewell rubbed his eyes. Upon opening them, his gaze fell on one of the small drawers in his desk. Perhaps this was the right time to speak of what he believed to be the cause of the Burgoyne family's current, far more deadly curse.

He raised his voice. "Please, my friends, enter."

As Elliott and the others seated themselves, Popplewell rang the bell and gave Ellis an order for some much-needed tea. After several minutes the footman returned, pushing a heavy, wheeled contraption laden with food. Thorne's eyes lit up at the sight of scones, finger sandwiches, and several thick slabs of seed cake.

Elliott looked at the vicar. "Popplewell, in the light of recent discoveries, is there anything you have not told us?"

The elderly man looked at Elliott in silence before moving to his desk and unlocking a drawer. Opening it, he removed a small envelope and held it out to his old friend. As

Elliott grasped the envelope, Popplewell didn't let go, and Elliott looked at him questioningly.

"I shall take this opportunity to apologise, my friend," Popplewell said quietly. "The images within this envelope are full of such evil that it makes me heartsick to reveal them."

Elliott frowned, took the packet from the older man and opened it, removing a number of photographs. Thorne stood behind him and they both took in the scenes that the grainy images displayed.

Thorne clamped his hand to his mouth and gripped the edge of the table as Elliott stared at the images, swirling green lights filling even the whites of his eyes as he gazed in horror at the scenes of death before him.

Giselle and Aquilleia leapt to their feet at their husbands' reactions to the photographs. Giselle touched Elliott's arm. "What is it? Elliott, let me see!"

He turned the images face down. "No!"

The sharpness of his response caused Veronique to growl. Aquilleia stroked the dog's ears as Elliott swallowed hard. "I am sorry, Giselle, but what is in these pictures is not for you, nor Aquilleia." He turned back to Thorne, his voice cracking. "It cannot be here — it was destroyed! It was sentenced to the Undoing!"

Giselle looked exasperated. "What was destroyed? What was sentenced to the Undoing?" She paused; her blue eyes suddenly widened. "I can remember only one Undoing in Astraea in my lifetime…" A horrified expression appeared on her face and she pressed her hand to her lips, her already pale face turning the colour of chalk. "Oh dear Gods, no!"

Aquilleia's voice was a whisper. "It is the Filicidae…it has returned!"

There was a horrified silence in the room; Elliott, Giselle, Thorne, Aquilleia, and Popplewell all knew of the crawling nightmare that was Filicidae.

Children were a rare gift in Astraea, and as such, the birth of a child was celebrated by the entire community and beyond, from the royal house to the healers and the champions. So, when the first child was found, their broken body discarded with callous contempt not only for the life so viciously taken, but also for the person who made the horrific discovery, the horror ran the full length and breadth of the kingdom. When the second, third, and fourth victims were discovered, the horror had turned into fear; a fear that kept children away from their play, their friends, and their schooling.

The authorities set their very best finders, trackers, and seers to discover the creature responsible. The king's own seer — Pythiacace, Aquilleia's mother — applied herself and delved into its mind. What she gleaned, before the contact drove her insane, was that the creature called itself 'Filicidae' and it was a form of changeling. In its human form it was utterly normal, behaving as the person it was born to be, male or female; but in its purest and preferred form, it had no sex, no morals, and no compassion…its purpose, its sole pleasure, was the destruction of children, and it fed off the fear and pain it inflicted.

The fear continued until the day it was witnessed attacking its last victim; it was finally caught by Versipellis, Shadavarian, Xenocyon, and their healer, Tamassian.

When it was dragged, screaming and foaming into the royal square in the centre of the city, huge black eyes spinning, needle-like teeth champing against its fetters, Filicidae opened its mouth and screamed in hatred as it was forced to its knees before the horrified king.

As Versipellis addressed the monarch before the people in the square, Filicidae began to change. The huge black eyes shrank, changing to a soft hazel; the bristling, needle-like teeth became small and neat, set in a sweetly smiling mouth;

the cracked, leather-like skin softened and golden hair appeared on the smooth brow, until the grotesque form of Filicidae had been replaced by the shape and features of Tamassian's wife, Zabathoria.

Elliott closed his eyes. The horror of the crimes would never lessen, but the utter loss in Tamassian's screams for his wife would never leave him.

Astraea was a just realm, but even there, it was apparent that there was no chance of redemption or rehabilitation for such a creature…the only punishment suitable for such abhorrent crimes against the innocent was the ultimate ending, and so the creature had been sentenced to the Undoing.

Few could carry out such a task; the ability to Undo was rare, and even then, very few were prepared to use the gift because of what it entailed. Elliott gritted his teeth; in his lifetime he knew of only two, and one was the man they had known as Phoenixus, his brother.

Phoenixus had been tasked with carrying out the Undoing on Filicidae. That should have meant utter destruction, with no chance of rebirth for the creature either in Astraea or in this realm. However, the events on the Island of Cove fifteen years earlier, and the photographic evidence that Popplewell had just given them, suggested Filicidae was still very much at large.

Elliott blinked, his mind flashing from thought to thought. His sister Chymeris's gift was that of a Skin Changer, just like him, unless…unless, just as she had taken over Phoenixus's body in the womb, she had taken a part of Phoenixus's gift too, his ability to Undo. But Filicidae had been reborn. Instead of carrying out the sentence of the Undoing, Chymeris had killed only Filicidae's physical form in Astraea, leading to their rebirth here — which meant that every time Filicidae died they were reborn into another life over, and over, and over again.

He turned to look at the others, his eyes bright with swirling green lights. "Hear me out!"

He explained the thoughts that had battered their way into his mind.

Thorne was the first to respond, with his usual aplomb. "Chymeris lies…it's what she does." He shrugged. "I'll be honest; in the years between then and now — and there are many, many years between then and now — I had forgotten that Phoenixus was the kingdom's Unmaker." he looked at Aquilleia, "I thought you said we weren't sure of Phoenixus' gifts."

"There was always something else there," Aquilleia replied. "He has another ability that Chymeris couldn't reach. I still don't know what it could be."

Elliott replaced the photographs in the envelope. "So, where do we go from here? If it is Filicidae it could be anyone. Male, female, family, servants — anyone."

Aquilleia shook her head, looking a little sick. "We know what my mother saw."

Popplewell turned to her. "My dear, your poor mother…"

Aquilleia continued, blinking back tears. "My mother saw it for what it was. That was what drove her mad…she saw what was in its mind." She took a deep breath. "She said it liked following families, not just for the deaths and the pleasure it felt, but because it enjoyed being worshipped and followed. I recall there were a few who followed it in Astraea…"

Elliott nodded grimly. "Yes — we dealt with them as we found them! Men and women who worshipped evil."

He looked at Aquilleia. "Looking at these photographs, and the similarities between the murders in Astraea and the murders here fifteen years ago, Filicidae must be responsible for the murders on the island."

Aquilleia paused before she answered. "I believe you are right, but there is something else. What my mother saw still stands. I cannot be sure, but I think there is another here...a follower."

Elliott nodded. "Evil always attracts a following. Some mistake fear for respect, and feel safe if they are on the side of the mighty, when all they are actually doing is ensuring they will be destroyed last."

He looked at Aquilleia. "Can you tell who Filicidae is?"

Aquilleia shook her head. "Unless they let their mask slip, I cannot see them." She looked at Elliott with a guarded expression. "And because of what happened to my mother, I will not look inside any mind here unless I am sure and prepared."

Elliott threw himself back into his seat, took a sip from his drink and grimaced. "Well, this rather prevents us from dealing with our investigation in a way that the police and government can accept!"

He looked at Thorne, who nodded as he bit into a scone. He took a gulp of tea before he spoke. "Elliott's right. We can't have the police traipsing around, and I think this also cuts out our contact with the government. With the best will in the world, telling the police and Lapotaire that a two-thousand-year-old creature from another world is responsible for multiple murders and child sacrifice will get us nothing more than a one-way ticket to Bedlam!"

Elliott nodded as he too took a bite out of his scone. "We must deal with this as best we can, without the assistance of either the police or Lapotaire." He leaned forward and poured himself another cup of tea. "If it is Filicidae, I don't think we have very much choice."

Popplewell walked to the window and stared out at the

winter-bare garden for a moment. Then he turned to Elliott. "The family may balk at the more...unsettling facts; it would probably be best to show them rather than tell them certain things. As for Filicidae, I am of course at your disposal. Anything that you need...I am here."

Aquilleia sipped her tea. She looked at Popplewell, her expression was apologetic. "There is something else. I am sorry, Mellior...but I believe the gift you have kept hidden will be needed before this ends."

Popplewell closed his eyes and slowly nodded. "I thought I had managed to keep it hidden all these years!" He looked at Aquilleia with a slight smile. "Your mother told you, didn't she, my dear?"

As Aquilleia nodded, Elliott's gaze flickered between them. "Would either of you like to share this information with the rest of us?"

Aquilleia looked at Popplewell, who paused then nodded slightly. When she spoke, her voice was soft. "Mellior is an Unmaker...and he also bears the gift of Making..."

Thorne's mouth, full of scone dropped open; he closed it hurriedly as he and Elliott gazed at Popplewell in genuine shock. The gift of Undoing was rare, but the gift of Making *and* Undoing; the ability to wield the power of both creation and destruction, was the rarest of all gifts in Astraea – and the most feared.

The gift of a Maker always led to a life of luxury: hand-crafted flowers, rare hides, furs, metals, and flesh were all created by the hand of the gift's weaver, and they could charge any price for their wares. The gift of an Unmaker, however, nearly always led to their employment as the kingdom's executioner. Elliott knew that Mellior had always been a very spiritual man, and would have rejected that line of work; but the fact that he had managed to keep both sides of his gift a secret from most of the people who knew him spoke to Elliott of a deep desire never to be employed in either capacity. He raised his voice. "I'm afraid Aquilleia is right, my friend; we may well need your gifts to see this case to its conclusion."

Popplewell nodded slightly. "I understand."

He sat down heavily in his armchair. "Since my gift is now known to you all, there are some things that I must say: things I have kept hidden for many years. I shall tell you the tale of the Burgoyne family, and the part I have played in a vast game of strategy, logic, and loss that has encompassed eons."

Aquilleia held up her hand. "I have a question, Popplewell."

"Yes, my dear?"

"How have you managed to keep your identity a secret? Surely at least some of the family are aware of your immortality?"

Popplewell smiled gently and spread his hands in a self-deprecating manner. "As a monk, and now a vicar, I am the chief archivist of the family's paperwork. This made it exceptionally easy for me to create a false identity for myself. A quiet visit to a remote church community under the care of a poor priest who would turn a blind eye for a small remuneration…a false declaration of marriage, the birth of a non-existent son, and the sudden death of a non-existent wife. I made a sorrowful return, having placed the non-existent child with friends, then several years later, on another visit far away, news was conveyed of my sudden death, followed by the rapid appearance of my son, primed and ready to take over his father's duties. Quite simple, really!"

He paused. "Then, after so many years…I found her: my Other…" Popplewell's jaw clenched. "We travelled to Astraea and retrieved her memories, and then we settled here on the island. Eight years after I found her, Thomas Burgoyne and the Inner Sanctum murdered our son, and she…she couldn't continue living. I found her at the foot of Horseman Falls."

He looked up at Elliott, a single tear sliding down his cheek. "So, I destroyed the Inner Sanctum, and punished them the only way I knew how…"

Elliott's eyebrows met, and he leaned forward. "What did you do, Popplewell?"

Popplewell took a sip of his drink. "I stabbed Thomas Burgoyne through the heart with his own sacrificial dagger: the one he had used on my son. Jerome Burgoyne, I left alive because he alone of the family was untouched by the curse. He was a hedonist, but in no way as cruel as his father or sister."

Elliott nodded. "And Josephina? Popplewell, what became of Josephina?"

There was a long silence as the elderly vicar stared at the glass in his hands. He raised his eyes to Elliott and cleared his throat. "I would really rather not say."

○

Sebastian and Theodora's Suite.
4:30pm

Theodora stared silently into the face of her personal maid. Rose stared back at her, the young servant's wide-eyed fear very obvious as she twisted her starched apron in nervous silence.

Theodora turned to gaze out of the window, allowing her the space to consider the best way of dealing with the distasteful issue that had been brought to her attention.

A light snowfall dusted the scene beyond her window, the clouds in the far distance appearing almost black in the dimming afternoon light. As she watched the gathering darkness, a sudden sound below caught her attention. Leaning forward, she gazed at her husband, walking across the drawbridge with Araby, both deep in discussion. A stillness came over her as she watched them walk towards the small terrace to left of the castle, then disappear from sight.

Her eyes darkened and she turned to face her servants. Harriet Marshall, their nanny, had given satisfaction since Leander's birth. Her cousin Rose, on the other hand, had only been given the position because she was Harriet's relation. She was headstrong and not as intelligent as she thought she was, with occasional drifts into very foolish behaviour.

Theodora flicked a glance at the far window, which overlooked the terrace where her husband walked with Araby. She forced herself to stay where she was. "You may leave us, Marshall; please take Leander for his daily walk."

The nanny bobbed slightly. "Yes, ma'am."

As the nanny left the room, she darted a quick glance at Rose; the young girl's face was pale as she braced herself for the severe dressing-down she knew was imminent.

As the door clicked shut, Theodora sat at the desk and looked at the terrified young woman before her. The fact that she had been silly enough to accept an invitation to walk out with one of the castle's young footmen after one day in his company was not a problem, since they wouldn't be there long enough for anything permanent to take root. The more troubling aspect was that she had stayed out extremely late. Such behaviour was enough to end in her immediate removal from their household with no character references — and yet...

Theodora looked hard at the young girl's pale, slightly puffy face, and leant back in her chair. "Explain."

The young girl immediately burst into frightened tears. "Oh ma'am, I'm so sorry! He said it was just a walk to the village and a drink in the snug at the pub, but it was the pub at Penwithiel, ma'am, on the mainland, and the causeway was under the sea...there was no boat to bring me back, so he said I would have to stay at his grandma's house." She gulped. "There was nothing improper, ma'am. When she found out what he'd done, his grandma sent him to Mr Stumps with a flea in his ear and he brought me back in the boat. And it was such a long walk back to the castle in the dark that I got lost. I'm that sorry, ma'am — please don't let me go! If I have no character references, I can't get another position!"

Theodora tapped her long fingers on the desk, pausing to trace the fine marquetry inlay as she thought, her mind dancing between the issue with her maid and the thought that made her nerves jangle: her husband's reunion with, and growing affection for, Araby Burgoyne.

She looked up at the young maid, her dark eyes unreadable. "I am prepared to allow you this one error in judgement, Rose." A faintly sardonic smile touched her lips. "We all make silly mistakes when we are young, but do not take this chance for granted: there will not be another. You may go."

The maid's tears flowed as she bobbed a grateful curtsy. "Oh, thank you, ma'am, thank you!" She hurried to the door.

As the door clicked shut behind her, Rose's tears disappeared. She wiped her eyes with her apron, and with a smug smile, headed down to the kitchens for a cup of tea.

Eliza's Room
4:40pm

Eliza sat on the edge of her bed and wept bitterly. All her work, all the liberties she had allowed, and for nothing!

She threw herself backwards onto the pillow with a wail.

She would have to go back into the employ of stiff, cold, rich people when she had been so close, so very close, to becoming part of the class she so desperately wished to join.

As she hugged the thin pillow to her chest and wept, a sudden thought caught her mid-sob and turned it into a hiccough. The gentleman visitor she had seen that night — was he just visiting, or could he be responsible for the murders?

Eliza placed the pillow back on her bed, pressed her apron to her swollen eyes, and thought carefully about what she had seen that night. It had been dark in the corridor, since most big houses were stingy when it came to lighting the servants' quarters — too dim to see either the room he had come from or make out the man's features. A shame, that, since if she had seen him, she could have blackmailed him too. Never mind; remember what Marcus always said: start slow, just the one would be enough, for now...

She thought hard. She knew the room was either Rose Marshall's or Mrs Burnthouse's, though she couldn't be sure which. She frowned; perhaps she could write two letters suggesting a meeting, see which one came, and then they could come to a financial arrangement to their mutual benefit. She gave a hiccoughing laugh; Marcus and Sybilla had trained her well!

Eliza wiped her face and smiled as her mind handed her another thought. If she could get them to allow her into their suite to pack, she knew where Marcus kept large amounts of banknotes, and where Sybilla's jewellery case was kept!

She paused, thinking hard. No, no...think long-term, not small-time! They might not know about the deaths at the London house yet. If she sent a telegram, ostensibly from Sybilla, telling that stuck-up butler Dagenham to take the servants to the Yorkshire estate immediately, she could return to London, pack all the belongings she wanted and leave the country...

That was it! That was the answer: She could ask for the family's leave at the castle to pack her master's and mistress's belongings and return to the empty London house, where she could pack all the things she wanted, take a ship somewhere new and exciting, and recreate herself in the image she had always dreamed of...

Eliza blew her nose and hurried to the tiny chest of drawers. Pulling out a small writing case she began to write the first of her letters.

○

Popplewell's Suite
6:00pm

There came a light tapping at the door. Popplewell looked up from his glass and shared a look with Elliott, before raising his voice. "Who is it?"

There was a pause then Cornelius' voice was heard. "It's me, Popplewell...Mayberry is with me. May we come in?"

Popplewell raised his eyebrows at Elliott who nodded and walked to the door. Opening it, he swept his hand in a gesture of welcome. "Gentlemen, please do come in."

As the two men sat on one of the settees, Elliott ran a sharp eye over them; they both looked extremely tired. "Would either of you gentlemen like a drink? Tea...or perhaps something stronger?"

The two men expressed a preference for double whiskies which were poured with speed, and received with gratitude.

Cornelius stared at the Persian rug and coddled his drink. "Well, young Alistair is finally back in the family fold." He looked at Dr Mayberry. "I asked Davaadalai to keep a lit candle in the room with him."

Mayberry blinked rapidly as he nodded. "Aye, it's only right, only right." He paused to take a sip of his own drink. "And how is Araby taking it? Both the discovery of her brother's death, and the appearance of the detective amongst us?" He glared at Elliott, who smiled faintly in response.

Popplewell cleared his throat; he had broken the news to Araby. "She was shocked, of course, and horrified." He took a sip from his glass. "When I explained about Elliott taking her brother's place to try and find out more about the deaths, her behaviour was, well, a little worrying, to be honest. She became incredibly quiet…she hardly said a thing." He sighed as he sat back in his armchair. "I believe the shock of finally knowing what happened to her brother has greatly upset her. We all believed in Alistair's guilt…" He paused at the harrumph from Mayberry. "I beg your pardon, *some* of us believed in his guilt, including Araby — and the fact that it has ended like this…"

Mayberry nodded. "Aye, and for Sebastian to appear with a wife and child — that wouldnae have done her any good!"

Cornelius nodded thoughtfully as he sipped his sherry. "Rather odd that Sebastian married; we all thought that… well, you know!"

Popplewell nodded sagely in response. "Yes, yes, I know what you mean."

Giselle looked at the men, her head describing a similar movement to the spectators at Wimbledon during a particularly thrilling rally. With an irritated sniff, she spoke. "You know what, exactly, gentlemen? We aren't all privy to inside gossip and tittle-tattle!"

Cornelius's walrus moustache flapped slightly as he harrumphed at the thought of being linked to common gossip. "It isn't gossip at all! Nothing was hidden; it was all quite open and above board. The simple fact is that when they were children, we — that is to say Ami and I, and Sebastian's parents — were all of the belief that when Araby and Sebastian reached adulthood, they would marry each other! It was quite a surprise to meet Sebastian's wife and child."

Thorne nodded as he ate his cheese scone. Breaking off a small piece, he passed it down to Veronique, who rapidly demolished the morsel then spent some time licking the carpet for crumbs. "I imagine that came as quite a shock to Araby!"

He caught Aquilleia's eye and she nodded almost imperceptibly; the appearance of Sebastian's wife had indeed been an unpleasant surprise for the stunned young woman.

○

The Great Hall
6:00pm

Araby descended the stairs and tiptoed to the open dining-room doors. Peering around the edge, she watched silently as Davaadalai and several maids finished setting the table for the evening meal. Hopefully she would be back before anyone noticed she was missing, but there was the important matter of organising the rest of her life. Hopefully, a short visit to an old friend would help her in her plans.

Dodging the heavily decorated Christmas tree, she hurried to the front door and reached for the handle, biting her lip as the squeaky hinge protested. She squeezed through the narrow gap before Davaadalai could hear, and see her.

Taking care not to make too much noise, she carefully pulled the massive door too; just catching the latch so she would be able to enter later without ringing the bell.

Araby tucked her gloved hands inside the wool muff

Nanny had knitted for her and shivered as she walked briskly along the dark path that wound its way down the hill. The evening air was bitterly cold; its chill, damp fingers plucked at her short hair as she continued along the path and into darkness. The snow that had started to fall mid-afternoon covered the landscape with a thin white blanket, giving off its own strange blue light that enabled her to find her way down the old, familiar path.

Her simple dark-blue frock and heavy fur-lined cloak brushed the edges of the path as she made her way through several fallow fields towards her final destination: Luci's cottage in the harbour. Only he could help her...he had to — he must!

She walked through the last field, climbed over the stile and continued down the narrow lane that led to his cottage. Arriving at his front door she swallowed hard and knocked, her breath misting around her in the freezing sea air.

After several minutes passed with no response, she knocked again, this time with more force.

One of the windows directly above the front door swung open and crashed against the outer wall. "Good Gods and little fishes!" bawled Luci. "Do you have any idea what the time is?" He stared blearily out of the window and spotted Araby standing below. "Araby? What on earth...er, wait, just...wait."

She stood on the path and waited. After several more minutes had passed, the ornate front door opened and Luci appeared; clad in a garish deep-orange dressing gown covered with elephants. He looked at her curiously as he tied the belt around his waist. "Good evening, Araby. Well, perhaps it could be better, given what happened earlier today! Are you all right?"

Araby nodded jerkily and took a deep breath; she knew

that if she didn't ask now, she would lose her nerve and never ask at all. "Luci, may I come in?"

Luci nodded, then stepped outside and looked down the garden path, then along the little lane. He frowned. "Araby, where is your chaperone?"

"I came alone…please, Luci."

He looked at her, concern on his handsome face. "Araby, you have to think of your reputation. Visiting someone who is, to be utterly honest, a dissolute and rather louche male friend, in the evening, without Nanny or any other female companion, will cause talk. I'm concerned for *your* reputation, Araby, not mine — that ship has most definitely sailed!"

She shook her head. "Please, Luci…I need your help."

He paused, then nodded reluctantly. "Very well, come in."

As Araby entered the small cottage, Luci scanned the row of cottages opposite; was that a twitching curtain? He groaned inwardly. Trust the Pepperbelles to spot Araby entering his home — it would be all over the village before supper!

He gritted his teeth and slammed the door, then entered the parlour and realised Araby was not there. He walked down the short hallway to the kitchen and found her seated at the table, staring at the piles of unwashed crockery, empty wine bottles, and dirty clothes piled by the sink.

He looked at her self-consciously as he kicked the pile of laundry into the corner and sat down opposite her. "It's the maid's day off. How can I help you, Araby?"

Araby looked at him and took a deep breath. "I remember your gift."

Luci flinched. Of all the things she could have said to him, that was not what he would have chosen!

He sat back in his chair and stared at her. When he spoke, his voice was quiet. "What of it?"

Araby swallowed hard. "I want you to use it for me...just once."

Luci stared at the far wall. After a few moments had passed, he muttered, "On whom, and why? As if I didn't already know..."

Araby's voice faltered as she forced out the words. "I want Sebastian to leave Theodora and return to me...you can make her accept this!"

He turned back to her, his dark eyes searching her face. "They have a child, Araby. What you ask of me is cruel and wrong!"

Araby's face crumpled and she started to weep. "You must help me — you know he's all I ever wanted! If you won't make her accept a divorce, then make him forget her, and their son! Please, Luci, for me?"

Luci placed his hands on the table and shook his head. "No, Araby, I will not. You are upset because of everything that has happened; you need to go home and rest. We will never speak of this again."

Araby stood up and stared at him through teary eyes, then turned with a sob and fled down the hall. Throwing the front door open, she hitched up her skirts and ran down the lane. Luci stood by the front door and watched her, a thousand questions racing through his mind.

As he turned to close the door, he saw Fern Pepperbelle standing opposite, watching. She turned her attention from the fleeing Araby to Luci and smiled at him: a nasty, spiteful, threatening little smirk.

A feeling of anger washed over Luci, followed by an idea. He left his front door and walked across the dimly lit road. Opening the Pepperbelles' garden gate, he smiled as a faint tingle began under his skin. Fern looked at him strangely as a faint pink light appeared in his brown eyes.

When Luci spoke, his voice had a curiously compelling

hollow timbre, as an echo of many voices overlaid his own. "Fern, I want you to forget ever seeing Araby this evening. Do you understand me?"

The bony woman's eyes widened and her thin lips parted as she whispered. "Forget...yes...forget."

He walked back to the gate, then turned; when he spoke, his voice had returned to its usual tone. "Good evening, Miss Pepperbelle — such a lovely evening, don't you think? By the way, have you seen Araby? She said she'd deliver some of Mrs Burnthouse's marvellous seed cake for me; I was rather hoping to have it for a late supper."

Fern started and blinked rapidly. "Oh, you did make me jump...I didn't see you there. Araby? No, I don't think so... no, I haven't seen her this evening."

Luci nodded, a slightly smug expression on his face. "Thank you, Miss Pepperbelle. How is Felix's latest piece coming along?"

The thin woman before him softened at the mention of her brother. "Oh, it's marvellous — Felix believes it to be one of his greatest pieces! He says the bourgeois nature of the murder up at the castle gave him the final pieces he needed to complete it He's called it 'The Tyranny of Non-Comradely Living'."

Luci grasped at the good manners he had been taught by his solidly middle-class parents and just managed not to laugh in her face. Instead, he nodded with an expression of knowledgeable seriousness. "Wonderful: the creation of art is a fundamental truth in the progression of the naïf from unthinking capitalist, to fully functioning comrade! Well, I do believe I shall go and declare my wish for a pot of coffee to my pantry, in the hope of finding the necessary supplies therein! Good evening to you, Miss Pepperbelle." He bowed his head and jauntily wandered back to his cottage, leaving the discombobulated gossip standing on her doorstep.

As Luci closed the door behind him, his air of amusement disappeared. He headed to his kitchen, poured himself a large glass of wine, and thought about Araby's desperate request.

○

The Cocktail Hour
6:40pm

Araby ran back along the path to the castle, raced across the drawbridge and flung herself against the front door, past caring if anyone saw her.

As she shot through the hall, Cornelius watched her from his position by the lounge doorway, his expression concerned as she took the stairs in a most unladylike fashion and disappeared.

He turned his attention back to Merric, who had put his evening plans on hold to make the necessary arrangements for the internment of Alistair, Sybilla, and Marcus. Ami had been approached for her thoughts on the funeral arrangements, but had succumbed to an immediate fit of hysterics that had led to Mayberry giving her another sedative.

Cornelius sighed and took another sip of his champagne as he walked back into the lounge and sat down next to Merric. He'd had such hopes for this weekend...what a bloody shambles!

He raised his voice. "I suspect something has upset Araby."

Merric looked up from his tired study of the map detailing the remaining shelves in the family mausoleum and sat back in his chair with a sigh. He drained his glass of champagne, refilled it, and held the bottle out to his uncle, who topped up his own coupe. Merric raised a tired eyebrow. "Something other than her cousin and her cousin's husband being brutally murdered at the family home where she herself was attacked fifteen years ago? Something other than discovering that the man claiming to be her brother is actually a private enquiry agent, and that said brother, whom we all thought was a murderer, was himself murdered and has been dead these last fifteen years? Something other than that?"

Cornelius looked hurt. "I say...that was a bit harsh, Merric — I didn't mean it like that!"

Merric held up a hand. "Sorry, Uncle. I'll have a chat with her after dinner." He glanced at the clock on the mantle and grimaced. "If we go over these papers once more, it will then be time to dress for dinner. We're running a bit late, so I won't be able to bathe, but needs must and all that."

The two men returned to the grim business of arranging the funerals as above stairs, Araby ran into her room, slammed the door, and flung herself across the bed with a sob. How could Luci deny her? He had promised years ago that he would always look after her. Now, when she wanted something so badly that it hurt, he had refused her plea.

She sat up and hiccoughed. Wiping her eyes, she took a deep breath and tried to calm her heart as it thudded painfully in her chest. There was, of course, another way...

She climbed off her bed and sat at the little desk by the window. Opening one of the drawers, she removed a sheaf of ribbon-tied billets doux. Letters Sebastian had written to her when she had turned sixteen; letters promising undying love and devotion if she would consent to be his wife; letters that had stopped shortly after her nineteenth birthday in July, 1892 — the month he had first met Theodora.

Placing the letters on the table, she removed a small bank book and turned to the total amount. After various unforeseen expenses, there wasn't much left of the inheritance her mother had left her, yet it was still a tidy sum that might be enough for her to achieve her dreams.

She placed the little book back in the drawer, removed her cheque book, and wrote out a cheque for nearly the full amount left in her account. Blotting the cheque carefully, she pulled out a piece of writing paper, wrote a concise list of terms, and blotted it. She put it to one side and turned to her reflection in the mirror; staring at her blotchy countenance, she set about repairing her appearance, applying balm and a little powder to try and disguise the patches of redness still visible around her lips and eyes.

She brushed the kinks out of her short dark hair and took a deep breath to settle her nerves. Standing, she smoothed her blue dress, gathered the letters, cheque, and list, and left her room. Hopefully her quarry was alone; it wouldn't do if Sebastian was also there.

She made her way to the suite, paused outside the door, straightened her back and knocked. The door was opened by the maid, Rose, who looked at her with a questioning expression. "Yes?"

Araby cleared her throat. "I need to speak with Mrs Lees; it is a matter of some import. Kindly inform your mistress that Miss Araby Burgoyne wishes to speak with her."

The maid nodded. "Yes, ma'am, please wait here."

The door was politely shut in Araby's face. She clenched her jaw as she waited on the whim of a woman whose very existence she had come to loathe over the last two days.

The door opened and the maid stood to one side. "Mrs Lees will see you."

Araby nodded stiffly as she entered the private sitting room. Theodora Lees was sitting by the window; the flickering gaslight caught the blue-black notes in her dressed hair and the oily green and purple lights in her dark silk gown.

The maid closed the door. "Miss Araby Burgoyne for you, ma'am."

Theodora nodded distantly. "Thank you, Rose, you may leave us."

"Yes, ma'am."

The maid curtsied and disappeared through the door that led to her small bedroom.

As the door closed, two things occurred. In the maid's room, Rose, still gripping the handle, inched the door open and pressed her ear to the gap. In the sitting room, Theodora Lees placed her book on the small table next to her and politely greeted Araby with a smooth, expressionless face. In spite of her mask-like demeanour, it dawned on Araby that as much as she despised Theodora, it was nothing compared to the utter disdain and contempt in which Theodora held her.

The older woman gestured to a chair. "Please take a seat. Rose said you wished to speak with me about something important."

Araby sat down and arranged her dress, thinking about the best way to begin the conversation. She looked up to find Theodora gazing at her in silence, her dark almond-shaped eyes inscrutable above her aquiline nose and wide-lipped mouth.

Araby decided that bluntness was perhaps her best chance. She took a deep breath, lifted her chin and looked Theodora in the eyes. "I want you to leave your husband. I am prepared to pay you well."

Her words came out slightly louder than she had expected. In the silence that followed, she swallowed hard as Theodora's face remained still. Sebastian's wife sat quietly in her chair, looking at the now-flustered Araby. Several interminable minutes ticked away as the older woman studied

Araby rather as a lepidopterist might study a subject fresh from the bell jar.

Araby, now rather unsettled, spoke. "Well? Aren't you going to say something?"

Theodora leant back in her chair and draped her arm over the armrest as she continued her silent study of the jittery young woman before her. "Indeed?" she said.

Araby swallowed. "You have been married to Sebastian for several years and you have given him a son…it's my turn now! He was always mine — eleven years ago he promised to be mine — and now I hold him to that promise!"

She pulled the sheaf of letters from her reticule and threw them onto the table, a look of triumph on her face. "These letters prove my status as the woman he should have married. His proposal to me predates his subsequent marriage to you and proves a breach of promise!"

She removed the cheque from her reticule and held it out to Theodora, who showed no sign of taking it from her, but instead continued to gaze at Araby with an inscrutable expression.

Araby gritted her teeth and flung the cheque on the table next to the letters. Reaching into her reticule, she removed the second piece of paper. "These are my terms; everything is laid out. It sets out when and how you will leave him. The cheque is a one-time payment, but as I state in the terms, more money will be forthcoming for you and your son on a yearly basis if you agree and adhere to my terms." She placed the paper on the table.

Theodora glanced at the paper, then raised her dark eyes to Araby's face. "My, my…you have been thorough in your plans for the destruction of my marriage, and the removal of my son from his father's life."

Araby glared at her. "You have no right to deny me — the law is on my side! Take the money and your son, and leave

Sebastian." Araby leant forward, her young face set in hard lines. "Otherwise, I shall do whatever is necessary to take him from you and leave you and your brat with nothing! I have the power to ruin and destroy you, Theodora Lees — don't think I won't!"

Standing, she snatched the letters from the table and stuffed them in her reticule. Without waiting for the maid, she flung the door open and left, slamming it behind her.

As Theodora sat in her chair, an expression of deep thought on her face, the door to the maid's room opened and Rose entered. She looked at her mistress with raised eyebrows; the conversation she had overheard had intrigued her greatly. "Is there a problem, ma'am?"

Theodora leant forward and picked up both the cheque and the list of terms that Araby had thrown down. She read through the list, a faint smile appearing on her usually enigmatic face. "Nothing I can't handle, Rose. I must speak with my husband. Would you please find Harriet and send her to Leander's room; it's nearly time for him to have his supper and be put to bed."

As Rose bobbed and bustled off to find her cousin, Theodora again ran her eyes down the listed demands: that the divorce be formally requested by her husband and go unchallenged; that she would never mention her marriage again in society; that she would refuse any invitation to a party or ball that Sebastian and his new wife were also invited to. The list of demands was exhaustive, but boiled down to one basic demand: the complete erasure of Theodora and Leander from both the life of Sebastian Lees and wider society, with no possibility of their return.

She stood up, walked to the window and gazed into the darkness. This situation would take a great deal of thought and consideration to deal with…luckily, she was known for her calmness in the face of adversity, the past few months being a testimony to that quality after her father's death, and those of her younger brother and her mother.

Theodora gazed outside, seeing nothing; the police still hadn't discovered who had stolen the carriage and driven it with such reckless abandon in London that day. Part of her wished they would never be found, so she could lock the pain away and never have to face it again; but another part of her wished she could find those responsible first...

Placing the documents on the table, Theodora walked to her jewellery case, lifted out a single cufflink and held it up to the light. When the police had discovered the abandoned carriage at Euston station, this had been the sole clue to the identity of the person who had murdered her father and brother, and brought about her mother's death from grief. Theodora gazed intently at the simple golden link with its single quarter-carat diamond centrepiece as though her attention would force it to reveal its owner. A simple design, but of good quality — possibly a wedding gift for a middle-class man on his wedding day...

She flung the link back into her jewellery case and slammed the lid shut. Collecting Araby's list of demands, she left her rooms and made her way to the lounge, where Merric and Cornelius had been joined by Dr Mayberry. The three men were sitting in companionable silence, the resting places of Alistair, Sybilla, and Marcus now finally arranged.

They looked up as she entered and hurried to rise. Cornelius was the first to speak. "My dear Mrs Lees, good evening."

"Good evening, Mr Burgoyne. Have you seen my husband?"

"Yes, he's in the library."

She nodded. "Thank you. Do please excuse me." She went to the library, various ideas formulating in her rapidly moving mind.

She found Sebastian sitting in an armchair, reading the latest edition of Punch. As she approached, he glanced up, put the magazine to one side and stood, his face slightly strained. "Theodora."

She looked at him quietly before responding. "Husband."

He looked suddenly exasperated. "Why do you insist on calling me that?"

She sat down opposite him. "Because that is what you are: my husband."

As he sat back down, she said, "I have just been visited in our suite by Araby."

He looked at her sharply, his blue eyes searched her face. "Oh?"

"Yes. She had a rather interesting proposition for me… and Leander."

She placed the two pieces of paper on the table between them. Sebastian looked at them, then back at his wife. "What's this?"

Theodora's dark eyes were calm. "I thought you might like to know how much she believes you are worth to me… and what her terms are."

Sebastian stared at her in silence. His first thought was that his wife was joking; but she very seldom joked. He looked at the calm face before him as he leant forward and picked up the papers.

Araby's suite
7:00pm

Araby brushed her hair and smiled at her reflection. That had actually gone rather well. Using the letters was an excellent idea…there could be absolutely no doubt of her position as Sebastian's true love. Theodora simply needed to understand that her place was in Sebastian's past, like Leander.

She looked at the letters that lay like scattered petals on her dressing table, and picked one up with a soft smile. She read the words that had made her heart soar the first time she had read them, and still did.

My dearest Araby,

You are now of an age where I feel I can no longer hide my adoration and admiration from you. I am now in a position where I am able to ask for your hand in marriage.

My darling Araby, will you do me the utmost honour of consenting to be my wife?

Araby picked up the next letter.

My Darling!

Your answer has made me so very happy. I will endeavour to spend the next few years earning enough to keep you in a style suitable for the wife of a London diamond broker!

I am soon to start a new position with Piotr Rose, one of the foremost diamond merchants here in London. He is firm but fair, and very family-oriented. Both his son and his daughter work for their father, and Mr Rose has invited me to dine with his family a week on Thursday.

Darling Araby, I believe that my future and yours are linked to my new position here in London.

Yours as ever,

Sebastian

Araby held the paper to her lips and smiled at the familiar scent. Yes, their future had seemed linked to that family business…and then came the arrival of his last letter: a terse note breaking off their engagement, with a brief apology that explained nothing. Araby took a shuddering breath; all their plans had come to nothing thanks to that Jezebel, who had obviously used her family's wealth and connections to capture Sebastian's affections!

Araby's hand clenched and the thin paper of the letter rustled in protest. Realising she was damaging one of Sebastian's letters, she hurriedly placed the paper onto the table and smoothed the creases out.

She smiled: it was over now. Sebastian would finally be hers, and all her plans, their plans, could now come to fruition…

As she read the letter through again, the door to her bedroom was violently flung open, hitting the wall with a jarring smash. Araby spun round in her seat as Sebastian, his face deathly white, thundered in, slamming the door behind him.

He saw the letters on the table, and with a savage curse he stalked towards them. Araby stared in disbelief as he gathered them up and ripped the letter she held from her hands, then walked to the fireplace, where a spitting fire danced in the grate. Sebastian tore the letters into confetti and flung them into the fire, then stood watching them burn.

He turned his burning gaze on Araby, who stared at him in shock. "But I — I thought, after everything you had said…I thought you wanted to be with me?"

Sebastian stared at her, breathing hard. "I did…in the beginning — but then I met Theodora, and my feelings for her were instant and all-encompassing. I felt great guilt for breaking our engagement, Araby...I always have. I wanted to meet you again this Yule, and see if you were still the girl I remembered." His gaze was hard, unblinking. "God help me, I thought you were — but your attempt to destroy my marriage helped me realise at last that Theodora was right about you." He walked to the door and turned to look at her. "Don't ever approach my wife or my son again, Araby; I will not guarantee your safety!"

As he disappeared through the door, Theodora appeared on the threshold and gazed at Araby with her dark eyes. A faint smile curved her lips as she too turned and walked away.

Araby ran to the door and slammed it shut, and flinging herself across her bed, she wept. Sobs racked her slender frame, echoing though the room as she realised that she had finally, irretrievably lost the one thing she had always believed would be hers.

She curled into a ball, clutching a pillow to her chest, as her mind turned back to the last time she had wept so much...

○

Christmas Eve
1885

"Alistair? Alistair, where are you?"

Ami paused at the foot of the staircase and looked up at her great-niece on the landing above. "Araby? What's the matter, child?"

Araby stood at the head of the stairs and pouted. "I wanted to show Alistair something, but I can't find him...he isn't in his room."

Ami smiled. "I'm sure he's around here somewhere; he

might be tinkering with your Uncle Merric down in the cellars. Now, it is very nearly your bedtime. Go and say goodnight to your great-uncle, and don't worry about searching for Merric either — he probably doesn't even know it's December, let alone Christmas Eve! After that, it's time for bed."

Araby nodded, looking a little downcast. "Yes, Aunt Ami."

She ran downstairs and entered the lounge, where Cornelius was sitting with a large whisky. "Goodnight, Gruncle! It's nearly Christmas!"

Cornelius laughed as he stood up and kissed the top of Araby's dark head. "Goodnight, my dear. Did you remember to hang up your stocking?"

Araby blinked. "No! I shall hang it as soon as I get to my room!" She turned and ran, her young legs carrying her up the many stairs to her bedroom on the fourth floor. Running along the short hallway, she entered her room, shut the door, threw open her linen chest and began to rummage through the neatly folded blankets and sheets for her Christmas stocking.

Finding it, she draped it across the end of her bed, turned down most of the gaslights, adjourned to the little bathroom, and began her usual nightly ablutions. While brushing her hair, she paused as a strange sound came to her ears. It sounded almost like...singing.

Araby cocked her head to one side and turned to look though the open bathroom door. The voice was soft and low...the song sounded like a child's lullaby...

"Lully, lullay, thou little tiny child, bye, bye, lully, lullay. Lully lullay, thou little tiny child, bye, bye, lully, lullay."

Araby set her hairbrush down on the sink and moved towards the door. There was a sudden flicker in the shadowy light beyond as a figure suddenly appeared in the dimly lit room. With a silent gaping scream and bloody hands outstretched, it ran towards her.

○

Araby's Suite

Araby jumped as a dying ember in the fire spat, rousing her from her unwanted memories. She shivered; that was more than she had ever been able to remember before.

She could now remember her screams: piercing screams that had brought Davaadalai and Gruncle running to her room...the horror on their faces as they wrapped her bloodied body in the blankets from her bed and carried her down to the village, desperate to get her to Dr Mayberry.

Araby traced one of the many pale marks on her collar-bone that stretched across her shoulder into darker, deeper scars across her back, then tugged at the neck of her dress violently. The extent of her injuries had forced her to spend several weeks in a private hospital on the mainland, and then the decision had come to send all the children away from the island. Araby drew a shuddering breath as she recalled the terrible ache of not being able to say goodbye to Sebastian, and then her utter euphoria when he began to write to her.

She wiped her face with the back of her hand as she thought about her recovery. Physically it had taken months for the scars to heal, but that cursed day haunted her dreams, where memories of pain and fear of something she couldn't remember danced around her mind. How could she feel such terror, such mind-numbing fear, for something she simply couldn't remember?

She could, however, clearly remember how terrified Perry had been when he arrived at the little cottage she was recuperating in, and how long it had taken her and Nanny to let him know he was safe and protected.

She took a sip from the glass of water by her bed. Perry had only been eight when it all happened. His parents had wanted him to be safe, and with someone he knew, so the family had agreed that he should stay with her and Nanny.

Araby sighed softly. Perry's parents had died a few weeks after he had moved in, and a small box of their personal belongings had been delivered to their little cottage. It contained some photographs, his father's medals from the New Zealand Wars, his parents' wedding rings, assorted bric-a-brac including several books, and the family Bible. Araby sniffed, and reaching into her sleeve, she retrieved her handkerchief and dabbed at her nose. She could still see Perry's face as he had been handed the box.

She leant over and yanked on the bell pull; after a few minutes there was a deferential knock at the door. "Come in."

Ellis stood on the threshold. "Yes, Miss Burgoyne?"

"Ellis, I have the beginnings of a migraine; I will not be at table this evening. I would like a bottle of champagne and a late supper tray in my room, please…Aunt Ami has always insisted on champagne and a supper tray as a cure for a sick headache."

Ellis nodded. "Yes, Miss Burgoyne, right away."

He left, closing the door behind him, as Araby settled back on her bed and allowed her mind to wander through her memories.

○

The Path to the Village
7:30pm

Eliza's expression was smug as she tiptoed down the back stairs and into the servants' sitting room. Hurrying across the empty room, she let herself out through the servants' entrance; the staff were too busy in the kitchens dealing with the preparation, serving, and clearing of dinner to hear.

She made sure the door was on the latch so that she could get back in after her appointment. She smiled a wicked little smile; one of her letters had been a failure, but the other had been a success. Her prey had taken the bait — hook, line, and sinker!

As the door closed, a pair of eyes, watching from behind the door to the servants' lavatory, blinked. The door was pushed open, and Eliza's chosen victim walked into the sitting room with a smile. They had wondered who had sent the letter, and now they knew. They had spotted her at the start of the weekend, all sharp little glances and greedy eyes. The smile grew wider; rather a pert and saucy baggage, that one. They buttoned their coat; the evening might provide far more enjoyable entertainment than previously envisaged…

In the frosty cold of the castle gardens, Eliza walked briskly towards the village, her quick footsteps crunching in the pristine white snow. In the note she had received from her victim, she had been given instructions on exactly where the meeting would take place: follow the footpath towards the village and wait at the stile. Reading this, she had sneered at the attempt to get her to walk along the dimly lit, tree-lined footpath into the village. Who did they think they were dealing with? She was no amateur!

Eliza walked past the access to the narrow path with a

dismissive sniff and stayed on the somewhat wider lane leading to the stile. She shivered as she walked. Hopefully it wouldn't take too long to reach the stile; although the snow had finally stopped falling, the night air was still bitterly cold.

She saw lights in the distance and hurried. On her right, several yards further down the lane, was the cottage which she knew belonged to Reverend Popplewell who was staying at the castle. On her left was the stile, the agreed rendezvous with her blackmail victim.

Eliza smoothed her hair under the flimsy little hat she had pinned at a daring angle, and fingered the long hatpin that held the cheap-looking confection in place. Then she turned her attention to the contents of her reticule. Opening the little bag, she removed a second hatpin and concealed it in her gloved hand. If her patron, for want of a better word, had invited her there to be a victim, their plan would fail!

As Eliza waited for her victim to arrive, she allowed herself to consider her future plans. Her first step was to take what she wanted from Marcus and Sybilla's home. When she was in possession of money, clothes, and Sybilla's substantial jewellery collection, she would finally be free of her position as maid. Then, perhaps, a ship to America: New York City, or perhaps even San Francisco!

Eliza's eyes shone; all her hopes and dreams, all her plans for her future would now come true. It was a shame about Marcus and Sybilla — they had taught her well — but with their money she could always find a playmate as prepared as she to push the boundaries. Perhaps, just perhaps, she would indeed hire a maid of her own...all she had to do was see this little meeting through. Blackmail was a lucrative business; it was sensible to use the next hour or so as a trial run for her future plans, and then she could leave and have the life she wanted.

As she stood there, dreaming about the fox-fur capes in

Sybilla's wardrobe that would soon be hers, she heard the distant sound of footsteps crunching in snow. Eliza shot a glance behind her, but the lane was empty. She could see no one, though the sounds were definitely getting closer. She turned to face the stile as she realised someone was approaching from the other side.

A dim figure appeared several yards away, slowly making its way towards where Eliza stood. She licked her suddenly dry lips and stepped away from the wooden fence separating the lane from the dark path, then tightened her grip on the hatpin as she waited for the woman to get closer.

As they paused on the other side of the stile, Eliza felt a sudden rush of confidence. She tossed her head. "Well? You'd better come closer if you want to do business."

The woman paused before carefully climbing over the stile and approaching the young maid, who held up her hand with a smile. "That's close enough for me! You've been naughty, haven't you? What would people think of you? Allowing a gentleman visitor into the castle at that hour, eh? Well, as it's only me what knows, your secret's safe enough — or is it? Did you bring my money?"

The figure before her laughed and held up an admonitory finger. "My dear young woman, when attempting blackmail, always make sure your victim is guilty of the crime you have accused them of, and not something far worse!"

Eliza blinked. "Look, you know they'll give you your marching orders if I tells them what I know. Just pay me what I asked for, and I'll be gone."

There was a soft laugh from the far side of the path and another figure appeared. The man's footsteps crunched as he walked towards the two women and stared intently at the now-frightened young maid.

Eliza turned to look at the woman from the castle. "I told

you to come alone! I said that in good faith, I did!" she blurted. "How's he so quiet?"

The woman smiled. "Trevenniss can be very quiet when he needs to be…and he's been waiting for you for the last hour. He has a great deal of patience, my dear…whereas I haven't!"

Eliza edged towards the reverend's cottage, and her voice took on a pleading tone as she brandished her hatpin. "Just — just give me my money and I won't tell no one. I promise — I'll go away and I won't tell no one!"

Chymeris smiled as Trevenniss moved to her side. "You will certainly be going somewhere, my dear! Such a pert little songbird, but you appear to have stopped singing. What's the matter? Cat got your tongue? Perhaps later! But first…"

At the bottom of the lane, Fern Pepperbelle stood in her front garden, hands on hips, waiting for her cat to decide if it wanted to come in or not. She let out an angry sigh and began to walk briskly up the lane, glaring at the reverend's immaculate garden as she walked past. He had won again for his sunflowers at the Cove Garden Competition that summer — if only she knew how he did it.

A slim white Persian suddenly appeared by her feet, and Fern picked the cat up with a happy smile. Holding the cat close, she kissed the top of the fluffy white head as a blistering scream rent the air, followed by the desperate sounds of a struggle. Fern let out a scream of her own, her sudden, jolting shock causing her to catapult the cat into the air, but not before the terrified animal had clawed at her arms and face. It landed and scrambled along the dark lane, its white coat glowing in the dim light as it ran towards its home, shot through the open door and hid in the kitchen.

Felix appeared on the doorstep, his pinched face somewhat paler than usual, then ran up the lane towards his sister, who was standing with her hands pressed to her face, staring up the lane to the field beyond the stile. "What the hell was that?" He looked at the scratches on her arms and cheek and his eyebrows knitted over his sharp nose. "That bleeding cat! I'll bloody drown it!"

Fern shook her head, her heart pounding in her chest. "Never mind the cat! The scream, Felix, it came from over there…"

Felix turned to the brown field, then shook his head. "Probably one of those bourgeois bastards from the castle—"

He looked at his sister, and a vicious little smile suddenly appeared on his face. "If it's one of them abusing a servant, Fern, we're made for life! That capitalist clan would do anything to protect themselves, and after the way that fat old fraud Cornelius treated us earlier…if we got something on them, we could make them accept us and get money out of them, too! It would be a spectacular revenge. What do you think?"

A second scream pealed out from the field as Fern looked at her brother, a greedy expression on her bloodied face. "They'd do anything, wouldn't they? They'd pay any amount to keep things quiet!" She nodded; a smile as vicious as her brother's appearing on her face. "Oh, the look on their faces!"

Felix took his sister's hand and the two of them headed towards the field, thoughts of money, position, and power blinding them to what was waiting on the other side of the stile.

○

The Lounge
7:50pm

Aquilleia smiled at Cornelius as he handed her a glass of champagne. As she sat, her face suddenly stilled and her eyes flickered with a faint silver light; in her mind's eye a flash of a snow-covered field appeared, followed rapidly by a woman's face, twisted in fear, the approaching shadows of two people...then, strangely, a white cat.

Thorne looked at her in concern from where he was chatting with Elliott and Giselle. Aquilleia caught his eye and mouthing the word 'vision'. He whispered to Elliott and Giselle and the three of them walked to her side, where in hushed tones, Aquilleia explained what she had seen. As she spoke, a sudden expression of uncertainty appeared on her face as a sensation of darkness came over her. She looked at Thorne. "They...they've disappeared from my sight!"

Thorne shook his head. "I don't understand..."

Aquilleia sent out the fingers of her mind, trying to find the place where she had seen the snow-covered field. She shook her head. "It's gone...someone is shielding themselves and what they have done from my sight."

Thorne frowned. "That suggests an Other."

Giselle nodded. "And one who knows enough of Aquilleia's gift to protect themselves."

They looked at each other. Thorne drained his glass. "I think I need another! Aquilleia?" His wife nodded, he took her glass and returned to the little bar area where Cornelius stood with Merric.

Cornelius leant into Thorne's side. "I say, is your wife well? She looks a touch peaky!"

Thorne shook his head. "I'm afraid Aquilleia is prone to migraines, she feels the approach of one now."

Cornelius nodded. "My dear wife Raine suffered from the damned things...so does Ami. She might have some of her powders."

Thorne nodded his thanks as Davaadalai struck the gong and announced dinner.

○

Sunday morning
The Drawbridge
1:45am

The black-robed figure stood by a bare tree, glared down the lane to the village, and drummed their fingers against a snow-laden bough before turning to their companions. "Private enquiry agents are always a worrying distraction; we have been very careful over the years…but I am still rather concerned about what this man and his associates could discover of our plans. It might be an idea if we took the island's telephone line and telegraph machine out of commission."

The grey-clad figure standing next to them bowed low. "Master, I can do it…please, let me!"

The massive figure of Filicidae sniggered, the rolling laugh thick and treacly in the snow-blanketed night. "You couldn't find your backside with a magnifying glass and both hands! *I* shall do it."

The Master smiled at the grey-robed acolyte as the lumbering form of Filicidae didn't wait for a response and began their slow, implacable walk into the village. The Master had a sudden thought. "No playing, Filicidae! Just destroy the line and return."

The creature didn't respond, but the position of their shoulders suggested a sulk had set in.

The Master turned to their equally sulking acolyte and placed a hand on their arm. "Filicidae will rip the machines from the wall and be back here in the time it would take you to break into the building and find the telephone. Take heart, my acolyte; there will be a time for your truth to be revealed, but here and now is not that time."

The grey figure nodded grumpily as they tucked their hands into their voluminous sleeves and fiddled with the material. In the flickering light of the lantern, the Master caught a sudden reflective flash at one of the acolyte's cuffs. The black-robed figure grasped the exposed cuff, and glared. "I told you to get rid of that damned cufflink weeks ago! If the other one is found it could link you to their deaths. You thoughtless idiot! You have put us all in jeopardy! Get rid of it as soon as you return to your room."

The acolyte bowed hurriedly, their cheeks burning as they stared at the frozen ground and pulled their sleeves back down; but in their mind a little voice was already suggesting where they could hide the cufflink to keep it from prying eyes…including those of the Master.

○

Cove Village Post Office
02:00 am

George Markson woke with a jump as his wife put her hand over his mouth, pressed her lips against his ear and hissed. "There's someone in the shop!"

Blinking rapidly in the dark room, the postmaster and his wife listened to the incredible cacophony of sound coming from the shop below their bedroom; it sounded like someone was taking the post office apart!

George slid out of his warm bed and pulled on his dressing gown. Wedging his feet into his winter slippers, he collected the key to the shop door and made his way down the stairs that led from their private quarters into the post office below.

Hearing a sudden noise behind him, he turned to see his wife following, bearing their best poker. He gestured angrily towards their bedroom, but his wife shook her head and brandished the poker at him. George turned resignedly; if whoever it was got past him, he wouldn't put money on them escaping her. He knew all too well just how good her aim was with that particular weapon!

The sounds of smashing glass and splintering wood were far louder than they had been; from their position on the stairs, they could now also hear the intruder moving around the little shop.

George placed the key in the lock as quietly as possible, but there was a sharp click as the door unlocked — a click that coincided with the sudden cessation of sound in the post office beyond.

George swore sharply under his breath and glared at his wife; the element of surprise had now gone. He took a deep breath, put his shoulder to the door, and flung it open.

As the door bounced back and hit him on his slipper-clad toe, George swore again, this time much louder as he gazed in horror at what had once been a neat and trim little shop. The entire room appeared to have been hit by an anarchist raid; the windows were smashed and the counter, a solid affair in oak that had taken several men to install, had been ripped off its supports and flung to the opposite side of the room. The telegraph machine, which had only been installed a few months earlier, was gone; a few bare wires were all that was left of that particular miracle of modern science.

George ran a hand through his thinning hair as he stared at the wreckage of his shop. A hideous thought suddenly came to him, and he pushed through the wreckage to the little telephone booth that had been installed with the telegraph. The booth itself was still standing, just; the glass and wood privacy panels had gone the same way as his windows, and the telephone had been ripped out of the wall. The strength needed to create such carnage was beyond his ken.

The front door stood open, hanging on one of its hinges. George retched as a rancid stench came to his nostrils; it smelt worse than his mother-in-law's cooking!

George caught his wife's eye, pressed a finger to his lips, pointed to the stairs, and made a shooing motion with his hand. For the first time in her life, Mary Markson did exactly what her husband suggested: she turned and made her way back upstairs.

As she went up to their rooms, George locked the door at the foot of the stairs, then ascended to the little landing, picked up one of their dining chairs, and wedged it between the door and the stair tread before walking to their bedroom and closing the door. There was a sharp click as the door was locked, then the sound of another chair being wedged against the door, The postmaster and his wife spent the next few hours in horrified speculation about what had demolished their little shop, and why it had destroyed the telephone and telegraph machines.

○

The Dining Room
10:00am

Giselle settled herself into her seat and graciously accepted a cup of tea from Davaadalai. Lifting the china cup to her lips, she looked at Cornelius and the doctor over the rim; they needed information, and Elliott and Thorne still hadn't decided how to elicit what was needed. She sighed; perhaps it was her turn to try.

She placed the cup down and caught her husband's eye. Elliott frowned, then nodded; he didn't know what she was about to do, but he trusted her implicitly.

"Dr Mayberry?"

The doctor turned to Giselle; his usual glare replaced with an expression as gentle as any likely to appear on his usually stubborn visage. "Yes, my dear?"

"I do beg your pardon, but I must ask you a question that is perhaps outside of what is socially acceptable. We are now investigating several murders, and we need to know as much as possible about the people in the castle and hereabouts. To start; what can you tell us about Lucius?"

Dr Mayberry frowned. "Lucius? Oh, Luci? I'm sorry, my dear, but I've known him for so long by his soubriquet that I tend to forget it's not his real name." He thought for a moment. "It is quite all right…I understand why certain… social niceties must be set to one side. Well, Luci Lutyens must be…thirty-two years of age now. Both his parents died when he was sixteen, and he became the sole breadwinner, if you'll pardon the term, for himself and his younger brother, Timothy…" The doctor cleared his throat. "Timothy was the youngest victim of the murderer who struck here fifteen years ago; Luci found his body. The child had been… tormented before death. I will not go into details, but Luci's last memory of his brother was, and still is, one of horror, brutality, and hideous loss." He stared at his teacup, then murmured, "I am ashamed to say that I had my fears for Luci."

Elliott looked at the doctor. "How so? I understand that the horror of his brother's murder made him dissolute, but—"

Mayberry sat up in his chair. "Oh no, you misunderstand me…I thought he might have been the killer!"

Cornelius stared at him. "My dear Tenniel! Impossible!"

The doctor sipped his now-cold tea and shook his head as he looked at his old friend. "He did have that strange ability to make people do what he wanted…remember, Cornelius? Remember that little incident when Felix Pepperbelle upset

Araby, and Luci told him to remove all his clothes and dance a solo foxtrot across the dry moat below Araby's bedroom window…and he did?"

Elliott exchanged sharp glances with Giselle as Cornelius gave a bark of laughter. "Oh yes, I'd forgotten that!" The smile vanished as he looked at the doctor. "An odd gift, I'll grant you, but that doesn't mean he committed those atrocities…"

Elliott nodded at his wife. "I think we might have to pay Mr Lutyens a visit."

Merric gently removed the cold tea from Mayberry's unprotesting grip, walked to the breakfast table, and replaced it with a cup that steamed. He handed the tea to Mayberry, who gruffed his thanks as Merric returned to his seat. "He should arrive in a short while for the church service," he said.

Cornelius tugged at his collar. "I'm afraid he might not, Merric; that little contretemps over inviting the Pepperbelles to the shoot led to me banishing him from the castle for a while…" He caught his nephew's sharp look and spread his hands in a conciliatory gesture. "Just for a little while. The Pepperbelles aren't nice; in fact, it is my humble opinion that they are intolerable, bigoted, and utterly devoid of any redeeming features whatsoever. I think Luci understood why I said what I did."

Merric nodded slowly as he sipped his tea. "Nevertheless, Uncle, I think it's time to bring Luci back into the fold…he's had time to regret his actions, and in honesty, because of what has happened, I would feel happier if Luci were included in our plans, if only to make sure that he is all right."

He turned to Elliott. "Mr Caine, a suggestion. It's too late to send for Luci now — the service starts in a little over an hour, and knowing Luci, he's probably still asleep! But if you do visit him, would you please ask him to come and see me as soon as is convenient?"

Elliott nodded as Thorne, Aquilleia, and Veronique entered the dining room, greeted everyone, and proceeded to lash into the hot plates. "We will walk down into the village after the service." He paused. "Just out of interest, how long will the service be?"

Cornelius laughed. "Oh, old Popplewell is very good at that sort of thing; his proselytizing never lasts for long and it's usually got a decent moral...he averages about thirty minutes."

Giselle smiled at her husband over her cup. "That sounds just about right."

Merric wagged a finger at his uncle. "However, it is the Christmas Sunday service...oh yes — because it is a special service, we usually dress for the occasion."

Elliott smiled. "Very well. We will retire to our rooms and change accordingly."

○

The Chapel
10:55am

Popplewell puffed as he stomped up the last few dozen steps to the Burgoyne family chapel that occupied the thirteenth floor of the castle. Pausing to catch his breath, he pressed a finger to his wrist, and counting the rapid and somewhat fluttery beats, he shook his head. His body was becoming more and more unsteady. The time was fast approaching for him to leave, renew, and return, but this time would be one of his most difficult ascensions. Would his friendship with Cornelius survive? Or should he continue with what had served him best in the past — the death of the old Reverend Popplewell, and the ensconcing of the new vicar in his place?

Popplewell shook his head and opened the heavy door;

the room beyond lay open before him. Popplewell smiled. He always experienced a feeling of deep peace in the family chapel, in spite of the fact that one or two of the family members commemorated on the wall plaque had gone to meet their maker at his hands.

Lifted quite literally from the ruins of Cove Abbey, the private chapel was a place of peace and beauty, the dark-stained oak pews, whitewashed stone walls, and glowing stained-glass windows creating a place of refuge from the outside world.

Popplewell was especially fond of the stained-glass panels depicting the Archangel Michael wielding his burning blade against a tide of demons. An unusual motif to find in a parochial chapel, but the original creator of the designs had not expected them to be viewed beyond the private rooms of the Abbot of Cove.

The windows looked out over the hidden gem that was the rooftop garden: a tiny space liberally planted with ferns which resembled a verdant green grotto, its inherent serenity and peace perfectly matching the tranquillity of the chapel.

Popplewell checked his fob watch and began to place copies of the King James Bible on the pews as chatter began to filter up the stairs, followed by the strange juddering whir of the mechanical floor as it carried Ami and Nanny to the foot of the three stone steps that led into the chapel. Cornelius, Merric, Elliott, and Sebastian each took a corner of the bath chair and lifted Ami over the threshold and into the chapel where Popplewell awaited them, a genial smile of welcome on his lined face. Merric wheeled Ami down the central aisle and settled her at the end of the front pew.

Popplewell bowed his head to Merric, kissed Ami's hand, and gestured to them all to be seated. The guests waited as the family took their usual seats at the front right of the chapel before seating themselves. Merric sat next to Ami,

Cornelius, and a very quiet Araby; one pew behind them sat Melisandre, Nanny, and Perry; on the front left pew sat Elliott, Giselle, and Dr Mayberry; on the pew behind were Thorne, Aquilleia, and Sebastian; Theodora, being of a different denomination, had no desire to be in the little chapel and so had taken the opportunity to read with her son in the library. At the back of the chapel, sitting in their Sunday best, were the family servants. The footmen, maids, and guests' servants sat in silence behind Mrs Burnthouse, dressed in her best black day frock, her straw hat with its large, waxy orange flower pinned with extreme force to her head. Next to her sat Davaadalai, resplendent in his dress uniform adorned with the silver Afghanistan Medal awarded to him after the Second Anglo-Afghan War, where he had served with Cornelius in the elephant and mule battery in Charasia.

As everyone settled into their seats, Reverend Popplewell ascended the pulpit, cleared his throat, affixed his glasses to his nose and began.

○

Midday

As they filtered out of the Chapel, Thorne leant in and whispered. "I thought it was going to be short? I need some serious fortifying to deal with the last hour!"

Elliott hid a smile. "You can't start drinking champagne yet!"

Thorne snorted as he took Aquilleia's arm. "Oh, yes I damn well can!"

The four of them went up to their suites to collect Veronique and dress in rather warmer clothing before walking to Luci's cottage.

Strolling through the well-tended garden to the front door of the trim cottage, Elliott considered the man who lived there. He was a louche, cynical, damaged alcoholic — but also a man who appeared to care for his home: the home he had lived in with his parents and his younger brother.

As Elliott knocked, the upstairs curtains in the house next door fluttered as the person within moved out of view, but continued to watch. Aquilleia gently squeezed Thorne's hand, and as he leant in, whispered a few words. Thorne shot a swift glance at the neighbouring cottage and nodded before nudging Elliott and Giselle, and gesturing with his chin.

Elliott cast a surreptitious eye over the neighbouring cottage. Similar in style and size to its twin, the sole difference between the other cottage and Luci's house appeared to be its shabby woodwork and the unwillingness of its unseen inhabitant to clean the dusty windows.

Elliott turned back to Luci's door and raised his hand to knock again. As he did so, the door was flung open and Luci, once again clad in his garish dressing gown, appeared in the doorway, a hand pressed to his forehead. He gave them a pained look. "Do you mind? I am currently trying to die with dignity in the kitchen, so if you would kindly cease that dratted hammering at my blasted door, I would be most grateful!"

Thorne raised an eyebrow. "A heavy night on the Rhine?"

Luci blinked. "Actually, rather a pleasant one to begin with…in the Rhône." He peered at Elliott. "So, Mr Policeman, what do you want?"

Elliott looked at the hungover young man with a tolerant expression; he had been there far too often to judge. "May we come in, Mr Lutyens? We need to speak with you about the events at the castle, and we also bring a personal message from the Earl of Cove."

Luci's hand dropped limply to his side. "In that case, I can hardly say no and send you on your way — even if that's how I feel on this miserable, cold, and revoltingly sober morning! Please come in, and don't mind the mess."

They entered the cottage and followed Luci into the kitchen, where Elliott immediately rethought one or two of his previous ideas. The kitchen resembled an explosion in a laundry house crossed with the aftermath of the proverbial bull in a china shop. Several days' worth of crockery, some of it broken beyond repair, sat in the sink, while empty wine bottles lay discarded around the kitchen table, itself piled high with a mixture of washed and folded clothing and haphazard piles presumably waiting for Luci's ministrations as washerwoman.

Luci hurriedly gathered several piles from the seats and dumped them unceremoniously onto the floor. "Ladies, please be seated."

As Giselle and Aquilleia settled in, Luci threw himself into a chair next to the sink. Veronique walked up to him and sniffed delicately at his hand, she turned back to Thorne and whined. Thorne nodded at Elliott. Luci was an Other; Veronique could smell it.

Luci looked at the Labrador with a strange expression as he gently stroked her ears. He looked up at Thorne. "Beautiful dog — I feel as though I have seen her before somewhere...just one of my many fancies, I suppose! So, ladies and gentlemen, what brings you down from the castle to my humble abode?"

Elliott stepped forward. "I take it you are aware that we were brought in to investigate the discovery of young Alistair Burgoyne's body?"

Luci nodded. "That little snippet of information had been brought to my attention — and also that you singularly failed to prevent the subsequent deaths of both the lovely Sybilla and her equally wonderful husband! Shame on you, Mr

Policeman!" He wagged his finger at Elliott with a mocking smile.

Elliott smiled back at him, and the dim gaslights in the kitchen caught his overly long canines in a sudden flash that made Luci sit back. "Mr Lutyens, we are here to communicate to you Lord Burgoyne's request that you be readmitted to the family gathering; he would like to see you later, but first we need to ask you one or two questions."

Luci looked at him, and the hangover that had been squatting in his head like a sullen lodger since the revoltingly early time of his awakening disappeared. As he looked at the guests sitting in his kitchen, he recalled the last time an official presence had made their thoughts about him clear: when they had accused him of murdering his own brother.

He leapt to his feet and stood by the sink; his smile replaced by a rather more concerned expression. "I was nowhere near the castle when Sybilla was killed; Cornelius banned me from the grounds and I came home." He paused and sighed. "He only sent me away because of my own stupidity. I had nothing to do with Alistair's murder, or Sybilla's death, or that of her equally revolting husband — you must believe me!"

Giselle eyed him. "Why do you refer to the De Banzies as 'equally revolting', Mr Lutyens?"

Luci's face paled. "I would rather not say in the presence of ladies."

Giselle's gaze did not waver. "Is it because of their… unusual personal practices?"

Luci's dark eyes flicked from face to face. "You found evidence?"

Elliott shared a glance with the others. "We did."

Luci sat back down and put his head in his hands before looking up at Elliott. "Did you find any evidence that they killed my brother?"

Elliott shook his head. "No."

Luci let out a shuddering breath. "I don't know about you, but I could do with a drink!" He poured a large glass of what appeared to be neat whisky and downed half of it.

Elliott sat back in his chair. "We would like to continue this discussion with you in a sober state of mind, Mr Lutyens."

Luci nodded. "I understand." His expression was fearful. "The evidence you found...was it by any chance a small book containing photographic images?"

In the sudden silence, Elliott's expression was carefully blank. "How do you know about the book, Mr Lutyens?"

Luci took a deep breath. "Several years ago, when they were looking for a suitable..." – he glanced at Giselle and Aquilleia – "playmate to join them, they needed to make sure that said associate was of a similar disposition. They used the book as a technique to weed out the less strong in stomach. Needless to say, I rejected their offer, and they never had much to do with me after that."

Thorne shared a look with his wife; the deaths of the De Banzies were rapidly becoming his idea of humane destruction!

"Did you not consider telling the police?" asked Elliott. "Or any of the family?"

Luci shook his head. "It would have killed Ami to find out that her adored step-granddaughter was such an evil, sadistic —" He took a deep breath to steady himself. "Please excuse me, ladies! The police never trusted me after they decided I was to blame for my brother's death and those of the other children on the island. All I could do was follow Sybilla and Marcus and try to prevent them from continuing their abuses."

Giselle nodded. "That was why you travelled to London

after the murders, wasn't it? To prevent Sybilla and Marcus from causing harm."

Luci nodded and sat up in his chair. "In the beginning, it worked. On several occasions I followed Marcus on his evening rambles into the darker and less wholesome parts of the city, and protected several ladies of the night who would have become their victims by hiring their services myself." Luci looked at Giselle earnestly. "Nothing untoward, you understand...I simply paid them for their time, usually spent at a bar in a public house. Believe me, if they had entered the De Banzies' townhouse, the harm done to them would have been incalculable!" He closed his eyes in remembered horror.

Elliott nodded slowly. The man before him was complex: louche, cynical, a drunkard...but also gentle, sorrowful, and lost. And also an Other; the best way to approach that might well take careful thought. "Mr Lutyens, we fear that the person responsible for the crimes committed in these last few days is equally guilty of more heinous crimes committed in the past."

Luci raised a somewhat jaundiced eyebrow, and executed a grand shrug that almost slopped the contents of his glass across the kitchen. "So they're unpleasant — what of it? And what does it have to do with me? Being very honest, Mr Policeman, whoever killed both Sybilla and Marcus did the world a favour. Humanity's moral standing jumped by several points after the De Banzies were removed from the world!"

Elliott shared a look with Thorne; this could take some time! "We believe the person to be guilty of the murders fifteen years ago, Mr Lutyens, including that of your brother, Timothy."

A sudden silence descended. As Luci looked at Elliott, pale pink lights appeared in his eyes. He leant forward and spoke, his voice echoing with the sound of many voices. "Tell me who they are!"

Elliott and the others exchanged glances at the sudden appearance of Luci's gift. Elliott, armed with advanced knowledge due to Mayberry's earlier comments, shrugged off the effects as he continued. "They are somewhat more than unpleasant, Mr Lutyens," said Elliott. "They have abilities that are...not quite human, if you understand me?"

Luci shot Elliott a sharp look; most people couldn't fight his strange ability...so far only two had succeeded, and both were now dead. He settled back in his chair and affected a bored expression to cover his unease; the conversation had taken a turn he had not foreseen. "When you say 'abilities', what exactly do you mean?"

Elliott looked at him steadily. "Some have the ability to change their appearance, some the ability to move between shadows, others..."

Luci's face paled until he was almost the colour of milk. "The ability to...to make people obey a command?"

Elliott sat back in his chair and studied the tense face before him. "Now why would you say that, Mr Lutyens?"

Lucius looked at the three of them silently before taking a large gulp of his drink. He coddled the glass between his hands, looking intently at it, before he answered. "When I was a child, I discovered that I could make people do what I wanted them to...just by asking." He looked at Elliott, his face desperate. "Not by threatening, you understand? Simply by asking. If it was something I really wanted, I would feel something, like a sensation of warm water rushing beneath my skin...and then they would do what I had asked." He sat back in his chair and stared at Elliott. "You are the only people I have told of this." He gave a bark of laughter that sounded strained. "I know how it sounds," he gabbled. "It sounds like I'm going mad, but—"

Elliott leant towards the frightened man. "You are not going mad, Lucius. You are an Other, like us."

Luci's eyes widened. "Like...you?"

Elliott smiled, his canines flashing as green lights appeared in his eyes. Luci's own eyes turned to the others', where he saw swirls of gold, silver, and lavender looking back at him. "What are you?" he whispered.

Giselle smiled gently. "We are like you, Luci; we have abilities that the average person would find...unnerving."

Elliott sat back in his seat and allowed his face to become that of Thorne, before returning to his own countenance. Luci stared at him; his breathing rapid. He swallowed hard. "I ask again; what are you? And why are you here?"

"We have much to discuss, Luci — you don't mind if I call you Luci, do you? I believe that after a chat, we will all become great friends! But first, perhaps a pot of tea might be a good idea?"

As Luci stood up slowly, Elliott spoke again. "Out of interest, you say your gift encourages people to do what you want them to?"

Luci swallowed. "Yes."

Elliott raised an eyebrow. "Why didn't you use your gift on Sybilla and Marcus? Why didn't you simply tell them to stop their abuses?"

Luci looked down at him. "I tried, but it doesn't seem to work that way. I can encourage someone to do something they themselves, might choose to do, but I can't force them to go against their will. When I used my gift, as you call it, to tell them to stop, Sybilla and Marcus looked at me as though I had wandered out of Bedlam!"

He stood silent for a moment, then took a deep breath. "Tea."

Thorne smiled approvingly. "And perhaps some cake?"

Elliott rolled his eyes as Luci nodded, and headed towards the range.

○

One Hour Later

As Elliott and the others left Luci's home, the curtains in the upper window of the house next door twitched as Trevenniss watched them walk back up the lane that led to the castle. Time to settle himself in for the evening and await his queen's commands...

As he was about to settle himself back in his chair, he heard a faint knocking; he frowned and glanced out of the window but could see nothing. The sound came again — light, but definitely the sound of someone knocking at a door or window...

He walked into the back bedroom, threw up the sash window, and stuck his head out to look into the small backyard, but again could see nothing. As he walked back to his own room, leaving the window open, he missed a faint movement from the roof above, as a slender figure crept through the open window and skittered across the ceiling behind him.

He sat back down and continued his watch. Chymeris hadn't told him what in particular to watch for, but he took his queen's orders very seriously; the notebook in his pocket was more than half full of information detailing the actions, appearance, and behaviours of the various villagers. He smiled — his queen would be very interested in Lucius Lutyens' actions, his most recent visitors, and the unusual quality of the young man's voice!

Trevenniss sipped his tea. As he placed the cup back in its saucer, the sound came again, this time a little louder, and definitely from somewhere below. Trevenniss scowled, stood up abruptly and headed downstairs.

When he reached the hallway, he smiled as he passed the bodies of the Pepperbelles and Eliza as he continued to the front door. He threw the bolt back and glared into the front garden, but no one was there.

Muttering some choice swearwords under his breath, the irritated man slammed the door shut and turned to the parlour. As he turned, the slender figure dropped from the ceiling and sank their fangs into his neck.

Trevenniss's scream was silenced even before it left him. He fell to the floor as the venom entered his bloodstream and began its work, bloody foam pouring from his open mouth.

The elegant man who had attacked him patted the convulsing man's pockets and removed the notebook. Flicking through the contents with a smile, he tucked the book into his own breast pocket, climbed up the smooth kitchen wall, and began to weave a cocoon in the corner. Several minutes later, perched in the corner of the ceiling, he turned from his work and extended a hand. A thin silken thread shot from his fingers to Trevenniss' chest.

As Eliza's dead eyes stared blankly from the hallway, the elegant man dragged the still-alive valet up the wall and into the cocoon.

The Stile
1:10pm

Aquilleia's eyes flashed with silver light and she turned to Thorne with a gasp. "Someone else is here — an Other!"

Elliott stared at her. "What can you see?"

Aquilleia sat down on the stile and pressed her hand to her throat; Veronique sat down beside her with a whine.

"A man, tall, slim and elegant. He bears fangs." She looked up at Thorne and swallowed. "He is weaving a trap for someone…a webbed trap"

Thorne looked at her sharply. "Aranea?"

She nodded as Giselle sat down next to her and took her hand. "I think so — yes."

Thorne looked at Elliott, his blond brows drawn down over his eyes. "What the hell is Jumping Jacques doing here? I though he was sentenced to a thousand years in the Boundary."

Elliott shook his head. "I haven't a clue, my friend – but if one of Asteraceae's favourite playmates has found a way to get out of the Boundary prison, we should be very careful." He looked at Aquilleia. "Can you see where he is? Or why he's here?"

Aquilleia frowned. "I cannot see where, as there is a veil over him. As to why…he wants the diamonds, the Lark and the Spur; he believes them to be near."

The others stilled; Giselle looked at Elliott. "If he believes the diamonds are here, then Chymeris is also here — and that is closer than I would like!"

Elliott nodded as Thorne helped Aquilleia to her feet. "We must return to the castle. Keep your eyes open, my friends; be aware of what you see and feel. We are now dealing with far worse than a mere human killer; we know that Filicidae is here, and now we know of the presence of both Chymeris and Aranea." Elliott sighed. "What did we do to deserve this kind of reunion?"

Thorne shrugged as they walked briskly back up the footpath, Veronique scouting the pathway before them. "Well, we did originally catch Filicidae, and we foiled Aranea's attempts to depose the king and put his half-sister Asteraceae on the throne, and we did rather get in the way of Chymeris' plans on one or two occasions…"

Giselle looked at Thorne as they walked up the snow-dusted track. "Your point being that if we did it once…"

Thorne nodded. "We can do it again."

○

Popplewell's Suite
2:00pm

Thorne accepted his fourth cup of tea that afternoon; he sincerely hoped his kidneys were appreciating the additional liquids that would enable that evening's intake of champagne to be significantly increased. He took a sip from the fine china cup and continued to take notes.

Popplewell sighed. "Aranea? If he is here, then things are rather more complicated than we thought. My friends, you must stay safe."

Elliott nodded as he sipped his tea. "We shall, but first we must deal with this case. Popplewell, is anyone here today who was alive when Thomas Burgoyne was Master of Cove?"

Popplewell shook his head. "Apart from me, no other was here during the time of the Priory." He paused. "Except Nannette."

Elliott raised an eyebrow. "Nannette?"

"Yes, she was not even sixteen when the Master died. And after I had witnessed the debauchery, the sadism revelled in by such a young girl, even after the pleas for understanding due to her age and naivety, I could never bring myself to call her by the ridiculous soubriquet of 'Nanny!'"

Thorne stared at him incredulously. "Miss Wyck was a member of the Priory?"

Popplewell nodded. "Oh yes. She's distantly related to the family, though a very poor relation, and as a girl she was thoroughly dedicated to the Master." He sighed as he shook his head. "I could never discover just how deeply she had fallen. The Master had originally limited the Inner Sanctum to a small number of his most dedicated followers, but where Nannette Wyck was placed, and if she was even included in that group, was beyond my knowledge, so I left her where she was. Jerome took pity on her and took her in. She had a knowledge of music and the arts, and she was very good with children, so a few years later, Jerome employed her as a nanny within the Burgoyne family, where she apparently lived up to her name and gave satisfaction." He raised his eyes to Elliott's. "That is not to say that I did not keep an eye on her over the years; I did." He rubbed his eyes. "After what the Inner Sanctum did to my son, I could not bring myself to trust her, but she seemed to take to her altered circumstances, and she aged along with the rest of us."

Elliott nodded. "And when the murders began fifteen years ago, there was never any suggestion…?"

Popplewell blinked. "She was quite elderly by then, seventy-five or so…that would make her nearly ninety now. And no, there was never any suggestion that she was involved, in spite of her past. Indeed, after the murders occurred, she was charged with caring for Araby, and Perry Challick, in a place of safety on the mainland." He smiled. "Though it is more accurate to say that over the last few years, Araby has taken care of all three of them; Miss Wyck is quite unsteady these days, and her mind is prone to wandering."

He settled back into his chair as Elliott plucked at his hairless chin thoughtfully. He caught his wife's eye and hurriedly placed his hand in his lap; the quicker his beard grew back, the better! With his particular gift, it could be regrown in a matter of seconds, but the other inhabitants of the castle might question the sudden and rather obvious appearance of a full and luxurious beard and moustache when such items had not existed one minute earlier.

As they sat in silence, a sharp rap sounded at the door. Popplewell cleared his throat. "Who is it?"

The voice of Cornelius sounded from the other side of the door. "It's me. May I come in?"

Popplewell smiled. "Come."

Cornelius entered and paused in the doorway when he saw the others. "I'm sorry, old chap, I didn't realise you had company. I'll call in later."

Elliott caught Popplewell's eye, and Popplewell nodded. "Not at all, Cornelius, please join us."

Giselle turned her brightest smile on Cornelius. "Shall I be mother with the tea?"

Cornelius faltered in the magnificent wattage of her smile; his face turned slightly pink as he accepted the freshly poured tea and allowed himself to be pressed into accepting a scone, a cheese savoury, and a chocolate éclair.

Elliott smiled, settled back into his chair, and looked at Popplewell. "If our thoughts are correct, the current killing spree is absolutely connected to the murders fifteen years ago. Who else was on the island at that time?"

Popplewell thought. "Myself, obviously. Cornelius, Ami, Alistair, Araby, Merric, Miss Wyck, Luci, young Perry — but he was only about eight years old at the time. Melisandre was here too, visiting with Sybilla and Marcus, who had only just been married and were on their honeymoon."

Cornelius blanched. "Oh, good God! It couldn't have been them…could it?"

Thorne looked at his wife with a raised eyebrow; it would certainly make their investigation somewhat easier if the killings fifteen years ago could be placed at the door of two dead sadists.

Aquilleia shook her head. "No, the killer is still very much alive. Alive, and gloating! They are enjoying the spectacle."

Cornelius frowned at Aquilleia's remark, but before he could say anything Elliott continued.

"What can you tell us about the servants?"

Popplewell blinked at the sudden change in the conversation. "How do you mean?"

"Could one of them be a suspect?"

Cornelius bellowed from his chair. "Absolutely bloody not! I do beg your pardon ladies, but really! I would trust Davaadalai with my life." He paused. "Actually, he did save my life back in Charasia..."

Popplewell nodded in agreement. "Davaadalai was here fifteen years ago, but I agree with Cornelius that he is beyond reproach. Mrs Burnthouse was here too — but she has been here nearly as long as I have! The footmen are mostly new, engaged within the last four or five years, and the same with most of the maids... Oh, but Parker was here."

Thorne looked up from his notes. "Parker?"

"Edith Parker, Ami's own maid; she has been with the family for over thirty years."

Cornelius helped himself to another scone. "She's been with Ami for closer to forty years; she was hired by our mother and never left."

Giselle nodded. "And what of the islanders, or people with very close connections to Cove?"

Popplewell considered. "There's Mossy, the fisherman... his father was from Cove. He's lived in Penwithiel since Methuselah was a boy..." Popplewell cast a quick glance at Cornelius. "Back in '25, Mossy helped bring an end to Thomas Burgoyne's reign of terror; he brought the mercenaries my, uh, father hired to the island...he smuggled them in on his father's boat. Mossy's wife Maybell and their grand-son, James live with him in Penwithiel. There's Luci, but we've already mentioned him — both his parents had already passed by that time; young Perry's parents, who both died shortly after the murders; the hideous Pepperbelles..." He huffed. "I understand that I am supposed to understand, love, and accept my fellow man, but they are too impossibly unpleasant to accept at all! Where was I? Oh yes, Sebastian was still with his parents at the time. His parents moved to Shrewsbury, I believe, and both died a few years ago. The Markhams moved here to run the post office less than ten years ago—"

Cornelius sat up in his chair. "Of course!" The others looked at him questioningly. "I forgot to tell you...your mentioning of the post office just reminded me; someone broke into the post office last night and destroyed both the telephone and the telegraph machine."

Elliott sat back and rubbed the bridge of his nose with a pained expression.

Thorne looked at the innocent éclair in his hand. "Well, that will make sending any further information to Lapotaire rather awkward!"

Elliott nodded, a faint green light appearing in his eyes. "It's too late to use the causeway to get to the mainland, and the weather is too unpleasant to take a boat out...we are trapped until the tide turns in the morning!"

He gestured to Popplewell. "Please continue...we were talking about the islanders."

Popplewell nodded. "The only other islander who was here at the time of the last murders is, of course, Doctor Mayberry."

Cornelius glared over his drink. "I do hope you aren't suggesting what I think, Popplewell!"

Popplewell smiled. "I wouldn't dare, old friend! We are

rather low on our numbers these days. Several houses in the village are empty now...quite a few families left after the murders and never returned — not that I can blame them. But I understand the cottage next to Luci's was rented by a gentleman from London just the other week."

Thorne exchanged glances with Aquilleia. "Do you happen to know the gentleman's name?"

Popplewell frowned. "I'm afraid I don't...I visited shortly after his arrival to welcome him to the village, and he wouldn't even open the door to me."

Cornelius nodded. "City-dwellers are always so rude, and they think we're standoffish to them! Damned cheek! However, I happen to know the chap's name since we own the house he rents. Now, what was it? Something rather local, although his accent definitely wasn't; it more Antipodean..." He worried at his moustache as he thought.

Elliott smiled suddenly. "It wasn't, by any chance, Trevenniss?"

"That's it, Trevenniss! A good Cornish name, I thought, but as I said, his accent was far more southerly."

"And he is in the cottage next to Luci's?"

Popplewell looked at him sharply. "Yes...is he a gentleman of some interest?"

Thorne nodded with a glint in his eye. "In more ways than you can possibly imagine!" He looked at the others. "It's getting late, but perhaps we should visit Trevenniss and see how he has fared these last few months!"

Elliott looked at Thorne. "I concur." He turned to Giselle and Aquilleia. "Ladies..."

Giselle held up a manicured finger. "We will accompany you...that is not up for discussion!"

Elliott smiled. "Understood. It is beginning to darken; let us go now, before it gets too late." He looked at Cornelius. "Do you have a spare key to the cottage, Mr Burgoyne?"

Cornelius nodded slowly as he stood up. "I'll get it for you." He paused and looked at them. "Would it be an idea if you took one of the carts? The lads can have it ready in ten minutes, and it would be far quicker."

Giselle nodded. "That would be very helpful, Mr Burgoyne, thank you."

Cornelius walked to the door. "Then I will see you in the great hall in ten minutes."

○

The Cottage
3:00pm

Thorne stepped down, assisted Aquilleia from the cart, and gave her a questioning look. She turned to the cottage, her eyes swirling with silver light as her mind looked inside the building. Then she shook her head. "I can feel no presence within."

Elliott produced the key Cornelius had pressed into his hand. Pausing, he looked at Giselle silently, then reached for the doorknob. The door swung open, revealing a narrow, unlit hallway that led into darkness.

Elliott looked at the two young lads on the cart. "Will you please stay with the horses, gentlemen?"

The two boys nodded as Elliott was joined at the door by Thorne, Giselle, Aquilleia, and Veronique.

There was a gas lamp just inside the door. As Elliott raised his hand to turn the jet on, Veronique began to growl, her hackles raised in a thick black ruff around her neck as she stared intently into the dark passageway.

Elliott paused. Looking at the guarding dog, he very carefully turned up the gaslights in the hall.

Three huddled bodies lay at the foot of the stairs. Elliott

peeped into the doorway on his left. It led to the parlour, which was empty.

Reaching the bodies, Elliott pressed his fingers against Felix Pepperbelle's throat in search of a pulse he knew he wouldn't find; from the coldness of the body, he had obviously been dead for some time.

As Elliott checked Fern and the second woman for signs of life, he was joined by the others. Giselle looked at him with a raised eyebrow, and Elliott shook his head; the Pepperbelles and the unknown young woman had been dead for some time.

Thorne moved into the kitchen and turned up the gaslight. At Aquilleia's gasp, he looked up. The shredded remains of a huge cocoon hung from a corner of the ceiling; bloodied clothing and thick strands of ichor and webbing dripped down the wall from a gaping hole in the cocoon, leaving a viscous puddle that was spreading across the black and white tiled floor.

As Elliott and Giselle joined them in the kitchen, Thorne nodded at the mess. "It would appear that Aranea is up to his old tricks again."

Giselle looked up at the cocoon in horrified disgust. "What came out of it?"

Aquilleia looked at her, her pale face the colour of chalk. "What went into the cocoon was Trevenniss…but what came out was something far worse!"

Elliott and Thorne looked at each other, and Thorne nodded. "We need to search the house. Aranea never stays in the same place as his food, or those he has bitten and turned to his will. He won't come back here…but we might find some information about Chymeris."

Elliott shook his head. "If there was any information about Chymeris, Aranea has it now. All we can do is work out why!"

The Garden
5:30pm

Marshall smiled as Leander battled his way through the rhododendron bushes, gleefully swinging a stick around his head as he fearlessly decapitated the enemies that surrounded him...or as they were usually known, nettles.

She sat on the rickety bench that overlooked where the young boy was playing and pulled some knitting out of her reticule, settling herself for a peaceful but chilly few minutes before the true battle of guiding him back to their suite, bathing the little terror, and getting him ready for his supper. As it was the Sunday closest to Yule, the cocktail hour had been moved up an hour to allow the twelve-course meal to start earlier, so her master and mistress would be in the lounge by the time they returned to the suite. She could get a few more minutes' peace there before Leander's bath, supper, and bed.

As she worked her way through a particularly fiddly set of stitches, her mind turned to her cousin Rose. Hopefully that little set-to with their mistress had knocked some sense into the pert miss, but she doubted it. Rose was rather a one for thinking she knew everything and not listening to advice until it was far too late.

She retched suddenly as a foul stench came to her nostrils. What in God's name was that smell? She opened her mouth to call Leander, but before a sound could escape her, a huge leathery hand clamped across her face and she was dragged backwards off the bench into the thick undergrowth behind.

Leander paused in his rallying of the troops and turned back to where Marshall had been sitting, but she wasn't there. He walked over to the empty bench and wrinkled his nose. What was that smell? It was worse than really bad eggs…

There was a rustle from the undergrowth behind him and he turned in relief. "Marshall, is that you? You scared me!"

A low, watery laugh came from the dark hedge as a figure slowly revealed itself. "I know…I can feel your fear!"

Leander stared in silent horror as the creature reached out a bloody hand.

○

Thorne and Aquilleia's Suite
5:40pm

Aquilleia sat up in the bed and pressed a hand to her chest; her heart was pounding. As she placed her feet on the floor, Thorne popped his head around the bathroom door. "Are you all right, my love?"

Aquilleia swallowed and shook her head. "It's here …Fili-cidae is here…" She turned to look at her husband. "There's been another death — I can feel it!"

Thorne hurriedly wiped the soap from his neck. "I'll get Elliott and Giselle." He turned to Veronique, a lavender light flashing in his eyes, "Guard her, Xenocyon…I'll be back!"

As the door closed behind him, Veronique leapt onto the bed and curled up next to Aquilleia, who gently stroked the Labrador's soft fur as her mind turned back to what she had seen and felt.

Cove Abbey Ruins

PART III

A Suite of Rooms
5:40pm

Chymeris hurried back to her rooms, closed and bolted the door, and came face to face with an unexpected visitor who had made themselves comfortable in her neatly appointed rooms, but not in one of her comfortable armchairs...her unexpected guest was instead perched halfway up the wall in a hammock made from opalescent webbing that had taken them just a few moments to spin.

The elegant, very slender man, resting with one evening-wear-clad leg dangling over the side, peered over the edge of the web and smiled, his perfect white teeth flashing. "Ahh, Chymeris...my dear, you're looking as lovely as ever!"

Chymeris gritted her teeth. Having to discard the nubile young body she had replicated only a few weeks earlier and replace it with the too-solid form of an ageing, stout woman with red hands and stiff hips had been a huge irritation to her. For Aranea to see her in this particular form simply added insult to injury!

She waved a dismissive hand as she settled in her armchair, taking great care not to turn her back on the unsettling figure smiling at her from his perch. "I know you, Jumping Jacques...I told your owner many years ago that I was no longer interested in an alliance, and that still holds true! I am not interested in anything they have to offer. Return to your buyer, lackey, and inform them of my response!"

The charming smile slid off the man's slender face almost as quickly as he slid out of his web and descended to the floor. His elegant features twisted in anger and razor-sharp fangs appeared, protruding like chelicerae from either side of his slim lips as he advanced towards her. He paused to control himself; his smile returned as he raised his light tenor voice. "How is your delightful manservant, Trevenniss? You have heard from him recently…or perhaps you haven't?"

Chymeris glared at him from her chair. "What do you mean?"

Aranea's smile widened unpleasantly and he licked his lips with a red tongue. "Delightful man — he tried so hard not to speak, but you know what a way I have with getting people to share! Did you think you could take the gems without the Child knowing? Many are aware of their true power — you should have known it would not be so easy!"

He stopped and his eyes flickered as though hearing something she could not. Aranea laughed suddenly and turned his full attention back to Chymeris, his fangs shrinking into his mouth as he flashed her his most charming smile. "The Child always gets what they want — especially when they have put so very much time and effort into a certain cause…you of all people should know that! Some other time, perhaps, Chymeris. For your future safety, it would be wise for you to remember just how much you owe, and to whom!"

He leapt out of the open window and landed gracefully on the lawn, more than thirty feet below. He turned and looked up at Chymeris, who stood at the window and glared at him. Her expression darkened as a second figure appeared at the edge of the lawn and stood next to Aranea. Hairless, skeletally thin, and with deep-red skin, what had once been Trevenniss smiled up at her. Aranea waved goodbye and walked towards the village, the gibbering red figure of her former servant cavorting around him as they walked.

Chymeris hissed through her teeth and slammed her hand down on the window ledge; things simply weren't going to plan! Her scheme for the eviction of Phoenixus from her mind had come to a sudden halt on their arrival in Cove, when he had fought her attempts to force him to activate his route to Astraea by hiding within deeply hidden ancient memories. Rapidly devising a new strategy, she had taken the place of someone well placed in the castle and had been wrestling with her brother ever since. She had though to return to London, until such time as she could find Phoenixus' hiding place and her will could once again override him…but the causeway was under water till morning, and in this weather, trying to hire a boat would be impossible!

She smiled. Perhaps a little visit to one of the fishermen and his family that night might be in order: a suggestion of something unpleasant befalling a man's wife and child could encourage even the wariest of fisherman into carrying her to the mainland regardless of the weather. Her smile widened; Aranea was right about one thing; it was always fun to play with one's food!

A terrible thought flashed into her mind, and in spite of the stiffness in her stolen hips she turned and ran to the wardrobe. Flinging the doors open, various items of clothing landed on the floor around her as she rummaged until she found what she was looking for: a simple wooden box. She sat back on her heels and opened it; a sigh passed her lips as she gazed once again upon the flawless perfection of the twin diamonds within: the Lark, and the Spur.

She jumped at a knock on her bedroom door and hurriedly pushed the box under her bed. Throwing the clothes back into the cupboard, she hurried to the door and flung it open. "Yes?" she snapped.

The young footman standing on the threshold started. "Er, Mr Davaadalai would like you to come to the kitchens, please."

She rolled her eyes and put her hands on her hips. "Why? It's my evening off, he knows that!"

He swallowed; this was his first placement in a big house, and he had an unpleasant feeling that it might be his last! "I don't know; he just sent me to tell you that they need you in the kitchen."

Chymeris chafed. The time to leave was now; she had what was necessary. Any more time spent needling Versipellis was losing her time she could have in Astraea — valuable time which she could dedicate to re-educating Abditivus!

She turned her glare on the young man. "Oh, very well. Tell him that I will be down shortly."

The footman looked relieved. "Thank you, Mrs Burnt-house." As the door closed in his face, he smiled.

Chymeris stood by the door and thought hard. She needed to overrule Phoenixus, and she needed to do it now! And then, one last journey to her old home and a pleasant reunion with Abditivus…at least on her part — and then she could concentrate on the utter destruction of what was left of Astraea!

With a satisfied smirk, she collected the few items she would need and placed them on the bed. An expression of concentration appeared on her face as slowly her features altered and her body began to change. She was reverting to the form of the young girl she had murdered just a few days before she and Trevenniss had arrived on the island and she had taken the old cook's place.

As the now far too large clothes fell from her slim frame, she smiled again and swiftly dressed in the clothes she had placed on the bed. Gathering up the wooden box and a small reticule, she left the room.

She decided to leave by the main stairs since she had no desire to run into Davaadalai — he was far too intelligent for his own good, and might have tried to ask questions she was in no mood to answer.

She arrived downstairs and headed for the front door, her low heels clicking on the parquet flooring of the great hall. Cornelius suddenly appeared at the door to the dining room and stared at her. "I say, who on earth are you?"

She didn't acknowledge him, instead walking slightly faster. She reached the door as Cornelius turned back to the people in the dining room and gestured with his whisky glass. "There's a girl — pretty thing, but dashed if I know who she is — making her way across the hall!"

He was joined at the door by Elliott. He took one look at her face. "Chymeris!"

She turned to look at him and laughed, then hitching up her skirts, ran out of the front door and across the drawbridge.

As Elliott and Thorne ran after her, Giselle turned to Cornelius, making a conscious effort to control the golden lights in her blue eyes. "Please don't worry...we'll be back in plenty of time for dinner."

The four friends pursued Chymeris, her laughter ringing in their ears as she ran through the snow-covered garden, following the path that led towards Phoenixus' portal to Astraea: the Horseman Falls.

They ran past the ruins of Cove Abbey; as they pushed through the rhododendron hedge, Elliott remembered the night of the séance. Realisation dawned as he suddenly understood the true meaning of Sybilla's terrible words: 'he must burn to be free'. His voice cracked as he screamed, "Phoenixus, we know it wasn't you — we know it was Chymeris! Brother, you must burn!"

As they heard their brother's words, the figure that was both Chymeris and Phoenixus stopped and turned towards him. Their face morphing between the two, their expressions changing as rapidly as their features as each sought dominance; pure hatred alternating with sheer despair.

With a strength born of desperation, Phoenixus wrenched himself to the front of his mind, using everything he could to force Chymeris back so that he could look upon his brother with his own eyes.

Elliott found himself staring into a face that was his... brown eyes gazed at him as he reached towards his brother. Phoenixus' face twisted sharply and he screamed as his features were replaced by Chymeris' full-lipped image. Her slanting eyes blazed a swirling dull-yellow light in triumph as she laughed at her brother's efforts to stop her.

"Did you really think either of you could be a match for me, brother? I have both the stones and I can travel by this route – you cannot! I hope you said goodbye to Abditivus the last time you saw him, brother mine…I will not guarantee his health, nor that of our dear brother Phoenixus, past this night!"

Her glowing eyes turned to Giselle. "You should have accepted me, my sweet…" She laughed again, malice and hatred ringing out as she turned to the falls and began to walk towards the edge. But as she placed one foot into the stream, she stopped as though she had struck a solid wall.

Dropping the small case that contained the stones, she paused, and her eyes widened in disbelief. She could feel rage — a rage that was not her own!

Horrified realisation struck her as her eyes slowly turned a deep, burning orange. She spun round and stared at Elliott, her eyes blazing as she was enveloped in a seething wall of orange and red flames that wrapped around her burning body like wings. She opened her mouth to scream as the flames turned a blinding ice-white and utterly consumed the body that contained both her and Phoenixus.

Elliott, Giselle, Thorne, and Aquilleia covered their eyes and turned away from the blistering heat. The billowing flames darkened to yellow, orange, and red before the heat disappeared as suddenly as it had arrived.

Elliott looked up from where he had buried his face in Giselle's neck. They turned to where Phoenixus and Chymeris had fought; on the smouldering patch of grass before them lay a naked, charred body. Elliott approached the prone figure.

Thorne raised his voice. "Be careful, Elliott!"

Aquilleia put her hand on his arm and shook her head, tears filling her eyes. "No…no, Shad, it's over!"

Elliott knelt by the still form, and reaching out a trembling hand, placed it on the blackened shoulder. The figure turned to look at him, and Elliott's fearful brown eyes stared into the living eyes of Phoenixus; twin pools of orange and red flame.

Slowly, the burned man sat up, his glowing eyes darting from side to side in his badly burnt face as though listening for something. He looked at Elliott and swallowed painfully. "She's gone…she's gone!"

Elliott held his brother close as the burned man wept, clutching at him as he realised that the millennia of torment he had suffered was over; Chymeris was destroyed.

Giselle ran to her husband's side and draped her winter shawl around the naked man. As she and the others watched, the hideous burns and blisters on Phoenixus' face and body began to heal, fading until they were completely gone.

Elliott raised his tear-streaked face to his wife and Thorne. "I have to get him to Abditivus. After all he has been through, he will need healing that only the Hidden One can offer. Help me, please!"

Thorne nodded, and helped Elliott and his brother to their feet. He picked up the discarded case and opened it; the Lark and the Spur twinkled up at him from their velvet bed. Thorne closed the case and looked at his old friend. "The falls are his way to Astraea, but not yours. Chymeris deceived us many times, but in this she spoke truth. Will Phoenixus be strong enough to trigger the doorway for you both to travel?"

Elliott gently guided his brother to the head of the falls. "He has to be! Giselle, Thorne, keep a watchful eye on things. Aquilleia, I believe you are right. I too have a bad feeling about tonight, but I must get my brother home."

Thorne nodded and held out the case. "The Lark and the Spur; take the gems with you. Whatever Chymeris was planning, they were somehow a part of it. Hopefully, they will be safe with Abditivus."

Giselle kissed Elliott. "Take care, my love; you know where we are if you need us."

Elliott faced the spot where the stream plunged off the edge of the cliff and advanced towards it, gently encouraging his brother to walk with him. As Giselle, Thorne and Aquilleia watched, the two men walked over the edge of the water and disappeared. Giselle hurried to the edge and saw her husband and Phoenixus walk down the waterfall and enter the glowing doorway beyond.

She turned back to Aquilleia and Thorne, tears streaming down her face. "After everything Chymeris did to Phoenixus, will Abditivus be able to help him?"

Thorne put an arm around his wife's shoulders, and shook his head, a look of uncertainty on his face. "Two thousand years of being trapped inside your own mind while another used your body to commit atrocities…two thousand years of witnessing their actions, unable to prevent them. Giselle, it would drive anyone to madness! But if he can be helped, then Abditivus is the one to do it."

He looked up at the clear night sky. The lights were on in the castle, but no one other than themselves seemed to have witnessed the familial contretemps on the cliff edge. He looked at Giselle and gently nudged his wife. Aquilleia placed her arm around her friend as Thorne smiled sadly at them both. Then he frowned. "We need to come up with something to explain Elliott's sudden disappearance."

Aquilleia thought for a moment. "Malaria? Relapses can occur; some last for weeks, others for no more than a day. Sufferers need peace and silence to recuperate…we can say he needs to be left to rest in his room. That should buy us enough time."

Thorne considered the suggestion, and nodded. "I concur." He glanced at his fob watch, "I think we must put on our best smiles and face the family; we still have to be good guests for the Burgoynes. I suggest we don't speak of what happened here…that might well be a truth too far! Perhaps we could suggest that the woman Cornelius saw was a maid, and had nothing to do with the case." He pinched the bridge of his nose. "Elliott is far better at these little lies than I am! Let's go back and tidy ourselves for the Yule celebrations, with a few healthy chargers of champagne to bolster us before dinner. After yesterday's festivities, this evening's meal should be truly exceptional!"

Giselle's laugh was part sob as she allowed herself to be led back along the path to the safety of the castle, and the evening to come.

As they disappeared, Aranea stepped out of the shadows and tapped a finger against his lips. "So, she did have the gems...and now they have been returned to Astraea." He shook his elegant head. "The Child will not be happy!"

He turned to look at what had been Trevenniss. "Such things are sent to try us. We have our orders; now we sit back and wait." He sighed. "A shame about Chymeris: say what you will, she certainly knew how to enjoy herself! We shall return home tomorrow, but first we must see about giving you a new name..."

He looked at the strange figure and stroked a slender finger down the hairless red temple with the proud smile of a creator. "One can never quite tell how the venom will affect people; it all rather depends on the individual. You look quite spectacular, though; hmm...what do you think about 'Red Spider'?"

The figure let out a high-pitched giggle that made Aranea smile as they made their way down to the village to await the turning of the tide.

The Dining Room
7:30pm

The meal was in full swing, since the amassed ranks of family and friends had decided that in spite of the hideousness of the previous day's events, every effort should and would be made to celebrate the first Yule at Cove Castle with the returned children.

Luci was at his mocking, biting best, trading caustic insults with a relaxed Sebastian, who smiled a great deal more than he had before and who shared most of those smiles with his wife Theodora, who was deep in discussion with Popplewell about a suitable replacement for the work-house in Whitechapel, both agreeing that it was no place for children nor the elderly; Cornelius and Mayberry had decided that their earlier conversation about the murders of Jack the Ripper might not be suitable for polite company, particularly given the current state of affairs, and were instead discussing the pros and cons of investing in tea plan-tations in Assam; Melisandre and Merric were attempting to manage their overwhelming urge to bill and coo with stiff-lipped aplomb; Araby appeared distant, she had looked terribly pale when she walked into the lounge for the cock-tail hour, but had realised that for her own happiness, she had to accept things and move on. After quaffing two large coupes of champagne in rapid succession, much to the audible irritation of Nanny, she felt she might actually be able to do so; Perry was again doing his best to drain the bottle of champagne before it left his immediate vicinity; while Ami had made her first appearance at table since Sybil-la's death. She was paler than Araby, and seemed a great deal smaller than before, but seemed insistent on maintaining the correct social standards despite her heartbreak.

Ami had been informed that morning of the true identity of the man who had been presented as her nephew, and the real whereabouts of Alistair. Cornelius had been concerned about her reaction, but she had simply said. "I knew Alistair couldn't have committed the murders, Cornelius…I always feared that something had happened to him. As to the young man you hired to investigate…if that was what you were keeping from me, don't ever treat me like an idiot again, brother!"

As Davaadalai removed her plate, she turned to Thorne. "I do hope Mr Caine is all right; it's always so worrying when malaria returns."

Thorne smiled suavely and finished his coupe of champagne, which was instantly refilled by Davaadalai. "I'm afraid Elliott's constitution is rather poor. He suffers from reoccurring bouts of malaria when he is exposed to extreme stress, and one has to say that this weekend's events have been extremely stressful!"

Ami turned her concerned face to Giselle, who was pushing her food around her plate. "Giselle, will he — that is to say, has he recovered well in the past?"

Giselle looked up, her blue eyes giving off a faint gold light. "Oh yes, these things never keep Elliott down; he simply fights them until they give in!" She took a gulp from her coupe, which was smoothly refilled by Davaadalai almost before she placed it back on the table.

Aquilleia looked at her friend, then turned a worried look on Thorne, who gave a minuscule shrug. Elliott had told them to keep an eye on things until his return; frankly, he would be far happier when it was all over and he, Aquilleia, and Veronique could finally travel to Egypt for their long-overdue honeymoon!

The champagne-driven meal was to continue in the usual fashion; entremets, soup, rum punch, boar's head in apple aspic, a delightful selection of fowl in mayonnaise, and then the desserts.

Shortly after the boars head arrived at table, Aquilleia became suddenly still; a soft chill descended her spine as in her mind's eye the colour in the room ebbed away, leaving only stark tones of black, white, and grey. She recognised the signs; a vision was imminent and she had no means of leaving the room without drawing unwanted attention.

A rushing sound like that of a fast-flowing stream filled her ears. She sat back and relaxed into the sensations that were beginning to make themselves felt; if she tried to force the vision away, it would only cause her harm. As she relaxed, thin lines slowly appeared across the faces before her, turning the people at table into a stiff tableau where their faces appeared to have been painted on wooden planks.

Aquilleia allowed her gaze to touch every person at the table. As she looked at each of them, the flimsy, painted planks slowly peeled back like the doors on an advent calendar, revealing the true face each person kept hidden beneath the thin veneer of civilised behaviour.

Her eyes moved slowly from face to face, witnessing the truth behind each person's façade. But as one person's true face was revealed to her, Aquilleia's mind blenched and her breath caught in her throat. She forced her face to remain still as she fought an almost overwhelming sense of horror. They were right; their very worst fears were true. It was Filicidae, the killer of children, the creature that fed on the terror, fear, and pain of the innocent.

Aquilleia averted her gaze as the exposed face before her smiled through needle-like teeth, abnormally large black eyes staring out of the leathery, slavering face, as the dinner party continued around them unaware. Aquilleia swallowed hard; the juxtaposition of polite chit-chat with the creature's sadistic ugliness made her feel utterly sick.

She stood up suddenly, and holding her napkin to her lips, looked at Thorne, who leapt to his feet. She turned to Cornelius. "I'm afraid I feel a little unwell...a migraine. Do please excuse me." She hurried out, followed by Thorne and Giselle.

Pausing only to close the dining-room doors, they caught up with her at the foot of the stairs. Aquilleia gripped the bannister as though it were the only thing preventing her imminent collapse. Thorne gently touched her elbow and she raised her eyes to his; swirling pools of silver light seemed to fill her face. She took a deep breath and sat down on the stairs. "Shad, we were right — Filicidae is one of the guests!"

Thorne stared at her, his expression of shock mirrored by

Giselle. Even after the discovery of the photographs, they had hoped desperately that they were wrong. Facing Filicidae was not something to be undertaken lightly, and certainly not when they were a person down. His face became still, and his voice was soft. "When you say you are sure, you are sure." He thought for a moment. "In the dining room, did you get any thoughts or feelings about another murder? Anything at all?"

Aquilleia shook her head. "They weren't thinking about the murders. They were pleased they had managed to stay hidden for so long..." She bit her lip as Thorne gently brushed her hair from her face. "Oh Shad, it was awful! It sat there so polite and attentive as a human, but on the inside it was gibbering! It loves nothing but pain and suffering!" She took a shuddering breath. "I saw what was in its mind. My mother was right; it likes following families, spreading sadism and evil. It encourages followers..." She looked at them with a disturbed expression. "It knew Thomas Burgoyne, the old Master, and encouraged him. It was far worse than he ever could be, and I saw inside its mind!"

She swallowed hard. "It is entertained by the fact that no one knows what they truly are..." She looked up at them. "Except two people, there are two here who are willing helpers. They know what Filicidae is, and yet they help!"

Thorne swore under his breath; Giselle's face was incredulous. "Someone knows what they are, and is protecting them?"

Aquilleia shook her head. "Worse...they are worshipping them and assisting in their evil! I can't see who they are, but I know of them now. One is of no consequence to the creature, but the other is Filicidae's most fervent pupil, and Filicidae is protecting them in turn!"

Thorne wrapped his arms around her as she burst into tears. He looked up at Giselle, who took a deep breath and wiped her own eyes. She tapped her lip with a manicured nail, her blue eyes flashing with a golden light as she looked at her friend. "You saw the human form of Filicidae…you saw who it is?"

Aquilleia nodded, her gorge rising at the thought of the two frighteningly different faces of the creature.

"You saw them clearly?"

Aquilleia nodded as Thorne held her tightly and pressed a kiss to her forehead. "Yes, oh Gods, yes!"

"Tell us!"

Aquilleia whispered the name; both Thorne and Giselle looked sick. Thorne shook his head. "When we caught Filicidae in Astraea, there were four of us — Versipellis, Xenocyon, Tamassian, and me — and even then it wasn't easy!" He smacked his hand against the bannister. "If only there were a way of getting a message to Elliott. We need him here; we can't take down that creature without him!"

Giselle opened her mouth, then hesitated; Aquilleia looked at her friend. "Go on, Giselle; you were going to say something?"

Giselle nodded slowly; her expression uncertain. "My own gift has been slow in returning, but I have been practising. Elliott and I can communicate across long distances."

Aquilleia smiled. "I mentioned this in New Zealand; our names show our gifts. Angellis means 'Messenger'."

Thorne looked at Giselle through narrowed eyes. "Can you get a message across the divide? Across the boundary to Astraea?"

She shrugged helplessly. "I don't know…I've never tried, but there's a first time for everything."

As they stood by the stairs, Aquilleia looked at them with a strained expression. "I can't go back in there…not now that I have seen it for who and what it truly is…"

Her voice faded as the images returned. Thorne pressed a

gentle kiss to her hand. "That won't be necessary, my love; perhaps, as you said in the dining room, a migraine?"

As Aquilleia nodded, he turned to Giselle. "What do you need to speak with Elliott?"

Giselle thought. "Peace. It also takes rather a lot of energy, so a little food as well." She sighed. "I was rather looking forward to dinner."

Thorne nodded firmly. "In that case, I shall escort you back into the dining room to finish your meal, and then you can return to your suite and contact Elliott. I shall give the family Aquilleia's apologies, plead a sick headache, and escort her back to our rooms. Let us know when you are retiring; will you need us there?"

Giselle shook her head. "It's best if I am alone...I will let you know his response."

The three of them nodded at each other; it was a plan.

○

The Dining Room
7:45pm

Ami turned to Merric. "I do hope Aquilleia is well."

Merric sipped his drink, a faint frown on his features. "Yes, yes indeed."

They all looked up as Thorne and Giselle re-entered the room. As Giselle took her seat, Thorne cleared his throat and addressed Cornelius. "I'm afraid it is a severe migraine, Mr Burgoyne, and my wife has retired to our rooms for the evening. Hopefully, if she has caught it in time, she will be well again by morning. If you will excuse me, I must be with her."

Ami gestured at Davaadalai. "See that a supper tray is sent up, please, Davaadalai." She turned to Thorne with a tentative smile. "A little light food and a medicinal glass or two was always a help to me during my attacks."

Thorne bowed and left the room. Closing the door behind him, he ran up to the first-floor landing where Aquilleia stood waiting, and gently taking her arm, he guided her back to their suite. Opening the door, they were greeted by a joyful Veronique, who swiftly realised that something was wrong and pushed her cold, wet nose into Aquilleia's hand.

Aquilleia smiled shakily, sat down on the edge of the bed and gently squeezed the Labrador's silky ears. Thorne closed the door, then began to unlace her boots.

A polite knock sounded at the door. Thorne caught Aquilleia's eye, and she tilted her head to one side before leaning against the profusion of pillows on the bed. "It's the butler."

Thorne smiled. "Who is it?" he called.

A rumbling baritone responded from beyond the carved oak door. "It is I, sir, Davaadalai. I have the tray Mrs Burgoyne requested for you."

Thorne smiled at his wife. "We don't want him knowing that we knew who it was before I opened the door." His face set in hard lines. "I remember dealing with Filicidae back in Astraea; just thinking about what happened then is enough to make me need a drink, and I'm pretty damn sure that after seeing that creature's face, you do too!"

He walked over to the door and flung it open with a flourish. The butler standing on the threshold looked somewhat less than impressed, and nodded at Thorne before walking into the room with a large tray that contained not one, but two bottles of champagne, caviar on ice, water biscuits, sour cream, chopped egg whites, a plate of gingerbread, and a large covered dish. He placed the tray on the table and opened the first bottle. The discreet pop was rapidly followed by the filling of two champagne coupes. Davaadalai turned, bowed, and left the room as silently as he had arrived.

Thorne followed him to the door and after a few seconds, shot the bolt. He smiled at Aquilleia as she uncovered the large dish to reveal a meaty-looking mutton bone that at once became Veronique's sole focus of attention.

"A supper tray fit for a king and his queen. I suggest we start with the gingerbread, then work our way through everything else from there."

Aquilleia smiled faintly. "As you say, my love."

He handed her a full coupe. "To us, my darling." He paused; his eyes moist. "And to Elliott, to Giselle...and to Phoenixus — in hopes that Abditivus can save him."

○

Elliott and Giselle's Suite
9:45pm

Dinner had been interminable. Giselle had spent most of it bristling at the social niceties that prevented her from leaving the table and contacting her husband.

She took a gulp of her champagne and cast a quick glance around the table; Ami appeared to be flagging. Giselle bit her lip and hoped that Merric or Cornelius would notice without her having to commit a faux pas by bringing it to their attention. Thankfully, Merric was looking at his aunt with concern. He stood and tapped his glass with a spoon. "Ladies and gentlemen, given the, ah, peculiar nature of the events of the last few days, I think it might be acceptable to allow the usual pleasantries to be optional for this evening. Coffee will be served in the lounge for those who would like it, but some of you may wish to retire instead."

There was a faint murmur from the guests, and chairs scraped back as they made their way either towards the lounge or the stairs. Cornelius escorted an indignant Ami — who was insisting that she wasn't at all tired — to the mechanical platform where they were joined by Nanny and Mayberry. As Merric and Melisandre left the table, Luci drained his champagne coupe and on entering the lounge, ignored the coffee cups that had been set out and instead headed towards the bar at speed where he was joined by a smiling Sebastian who accepted drinks for Theodora and Popplewell, who had both decided to continue their earlier discussion in the more comfortable and relaxed surroundings of the lounge.

Giselle smiled at Araby, who still looked a trifle pale, as they walked up the stairs and along the corridor; from the hall below came the sound of a truculent Nanny being loaded into the lifting mechanism alongside Ami. As Giselle and Araby paused on the landing, the platform sailed past them with many protesting creaks and whining noises; most of which seemed to be coming from the more elderly of the two ladies.

Giselle nodded at the young woman. "Goodnight, Araby."

Araby turned from watching the platform disappear through the ceiling and blinked. "Oh yes, goodnight". She went down the little hallway that led to the second flight of stairs. She paused at an archway in which was set a tiny spiral staircase and, as Giselle watched, Araby pressed her hand gently against the ornate wrought iron before continuing to her room.

Giselle turned and jumped as she came face to face with Perry, his young face flushed from the champagne he had been putting away at table. He leant towards Giselle, nodded towards Araby and whispered huskily, "Those are the stairs to her old room...where it happened; you know — the attack."

Giselle leant away from the alcohol fumes and assumed a polite but distant expression. "Indeed, Mr Challick." She paused. "What do you remember about that night?"

Perry swayed slightly and tried to focus on one of the several Giselles dancing across his vision. "Gosh, not much. I was only a child at the time, and certain details were kept from me..." His eyes became distant. "Kept from me for good reason."

His slender fingers plucked at his cuffs as his mind returned to a time that he had spent a considerable amount of effort to forget. As he fidgeted, Giselle noticed that his cufflinks were odd: one was plain gold, while the other was set with a small diamond.

He suddenly raised his eyes and gave her a somewhat glassy smile. "Good evening. I hope your husband and friend will be well tomorrow." He looked a little shamefaced. "I think I need some water...please excuse me." He weaved down the corridor to his own room.

As his door clicked shut, Giselle turned to the stairs leading to the room where Araby had been attacked. She narrowed her eyes as she walked back to her suite. There was a great deal to tell Elliott; things were moving towards a conclusion rather too fast for her taste.

As she passed Aquilleia and Thorne's suite, she slowed and gave the door a sharp knock. It was almost immediately opened by Thorne, who nodded as she swept towards the room she shared with her husband. Thorne continued to watch until Giselle had entered the room and closed the door behind her.

Giselle quickly bolted the door, removed her jewellery, and placed it on the bedside table. Sitting on the edge of the bed, she unbuttoned her boots and then the real effort began.

Twisting her arms behind her, she began the painstaking process of taking off her evening gown and undoing her stays. She caught a fingernail on one of the fine lace panels; the tearing sound made her grimace and she swore to herself that, regardless of the peculiarities of their household, she would most definitely hire a maid in the next few weeks!

After much puffing and blowing, various smart remarks about Lilith's abandonment of her service, which she immediately regretted, and a definite straining of her stomach muscles, Giselle finally stood in the centre of the room clad in her chemise, bloomers, and stockings. She took in an unrestricted deep breath, scratched her ribcage with pleasure, and relaxed. Wrapping Elliott's dressing gown around her shoulders, she plumped up the pillows, settled herself on the bed, and began the process of contacting her husband to inform him of the evening's events.

○

Thorne and Aquilleia's Suite
11pm

Veronique appeared at the side of the bed and whined faintly. Thorne raised his head from the pillow and smiled at the Labrador. "That time, is it?"

As she whined again and patted the bed with her paw, Thorne climbed out of bed and threw on the clothes he had been wearing for the abortive dinner. He turned to look at his wife. "I need to take her out for her last trip. Will you be all right here, or shall I ask Giselle to—"

"I might just go to Giselle's room and see if she's all right," Aquilleia replied. "She said that she needed to contact Elliott alone, but it has been over an hour now."

Thorne smiled at Aquilleia as he lit the small lantern and

led the whining dog to the door. "We'll be right back." He paused. "Actually, all things considered, I think I should escort you to Giselle's room."

Aquilleia left the bed and put on her warmest peignoir, then the three of them headed to the suite Giselle shared with Elliott.

Thorne knocked on the door and waited. There was a faint clicking on the other side, then Giselle's voice. "Who is it?"

Thorne placed his mouth close to the door. "It's us."

The door moved a crack and a suspicious blue eye peered around the edge, then Giselle opened the door and tucked the small pistol in her dressing-gown pocket.

As the door clicked shut, Giselle gestured to the little sitting area by the drawn curtains. "I managed to contact Elliott; I asked him about Phoenixus…"

Thorne shared a glance with his wife. "What did he say?"

Giselle pulled her wrap around her shoulders. "His body has healed, but his mind is…" She sighed and made a helpless gesture. "Millennia of seeing what she did, fighting her, witnessing her evil while being unable to stop her, has left Phoenixus damaged. Some of the worst memories of Chymeris' brutality might have to be Unmade. Elliott told Abditivus of Mellior's gift. Abditivus wants to discuss the situation with him, but he believes that with time and patience Phoenixus *can* be saved."

Thorne let out his breath and shared a relieved look with Aquilleia. "That is excellent news. What did Elliott make of the identity of Filicidae?"

Giselle paused, then walked to the open bottle of champagne on the dressing table. "I don't know about you, but I definitely need a drink. It's been a very strange day."

She poured a glass of champagne and held it out to Aquilleia, who accepted it. Giselle raised her eyebrows at

Thorne, who shook his head with a smile. "I've already had one or two extra glasses, and Veronique would appreciate it if I were able to find my way through the front door to the garden and back without weaving! So, what did Elliott say about Filicidae?"

Giselle disappeared into the bathroom and returned with a tooth glass. She filled it and sat down opposite Aquilleia with a sigh. "I told him what Aquilleia had seen and who Fili- cidae was, and his exact words were 'Of course, who else could it be?' I hate it when he does that!"

Thorne smiled. "Did he suggest a plan of action?"

Giselle took a sip of her drink. "He asked us to be vigilant, and said we should keep an eye on young Leander." She shared a worried look with Thorne and his wife. "He is the only person here in whom Filicidae and their followers would be interested. Elliott will try and return as soon as possible." She looked at Aquilleia, "He knows things are moving quite fast, and he doesn't like it any more than I do."

Thorne leant across the settee and took possession of his wife's glass of champagne. Taking a hefty gulp, he then walked to the door. "I must take Veronique for her last perambulation of the day. Lock the door after us; I'll knock when we return."

Closing the door behind him, he waited until he heard the shooting of the bolt before leading Veronique down to the front door. As he pushed the door open, the chill blast from the darkness beyond made him shiver. He turned to look at Veronique with a raised eyebrow. "Are you sure you need to do this?"

Veronique whined softly as Thorne turned up the collar of his coat resignedly and the two of them headed out across the snow-covered drawbridge and down into the rose garden. They crossed the garden to an area more conducive to Veronique's personal requirements, with an expanse of lawn, thick hedges, and a rhododendron walk that led to the Burgoyne family mausoleum.

As Thorne and Veronique strolled down one of the dark little paths that was Veronique's favourite evening jaunt, Thorne thought through the events of the past few days and shook his head in disgust. Filicidae! Of all the creatures that could have escaped the Unmaking, why on earth did it have to be that? It had taken them months to track, and the truth of the creature's identity had devastated Tamassian. Thorne sighed. The taking of one's own life was a very rare occurrence amongst their people. Apart from Tamassian, he knew of only one other, and that had been Mellior's wife; the tragic loss of their son in such a hideous fashion had utterly destroyed her...

A sudden sound beyond the path caused Veronique to prick up her ears; she bounded from Thorne's side and disappeared into the thicket. Thorne waited on the path with a smile. The local rabbit population was about to find itself one short!

There was a rustling in the trees to his left, followed by a sudden high-pitched yelp that made his blood run cold.

Thorne immediately leapt into the undergrowth, the thick-leaved rhododendron bushes fighting him as he forced his way towards where the awful noise had come from.

He found himself in a small clearing. He raised his lantern and saw the dark outline of the Burgoyne family mausoleum, but before it a black furry shape lay still and silent on the snow-dusted grass.

Thorne's breath caught in his throat as he ran to Veronique's side. Placing the lantern next to her, he carefully turned her over. A bloody wound stretched from her left ear across the top of her brow and down onto her snout...a snout that was still moving in time with her breathing. Thorne took a shuddering breath, his heart pounding in his ears; she was breathing! It was laboured, but she was still breathing!

As Thorne placed his arms under her body to lift her, he heard a sound behind him. He turned, as a heavy weight struck his head, knocking him forward over Veronique.

There was silence, then a voice, sharp and cool. "Filicidae, bring him. Acolyte, bring the child, but leave the animal."

One of the figures in the clearing immediately moved to Thorne's side and crushed the guttering lantern beside him with one leathery foot. With no apparent effort, they lifted him and slung his silent form over their shoulder. The acolyte, garbed in a grey robe, walked to the mausoleum, unlocked the iron-bound door and disappeared within. After a few moments they reappeared carrying Leander Lees. The little boy lay limp in the acolyte's arms, the sleeping draught that had been forced upon him rendering him almost catatonic, as the Master walked towards the hidden door that led to the catacombs.

○

Giselle and Elliott's Suite
11:20pm

As the two friends sat in companionable silence with their drinks, Aquilleia lifted her champagne to her lips. Her eyes began to flicker from side to side, and with a gasp she dropped the glass. As the coupe smashed on the floor, she turned to face Giselle, her horrified eyes full of swirling silver light.

"It has him, Giselle! Filicidae has Shad!"

The Garden
11:25pm

In the damp, dark undergrowth by the mausoleum, Veronique slowly woke. The black Labrador whimpered softly as she blinked away the blood that had run from the deep wound into her brown eyes. In the dim light afforded by the snow, she made out the crushed shape of the lamp Thorne had been carrying; she sniffed at the ground where he had fallen and found a second scent...a scent of leather, and cruelty, and pain; a scent she remembered all too well from days long past. Realising what had taken Thorne, Veronique sat beside the lamp, threw back her head and howled.

She stood slowly, her legs wobbling as she made her way back and forth across the clearing, her nose pressed to the ground. Another scent, of sadness tinged with alcohol; another of pride and paper; and yet another...the scent of a terrified child.

Veronique stood still; her dark nose still pressed to the chill ground. She remembered when they had caught the creature in Astraea, and what she and the others had found... what it had done to its victims...

Growling, she turned back to her search. She paused at another scent she recognised: the scent of death. She followed it to the dark side of the mausoleum, where she discovered the body of Leander's nanny, Harriet Marshall.

Veronique pressed her sensitive nose against the young woman's cold hand, then sat down with a thump as a wave of nausea hit her. Turning her head slowly, she saw the narrow beginning of the stream that turned into Horseman Falls. Veronique padded to the water and dipped her head into its chill depths; the blood from her wound was washed away as the coldness of the water helped ease the pain in her head.

Taking several laps of the bitterly cold stream, Veronique moved back to the last place she had seen Thorne. Her eyes were clear now, her manner calmer, as she paced along the ground, following the scent to an old door that was not quite closed. Veronique worked her nose into the narrow gap and forced the door open.

As she entered the passageway beyond, she caught Thorne's scent. With a faint wag of her tail, she followed it into the dark.

○

The Inner Sanctum
11:50pm

The three figures made their way through the catacombs in silence. The grey-clad acolyte, clutching the slight form of young Leander to their chest with one arm, marched at the front as light-bearer, a flaming torch high above their head as they led the procession towards the ancient room of power where the old Master had received his teachings from Filicidae so many decades before. Second in line came the new Master, swirling black robes brushing the ground, wearing a look of supercilious pride as they swept along. Third came the creature Filicidae, carrying the unconscious Thorne.

The three entered the room of power, and the acolyte used their torch to light the four braziers surrounding the altar in the very centre of the cavernous room.

The Master snapped their fingers at the acolyte. "Bind the child and place them on the altar."

As the acolyte hurried to do their Master's bidding, the black-robed figure looked at Thorne with an unpleasant smirk. "Put him over there, Filicidae, out of the way; we will deal with him later."

The massive creature walked to the far side of the room where they dropped Thorne's body onto the cold stone floor. They paused, and reaching down a leathery, black-taloned hand, they turned his face to the flickering light and examined his pale features. Something about him was familiar, but the creature couldn't place it. Shaking their head, they made their way back to the altar where the Master stood.

Approaching the bound child, the creature began to giggle. The obscene laughter echoed around the cavernous room, increasing in strength as the little boy came to, woken from his drugged slumber by the sheer evil of the sound. Leander turned his head to look at the approaching figure and his blue eyes grew wide with fear as Filicidae smiled, needle-like teeth dripping as they reached towards the boy's neck—

"No!" The Master slapped Filicidae's hand. "Not yet. You know what must be done first."

Filicidae looked disgruntled but slowly stepped away from Leander. As the creature stood against the wall its eyes narrowed; there was something about the child that was also familiar...but again, they couldn't place what it was.

Filicidae flicked a glance at the Master before focusing its gaze on the child. The little boy was silent, lying deathly still on the altar and staring sightlessly at the ceiling. His fear had overtaken his senses, his mind hiding from what was happening around him.

The Master turned their attention to a small wooden chest sitting in a carved niche in the wall. They nodded at the acolyte, who hurriedly placed a silver salver covered with bay leaves on the altar. They fell to their knees and began to chant as the Master opened the chest and removed the glittering, jewelled knife that lay within. With a proud smile, the

Master presented the blade to the chanting acolyte and Fili-cidae, who both nodded encouragingly.

The Master turned back to the child on the altar and raised the curved blade high above their head. "Masters of the Inner Sanctum, Lords of Pain and Sorrow, behold my offering of flesh, and blood, and fear!"

A deep growl came from the shadows as Veronique slowly padded into the cave. The injured Labrador looked at the silent child on the altar, then the massive figure standing in the shadows on the opposite side of the room. Filicidae hissed as a dim, distant memory returned: of who the hound was, her connection to the man on the floor — and just how sharp her teeth could be!

The black dog turned back to the dark figure with the gleaming knife in its hand and continued to growl.

The Master glared at the injured dog and snapped their fingers at the kneeling acolyte. "Deal with that bitch!"

The grey-robed figure stood up and drew their ceremo-nial dagger. Veronique growled again, but this time the growl had a strange, echoing timbre. On the altar, Leander blinked. Waking from his stupor, he turned to stare at her and his terrified blue eyes were suddenly touched with a flickering white light. "Xenocyon!" he whispered.

The acolyte and the Master felt a deep shiver at the base of their spines as the black dog raised her hackles and slowly moved towards them. Veronique bared her teeth as she advanced, until she stood between the robed figures and the child.

The acolyte looked at their leader uncertainly. The Master again snapped their fingers and gestured at the dog. "Deal with it, or I shall deny you your truth!"

The acolyte's face set, they turned back to Veronique and again raised the blade.

Veronique raised her head and sniffed the air, the wound

on her temple reopened as she slowly turned her attention from the acolyte to the prone figure of Thorne huddled by the far wall. She stared at him, then flung back her muzzle and howled.

The acolyte smiled, they threw back their head and laughed in a mockery of the dog's distress. But their amusement disappeared as the dog's howl became a shockingly human scream of rage...Veronique snapped at the air before her; those were not the teeth of a Labrador!

As Veronique snarled, her brown eyes swirled with a deep-red light. The skin around her snout and muzzle stretched, the fur around her shoulders became thicker, her forelegs shortened, her paws became longer as her claws extended and her Otherness took over...

The acolyte dropped their knife and reached into their robe, their shaking fingers grasping desperately for the pistol they had used to frighten Marcus, but it was too late. Veronique launched herself at the grey-robed acolyte, her form increasing massively in size as she flew through the space between them and smashed the terrified follower to the ground.

The Master pressed themselves against the wall, their proud, pale face frozen in shock at this unexpected alteration to their plans. They staggered away, gazing in horrified fascination as the now fully changed battle hound's teeth ripped into the screaming acolyte's throat.

On the far side of the room, Filicidae watched the death of their youngest follower with both anger and visceral enjoyment. With a snarl, they made their way to the side of the Master, and grasping their arm, dragged the unprotesting figure towards one of the many passageways that led back to the castle.

As Filicidae dragged them away, the Master looked back as what had once been a docile Labrador viciously dispatched their assistant. Filicidae was right — now was the time to flee!

Turning in blind panic, the Master and Filicidae abandoned their follower to their fate and fled through the catacombs, pursued down the dark passages followed by the echo of the acolyte's dying screams.

Hearing something running towards them, Filicidae dragged the Master through a door on the left side of the passage, and swung it shut behind them. The Veronique threw herself at the barred door, tearing at it with her talons as the figures fled to the safety of the rooms above.

They came to a fork in the passageway; one branch led to a set of stone steps that disappeared into the upper regions of the castle, the other to a secret passage into the library. The Master turned to Filicidae. "I will continue upstairs. Make for your room, and meet me in my suite by your usual route as soon as you can; we need to talk about what has happened and change our plans. Take my robe; we left your clothes in the Sanctum." They hurriedly undid their robe and handed it to Filicidae before continuing along the secret passage that led to the library.

Filicidae made their way up the steps toward the passageway to the upper floors. As they made their way up several flights of stairs that would lead them to their floor, Filicidae considered whether or not to change back, before deciding to stay as they were…changing back to their human form would make their journey take far longer.

They draped the robe around them and pausing at the secret door that led into one of the empty suites on the fourth floor, they pressed their ear to it. Hearing no sound in the room beyond, they pushed the panel open, entered the room and crossed the dusty floor. Again, at the door they listened carefully, then hearing nothing, they opened it, entered the silent hallway and hurried to their room before returning to the Master's suite to discuss what had happened in the Inner Sanctum.

○

The Inner Sanctum
12:05am

Several floors below, beyond the flickering gaslights and the veneer of civilised behaviour, Thorne slowly returned to consciousness. As he pressed a trembling hand to his bloodied head, he heard the unmistakable laboured breathing of a dying man, which eventually stopped altogether.

Opening his eyes, he saw Veronique appear from a passageway and worry at what was now a corpse. He held out his hand and gently clucked at her. As she raised her head from her feeding and padded towards him, she began to lessen in size; as she reached Thorne's side, her tail wagged. He gently stroked her ears and wiped the more obvious gore from her chops, wincing at the pain from his wound, and smiled wryly. "We shall have to rinse you off before we walk back into the house, old girl; you'll terrify them into fits!"

He stood up slowly, swaying slightly as he caught his balance, and spotted the young boy strapped to the altar. "Let's get you somewhere safe, shall we?" He swiftly untied the leather straps and gathered the child into his arms.

The boy reached down to Veronique and gently stroked her bloodied fur. "Xenocyon." Thorne stared at the little boy; very few knew Veronique's real name...

As the child touched Veronique's injured head, a brilliant white light sparked from his fingers. Thorne gasped as the bloody wound on Veronique's temple began to knit. He looked at Leander's face; the child's eyes, usually a light blue, were pools of swirling white light as the young boy healed Veronique.

The little boy laughed delightedly, then looked up at Thorne and prodded him in the chest. "Shadavarian!" Thorne blinked in shock.

Then Leander slapped himself on the chest. "Tamassian!"

Thorne's green eyes filled with sudden tears: Tamassian! He wrapped his arms around the little boy, who clung to him in return, Leander's eyes glowing as Thorne's wounds healed at his touch.

Thorne took a deep breath as he stroked the child's hair. After so very long, they had found the last of their group. In Astraea, their small band of investigators had been considered the greatest, bravest, and most gifted; that was why they had been brought in to track down Filicidae. Versipellis had been investigator and leader, Shadavarian their investigator and rescuer, Xenocyon their tracker and battle hound, and Tamassian their healer...

For those who had died in Astraea and been reborn in this new world, it was always a fight for their other halves to find them. It was far better to discover them when they were still children, for children always remembered who they had been; no new life events had forced out the memories of who they were.

Thorne wiped the blood from his face, the ugly wound that had cut across his temple now healed. He looked down at the smiling child; the discovery of another who had been lost was something they would have to deal with later. Now, however, he was rather more concerned with getting them out of the catacombs safely.

He looked at the passageway that led up to the castle and turned to Veronique. "You know the way better than I; you find our route back to safety."

As Thorne lifted the burning torch from its bracket on

the wall, the now fully healed Labrador wagged her tail before pressing her nose to the floor and leading them from the Inner Sanctum. Dismissing the routes that carried the more recent scents of the Master and Filicidae, she led them back to the doorway that opened into the garden, beside the mausoleum.

○

The Library
12:20am

The Master hurried along the convoluted route that would lead them to the secret passage into the library. Pausing at the door, they carefully smoothed their clothes before stepping through. A tired-looking Ami was reading by the fireplace; she was so engrossed in her book that she hadn't realised she now had company.

The new arrival cleared their throat. "Good evening, Aunt Ami, you're up late."

The lady looked up from her book and smiled tiredly. "Hello, Araby, I didn't hear you come in." She held up her book. "With everything that has happened, I simply couldn't sleep, I'm afraid." She paused, concern on her strained face. "Are you well, my dear? You look quite flushed!"

Araby smiled comfortingly, her mind flying. She had hoped the library would be empty; the presence of her great-aunt was an issue she would have to deal with, and quickly!

She came up with and discarded several ideas before realising there was only one possible option. She walked to the fireplace and picked up the cast-iron poker. Weighing the sturdy length of wrought iron in her grip, she turned to face the elderly lady. "I'm absolutely fine, Aunt Ami...and I'm going to feel even better very soon!"

She advanced on her aunt, raising the poker, before swinging it at the elderly lady's head with all her strength—

A metallic clang rang out as the poker met the tang blade of Elliott's red Malacca sword stick. As Ami fell away from her great-niece in horror, Araby turned to gape at Elliott. He ripped the poker from her numb hand and threw it towards the fireplace.

He wagged his finger at her. "For shame, Miss Burgoyne! That is no way to treat a lady."

Araby smiled winsomely. "Why, Mr. Caine, whatever can you mean? I was simply about to..."

"Strike your great-aunt with a poker? Yes, Miss Burgoyne, we are quite aware of what you were about to do!"

She gave a light laugh. "I don't know what you—"

The library door opened and the company assembled: Cornelius, Merric, Mayberry, Giselle, Aquilleia, Thorne, Veronique, Luci, Sebastian, Theodora, Leander, Popplewell, and Davaadalai. Theodora was holding her son as though she would never again let him go, her dark eyes blazing as she glared at the young woman before her. Sebastian put a protective arm around his wife's shoulders as he looked at Araby; whose smile faltered as she saw the hatred burning in his eyes.

Elliott kept his blade poised as Thorne walked past the others and pushed Araby none too gently towards the door. As she passed Sebastian, Araby reached out to him. The young man jerked backwards, pulling Theodora and Leander away from the woman he once thought he had known, his expression a mixture of hate and disgust. Araby's face paled, and an expression appeared on her mobile face that Popplewell immediately recognised. He had seen it many times over the course of several centuries dealing with the Burgoyne family. Pride: savage, overwhelming, unreasoning pride.

Popplewell left the room and made his way down the servants' stairs to the ground floor. Entering the great hall, he looked around him before opening the narrow door that led into the under-stairs cupboard. Pausing only to light a candle stub and place it in a cobweb-covered lantern, he closed the door and walked to the back of the dusty, flotsam-filled storeroom. Reaching up he pulled an unseen lever; with a painful squeal, a portion of the back wall slowly swung open to reveal the dark beginnings of a spiral staircase.

Popplewell stared at the black hole that disappeared into the bowels of the castle for several long moments before walking into the gloom beyond. The secret panel swung shut behind him as he made his way towards his destination: a room he had hoped never to enter again.

○

The Lounge
12:45am

As everyone settled themselves, Elliott looked at the smirking young woman with a set face. "I will ask you once, Araby. Where is Filicidae?"

Araby's proud expression faltered as Elliott used the creature's real name; then her smile returned and she shook her head.

Elliott cast a glance around the room and frowned. Where was Popplewell?

Shaking his head slightly, he conferred with his wife, Thorne, and Aquilleia. After a few moments they came to an agreement, and he turned to the butler. "Davaadalai, please escort Miss Araby Burgoyne to her rooms, then return here.

Take Ellis and Poulson with you, and leave them to guard her door."

The butler turned to look at Cornelius and Merric, who both nodded. He bowed and turned to the still-smirking young woman. As he reached out his hand, she slapped it away. "Keep your filthy hands away from me! How dare you attempt to touch me, you revolting half-breed!"

A shocked silence fell. Davaadalai gritted his teeth and looked at Cornelius who had an expression of incandescent rage on his face, but it was Merric who addressed the butler. "Davaadalai, on behalf of my family, I apologise. I give you absolute permission to place your hands on my niece and escort her to her room, where you will lock the door and set a guard upon it." He looked at his niece with hard eyes. "You attempted to murder your own great-aunt, Araby. Why?"

Araby laughed; a touch of hysteria now evident as she glared at her family. "I have no regrets. What I have done, I did for the greater glory of the Inner Sanctum, and for the Teacher of the Masters of Cove!"

Elliott looked at the young woman and a faint green light appeared in his dark eyes. It vanished as he leant towards her. "And were you as proud when you and your accomplices murdered the children of Cove fifteen years ago?"

In the sudden, horrified silence, Luci shot from his chair, staring incredulously at Elliott. "No! No, that's not possible — it can't be!" He turned his eyes to Araby with a pleading look. "Araby, please say you didn't…please!"

Araby looked at him, a faint smile on her lips as she recalled the night so many years earlier when she had committed her first murder: poor little Timothy! She giggled at the memory as her family and friends stared at her in horror.

Luci fell back into his seat, and placing his head in his hands, he wept. Araby's smirk broadened into a smile of malicious delight as she watched the man who had called her a friend suffer the pain of his brother's death yet again.

Davaadalai blinked rapidly, his gaze sweeping from face to face as he tried to understand just what had been said. As his eyes fell upon Elliott's face, the butler thought he saw a green light appear in his eyes.

Merric held up his hand as he looked at his niece. His face was deathly pale, and his hand trembled, but his voice was firm. "Enough. I don't know who you are, Araby, but I know what I can do to begin healing our family." He drew himself up. "Araby Burgoyne, you are hereby cast out of this family. When the police come for you, we will not raise a hand to protect you or help you. Justice must be done for the innocent children whose lives you took; you are nothing to us now." He paused, and his voice was harsh. "Take her away!"

Davaadalai bowed again, took Araby's wrist in a firm grip, and dragged the now silent, white-faced young woman out of the room, followed by the two footmen.

As they left, Giselle shared a look with Aquilleia. "It might be an idea for at least two of the fairer sex to also stand guard at her door."

Elliott and Thorne looked at each other; they were unsure about this part of the plan. Baiting a trap was always a dangerous business, but their wives had insisted, and both Elliott and Thorne were well aware of the small but deadly pistols that both Giselle and Aquilleia currently kept in their reticules in case of a meeting with Filicidae. Giselle and Aquilleia also knew that if the creature made an appearance, they were to wound only, not kill. Elliott loathed the idea of either of them meeting the creature while he and Thorne were not there, but if this trap worked in flushing the creature out, it would definitely make things easier than the only possible alternative!

Elliott nodded briskly, his expression hiding his unease

and concern for both his wife and Thorne's. "Of course. You know what to do."

Giselle and Aquilleia swept out as Elliott faced the room. Thorne took a seat on the end of one of the settees, Veronique at his feet; Luci sat next to Thorne, his face desperately pale as the black Labrador gently pressed her nose into his hand; Sebastian, stunned, stood next to his seated wife, their young son dozing beside his mother; Cornelius and Merric sat on opposite sides of Ami, whose previously horrified expression had set into one of brittle anger; Dr Mayberry stood by the bar, a large whisky clutched in his hand as he stared at the others in the room.

Elliott cleared his throat and began. "Ladies and gentlemen, in spite of the lateness, or indeed the earliness of the hour, now is the time to reveal our discoveries regarding the murders here on the island. As you are now well aware, several weeks ago my friends and I were approached by Cornelius Burgoyne who, with Reverend Popplewell and Davaadalai, had made a chilling discovery: that of the mummified remains of Alistair Burgoyne, hidden in an oubliette in one of the sub-levels of the castle."

He surveyed the room. "We arrived as characters deliberately created with the intent of pushing Alistair's killer out into the open. That first night, we thought we had succeeded when Sybilla De Banzie reacted in such a dramatic fashion to our presence…but the following morning, both she and her husband Marcus were found dead." He bowed slightly to Ami. "I am very sorry for your loss, Mrs Burgoyne."

Ami nodded back as Cornelius and Mayberry stared at the floor, their agreement to keep Sybilla's and Marcus's sadistic practices from Ami sticking in their throats as they saw just how badly her step-granddaughter's passing had affected her.

Elliott patted gently at his cravat. "Almost immediately,

we found evidence pointing to a connection between the murders fifteen years ago and the crimes of the last few days. We realised that to solve the case, we had to understand how the most recent murders were intrinsically linked to the heinous murders committed on the island fifteen years ago, for linked they were. Therefore, we had to include those previous murders in our investigation."

In the utter silence of the room, Elliott's mind returned to the conversation they had had earlier. How on earth could he explain the reality of the murders when one of the guilty parties was an immortal killer who had the ability to turn into a monster? They would never be able to comprehend that — and it certainly wouldn't hold any weight with the local police, the judiciary, or the hangman! He sighed and rubbed his eyes. There might be a way; old evils die hard, and old hatreds die even harder...perhaps that was the best way to explain the events of the last fifteen years.

He turned to face the gathered guests. "Fifteen years ago, this island community was horrified by the sadistic murders of several children. But that is not the beginning of this case; for that, we must go back seventy-five years to the time of the old Master of Cove, Lord Thomas Burgoyne, to his debauched society, the Monks of Cove, and their secretive Inner Sanctum. This comprised men and women whose predilections for debauchery were not confined to just wine, women, and song; they were dedicated to the more inhumane crimes of torture, mutilation, and murder. Thanks in part to the knowledge of one who has been a party to the Burgoyne family history over many years, we were able to piece together a picture of the pride, malice, and sadism that runs through the Burgoyne family bloodline almost from its inception... The first victim of this stain was the first Earl of Cove, who was cursed by the abbot of the Abbey of Cove for his murder of the original monks. The abbot condemned him and his family line, decreeing that their blood be forever tainted with the madness of sadism — a taint that endures even today, as we have seen this evening!"

As his listeners digested this information, Elliott poured himself a drink. Davaadalai entered the room and addressed Merric. "My lord, as requested, I left both Ellis and Poulson to guard the door. Mlle Du'Lac and Mrs Thorne are across the hall, within sight of both footmen." He turned to Elliott. "Your wife asked me to bring you a message: 'We have checked, and they are not there.'"

Elliott nodded his thanks. So, the room was empty...it was only to be expected; if Filicidae had still been in their rooms it would have made everything too damned easy! Now, where could Filicidae be?

Ami frowned suddenly as she processed what she had just heard, then glared at her brother and Elliott. "When I first saw her, I said she looked like the opera singer Giselle Du'Lac!" She sat back in her bath chair with an aggrieved expression. "We will have words about this, brother!"

Cornelius nodded unhappily; Davaadalai walked to the bar and without a word poured him a double scotch.

Elliott tugged at his suddenly tight cravat. "Then we were presented with an incredible piece of information: a set of photographs from the murders fifteen years ago, showing a level of brutality and evil that we had only witnessed once before. Several years ago, my friends and I were part of an investigation that uncovered a murderer who referred to themselves as 'Filicidae'. The appalling images, which I will not detail here, left us in no doubt as to the killer's identity, since the methods of mutilation and murder were exactly the same. We realised that we were dealing with the killer we had stalked all those years before."

Sebastian spoke, his demeanour quiet as he stood beside his wife and their sleeping child. "Then if you had already caught this killer…this Filicidae before, you must know what they look like? Surely, if their crimes had left such an indelible imprint, you recognised them at once when you arrived?"

Elliott turned to face the young man. Thorne chimed in, leaning back in his seat. "I'm afraid not: Filicidae was known for their gifts in the art of disguise. When we caught them, they were wearing brown and red face paint and a bearskin complete with teeth. Needless to say, they were not exactly sane!"

He shared a look with Elliott; he had described exactly what Filicidae looked like, merely omitting the fact that they were immortal, could change between their human and Other form at will, possessed razor-sharp teeth and claws, and were well over seven feet tall. Other than those few details, it was the truth.

Elliott took a deep breath, but before he could speak, Dr Mayberry raised his voice. "You said Araby was the killer, and now you say this person, Filicidae, is. Which is it?"

Elliott caught Thorne's eye: so far, so good. He addressed the glowering doctor. "Both, I'm afraid, Dr Mayberry. You were the doctor here at the time of the murders, were you not?"

Mayberry nodded. "Aye…what of it?"

Elliott ignored the pugnaciousness that accompanied the doctor's response. "Would you name the victims for us, doctor?"

Mayberry blinked. "Well…the first was young Vanessa Carter. She was eleven. She'd been playing clock golf on the bluff above the waterfall; that was where she was found. Then there was…"

He glanced at Luci, who was staring at the Persian rug, his empty eyes and blank expression a far greater worry to Mayberry than any explosion of emotion. Mayberry continued. "Timothy Lutyens, he was the youngest...only six. He was found by his brother in the glade where the children played—"

"He was late for supper..." Luci's voice was husky. "I told him to be home by six o'clock...when he wasn't home by seven, I went looking for him. I met..." He clenched his teeth. "I met Araby on the footpath to the castle; she said they had been playing in the glade and she'd left to visit Popplewell..." He looked up at Elliott, his eyes tortured. "She told me where he was — she knew I would find him and see what they had done to him!" He covered his face and began to weep, deep sobs racking his thin frame. Ami hurriedly wheeled her bath chair to his side, and wrapping her arms around him, she held him tightly.

Mayberry emptied his glass, which was silently refilled by Davaadalai, and cleared his throat. "Then there was young Hugo Fletcher, who was eleven. He'd been down on the beach, searching the rock pools. He was found in the bathing machine."

Elliott caught Thorne's eye; that explained why the machine had been abandoned.

"James Kelly, was only seven; he was found in the ruins of the Abbey, where he'd been playing. George Smith—"

Dr Mayberry's voice cracked; his knuckles were white on his glass as he tried to compose himself, his eyes wet. "George Smith, nine years old, was found on the path between the castle and the village...he was the son of my partner, Dr Leonard Smith." He looked at Elliott. "It killed Leonard and his wife Mary; they were both gone within a year of their boy."

He took a shuddering breath. "Little Edith Granger was ten, and she was found in the harbour three days before Christmas. Then there was Jane Parsons..."

A sob escaped Ami; she closed her eyes as Mayberry

gently patted her arm. "Ami found her under the Christmas tree, just over there in the great hall." He paused. "And then there was Araby."

Elliott shook his head. "No, Dr Mayberry. Then there was Alistair."

Merric stared at him, incredulous. "Are you saying that Araby killed all these children, and her own brother?"

Elliott nodded. "That is exactly what I'm saying."

"But why? And how? He wasn't a child like the others; he was a sturdy young man of fifteen!"

"With respect, Merric, your nephew's head was crushed on one side. An unexpected blow, even by a child, could have taken Master Alistair by surprise. As he fell, he would have been vulnerable to a further attack and it is also likely that the impact from being rolled into the oubliette wouldn't have helped."

Merric shook his head stubbornly. "I disagree. He just wouldn't have been an easy target for a little girl!"

Elliott held up an admonitory finger. "A little girl working with the assistance of Filicidae, who I can assure you is more than capable of killing an adult. And they had the assistance of one other."

Merric blinked. "Who?"

Elliott smiled, his canines flashing. "All in good time, my lord."

Melisandre shook her head, her face deathly pale. "But the attack on Araby in her rooms…she couldn't possibly have attacked herself." She looked at Elliott in horror, "Or did one of her helpers do that to her?

Ami glared at them; her arms still wrapped around Luci. "I think it's obvious!"

Cornelius frowned. "I don't understand…"

Ami nodded firmly. "It was her: the Nightwitch!"

Mayberry pressed a hand to his forehead. "Ami, nae that again!"

Ami glared at him. "We know she comes for Burgoynes who turn to evil; why couldn't it be her? The injuries to Araby's back and arms were caused by razor-sharp claws — they were far too deep to have been caused by human nails!"

Mayberry shook his head, then caught Davaadalai's expert eye. The butler provided him with another refill, topping up Cornelius's glass as he returned the nearly empty decanter to the bar, then he left the room and walked swiftly to the kitchens.

As he entered, the servants who were still up stared at him. Ami's elderly maid Edith Parker was sitting next to a weeping Rose who had been told about the death of her cousin, Harriet. Edith put her hands on her hips. "Well?"

Davaadalai fetched a bottle of whisky and placed it on the scrubbed kitchen table, then poured himself a large glass of cooking brandy and downed it in one. He looked at the silent servants. "Fifteen years ago, the children — all of them — were killed by Araby."

As he picked up the bottle of whisky, he looked at the servants in the room and paused. "Do we have any idea where Mrs Burnthouse is?"

Edith looked at the others. "I don't know; we haven't seen her since before dinner. Tonight was her evening off, so she should be in her room."

Davaadalai nodded and hurried back to the lounge, leaving the servants staring silently at each other until Edith turned and wiped the tears from Rose's face. "Come on, my girl...kettle on."

As he walked back into the lounge, Davaadalai paid attention to the conversation. He had missed a few minutes of the denouement, but after some listening, he deduced that they had been continuing their discussion of the improbability of the Nightwitch being real and attacking Araby. Ami was adamant. "It was her — it had to be her! What else could have created such injuries?"

Cornelius leant forward, his face deathly pale. When he spoke, his words came slowly, as though afraid to leave his lips. "My dear, Araby's injuries were consistent with some of the injuries to the other children..." He turned to look at Elliott. "Is it possible that this Filicidae attacked Araby? Had Araby realised what they were doing was wrong? Did she try to escape their clutches?"

Elliott shook his head. "Araby knew it was wrong, Cornelius, but she enjoyed it! She would never stop; not when she had the attentions of her teacher, Filicidae, and the support of one who hero-worshipped her."

Ami pursed her lips. "Who?"

Elliott looked at the people in the room for one long moment. "The late Perry Challick."

There was a horrified silence; Ami gasped and pressed a hand to her mouth.

"Perry!" blurted Cornelius. "But — but the boy was a child; he was only eight when the children were killed..." His eyebrows met over his nose as he stared at Elliott. "What do you mean, 'the late'?"

Elliott was careful not to look at either Thorne or Veronique. "Down in the Temple of the Inner Sanctum, when Araby and Filicidae fled, Perry Challick chose to fight when he should have submitted."

Cornelius shook his head as Ami wiped a tear from her cheek. "We knew him from a child," she said. "What power could possibly have made him join Araby in committing these heinous acts?"

An opening – perfect! Elliott hid his relief. "A very good question, Ami. There was another in their group: one whose presence connected them to the crimes of eighteen-twenty-five, the crimes of fifteen years ago, and the most recent murders on Cove Island."

Ami shook her head, clutching Luci's hand. "But there's no one — a follower from the Inner Sanctum would be over one hundred years old now!"

Elliott shook his head gently. "No, Mrs Burgoyne…the youngest member of the Inner Sanctum would be only ninety years of age."

Ami looked aghast. "But there's only one person here of that age…"

Elliott nodded. "Indeed: Nanny Wyke!"

Cornelius looked sick. "She was a part of the Inner Sanctum; she was forgiven because of her age…"

"Yes," said Elliott. "Nanny, or Nannette Wyke, to use her full name, was indeed a member of the Inner Sanctum. She was nearly sixteen when the Master was killed, but she was not a naïve, easily indoctrinated child. No, Nannette Wyke was an enthusiastic and dedicated accomplice of Thomas Burgoyne." Elliott paused. "Not least because he did not teach her the abuses they inflicted on others; but because *she* taught *him*. She was the true Master of the Inner Sanctum, a secret of which only one or two within that small group were aware. The truth was denied to the families of the victims they murdered."

Ami pressed her hand to her lips. "Oh, God! Poor Popplewell!" She raised her teary eyes to Elliott's face. "How much of this does he know?"

Elliott's face was set. "Everything."

○

Beneath the Castle
1:10am

Deep in the bowels of the castle, beyond labyrinthine dark corridors, a figure bearing a candle approached a series of pitch-black rooms that had been hidden to nearly all memory. What had begun so many years ago must now be finished.

They paused before a sealed door, the edges of which seemed to blur into the wall. The figure gently ran a finger along the door handle, their finger leaving a faint blue trail as with a click, the door opened to their touch.

The room beyond was dark and deathly quiet, the utter lack of sound unnatural. The figure padded silently across the room, their memories of that place enough to remind them of where they had left everything on that night, fifteen years ago.

Sickened by the murders on the island, in the desperate belief that the killer could not possibly have been a Burgoyne child of such young years, and horrified by the thought that their creation may have tried to kill an innocent, they had sealed it into this hidden tomb on the night Araby had been attacked in her room. For the last fifteen years they had willed themselves to believe that the unknown killer had attacked her…when the truth was far, far worse.

The figure sighed. Their guilt at the actions of what they had created had eaten away at them for years…and now, to discover they had been right all along…

Placing their lantern on the small, round stone table in the centre of the room, the figure paused as a faint blue light began to emanate from a plain stone sarcophagus in the darkest corner. The soft light pulsed like a heartbeat in the tiny chamber as Popplewell approached the unmarked grave and raised his glowing hand.

"Awaken!"

Araby's Suite
1:15am

As the door closed behind her, Araby sat on the edge of her bed. So dear Merric thought he could cast her out of the family without any effort. He would soon find out just how wrong he was!

She smirked; they might know that she had murdered her brother and the other children fifteen years earlier, but they couldn't prove any of it. She considered the best way to play the situation to her advantage; the easiest way might be to push the idea that the family had always been against her... perhaps something along the lines of how her uncle, great-uncle, and great-aunt had never really liked her, and had set about trying to prove her guilty to get rid of her — or perhaps they were actually the killers and were trying to blame her to cover their own guilt?

Araby's smile widened. She could wrap any number of people around her little finger, and by the time she was finished they'd believe the queen herself was more likely to have committed the murders than poor little poverty-stricken Araby Burgoyne. Then she would deal with Gruncle and the rest of her damned family when they least expected it!

She giggled and wrapped her arms around herself with a happy sigh. They thought they could stop her, but they were very, very wrong. Nothing could stop her, not with the blood of her ancestors pulsing through her veins. They demanded fealty, loyalty, and blood, and she would give those offerings to them by the barrel!

She walked to the drinks tray on her dressing table and poured herself a large brandy. Taking a gulp of the burning liquor, she recalled how well Theodora had brushed off her attempts to take Sebastian. Araby sneered; she had decided early on that killing Theodora and getting her out of the way would be best, but had discarded the plan for fear that Sebastian might mourn her.

Her other plan had seemed better; kill Theodora's father and brother so that Sebastian and Theodora would inherit the family business, then pay Theodora off and take Sebastian for herself. Araby pouted; it had been such a good plan until that bitch Theodora had exposed her to Sebastian. Now she would just have to kill them all and make a new future without them.

She sat on her bed and gave some thought to her current predicament. Perhaps waiting for her family to present information to the police was a mistake; Filicidae's destruction of the telephone and telegraph had been a very sensible decision! They couldn't telephone for the police, they couldn't drive to the mainland because the causeway was still under water, and they couldn't contact Mossy to bring his boat. They would have to wait until past eight o'clock in the morning before the causeway was passable, then drive to Penwithiel to contact the useless Sergeant Hollis. Araby smiled and tapped her lips thoughtfully; that left nearly seven hours in which a great deal of planning could be done!

As she sat on her bed, a faint sound came to her ears and she frowned. She turned, and thought she saw a flicker of movement out of the corner of her eye.

Araby suddenly felt cold. As she rubbed her hands briskly up and down her arms, she heard the sound again, it was the sound of someone humming. As she strained to hear, the voice broke-off and gently crooned. "I know what you did…I saw what you did!"

Araby's breath stuttered down her throat as she turned to the end of the bed. Thick, hair-covered fingers were inching from the secret passage that opened through the panelled bookshelves. As the creature pulled itself through the hidden doorway, it smiled at her, bristling teeth dripping.

Araby gazed at the approaching horror and shook her head. "Put your normal face on. We have plans to make and though I enjoy our playtimes with you as Filicidae, you know I can't talk to you about boring, serious things when you look like that!"

Filicidae glared at her, then began to change. Cracking bones, snapping ligaments, and laboured breathing were the only sounds as slowly, painfully, the creature returned to their usual appearance.

Araby smiled as the changed figure tottered towards her, dropping the black robe she had lent them onto the bed. The naked figure struggled into the night attire they had remembered to bring with them before sitting down carefully in the wicker chair by the dressing table. As the figure settled into the cushioned seat, they giggled. "It was just a bit of fun. Well, my dear, we must think carefully. They know about you… but they may not know about your plans for the family."

Araby poured another glass of brandy and handed it to the figure before her. "You're right, Nanny, we have to move very fast. Now that they know about the fun I…that is to say, *we* had, fifteen years ago, I think we will have to finish things tonight before they get the chance to tell anyone else…we can't allow them to destroy our plans. Between the two of us, though, I think we can kill everyone in the house and dispose of them…it will just take a little careful planning."

Nannette Wyke raised her glass to her young protégée,

and an ugly smile appeared on her thin lips. "But this time I get the child…"

Araby smiled in response; her expression no less unpleasant than Nanny's. "Of course, and I shall deal with the mother!"

Nanny took a sip of her drink. "I did say, my dear, that we should have seen to her years ago!"

"Yes, Nanny, you did. I just didn't want her to become the perfect ghost, always there in the background." She sighed. "It's a shame about Sebastian, but I suppose it can't be helped."

Nanny leant forward and patted Araby's hand with a pale, wrinkled paw. "There-there, my dear. It's for the best, I'm sure. Would you like me to see to him for you?"

Araby took a sip of her drink and shook her head. "No, thank you, Nanny; I have something rather special planned for Sebastian…"

Nanny tittered again. "There are four rather delicious possibilities just outside the door, my dear…perhaps we should start with them?"

Araby shook her head with a smile. "No, Nanny…if we use the secret passage that links this room to the dining room, we can be amongst them before they realise their doom is upon them!"

She paused and the smile slid from her face as she thought about what had happened earlier. "Down in the temple, Nanny, what was that thing? That…dog? If it was a dog."

Nanny frowned at her drink as the memory of what she had felt in the temple came back to her. She shook her head. "I'm not too sure, my dear, but I think it comes from the same place as I do."

Araby nodded thoughtfully. "That would suggest that her

owner, Thorne, that bastard who claimed to be Alistair, and their wives are perhaps…similar?"

Nanny shrugged. The effect was frighteningly normal; an elderly lady sitting in her nightgown sipping brandy, with no sign of what lay beneath her thin, translucent skin. "I really couldn't say, my dearest. I know them, both the people and the dog…and the child too; but I can't say from where."

"We'll find out sooner or later, I suppose." Araby smiled at the elderly lady. "Remember all those years ago, when I caught you killing Luci's whiny little brother and I asked you to teach me?"

Nanny tittered. "Oh yes, my dear…you are the best and most apt pupil I have ever taught, and I include your dear great-great-grandfather in that!"

A faint pinkness came to Araby's pale cheeks. "Oh, Nanny!"

She settled back in her chair, a happy smile on her face, then took a sip of her drink and sighed. "It was so lovely that they sent me to the mainland under your care…all those lovely trips to visit the other children who were sent from Cove." She and nanny shared an ugly smile as they remembered the work they had continued on the mainland. The elderly lady nodded. "When one starts something, one must always finish it. Out of all the children of Cove, only you and Sebastian are left…now that we have lost Perry."

Araby nodded sadly. "Poor Perry just wasn't up to snuff, was he?" She finished her drink and refilled their glasses, then gave Nanny an arch look. "A suggestion: I know you want the child, but perhaps instead of killing him, we could keep him and train him to be like us." She ignored the pout that appeared on the elderly lady's face and continued. "Remember, we brought Perry into our playtime when he was eight years old. Leander is only six; it might not be that difficult to encourage any — abilities he might have."

Nanny narrowed her rheumy blue eyes and nodded. "It has possibilities." A dull red light appeared in Nanny's eyes. "And if he does not conform, we will have to break him."

Araby sat down with an evil smile. "Perhaps, if we kill his mother in front of him, that will break his mind — and then we can rebuild it to suit our purpose!"

Nanny raised her glass with a smile. "I'll drink to that, my dear!"

○

The Lounge
1:30am

The inhabitants of the lounge were sitting in tired contemplation of the events of the last few days when their thoughts were rudely interrupted by a sudden peal from the bell in the barbican.

Cornelius leapt to his feet and stared at the door as Davaadalai smoothed his waistcoat and walked towards it. "Who in God's name could it be at this hour?"

He sat back down with a thump and poured himself another cup of tea, then raised the teapot to his sister, who shook her head. Cornelius was about to insist that she have a cup of tea to warm her, but paused as Davaadalai entered the room, closely followed by a tall, elegant man he didn't recognise.

"His Excellency, the Comte de Us-Otiosus," Davaadalai intoned.

Cornelius blinked as Merric stood up. "Who?"

Elliott stood up. "I took the liberty of inviting someone who must be here to bear witness to the capture of the killer who has terrified this island for so long." He shook the gentleman's hand before turning to Merric. "May I present our dear friend, Comte Abditivus de Us-Otiosus? Abditivus, this is Lord Burgoyne of Cove, his aunt, Amicarella Burgoyne, and his uncle, Cornelius Burgoyne."

"My lord, madam, gentlemen, my pleasure." The dark newcomer shook hands with both men before turning to Thorne with a smile. "My dear Abernathy, it has truly been far too long. Xenocyon, how lovely it is to see you as well." The delighted Labrador received a great deal of attention before Abditivus shook hands with a smiling Thorne. He looked at the two men. "And where are Giselle and Aquilleia?"

"They are keeping a watch at Araby's door." Elliott sighed. "It's been rather a mess, my friend."

Abditivus nodded. "I don't doubt it!"

There was a faint cough from the door. "It's been a long time since I heard that voice."

Abditivus turned as Popplewell entered the room. The two men greeted each other warmly as Cornelius looked on, his head swivelling from his old friend back to the newcomer, his expression nonplussed as he tried to understand how the two men could possibly know each other.

Mayberry leant towards and muttered, "I have a question!"

Merric looked at the frowning man. "Oh?"

"Aye! The causeway is under water and the telephone line is down, so just where on this green earth did that fancy gentleman arrive from?"

Merric frowned, then turned to look at the tall man chatting so familiarly with Popplewell. He nodded slowly. "And how does he know Popplewell?"

○

The Kitchen
2:10am

Davaadalai yawned tiredly as he made another pot of tea. He had no idea where Mrs Burnthouse was, but after the previous day's events, if she turned up married with a slew of children behind her he wouldn't blink. He just wished she was there to help him deal with the kitchen! He sighed as he swilled the pot out; if she hadn't returned by breakfast time, that would make for a very interesting morning!

As he measured a heaped teaspoon of tea into the pot, the heavy curtain across the door to the servants' staircase billowed out as the door was pushed open from the other side. Davaadalai glared as the boot boy, Martin, slid into the room. The young lad swallowed hard. "Uh, mornin' Mr Davaadalai, sir. I thought that as there's a lot of work to do, I'd get in early like and see to it."

Davaadalai waved a hand and returned to his teapot as Martin hurriedly cut a wedge of bread for his breakfast. Davaadalai looked at Martin, then turned to the hidden door that led to the servants' quarters. He blinked, then the china teapot smashed on the floor as Davaadalai ran out of the kitchen and sprinted to the lounge. Arriving in the doorway, he looked at Cornelius. "There's a secret passage in the room Araby's in!" he blurted. "I've only just remembered!"

Elliott and Thorne swore violently as they ran up the stairs to Araby's suite, followed rapidly by Veronique. Arriving at the door, they were greeted by Ellis and Poulson, both still awake and on guard. To the relief of both Elliott and Thorne, Giselle and Aquilleia were also awake and safe on the opposite side of the passage.

Ellis opened his mouth, but Elliott held a finger to his

lips, then beckoned to the two footmen, nodded at the suite of rooms where Araby was being held, and dropped his voice to a whisper. "Has anyone tried to get in?"

Ellis shook his head. "No sir. But it's a bit strange…"

Elliott looked at him sharply. "Strange? How so?"

Ellis shrugged. "It sounds like she's talking to someone in there, but no one's got past us."

They were joined by Giselle and Aquilleia, and Elliott explained their concerns about the secret passage. Davaadalai joined them, and Elliott looked at the butler. "Do you know where the secret passage from that suite leads?"

Davaadalai looked at him, an expression of deep concern on his face. "It leads everywhere! It disappears into the walls and joins with other passageways that lead into other rooms and cupboards. It's a rabbit warren!"

Thorne swore as Merric and Abditivus joined them, followed by Cornelius, puffing heavily. The elderly man was joined by Dr Mayberry, who looked at him with a very judgemental expression. "Gout!" he pronounced.

Cornelius wagged his finger at the doctor as he got his breath back. "Good food, good wine, and good cheer are all I have left at my age, Mayberry, and you're not taking that from me!"

Thorne shushed them and hurriedly explained the situation. Davaadalai looked at Cornelius and cleared his throat. "Shall I retrieve your blunderbuss, sir?"

"Yes, thank you, Davaadalai."

As the butler headed to Cornelius's suite, Elliott held up a warning hand. "Gentlemen, if Filicidae is in there with Araby, please do not kill them — the paperwork can be rather an issue! If you must loose your weapon, aim to incapacitate. Agreed?"

Merric nodded. Both Cornelius and Mayberry looked

slightly disappointed, but grudgingly signalled their agreement.

Davaadalai returned, handing the blunderbuss to Cornelius and a second firearm to Merric, who looked at him with a raised eyebrow. Davaadalai bowed. "Just in case, my lord."

As Elliott and Thorne edged away from the rest of their group, Thorne whispered, "I take it you are armed with something more than that blessed sword stick?"

Elliott grinned, his canines flashing as he lightly patted his breast pocket. "You?"

Thorne grinned back and removed a well-polished revolver from his own pocket. Across the hallway, Giselle and Aquilleia removed their pistols from their reticules.

The two men crept towards the door. As they reached it, they could hear Araby's voice on the other side. Elliott placed his hand on the key and nodded at Thorne. "Ready? One... two...three!"

He twisted the key in the lock and flung the door open. They rushed in and Elliott saw Nanny. He raised his gun. "Filicidae, stay where you are!"

Thorne trained his weapon on Araby as Cornelius and Merric pushed their way into the room behind them. Merric looked at Nanny, who smiled back at him through rheumy eyes. He turned to Elliott. "For God's sake, man! You said Filicidae would be here."

Nanny tittered. "And they are..."

Her change earlier had been slow...this time it was hideously swift; the harsh snapping of her bones was almost drowned by the creature's guttural screams as her pink flannel nightdress was ripped into shreds by her rapid transformation.

Filicidae leapt from the edge of the settee and ran towards Elliott, blackened talons reaching for his throat. A sharp retort was followed by the bitter, stinging odour of gunpowder as Thorne fired his revolver. A splash of red suddenly appeared on Filicidae's shoulder as the creature turned and ran to the secret passage. Throwing the door open, they fled into the dark corridor beyond.

Merric stared at Elliott, his face deathly pale. "I don't understand...what in God's name was that thing?"

Elliott looked at Araby's laughing face. "Davaadalai, take her and lock her in a room with no secret passages; I will leave the choice of room to your discretion. The rest of you, come with me; we need to gather everyone in a room that the creature cannot infiltrate. Davaadalai, which of the main rooms have no secret passages?"

Davaadalai thought. "The lounge, sir...no passages lead to that room."

"Right, we need everyone in that room, including the servants, while we work out how to flush Filicidae out."

Merric pushed past Thorne and grasped Elliott by the arm. "Answer my question! What was that...that thing?"

The young lord's anger faltered as green light swirled in Elliott's eyes. "That, my lord, was Filicidae, an immortal creature of murderous appetites that feeds off the pain it causes. It has followed this family for years, and we must end its existence tonight!"

◯

The Lounge
Ten minutes later

Cornelius walked to the bar and poured a large whisky with shaking hands. He was joined by Merric, who did the same before addressing Elliott.

"I'm sure you understand that this is quite a thing to be asked to believe…It seems utterly impossible!"

Cornelius nodded, his usually ruddy face pale. "I have hunted many times, but not for a being such as this. How do we flush it out?"

Elliott looked at him with a grim expression. "The same way we did the last time; we set and bait a trap!"

Melisandre shook her head, her blue eyes huge, as Merric sat next to her and took her hand. "But how? What would such a hideous creature want?"

Thorne looked at her, his face pale. "The same thing it wanted when we searched for it many years ago. A child — and there is only one on the island!"

The room fell silent as everyone turned to look at Sebastian, who was sitting by the fire. He raised his eyes as Elliott placed a gentle hand on his shoulder. "I dread to ask this of you and your wife and son, but there is no other way."

Sebastian looked up at him, his face set in stern lines. "I am loth to expose my son to more horror — but if it will prevent that bitch and her creature from harming anyone again, I agree to your request. We must ask Theodora first; if her answer is no, we must abide by it."

Elliott nodded. "Understood. Let us ask her now."

Elliott, Thorne, and Sebastian walked quickly to the far side of the lounge, where Theodora was sitting with her son. Leander smiled at them from his seat at the table, where he was tucking into a hearty feast of bread and strawberry jam.

Theodora looked at her husband with a set expression. "Well?"

Elliott stepped forward. "I'm afraid it isn't yet over, Mrs Lees. As I explained earlier, Araby had another helper besides young Perry. We need your help, and the help of your son, to stop this creature from killing again and again."

There was a faint cough from behind them. Abditivus

bowed his head to Theodora and Sebastian before addressing Elliott. "My friend, I trust you know what you are doing?"

Elliott nodded. "I certainly hope so!"

He turned back to the silent young woman. "Mrs Lees, do you agree?"

The silence lasted for many minutes before she spoke. "Before I agree, I need to know exactly what you want him to do." She turned to Sebastian. "Know this, husband: if anything happens to our son, I will hold you responsible."

Sebastian nodded, a look of shame on his face, then turned to Elliott and Abditivus. "Will you give my wife and I a little time alone, please?"

"Of course."

As the three men walked away, Elliott turned to Thorne. "We must ask Davaadalai if they have anything like a net in the castle…if not, we might be able to borrow a net from one of the fishermen."

Thorne raised an eyebrow. "That would mean some of us heading into the village…in the dark! It may be safer to stay here and make do!"

The two men reached the settee where Giselle and Aquilleia were sitting with Veronique. Abditivus poured several cups of tea as they discussed their plans for the demise of Filicidae.

The Thirteenth Floor
2:45am

The small figure, clad only in his oversized nightshirt, crept along the dim passageway. He clutched his most treasured tin soldier in one hand and an ornate walking cane in the other as he approached the narrow spiral staircase leading to the chapel, the observatory, and the roof garden beyond.

There was a sudden movement in the darkness behind him as Nanny stepped out and smiled at the young boy, her billowing black robe covering her from ankle to neck. A faint trickle of drool appeared at the corner of her smiling lips as she cast a quick glance down the dark corridor. All was silent: perfection. "Now, young man, what are you doing out of bed so far past your bedtime?"

Leander gripped his tin soldier and looked back down the corridor behind him. He looked at Nanny and whispered, "I wanted to show my soldier the chapel gardens…"

Nanny nodded in a conspiratorial manner. "So, you decided to leave your room for a little adventure?"

Leander nodded. "Yes… Mama wouldn't let me go to the chapel, but I heard about the garden. I've never seen a garden that wasn't on the ground before."

Nanny became aware of the strand of drool dripping off her chin and hurriedly wiped it away. "I might be able to help you, young man. You need someone to help guide you. If anyone asks, you were helping an elderly lady see the garden one last time before she leaves the castle tomorrow. Agreed?"

Leander nodded happily as the elderly lady offered him her arm. Linking elbows, they made their way towards the spiral staircase at the far end of the corridor.

Helping the puffing, doddery lady up the narrow stairs, the little boy guided her towards the chair by the two steps leading into the consecrated room beyond. Nanny sat down with a happy sigh and watched Leander run up the two steps that led to the chapel door. Her smile widened as the little boy pushed fiercely against the doors but could not open them. She settled into her seat as she watched him; a frown suddenly touched her wrinkled face; there *was* something familiar about him — she shook her head; no, it was gone.

As Leander lay on the floor and peeked under the chapel door, Nanny licked her lips; Araby may have wanted to break the boy in to replace Perry, but Araby wasn't there to stop her...and accidents did happen.

Nanny smiled as she began to consider just what she would do to the boy first...

A sixth sense made the child turn; as he caught her expression, his eyes widened in fear.

Nanny laughed, the sharp tang of anticipated pleasure moving under her skin as she stood up and walked towards the trembling child.

Leander dropped his tin soldier, unsheathed the sword stick, and brandished the gleaming blade at the elderly lady, who raised her eyebrows in response. She wagged a finger at Leander. "Now, now, young man...this is no way to treat a lady, especially an elderly one." She laughed as the child slashed at the air with the blade. "How sweet: you actually think that will stop me."

Leander shook his head as he looked up at the elderly lady. "It is over, Filicidae."

Nanny smiled and shook her head. "It is never over, young man." A faint frown creased her face, "How do you know my name?"

Leander stepped away. Keeping a tight grip on the sword stick, he watched her...and began to change. His blond hair began to darken and curl, his limbs stretched, and the snapping sounds of his thickening joints echoed in the corridor as the child Leander was replaced by the grim form of Elliott. He stood in the middle of the corridor clad only in his nightshirt, his sword stick gripped in his hand. "Surrender, Filicidae...it *is* over."

Nanny shook her head. "I recognised you and your friend...I wasn't sure how I knew you, but I only recognised that infernal dog after it attacked Perry!" She shrugged, the thick black robe rippling as she moved her shoulders. "Never mind...where you came from can't be as important as where I'm going to send you!"

She stood and gently flexed her wrinkled fingers, an evil smile twisting her thin lips. "I'll see your change, young man...and I'll raise you mine!"

The movements that rippled her robe increased in speed as the elderly woman's face began to split; thick tufts of rust-coloured hair sprouted through the cracks in her skin as Nanny's Other appeared.

Elliott raised his voice. "Thorne, Davaadalai — now!"

The door to the chapel was suddenly flung open and the two men, joined by Cornelius, Merric and Abditivus, appeared on the threshold. Thorne and Davaadalai were armed with a net from the under-stairs cupboard, the tightly woven lengths of knotted rope stretched between them.

Nanny flung back her head and laughed, the sound a grotesque liquid gurgle as her massive black eyes met the horrified gaze of Cornelius and Merric.

Cornelius blenched as the tottering form of Nanny changed before him; he swung the blunderbuss up to his shoulder.

Elliott threw up his hand. "Cornelius, no! If you kill it here, we will never be rid of it! Thorne, Davaadalai, rope her!"

Davaadalai took one look at the creature and froze; in a split second of horror, his mind gave him a name from his faith: Rakshasi! Gritting his teeth, he leapt forward with Thorne and the two men threw the net over the thrashing and screaming form of Filicidae. They were joined by Veronique, who had listened grudgingly to Thorne's polite suggestion about not changing fully in front of the family, and had only allowed a partial change to occur. Her body and head were those of a Labrador — her teeth and her claws were not!

Elliott leapt into the fray. Dropping his sword stick, he shouted above the creature's screams. "Get to the chapel! Abditivus, help us!"

Abditivus moved from where he had been observing the battle and flung both doors wide as Thorne, Elliott, Veronique, Cornelius, Merric, and Davaadalai herded the screaming creature into the chapel where Popplewell, Giselle, and Aquilleia waited.

Popplewell raised his eyes from the tiny portrait of his wife and son that he kept in a gold locket around his neck. He kissed the image and carefully tucked the locket back into his collar as he gestured to the others to bring the creature closer.

They dragged Filicidae towards the elderly man. A flicker of dread appeared in the black, black eyes as Popplewell reached out to touch the creature's face.

○

Araby's Suite
3:00am

Several floors below, Araby paused in her pacing and pressed her ear to the door as Filicidae's inhuman screams erupted from far above, the hideous sound travelling through the castle, echoing down the stone corridors, passing through the very walls in unending peals until it reached Araby ears. Araby screamed in response, hammering at the door in a desperate attempt to free herself and save her teacher, her protector, her friend.

The screams ricocheted through the castle. Sebastian and the others, having been told not to leave the lounge, could not bring themselves to ignore the sound and hurriedly made their way to the chapel.

On the thirteenth floor of the castle, Popplewell placed his hands upon the leathery skin of Filicidae's temples. The creature became still at Popplewell's touch; as the net was removed, Filicidae stood silent, unable to move or make a sound as the reverend began their Undoing.

A soft mist appeared around Filicidae as Popplewell kept his hands pressed to the creature's temples, but slowly, implacably, began to move away, pulling a fine mist from the creature's body. Filicidae's eyes flickered desperately as they realised what was happening, but it was too late. As Popplewell moved, the mist thickened around Filicidae before separating into many diaphanous and disparate forms: the huge, twisted figure of Filicidae, numerous unidentifiable men and women who were Filicidae's previous incarnations on earth, the frail outline of Nanny, a thin and damaged layer of the soul that had been left within, and finally, the figure of Zabathoria, Tamassian's wife.

Popplewell concentrated, pulling the form of Filicidae free from the others. He looked the creature and swirling lights of black and white appeared in his eyes. "Be Unmade!"

There was a sudden, vast silence and the lights in the house dimmed as a creation was irreparably altered and removed from both time and space. The forms of Filicidae, Nanny, and the multitude of earthly incarnations faded into a thick, dark red mist that wrapped around Popplewell's raised hand and which he slowly pulled into fine strands. They solidified into threads of red cotton that he let fall to the ground.

He turned to Elliott. "Energy can never be destroyed...it simply becomes something else."

Turning his attention to the figure of Zabathoria, Popplewell focused on the ragged fragments of the soul that had been trapped within the body of Filicidae. Reaching up with his right hand, he pulled a golden thread from the air and wove the glowing cord into the faint outline of the damaged soul, using the golden light to repair the tears and rents in the energy's fabric before gently pressing the now healed soul back into Zabathoria's body.

Zabathoria blinked as though waking from a deep sleep as her soul was renewed and returned to her, free of the taint of Filicidae. She gazed at the people in the room, and as her eyes fell upon Elliott, Giselle, Thorne, and Aquilleia, a smile of recognition appeared on her face. Then her gaze fell upon a group of people who had suddenly appeared in the doorway, and rested on one in particular; Leander, held in his mother's arms.

Zabathoria's hazel eyes filled with sudden tears; she raised a hand and whispered, "Tamassian!" Leander blinked, and reached out towards her...

Popplewell gently pressed the palm of his right hand against her forehead. "You must be reborn here, my dear, but we will search for you, as we search for all the Others. I release you, Zabathoria; you are free of Filicidae."

The beautiful face before him slowly faded, leaving a faint mist that gently gathered around Leander before vanishing.

Popplewell tottered to one of the pews and sat down heavily as the others stood in silence.

Araby's Old Suite
3:15am

Araby shivered as she stood by the door. It had been fifteen years since she had been in her old bedroom; trust that bloody bastard butler to choose this place to imprison her!

She looked at the dusty white furniture. The faded peach eiderdown still lay half on the floor, where Davaadalai had thrown it when he and Cornelius found her fifteen years ago...

Araby looked at the brown marks still visible on the rug in the bathroom. She had been standing there when she was attacked. The room had been closed up after the police investigation; the family had simply locked the door and left it untouched.

She wandered around the room aimlessly, then sat on the edge of her old bed and glared at it; the old decorations from that Christmas so long ago; cards from her friends...one or two of whom had not lived to see that particular Christmas; an ancient red and green paper chain whose links had fallen apart, and the stocking she had draped across the end of her bed just before...

She walked into the bathroom and her face stared back at her in the mirror. Leaning forward, she traced the outline of her face. "You've come this far; remember what she taught you and your great-great-grandfather. People are things, here to entertain and amuse us...the louder they scream and the greater their misery, the greater your life will become!"

She smiled at the mirror as she ran some water into the sink and splashed some on her face. The family would approach the authorities, but one look at poor, weak, badly treated Araby, abandoned by her family and the man she loved, set up by an obviously corrupt private enquiry agent, who had been hired by the equally unpleasant reverend...

Her smile widened unpleasantly as she patted her face dry with her handkerchief. She could act very well when she had to...her dear friend Sophie Havercroft had taught her on the many occasions when they had met for their special evenings at Sybilla and Marcus' home in London.

Araby gently ran her old hairbrush through her short dark tresses as she remembered several of the interesting lessons she had passed on to her willing acolytes. Perry had been most promising when he was younger, but sadly he had turned out rather a dunce...especially when alcohol was involved. Araby shook her head in irritation. Wearing his father's cufflinks when he took the carriage to kill Theodora's father and brother, then losing one in the dratted vehicle, had been the actions of an utter imbecile; and both she and Nanny had told him so. Araby studied her hands and picked at a sharp nail. Unfortunately, he had enjoyed his punishment too much, so what they tried to teach him hadn't really sunk in.

As to the others — Sybilla, Marcus, and their occasional followers, dear Sophie and the rather exquisite Mr Weatherly Draycott — they had all been marvellous fun. However, they had all made the error of thinking that they were teaching her, when she was actually teaching them.

Nanny had insisted on her finding her own little group and passing on her knowledge. She had expressed no desire to join the evenings with Sybilla and Marcus, or even Sophie and Weatherly, either in her guise as Nanny, or as Filicidae. Perry had only been an acolyte, so he didn't really count; Nanny had only ever shared her gift with *her*...

As Araby brushed her hair, a single tear coursed down her pale cheek; she would miss Nanny. Filicidae had taken the act of murder and turned it into a feast of pleasure, but Nanny had also protected and nurtured her willing protégée with tender care, taking a curious child and broadening her mind beyond all expectation. Araby nodded...she would always remember Nanny.

As she replaced her brush, a low sound came to her ears. It sounded almost like...singing.

Araby cocked her head to one side and looked though the

open bathroom door. The voice was soft and low; it sounded as if it were crooning a lullaby…

Araby's brown eyes widened in horror and as she stared at her reflection in the mirror, the blood drained from her face. Her breath caught in her throat as she remembered when she had last heard that song.

Her legs began to shake as she stood by the sink, her mind replaying the memories of that day fifteen years ago. Just a few hours after she had murdered her brother and Filicidae had abandoned his corpse to the oubliette, she had said goodnight to the family, smug in the knowledge that only she, Nanny, and Perry knew what she had done. But she had been wrong. Someone else knew of her crimes, and that night they had sought her out and begun her punishment, but the arrival of Cornelius and Davaadalai had saved her from their tender ministrations…

Araby's blood pounded in her head as the soft voice continued its song; "Lully lullay, thou little tiny child, bye, bye, lully, lullay. Lullay, thou little tiny child, bye, bye, lully, lullay."

In the dim room beyond, there was a sudden flicker as a red-robed figure that had been a repressed memory in Araby's mind for fifteen years suddenly appeared out of the dark; the too-red lips peeled back in a twisted semblance of a smile to expose rank after rank of pointed, blackened teeth, as with sudden, horrifying speed, the figure held out its claw-like hands and ran towards her.

The Chapel
Same Time

Cornelius stared at Popplewell, everything he thought he knew about his old friend thrown into the air. He shook his head. "Popplewell...how?"

Popplewell sighed, and removing his eyeglasses, he stood and faced Cornelius. "Have you ever wondered, my old friend, just how I knew so very much about the Burgoyne family's more unpleasant foibles?"

Cornelius looked nonplussed. "I assumed your father told you in his letters. He was most insistent on sending them each week, much like his father before him..." He mused. "How strange; we have an unbroken family line, and so do you. Same name, same position, same strengths: we are quite similar." He looked at Popplewell, a questioning expression on his lined face. "Or are we?"

Popplewell shook his head sadly and closed his eyes. Slowly his face began to change, becoming smoother, unlined, younger. His sparse silver hair thickened and darkened to its original fullness and colour, and his back straightened as the elderly man before them returned to his true identity: Mellior, the original monk of Cove, who had destroyed the first Lord Burgoyne, become Reverend Newton Popplewell, and avenged himself upon the Master of Cove seventy-five years earlier for the murder of his son.

Ami shook her head as she stared at him. "What are you?"

Popplewell swallowed. "I am what is known as a Maker and Unmaker...I can alter people and things, and make them into something new."

Ami stared at the man she thought she had known and a terrible thought entered her mind. She looked at Elliott then turned back to Popplewell, her face pale. "It was you…you were Newton Popplewell. All these years. The family monk…"

Popplewell nodded gently. "Mellior. Yes, Ami, it has always been me. I have lived several lifetimes with this family, watching over you, protecting you, and yes, punishing those who required it."

Ami gasped, and tears filled her eyes as she looked at the young man. "You were there all those years ago when Thomas Burgoyne — Oh! It was your son! It was your son he killed, and you killed him!"

Popplewell blinked and nodded again. "Yes."

Ami's wet eyes narrowed. "That was the night Josephina Burgoyne disappeared; what happened to her?"

Popplewell swallowed hard before he spoke. "I have not mentioned other things that I have done, and how I used my gift to protect the family." He took a deep breath. "I Unmade her, piece by piece, and rebuilt her as a guardian: a watcher to protect others from the family curse. She became the Nightwitch, something I hoped would prevent the family curse from causing more suffering…"

He looked at the silent group. "But I made one error; I set a boundary to prevent my creation from ever leaving this house. After Araby committed her vile acts against the island's children and was sent to the mainland, she was free, without the threat of punishment for her evil actions, until such time as she returned home!"

Merric shook his head. "The events of the last few days and the discovery of the murderer is too fantastic for the police to believe, and there is no evidence to prove it was Araby. We can do nothing!"

Popplewell lifted a shaking hand to his face. "It really doesn't matter now…"

Elliott's head snapped around; green lights appeared in

his eyes as he looked at his old friend. "Mellior, what have you done?"

Aquilleia frowned, then clamped her hand to her mouth and retched. She turned her eyes, swirling with sliver lights, to Thorne. "She's here! The Nightwitch is here!"

Sudden screams erupted from downstairs; horrifying screams of sheer terror that echoed up to the very rafters of the castle. In the shocked silence they stared at each other, then ran to Araby's bedroom.

As they ran, Davaadalai reached into his pocket for the skeleton key. Arriving at the locked door Davaadalai fumbled with the key in his haste, the screams throwing his mind back to the day when Araby had been attacked, and what he and Cornelius had discovered within. He fought with the lock as the screams became impossibly high; joined by hideous tearing and rending sounds that thrummed on the ears.

Merric took the keys from the butler's trembling hands and swiftly unlocked the door. As it swung open, the sounds beyond ceased. They entered the room and stared in horror at the tall, blood-soaked figure who stood in the centre of the chamber.

Her long red robe was saturated with gore, her razor-sharp talons hung dripping by her sides as she looked with pleasure at the remains of her work on the floor before her; Araby's cooling blood pooled around her broken body, as she lay at the feet of the Nightwitch.

Josephina Burgoyne smiled through pointed, bloody teeth at what was left of her father's descendants. A mass of tumbling dark curls framed what had once been a proud and commanding countenance, now filled with sadistic malice and visceral enjoyment of the purpose she had been recreated for.

Her gaze flicked from Merric to Cornelius before falling

upon Popplewell. A look of uncertainty appeared in her dark eyes as Popplewell approached her, keeping his face turned away from the wretched remains of Araby that lay by the bed.

As his creature, the Nightwitch, moved towards him; he raised his hand. "It is done, Josephina, it is over: Your punishment is fulfilled, and you are released from your curse: you are the Nightwitch no longer. Become Josephina once more, and go in peace."

Reaching out to the blood-soaked figure, he placed his hands upon her temples and a soft sound, as of a hundred voices sighing, filled the room. Popplewell slowly moved backwards while seemingly keeping his hands pressed to Josephina's temples... As he moved away, the air around Josephina became dense and her body, soul, and spirit were pulled into three separate layers displaying different aspects of her nature, with a fourth layer acting as an overlay that bound the other three together: the overriding and terrifying presence of the Nightwitch.

Before the stunned eyes of the gathered family, the essence that had been both Josephina and the Nightwitch dissolved into a thick mist that slowly gathered around Popplewell, wrapping around him like smoke before fading into the air.

He turned to Merric and Melisandre, a look of exhaustion and exultation on his face. "It is over!"

THE END

The Versipellis Mysteries will continue in Book Four

Death in Eau de Nile...

Coming Yule, 2022

www.rhengarland.com

ABOUT THE AUTHOR

Rhen Garland lives in Somerset, England with her folk-singing, artist husband, 4000 books, an equal number of 1980's action movies, and a growing collection of passive-aggressive Tomtes.

"I thought when I finally started writing that my books would be genteel "cosy" type murder mysteries set in the Golden Era (I love the 1920's and 30's for the style, music, and automobiles), with someone being politely bumped off at the Vicar's tea party and the corpse then apologising for disrupting proceedings. But no, the late Victorian era came thundering over my horizon armed with some fantastical and macabre plotlines and planted itself in my stories, my characters, and my life, and would not budge."

I enjoy the countryside, peace, Prosecco, and the works of Dame Ngaio Marsh, Dame Glady Mitchell, John Dickson Carr/Carter Dickson, Dame Agatha Christie, Simon R Green, and Sir Terry Pratchett. I watch far too many old school murder mystery films, TV series, and 1980's action movies for it to be considered healthy.